UNIDENTIFIED
FUNNY
OBJECTS
4

Edited by
Alex Shvartsman

UFO Publishing
Brooklyn, NY

PUBLISHED BY:

UFO Publishing
1685 E 15th St.
Brooklyn, NY 11229
www.ufopub.com

Trade paperback ISBN: 978-0-9884328-6-4

Cover art: Tomasz Maronski
Interior art: Barry Munden
Typesetting & interior design: Melissa Neely
Graphics design: Emerson Matsuuchi
Logo design: Martin Dare

Copy editor: Elektra Hammond
Associate editors: Cyd Athens, James Beamon, Frank Dutkiewicz, Nathaniel Lee

Visit us on the web:
www.ufopub.com

TABLE OF CONTENTS

FOREWORD

ALEX SHVARTSMAN

Over the last three years my team and I have done our best to showcase a wide variety of stories and cover as many different types and styles of humor as possible. This year, we're doing something different: there is an overall theme to the book, and that theme is dark humor.

What's dark humor? I'm open to a rather wide interpretation of the theme. It can be black comedy, touching on subjects that are normally taboo or painful to talk about. It can also be biting satire, or morbid irony. When I presented the idea to our authors, I told them that I still wanted each story to be humorous first, with varying shades of darkness in the mix. I gave them plenty of freedom to do what they will with the prompt.

The resulting collection is almost as varied as the previous volumes, even though—and I hope you will agree upon reading it—the dark humor theme is consistently present. Among the twenty-three stories collected within there are horror tales with a touch of humor, such as "The Monkey Treatment" by George R. R. Martin and "Armed for You" by Anaea Lay. There are lighthearted yarns by Esther Friesner and Piers Anthony that inject just enough darkness to hide the banana peel. And there's everything in between.

Inside this volume you will also find time-traveling ghosts, Faustian bargains gone awry, talking hamsters, flawed supervillains... I could go on, but really, the stories themselves are more fun than anything I can say about them here. So I will step aside, and let you enjoy them.

Happy reading!

1

WE CAN GET THEM FOR YOU WHOLESALE

NEIL GAIMAN

P eter Pinter had never heard of Aristippus of the Cyrenaics, a lesser-known follower of Socrates who maintained that the avoidance of trouble was the highest attainable good; however, he had lived his uneventful life according to this precept. In all respects except one (an inability to pass up a bargain, and which of us is entirely free from that?), he was a very moderate man. He did not go to extremes. His speech was proper and reserved; he rarely overate; he drank enough to be sociable and no more; he was far from rich and in no wise poor. He liked people and people liked him. Bearing all that in mind, would you expect to find him in a lowlife pub on the seamier side of London's East End, taking out what is colloquially known as a "contract" on someone he hardly knew? You would not. You would not even expect to find him in the pub.

And until a certain Friday afternoon, you would have been right. But the love of a woman can do strange things to a man, even one so colorless as Peter Pinter, and the discovery that Miss Gwendolyn Thorpe, twenty-three years of age, of 9 Oaktree Terrace, Purley, was messing about (as the vulgar would put it) with a smooth young gentleman from the accounting depart-ment—*after*, mark you, she had consented to wear an engage-ment ring, composed of real ruby chips, nine-carat gold, and something that might well have been a diamond (£37.50) that it had taken Peter almost an entire lunch hour to choose—can do very strange things to a man indeed.

After he made this shocking discovery, Peter spent a sleepless Friday night, tossing and turning with visions of Gwendolyn and Archie Gibbons (the Don Juan of the Clamages accounting department) dancing and swimming before his eyes—performing acts that even Peter, if he were pressed, would have to admit were most improbable. But the bile of jealousy had risen up within him, and by the morning Peter had resolved that his rival should be done away with.

Saturday morning was spent wondering how one contacted an assassin, for, to the best of Peter's knowledge, none were employed by Clamages (the department store that employed all three of the members of our eternal triangle and, incidentally, furnished the ring), and he was wary of asking anyone outright for fear of attracting attention to himself.

Thus it was that Saturday afternoon found him hunting through the Yellow Pages.

ASSASSINS, he found, was not between ASPHALT CONTRACTORS and ASSESSORS (QUANTITY); KILLERS was not between KENNELS and KINDERGARTENS; MURDERERS was not between MOWERS and MUSEUMS. PEST CONTROL looked promising; however closer investigation of the pest control advertisements showed them to be almost solely concerned with "rats, mice, fleas, cockroaches, rabbits, moles, and rats" (to quote from one that Peter felt was rather hard on rats) and not really what he had in mind. Even so, being of a careful nature, he dutifully inspected the entries in that category, and at the bottom of the second page, in small print, he found a firm that looked promising.

"*Complete discreet disposal of irksome and unwanted mammals, etc.*" went the entry, "*Ketch, Hare, Burke and Ketch. The Old Firm.*" It went on to give no address, but only a telephone number.

Peter dialed the number, surprising himself by so doing. His heart pounded in his chest, and he tried to look nonchalant. The telephone rang once, twice, three times. Peter was just starting to hope that it would not be answered and he could forget the whole thing when there was a click and a brisk young female voice said, "Ketch Hare Burke Ketch. Can I help you?"

Carefully not giving his name, Peter said, "Er, how big—I mean, what size mammals do you go up to? To, uh, dispose of?"

"Well, that would all depend on what size sir requires."

He plucked up all his courage. "A person?"

Her voice remained brisk and unruffled. "Of course, sir. Do you have a pen and paper handy? Good. Be at the Dirty Donkey pub, off Little Courtney Street, E3, tonight at eight o'clock. Carry a rolled-up copy of the *Financial Times*—that's the pink one, sir—and our operative will approach you there." Then she put down the phone.

Peter was elated. It had been far easier than he had imagined. He went down to the newsagent's and bought a copy of the *Financial Times,* found Little Courtney Street in his *A-Z of London,* and spent the rest of the afternoon watching football on the television and imagining the smooth young gentleman from accounting's funeral.

IT TOOK PETER a while to find the pub. Eventually he spotted the pub sign, which showed a donkey and was indeed remarkably dirty.

The Dirty Donkey was a small and more or less filthy pub, poorly lit, in which knots of unshaven people wearing dusty donkey jackets stood around eyeing each other suspiciously, eating crisps and drinking pints of Guinness, a drink that Peter had never cared for. Peter held his *Financial Times* under one arm as conspicuously as he could, but no one approached him, so he bought a half of shandy and retreated to a corner table. Unable to think of anything else to do while waiting, he tried to read the paper, but, lost and confused by a maze of grain futures and a rubber company that was selling something or other short (quite what the short somethings were he could not tell), he gave it up and stared at the door.

He had waited almost ten minutes when a small busy man hustled in, looked quickly around him, then came straight over to Peter's table and sat down.

He stuck out his hand. "Kemble. Burton Kemble of Ketch Hare Burke Ketch. I hear you have a job for us."

He didn't look like a killer. Peter said so.

"Oh, lor' bless us, no. I'm not actually part of our workforce, sir. I'm in sales."

Peter nodded. That certainly made sense. "Can we—er—talk freely here?"

"Sure. Nobody's interested. Now then, how many people would you like disposed of?"

"Only one. His name's Archibald Gibbons and he works in Clamages accounting department. His address is..."

Kemble interrupted. "We can go into all that later, sir, if you don't mind. Let's just quickly go over the financial side. First of all, the contract will cost you five hundred pounds..."

Peter nodded. He could afford that and in fact had expected to have to pay a little more.

"...although there's always the special offer," Kemble concluded smoothly.

Peter's eyes shone. As I mentioned earlier, he loved a bargain and often bought things he had no imaginable use for in sales or on special offers. Apart from this one failing (one that so many of us share), he was a most moderate young man. "Special offer?"

"Two for the price of one, sir."

Mmm. Peter thought about it. That worked out at only £250 each, which couldn't be bad no matter how you looked at it. There was only one snag. "I'm afraid I don't *have* anyone else I want killed."

Kemble looked disappointed. "That's a pity, sir. For two we could probably have even knocked the price down to, well, say four hundred and fifty pounds for the both of them."

"Really?"

"Well, it gives our operatives something to do, sir. If you must know—" and here he dropped his voice "—there really isn't enough work in this particular line to keep them occupied. Not like the old days. Isn't there just *one* other person you'd like to see dead?"

Peter pondered. He hated to pass up a bargain, but couldn't for the life of him think of anyone else. He liked people. Still, a bargain was a bargain...

"Look," said Peter. "Could I think about it and see you here tomorrow night?"

The salesman looked pleased. "Of course, sir," he said. "I'm sure you'll be able to think of someone."

The answer—the obvious answer—came to Peter as he was drifting off to sleep that night. He sat straight up in bed, fumbled the bedside light on, and wrote a name down on the back of an envelope, in case he forgot it. To tell the truth, he didn't think that he could forget it, for it was painfully obvious, but you can never tell with these late-night thoughts.

The name that he had written down on the back of the envelope was this: *Gwendolyn Thorpe.*

He turned the light off, rolled over, and was soon asleep, dreaming peaceful and remarkably unmurderous dreams.

KEMBLE WAS WAITING for him when he arrived in the Dirty Donkey on Sunday night. Peter bought a drink and sat down beside him.

"I'm taking you up on the special offer," he said, by way of greeting.

Kemble nodded vigorously. "A very wise decision, if you don't mind me saying so, sir."

Peter Pinter smiled modestly, in the manner of one who read the *Financial Times* and made wise business decisions. "That will be four hundred and fifty pounds, I believe?"

"Did I say four hundred and fifty pounds, sir? Good gracious me, I do apologize. I beg your pardon, I was thinking of our bulk rate. It would be four hundred and seventy-five pounds for two people."

Disappointment mingled with cupidity on Peter's bland and youthful face. That was an extra £25. However, something that Kemble had said caught his attention.

"Bulk rate?"

"Of course, but I doubt that sir would be interested in that."

"No, no, I am. Tell me about it."

"Very well, sir. Bulk rate, four hundred and fifty pounds, would be for a large job. Ten people."

Peter wondered if he had heard correctly. "Ten people? But that's only forty-five pounds each."

"Yes, sir. It's the large order that makes it profitable."

"I see," said Peter, and "Hmm," said Peter, and "Could you be here the same time tomorrow night?"

"Of course, sir."

Upon arriving homes, Peter got out a scrap of paper and a pen. He wrote the numbers one to ten down one side and then filled it in as follows:

1 ...*Archie G.*

2 ...*Gwennie.*

3 ...

and so forth.

Having filled in the first two, he sat sucking his pen, hunting for wrongs done to him and people the world would be better off without.

He smoked a cigarette. He strolled around the room.

Aha! There was a physics teacher at a school he had attended who had delighted in making his life a misery. What was the man's name again? And for that matter, was he still alive? Peter wasn't sure, but he wrote *The Physics Teacher, Abbot Street Secondary School* next to the number three. The next came more easily—his department head had refused to raise his salary a couple of months back; that the raise had eventually come was immaterial. *Mr. Hunterson* was number four.

When he was five, a boy named Simon Ellis had poured paint

on his head while another boy named James somebody-or-other had held him down and a girl named Sharon Hartsharpe had laughed. They were numbers five through seven, respectively.

Who else?

There was the man on television with the annoying snicker who read the news. He went on the list. And what about the woman in the flat next door with the little yappy dog that shat in the hall? He put her and the dog down on nine. Ten was the hardest. He scratched his head and went into the kitchen for a cup of coffee, then dashed back and wrote *My Great-Uncle Mervyn* down in the tenth place. The old man was rumored to be quite affluent, and there was a possibility (albeit rather slim) that he could leave Peter some money.

With the satisfaction of an evening's work well done, he went off to bed.

Monday at Clamages was routine; Peter was a senior sales assistant in the books department, a job that actually entailed very little. He clutched his list tightly in his hand, deep in his pocket, rejoicing in the feeling of power that it gave him. He spent a most enjoyable lunch hour in the canteen with young Gwendolyn (who did not know that he had seen her and Archie enter the stockroom together) and even smiled at the smooth young man from the accounting department when he passed him in the corridor.

He proudly displayed his list to Kemble that evening.

The little salesman's face fell.

"I'm afraid this isn't ten people, Mr. Pinter," he explained.

"You've counted the woman in the next-door flat *and* her dog as one person. That brings it to eleven, which would be an extra—" his pocket calculator was rapidly deployed "—an extra seventy pounds. How about if we forget the dog?"

Peter shook his head. "The dog's as bad as the woman. Or worse."

"Then I'm afraid we have a slight problem. Unless..."

"What?"

"Unless you'd like to take advantage of our wholesale rate.

But of course sir wouldn't be..."

There are words that do things to people; words that make people's faces flush with joy, excitement, or passion. *Environmental* can be one; *occult* is another. *Wholesale* was Peter's. He leaned back in his chair. "Tell me about it," he said with the practiced assurance of an experienced shopper.

"Well, sir," said Kemble, allowing himself a little chuckle, "we can, uh, *get* them for you wholesale, seventeen pounds fifty each, for every quarry after the first fifty, or a tenner each for every one over two hundred."

"I suppose you'd go down to a fiver if I wanted a thousand people knocked off?"

"Oh no, sir," Kemble looked shocked. "If you're talking those sorts of figures, we can do them for a quid each."

"One *pound?*"

"That's right, sir. There's not a big profit margin on it, but the high turnover and productivity more than justifies it."

Kemble got up. "Same time tomorrow, sir?"

Peter nodded.

One thousand pounds. One thousand people. Peter Pinter didn't even *know* a thousand people. Even so... there were the Houses of Parliament. He didn't like politicians; they squabbled and argued and carried on so.

And for that matter...

An idea, shocking in its audacity. Bold. Daring. Still, the idea was there and it wouldn't go away. A distant cousin of his had married the younger brother of an earl or a baron or something...

On the way home from work that afternoon, he stopped off at a little shop that he had passed a thousand times without entering. It had a large sign in the window—guaranteeing to trace your lineage for you and even draw up a coat of arms if you happened to have mislaid your own—and an impressive heraldic map.

They were very helpful and phoned him up just after seven to give him their news.

If approximately fourteen million, seventy-two thousand, eight hundred and eleven people died, he, Peter Pinter, would be *King of England.*

He didn't have fourteen million, seventy-two thousand, eight hundred and eleven pounds: but he suspected that when you were talking in those figures, Mr. Kemble would have one of his special discounts.

MR. KEMBLE DID.

He didn't even raise an eyebrow.

"Actually," he explained, "it works out quite cheaply; you see, we wouldn't have to do them all individually. Small-scale nuclear weapons, some judicious bombing, gassing, plague, dropping radios in swimming pools, and then mopping up the stragglers. Say four thousand pounds."

"Four thou—? That's in*cred*ible!"

The salesman looked pleased with himself. "Our operatives will be glad of the work, sir." He grinned. "We pride ourselves on servicing our wholesale customers."

The wind blew cold as Peter left the pub, setting the old sign swinging. It didn't look much like a dirty donkey, thought Peter. More like a pale horse.

Peter was drifting off to sleep that night, mentally rehearsing his coronation speech, when a thought drifted into his head and hung around. It would not go away. Could he—could he *possibly* be passing up an even larger saving than he already had? Could he be missing out on a bargain?

Peter climbed out of bed and walked over to the phone. It was almost 3 A.M., but even so...

His Yellow Pages lay open where he had left it the previous Saturday, and he dialed the number.

The phone seemed to ring forever. There was a click and a bored voice said, "Burke Hare Ketch. Can I help you?"

"I hope I'm not phoning too late..." he began.

"Of course not, sir."

"I was wondering if I could speak to Mr. Kemble."

"Can you hold? I'll see if he's available."

Peter waited for a couple of minutes, listening to the ghostly crackles and whispers that always echo down empty phone lines.

"Are you there, caller?"

"Yes, I'm here."

"Putting you through." There was a buzz, then "Kemble speaking."

"Ah, Mr. Kemble. Hello. Sorry if I got you out of bed or anything. This is, um, Peter Pinter."

"Yes, Mr. Pinter?"

"Well, I'm sorry it's so late, only I was wondering... How much would it cost to kill everybody? Everybody in the world?"

"Everybody? All the people?"

"Yes. How much? I mean, for an order like that, you'd have to have some kind of a big discount. How much would it be? For everyone?"

"Nothing at all, Mr. Pinter."

"You mean you wouldn't do it?"

"I mean we'd do it for nothing, Mr. Pinter. We only have to be asked, you see. We always have to be asked."

Peter was puzzled. "But—when would you start?"

"Start? Right away. Now. We've been ready for a long time. But we had to be asked, Mr. Pinter. Good night. It *has* been a *pleasure* doing business with you."

The line went dead.

Peter felt strange. Everything seemed very distant. He wanted to sit down. What on earth had the man meant? "We always have to be asked." It was definitely strange. Nobody does anything for nothing in this world; he had a good mind to phone Kemble back and call the whole thing off. Perhaps he had overreacted, perhaps there was a perfectly innocent reason why Archie and Gwendolyn had entered the stockroom together. He would talk to her; that's what he'd do. He'd talk to Gwennie first thing tomorrow morning...

That was when the noises started.

Odd cries from across the street. A catfight? Foxes probably. He hoped someone would throw a shoe at them. Then, from the corridor outside his flat, he heard a muffled clumping, as if someone were dragging something very heavy along the floor. It stopped. Someone knocked on his door, twice, very softly.

Outside his window the cries were getting louder. Peter sat in his chair, knowing that somehow, somewhere, he had missed something. Something important. The knocking redoubled. He was thankful that he always locked and chained his door at night.

They'd been ready for a long time, but they had to be asked....

When the thing came through the door, Peter started screaming, but he really didn't scream for very long.

Neil Gaiman

Neil Gaiman is the bestselling author of books, short stories, films and graphic novels for adults and children.

Some of his most notable titles include the novels *The Graveyard Book* (the first book to ever win both the Newbery and Carnegie medals), *American Gods* and the UK's National Book Award 2013 Book of the Year, *The Ocean at the End of the Lane*. His latest collection of short stories, *Trigger Warning,* was an immediate *New York Times* bestseller and was named a *NYT* Editors' Choice.

Born in the UK, he now lives in the US with his wife, the musician and writer, Amanda Palmer.

THE TIME-TRAVELING GHOST MACHINE OF PROFESSOR JAIME PELIGROSA

Andrew Kaye

D r. Peligrosa hated his meetings with the senior faculty.

As Professor of Advanced Temporal Locomotion, he presided over the most technologically advanced discipline in the university's esteemed School of Esoteric Studies. He considered very few of the men and women around the table to be his peers, and considered even fewer to be his friends. If he was going to be honest with himself—Dr. Clarissa Blackheart, Professor of Applied Necromantic Sciences, was the only person at the table he actually *liked.*

This said a lot about his colleagues, because aside from the turtleneck sweater and the stylish glasses, Dr. Blackheart was the very definition of a mad scientist. Dr. Peligrosa recognized all the signs. The blood under her fingernails. Her tendency to cackle during electrical storms. Her frequent social media updates from local graveyards. And yet despite all that, he found Dr. Blackheart—dare he say it?—delightful. He enjoyed every moment in her (probably literally) intoxicating presence.

Dr. Blackheart winked and smiled at him as she took her place at the table. Dr. Peligrosa's heart fluttered—affection, maybe, or possibly black magic. It was sometimes hard to tell.

Dr. Lilywhite, Professor of Cryptozoological Affairs and the school's assistant dean, did not wink and was probably genetically predisposed not to smile. "Well, Jaime?" he said, displaying the warmth that had earned him the nickname 'Dr. Chillywhite' among his students. "You called this meeting. Are you going to tell us what this is all about?"

"I wanted to discuss... the clause."

"Dr. Kringle has already apologized for the break in, Jaime. He'd never heard of a Sephardic Jew before."

"The clause in my *contract*, Richard."

Dr. Lilywhite groaned. "Not this again. Jaime, you signed the contract and every clause along with it. We can't have you irreparably damaging the timeline. Until you find a paradox-proof time traveler, your work will remain theoretical and your time machines will be for display purposes *only*. The last thing we need is someone going back in time, killing their ancestors, and preventing their own birth. A paradox of that magnitude will cause reality to fold in on itself like... like..."

"...An origami swan," said Dr. Peligrosa, smiling. "You'll recall I wrote a paper on it. Luckily for us and reality as we know it, I've finally found a way around the paradox."

He reached into his jacket pocket and—resisting the urge to flourish—placed an eyeball on the table.

Not an actual eyeball, of course, but something closely resembling one—it was spherical and soft, with a single aperture. Most of the professors recoiled, except Dr. Blackheart, who had seen far worse things rolling across tabletops. Dr. Peligrosa cleared his throat. "This is my latest time machine."

Dr. Lilywhite leaned in for a closer look. "A bit small, isn't it?" he said—overly critical, as usual. "Your previous efforts were much larger."

"Nowadays seventeen different devices can fit onto a single cell phone," he said, noting with some satisfaction that Dr.

Lilywhite appeared to be trying to figure out which seventeen devices he meant. "I admit that this time machine isn't as sexy as ones shaped like cars or phone booths, but those were designed for living things. This is designed for ghosts."

Dr. Lilywhite sniffed importantly through a beard worn more convincingly on cartoon lumberjacks. "*Ghosts*, Jaime? Don't be preposterous."

"If a professor in the School of Esoteric Studies can't dabble in the preposterous once in a while, Richard, where would we be? I've been looking for a paradox-proof time traveler for years! I ran scenarios, for example, with the Professor of Abrahamic Xenobiology to see if angels or djinn would be suitable candidates. And before that, I was assisted by the Professor of Cuteness Theory until we found out how much damage a duckling with a camera strapped to its head could cause. But ghosts... ghosts won't interrupt an experiment to proselytize and won't go berserk at the sight of bread crumbs. More importantly, ghosts are incorporeal. No bodies. No voices. They can't even be seen by the naked eye. A ghost can go back in time without changing the past."

"That's an ingenious idea," said the Professor of Complimentary Psychology.

"Thank you, Dr. Wu. With Dr. Blackheart's help, I've designed this time machine to hang unobtrusively in a ghost's ectoplasmic matrix." He glanced uncertainly at Dr. Blackheart, who gave him a thumbs-up. "The ghost will be able to operate the machine with minimal willpower, opening a portal in time that it can then float though. The machine even includes a small video camera to record the trip."

Dr. Lilywhite narrowed his eyes. "It sounds... plausible, Jaime. But why call us here? You seem to have figured out a way to use your machine without breaching the clause—"

"That actually wasn't the clause I wanted to talk about, Richard. I was referring to the *other* one. The one that guarantees the full support of the senior faculty as long as I adhere to the *first* clause."

"But I just *gave* you my support—"

"I need to kill a student, Richard."

The other professors looked at each other nervously, except Dr. Blackheart, who never looked at anyone without leering. Finally, Dr. Lilywhite managed to say, "Why in the world would you think we would let you do *that*?"

"I need a fresh ghost," he said, with a shrug. "They have a short shelf life."

"You most certainly may *not* kill a student!"

"But Dr. X430 has killed *dozens* of students," he said, pointing a damning finger at the Professor of Expendable Humanities. Dr. X430, the only robot among the faculty, regarded Dr. Peligrosa with its expressionless red lenses and beeped.

Dr. Lilywhite scoffed. "Those deaths were accidental."

"It was studying the flammability of human tissue!"

"The students filled out liability forms," he said. "Honestly, Jaime, this is ridiculous. In order to prevent a time traveler from killing someone in the *past* you're going to kill someone in the *present*?"

"Killing someone in the present won't destroy reality."

"It will for the person you kill!"

"Actually, *I* won't be killing anyone," he said. "Dr. Blackheart has offered to take care of the details."

"Absolutely not, Jaime. That's even worse."

"Worse? We only need *one* ghost!"

"Frankly, Jaime, your cooperation with Dr. Blackheart calls the entire project into question. I don't trust her. I'm not convinced she could stop at just one student. You know how necromancers are."

"Richard, I hardly think that's fair—"

Dr. Blackheart cut him off with a wave of her hand and said sweetly, "I can defend myself, Jaime, thank you." Then she snapped her head angrily toward the end of the table. "Fuck off, Lilywhite!"

"Clarissa, please..."

"I'm not a *necromancer*. I'm the Professor of *Applied*

Necromantic Sciences," she said. Dr. Peligrosa noticed that she was getting so irritated that a dark nimbus of applied necromantic sciences was forming around her hands and blackening the tabletop. Her expression took on an arctic chilliness that put Dr. Lilywhite to shame. "I have PhDs in ghostwhispering and ambulant cadaver studies. Don't compare me to some dime-store sorceress with a fondness for skulls and costume jewelry. I'm a *professional!*" A smiled crawled across her face like a crack in an ice floe. "And, might I add, that while I *study* ghosts and reanimated corpses, I haven't *married* any of them."

Dr. Peligrosa winced at that. It was well-known among the senior faculty that Mrs. Lilywhite was, in fact, a sasquatch.

He pinched the bridge of his nose. Voices were being raised. Chairs were being pushed back. The discussion had gotten away from him, grown, leveled a small city with its radioactive breath. It was time to put this monster down. "Insults and arguments will accomplish *nothing,* ladies and gentlemen. I didn't call you here to ask for permission. My contract gives me all the permission I need. I came here with a spirit of full transparency—pun not intended—so you could start planning for any potential... unpleasantness."

Dr. Lilywhite's face collapsed into a scowl so deep it threatened to swallow most of his beard. "Very well, Jaime. Very well."

The erratic buzz-saw whine of an 80s-era computer printer announced a comment from Dr. X430. Dr. Wu tore off the sheet that sputtered from the robot's chest. "It's a list of underperforming students."

Dr. Blackheart snatched it from her. "Very helpful. Thank you, Dr. X430."

It beeped.

"Keep this in mind," Dr. Lilywhite said. "Dr. Blackheart is your responsibility now, Jaime. There's no telling what she'll do once she's killed a student. This is setting a dangerous precedent. For years her studies have gotten by on corpses generously donated by Dr. X430, but this could convince her to take matters into her own hands. There's no mistaking that evil glint in her eye."

"That's my astigmatism—"

"Watch out for her, Jaime!" he continued, as he and the other professors filed out of the room. "Don't let her well-documented murderous tendencies go unchecked!"

Dr. Peligrosa waited until the door closed before leaning back into his chair. "That went well."

"Yes. Yes it did."

He paused. "Well documented...?"

"They were mostly teenagers," she said, rolling her eyes. "Honestly, it's not like any of them even belonged to him."

THREE DAYS LATER, Dr. Peligrosa settled behind the desk in his office and turned on his computer monitor. An uninspiring headline about the university's equally uninspiring basketball team featured prominently on the campus splash page. His eyes fell gloomily to the folder icon marked "Assignments to Grade," and he sighed as long and as mournfully as his lungs would allow. He sometimes wished he could be more creative with grades, like the Professor of Greco-Roman Divination (who graded everything with augury) or the Professor of Forgotten Realms (who used a sack of polyhedral dice).

He had nearly worked up enough courage to open the first file when Dr. Blackheart sidled in.

"Don't ask me where I put the body," she said, by way of hello.

She smelled of blood. It was not the strangest of her perfumes, but it was unusually strong today. She was wiping her hands clean with a damp paper towel, which had turned a soggy red before she dropped it into his wastepaper basket. She was followed though the door by the rust-colored Pomeranian she had named, against all reason, Muffin. Sometimes it was hard to remember that Dr. Blackheart was the kind of woman who had a favorite internal organ based on tactility.

Muffin was normally a happy creature—well-fed and never wanting for bones—but today he was out of sorts, even skittish. He was growling the low, menacing snarl of a dog twice his size and staring fixedly on a patch of empty space beside Dr. Blackheart.

"A few hours ago I acquired your ghost, Jaime." She tossed him a pair of green-tinted glasses. "Don't mind Muffin, he just gets nervous around the undead."

Dr. Peligrosa put the glasses on and saw the transparent form of a young woman floating dejectedly at Dr. Blackheart's side. "Dear God, Clarissa, when I said 'take your pick' among the listed students, I didn't honestly think you'd kill one of *mine!* That's Mia Thompson from my Time Travel 101 course!" There was no mistaking Mia's curly hair or her tendency to wear the T-shirts of obscure punk bands, which had apparently carried over into the afterlife.

Dr. Blackheart shrugged. "You wanted a ghost, I got you a ghost. I found her taking notes by your time machine exhibit in the Zeddemore Wing. She was a target of opportunity. The place was otherwise empty."

But Dr. Peligrosa's concerns were already forgotten. He started pushing furniture aside to give the time machine space to open its portal. Then he reached into his pocket. "I always keep this close to my heart," he said with a wry smile, handing Dr. Blackheart the time machine. "I'm thinking about calling it 'the Clarissa.'"

She nearly laughed. "You can name it after me once you prove it actually works, Jaime."

He watched as she installed the time machine into the chest of Mia Thompson's ghost. He exhaled loudly as it hung in place, surprising himself—he hadn't realized he'd been holding his breath. "Excellent," he said quietly. "This is perfect!"

"I need to clarify something before we begin, Jaime. Once the ghost goes through the portal, I won't have control over her anymore. If she forgets her orders or gets lost or confused, we may never see her or your time machine again. I'm telling you this because we decided to use an underperforming student."

"I knew the risks going into this, Clarissa."

"Then where do you want to send her? Ancient Rome? Tokugawa shogunate? Inca Empire?"

"Let's try the early Cretaceous. No humans to even worry about, and we'll hopefully get some good footage of dinosaurs. They're always a crowd pleaser." Although he tried to sound like he was choosing a safe option, he was really just trying to win a bet he'd made with Dr. Alhazred, who taught Dead Languages but whose fascination with extinction went well beyond words. Dr. Alhazred swore most dinosaurs were covered in blue and white feathers "because blue jays are fuckers, that's why, and they had to have gotten it from somewhere."

Dr. Blackheart made a series of strictly scientific and by no means magical gestures with her left hand, leaving faint trails of black-and-purple energy hanging in the air. Mia Thompson's ghost suddenly became alert, as if she had heard someone calling her name. "I have a job for you," Dr. Blackheart said, and the ghost nodded.

"I've inserted a time machine into your ectoplasm. Can you sense it?"

The ghost nodded again.

"Excellent. You can control it with an extension of your willpower—the same willpower that gives you shape. Think of a time and a place and the machine will calibrate itself accordingly. A portal will open. You are to go through it. Understand?"

Another nod.

"I want you to open a portal to the early Cretaceous—"

"—110 million years ago—"

"—Yes, 110 million years ago. And then I want you to come back in ten minutes. Can you do that?"

Mia's ghost hesitated, then nodded for a fourth time. Dr. Peligrosa watched with fascination as Mia's ghost rippled and the time machine shimmered. A misty, swirling cone of energy spread from the orb and formed a portal in the center of the room. It was small at first, but Mia's ghost frowned with effort and the portal expanded to a diameter of nearly five feet. Mia's ghost turned and narrowed her eyes at Dr. Blackheart. Then she floated though the portal, which abruptly closed behind her with a sound like paper tearing.

Muffin, already on edge, began barking furiously.

"It worked," Dr. Peligrosa said. "It worked!"

In his excitement he gave Dr. Blackheart a hug—a hug she did not return. He pulled back, embarrassed. Dr. Blackheart managed a weak smile and adjusted her glasses. "Sorry. I don't... I don't do well with physical displays of affection and DAMN IT MUFFIN SHUT THE HELL UP! Sorry."

"No, no. No need to apologize. I...." He tried to stand a little straighter. "How about a drink? A little celebratory bourbon?"

"I don't think we should celebrate just yet," she told him, but he was already heading back toward his desk. "Did you see the look the ghost gave me as she went through the portal?"

"I didn't think ghosts had emotions."

"Only two: misery and anger. She was glaring daggers at me."

"Are you sure she wasn't crying daggers?" he tried.

"This is serious, Jaime. Her last-minute flash of aggression might complicate things and I WILL TURN YOU INTO A LITTLE COAT, MUFFIN, IF YOU DON'T SHUT UP RIGHT NOW! Sorry. He's giving me a headache."

She looked down at the enraged Muffin, an uncharacteristic look of concern on her face. "This portal technology," she said, an apprehensive lilt at the edge of her voice. "If the ghost can go *through* the portal, could anything come back out?"

"The odds of that happening are infinitesimal," Dr. Peligrosa said, pushing his chair back and opening the filing drawer he had repurposed into a liquor cabinet. "You saw how it worked. The portal closes as soon as the ghost goes through. You don't need to be nervous. No body, no voice. Paradox proof, remember? She can't go back in time and prevent her own birth."

"No, no, I understand, Jaime. It's just... what if she tries to prevent her own *death*?"

Dr. Peligrosa was about to say something, but he had a momentary lapse in thought. What had he been doing again? Something about grading papers. And bourbon. The two were not always mutually exclusive. He shrugged, grabbing the bottle and very nearly two glasses from the back of his filing drawer. He placed them neatly on the desk and stared at them a moment, trying to focus. Then he turned to his computer monitor.

The university splash page glowered back at him in stark black letters. "Professor Killed By Dinosaurs!" screamed the headline, with "Dinosaurs Mysteriously Vanish After Grisly Kill" whispering loudly beneath it. Suddenly the bourbon made sense. His inbox was filling up with emails—accusations, mostly, and one from Dr. Alhazred demanding twenty dollars.

Dr. Peligrosa sighed. The school had a damned Professor of Crichtonian Cloning on staff, but the moment a pack of deinonychus materialize on campus it's the time travel expert that immediately catches all the blame.

It couldn't have been his fault. He never got a chance to use his latest time machine. He reached into his jacket pocket and pulled out the device, holding it up to the sunlight and watching the rainbows play across its surface. "Poor Clarissa," he said sadly, to the time machine as much as to himself. "I really thought we could get this to work."

Someone rapped on his office door.

"Come in."

One of his students—a young woman named Mia Thompson—crept into the room. Her clothes were torn, her knees were scraped, and the stack of papers clutched against her chest was spattered with blood. "I... I finished the extra credit assignment," she said, her voice wavering. "Sorry it's late. I... I was finishing some research down in the Zeddemore Wing when the dinosaurs showed up. I'm still a little shaken up about it. I saw... *everything*, sir. You ever have a brush with death?"

His heart fluttered sadly. "All the time."

"Sir?"

"Just reminiscing, Ms. Thompson."

"All of the time machines you had on display were destroyed, sir. What are you going to do now?"

"I can always build more, I suppose." He gave the ball one last, wistful look, then crushed his failure between thumb and forefinger.

It damn near broke his heart.

Andrew Kaye

Andrew Kaye is a professional ne'er-do-well from the suburban wilderness of Northern Virginia, where he lives with his wife, his three children, and a large, empty space in his basement that should probably be filled with a robot or something. Sometimes he writes speculative fiction, edits the humor magazine *Defenestration*, and draws the webcomic *Ben & Winslow*. He thought he traveled back in time once in 1987, but it turned out he was mistaken. You can find him lurking in his usual haunt on Twitter @andrewkaye.

PLEASE APPROVE THE DISSERTATION RESEARCH OF ANGTOR

CAROLINE M. YOACHIM

```
From:    ANGTOR.lastname@u.titan.edu
To:      hsrb@u.titan.edu
Date:    1:08am May 21, 2429
Subject: Please Approve the Dissertation Research of Angtor
```

Dear Ethics Review Board for Research on Insignificant Humans,

Angtor requests approval for dissertation research to test the theory: "Humans will destroy inhabited planets if Angtor screams death threats at them until they comply." This is a minor variation of the Milgram experiment and is therefore eligible for expedited review.

Angtor will be the first of its brood to obtain a PhD, so it is imperative that you approve this research.

Thank you,

Angtor

```
From:    jenna.wong@hsrb.titan.edu
To:      ANGTOR.lastname@u.titan.edu
Date:    9:45am May 23, 2429
Subject: RE: Please Approve the Dissertation Research
         of Angtor
```

Hi Angtor,

Your dissertation is not eligible for expedited review. The Milgram experiment asked subjects to administer an electric shock. Your proposed research involves shouting death threats at students until they destroy a planet. This is not a minor variation. You need to submit a full application.

Being the first of your brood to obtain a PhD is an admirable goal, so I will give you a tip: the board cannot approve research where undergraduates are subjected to death threats.

Good luck,

Jenna Wong, Chair

Human Subjects Review Board

University of Titan

```
From:    ANGTOR.lastname@u.titan.edu
To:      jenna.wong@hsrb.titan.edu
Date:    12:53pm May 23, 2429
Subject: URGENT: Please Approve the Dissertation Research
         of Angtor
```

Dear Jenna Wong,

Thank you for the helpful tip. Please provide approval for Angtor's much improved dissertation research: "Humans will destroy inhabited planets if Angtor asks them politely without making any overt death threats." This study assesses the benefits of a public service program, and therefore is eligible for expedited review.

Angtor needs a PhD by the end of this academic year to impress a mate, therefore Angtor asks you politely for approval without making any overt death threats.

Thank you,

Angtor

```
From:    jenna.wong@hsrb.titan.edu
To:      ANGTOR.lastname@u.titan.edu
Date:    9:33am May 24, 2429
Subject: RE: URGENT: Please Approve the Dissertation Research
         of Angtor
```

Angtor,

There are only three weeks remaining in the academic year, so even if your proposal is approved it is unlikely that you will be able to complete your research in time to graduate this year. If you start now, you might be able to finish in time for next year.

Quick clarification question: what is the public service program your research will be assessing?

Thanks,

Jenna Wong

```
From:    ANGTOR.lastname@u.titan.edu
To:      jenna.wong@hsrb.titan.edu
Date:    2:06pm May 24, 2429
Subject: RE: RE: URGENT: Please Approve the Dissertation
         Research of Angtor
```

Dear Jenna Wong,

Eliminating planets infested with undesirable life forms is a public service.

Thank you,

Angtor

```
From:    jenna.wong@hsrb.titan.edu
To:      ANGTOR.lastname@u.titan.edu
Date:    12:14pm May 25, 2429
Subject: RE: RE: RE: URGENT: Please Approve the Dissertation
         Research of Angtor
```

Hi Angtor,

Thank you for your clarification. Your research project, "Humans will destroy inhabited planets if Angtor asks them politely without making any overt death threats," is not eligible for expedited review. Please submit a full application.

Good luck (you'll need it),

Jenna Wong

```
From:    ANGTOR.lastname@u.titan.edu
To:      jenna.wong@hsrb.titan.edu
Date:    3:06am May 26, 2429
Subject: PLEASE APPROVE THE DISSERTATION RESEARCH OF ANGTOR
```

Dear Jenna Wong,

You seriously expect Angtor to fill out a 37-page application form to conduct one miserable study about whether humans will destroy inhabited planets? Angtor has many important things to do to prepare for mating and producing broodlings that will spread across the galaxy. Do you not wish for Angtor to have a mate? You have already wasted one precious week of Angtor's research time by not approving the initial proposal.

Angtor's kin have provided the university with money to build the Katrid Library and the Tannin Museum of Galactic Conquest. They will be most displeased to hear of your resistance.

Thank you,

Angtor, Broodchild of Katrid, Ruler of the Tannin Empire

```
From:    jenna.wong@hsrb.titan.edu
To:      ANGTOR.lastname@u.titan.edu
Date:    8:22am May 29, 2429
Subject: RE: PLEASE APPROVE THE DISSERTATION RESEARCH
         OF ANGTOR
```

Dear Angtor,

I am pleased to inform you that we can do an expedited review for your dissertation research after all, thereby saving you the trouble of filling out a full application form. I do have a few clarification questions, as the description of your study was not entirely clear:

1. Will the undergraduates in the study be destroying actual planets, or will they see a simulation of planets being destroyed?
2. Will assignment to the experimental group be randomized?
3. Do you plan to eat the undergraduates at the end of the study?

With sincerest respect for your parents,

Jenna Wong

From: ANGTOR.lastname@u.titan.edu
To: jenna.wong@hsrb.titan.edu
Date: 6:21pm May 29, 2429
Subject: RE: RE: PLEASE APPROVE THE DISSERTATION RESEARCH OF
         ANGTOR

Dear Jenna Wong,

1. Actual planets will be destroyed. Angtor does not care what puny undergraduate research subjects see. What will make the review board approve this dissertation research? Kittens? Undergraduates will see pictures of kittens.
2. Angtor will randomly put all the undergraduates into the group where they destroy planets.
3. Angtor will only eat the undergraduates that do not comply. The others are free to go out and live their insignificant lives until such time as Angtor selects a mate and produces a hungry brood.

Thank you,

Angtor

From: jenna.wong@hsrb.titan.edu
To: ANGTOR.lastname@u.titan.edu
Date: 4:55pm May 30, 2429
Subject: Application for Research Denied

Dear Angtor,

With sincerest apologies to you and your exalted parents, I am unable to approve your application for "Humans will destroy inhabited planets if Angtor asks them politely without making any overt death threats."

As a precaution for my personal safety, I have fled the university prior to sending this message. Please do not reply to this message, as I have requested this email account be deleted.

Goodbye,

Jenna Wong

From: ANGTOR.lastname@u.titan.edu
To: loretta.blaine@u.titan.edu
Date: 3:08am June 2, 2429
Subject: Please Approve the Dissertation Research of Angtor

Dear Puny Human Advisor,

Submitted in fulfillment of the graduation requirements of the PhD program is my thesis, "Human undergraduates will destroy the home planet of Jenna Wong if Angtor asks them politely without making any overt death threats." Retroactive HSRB approval was provided by Ulric Thurman, the new chair of the human subjects review board. Angtor spent two whole days working very hard on this research.

If you feel this dissertation does not meet the standards of the university, Angtor can add an additional test condition to see if human undergraduates will destroy your home planet when asked politely by Angtor. Earth is a very nice planet. It would be a shame if something happened to it. Angtor is confident that the human subjects review board would retroactively approve this additional research if asked politely without any overt death threats.

Thank you,

Angtor

```
From:    loretta.blaine@u.titan.edu
To:      ANGTOR.lastname@u.titan.edu
Date:    5:52am June 2, 2429
Subject: RE: Please Approve the Dissertation Research of
         Angtor
```

Dear Angtor,

Congratulations on finishing your thesis. I can assure you that although the official paperwork is still being processed, you will absolutely be receiving your PhD, and therefore there is no need for you to conduct additional research of any kind.

Purely as a formality, we have scheduled your thesis defense for Friday afternoon. Again, please rest assured that you need not do any additional research, and this is only a formality. Congratulations on your PhD.

Sincerely,

Loretta M. Blaine, PhD

Psychology Department

University of Titan

```
From:    ANGTOR.lastname@u.titan.edu
To:      loretta.blaine@u.titan.edu
Date:    3:42pm June 3, 2429
Subject: RE: RE: Please Approve the Dissertation Research
         of Angtor
```

Dear Puny Human Advisor,

Angtor is pleased that no additional research is needed.

On a personal note, Angtor has selected a mate and is filled with broodlings. Therefore Angtor will not be attending your thesis defense nonsense.

Thank you,

Angtor

From: ANGTOR.lastname@u.titan.edu
To: SCREEVE@u.tauceti.edu, LINGBAD@u.tauceti.edu,
          ZYNCHVAR@u.tauceti.edu
Date: 9:19pm June 7, 2429
Subject: Please Approve the Dissertation Research of Angtor

Dear Exalted Tannin Empire Dissertation Committee,

Angtor humbly submits for your approval a dissertation titled "Human University Will Grant PhD to Alien Student When Threatened With the Destruction of Inhabited Planets."

No sentient creatures were physically harmed in the execution of this research, but the humans seemed strangely troubled by Angtor's highly convincing simulations of planetary destruction. In debriefing, Angtor offset this psychological damage by showing the humans pictures of small furry Earth creatures called kittens.

Thank you,

Angtor, PhD

Caroline M. Yoachim

Caroline M. Yoachim lives in Seattle and loves cold cloudy weather. She is the author of dozens of short stories, appearing in *Fantasy & Science Fiction, Clarkesworld, Asimov's,* and *Lightspeed,* among other places. For more about Caroline, check out her website at carolineyoachim.com.

MATCH GAME

Esther Friesner

"**Y**our next client is waiting," said Toodles. "She tried to bite me."

"Hmm?" Mrs. Vera Knight, matchmaker extraordinaire in quite a few senses of the adjective, looked up from her morning must-haves—black coffee, an apricot danish, and the gossip column—to regard her secretary with that absent-minded, somewhat dismissive look that had driven her late husband Gerald to drink. "Well, darling, remember what I told you: if they bite, bite them back, otherwise they'll never learn. And what do we always say about clients who never learn?"

"Like I care," said Toodles, grooming his whiskers vigorously. Though his words were filled with indignation as hot and strong as his employer's morning cup of get-up-and-go, he could not hide the fact that his recent experience had jangled his nerves. He was, after all, just a hamster. More or less.

Mrs. Knight tsk-tsked, though merely for form's sake. She'd had Toodles on staff for a year and she'd never employed a better secretary/receptionist/rodent-of-all-work. Albeit the small, furry creature was useless at any task requiring muscle, once you put a SmartStik in his plastic runabout ball, the little fellow was all over what remained of the Internet in jig time. Any touchscreen, especially the teensy one provided on the SmartStik, was the hamster's bitch. It often amazed his employer to think of how badly humanity had underestimated the capabilities of *Mesocricetus auratus* over the centuries, and that it had taken the horrors of the Shift to open their collective eyes.

"Now, Toodles, let's not be like that," said Mrs. Knight. She broke off a fragment of danish and bent over to pick up the hamster ball. Holding the succulent crumb where Toodles could not fail to see it, she coaxed: "*What* do we say about clients that won't learn?"

"That it's up to us to teach them a lesson," Toodles recited obediently, enraptured by the promise of moist, flaky, jam-topped recompense for being a good scholar.

"That's correct." Mrs. Knight unscrewed the top of the plastic sphere and gave the hamster his reward. He promptly stuffed it into his starboard cheek pouch and looked at her expectantly, eyes glowing red with greed. She wagged an admonitory finger at him. "No, no, darling. No more until we take care of our client. Mustn't keep the undead waiting."

The hamster's nonexistent shoulders slumped. "Why not?" he grumbled. "They're not going anywhere."

"They could go to another agency," Mrs. Knight reminded him. "And that would be simply dreadful."

"You sure about that?"

"About them taking their business elsewhere? My sweet, it's a basic rule of business that if you don't give the customer what he wants, he will—"

"Nah, I mean the part about this one being undead. She doesn't look it, and I can usually tell. You got confirmation?"

A momentary sour expression flitted across Mrs. Knight's countenance. "When you reported that she tried to bite you, I simply jumped to the obvious conclusion."

"Oh. Well, uh, I kinda sorta mighta been making more out of it than there was. I mean, she did pick me up and hold me real close to her mouth—a little too close for my taste. Maybe she was just trying to make sure I got her name right when I checked her in, but she didn't wanna raise her voice to do it. That, or maybe something else, I dunno. I was the one who yelled 'Put me down!' But I did it in a totally professional way, I swear!" The hamster gave his employer a look that was at once apologetic and so adorable that forgiveness was assured.

"You know I've got comfort zone issues. It goes with being this size and this, um, edible."

"Edible?" Mrs. Knight was amused. "Dear Toodles, you forget that I *know* you. How can you still say that with a straight face?"

The hamster looked aggrieved. "Hey, once you're born prey, it don't go away!"

"Ah yes, quite right. How insensitive of me. I beg your pardon." She closed the hamster ball and set it back on the floor. "Now go see our caller in, and if she tries to bite you again, you know what to do."

"Yeah, but not *how* to do it," Toodles replied, knocking one hairy pink paw on the curved plastic wall enclosing him. "Darned if I know how you expect me to bite anyone when I'm sealed in this thing."

"I wouldn't say 'expect' is the proper word to describe your situation, precious. On the other hand, since you *are* in there, how can anyone manage to bite *you*?" The boss-lady's riposte was accompanied by an impish twinkle in her eyes. "Which makes me wonder whether sometimes—only sometimes, mind you—you complain about our clients' behavior for the sheer joy of hearing yourself complain."

An abashed hamster is a dismal sight. Toodles' whiskers drooped. "That transparent, am I?" he asked.

"Almost as much as your runabout ball," Mrs. Knight replied. "But I don't mind; I couldn't do without you for a moment. I hope you know that." Her affectionate words made the hamster perk up. He rolled out of the office at a brisk pace to fulfill his given task.

Left to herself briefly, Mrs. Knight prepared to greet the new client. According to the memo Toodles had entered on her e-genda, the person in question was Hortense Ingram. The antique charm of that name was endearing, but Mrs. Knight *did* wish she had more than that to go on before meeting the woman. When Toodles had first made the appointment, she'd asked him why there was no additional information about Miss Ingram included. The hamster had replied that the client declined to give any personal data besides her name, address, credit rating, and TagMe URL. Mrs.Knight had duly looked up said TagMe page, only to find it contained no images of its hostess and a scant handful of posts in which Miss Ingram revealed little beyond the fact that she liked reading F. Scott Fitzgerald novels and owned his skull.

"My goodness, that tells me absolutely *nothing* special about her!" Mrs. Knight had exclaimed in frustration. "Well, nothing except that she knows where to shop. I suppose I shall just have to wait and see."

Now the wait was over. In the last few instants before Toodles ushered in Miss Ingram, Mrs. Knight cudgeled her brain mightily in an effort to deduce any shred of factoid concerning the young woman. Her years of experience had taught her that the more she knew about a person before sitting down to do business, the more likely she would be to have the advantage during negotiations. Such knowledge was also a wonderful time-saver when reviewing her backlog of Availables (as she liked to think of them) allowing her to winnow out extraneous or inappropriate creatures before presenting the client with a nicely streamlined list of Possibles. Clever shortcuts like these continued to secure her reputation for astoundingly prompt customer service and satisfaction.

It also meant she was able to get clients the hell out of her office as fast as ever she could, and preferably faster than that. This was not done for their accommodation, but for her own. Despite her chosen field, Mrs. Knight truly could not stand to deal with most of her clients face-to-face for any appreciable length of time. It creeped her out beyond all bearing, and after interviewing some of them, she found herself unable to stomach more than weak tea and unbuttered toast for several days.

She glanced out of her office window as if some molecule of a sliver of a hint concerning Miss Ingram's nature might be found in the vulture's-eye view of smoldering buildings and ravaged corpses below. There had been a full moon the previous evening and to judge by the evidence still seeping in the gutters, the local lycanthropes had been making rather merry.

Mrs. Knight glowered at the sunlight. Brightly though it blazed, it did not mean she could discount Dracula from Miss Ingram's potential kin. The world-wide disaster known as the Shift had not only thrust unwanted waves of supernatural beings back into the waking world—including, but not limited to, vampires, werewolves, animate mummies, zombies, and the occasional pooka—it had also managed to change the rules that formerly governed membership in their numbers and limited their range for wreaking havoc. Oh, you could still kill most of them with a judicious application of the Li'l Marvel Pocket Flame-Thrower, but things like sunlight, religious symbols, garlic, the poetry of Gertrude Stein, and silver bullets were now mere ploys for bringing them up short without doing the fatal trick. Thus Miss Ingram's ability to walk abroad before sundown meant zip.

"Drat," Mrs. Knight muttered. "It would be so much simpler if she were a vampire. I know how to deal with vampires. Vampires are dead easy, but she might be any of those other awful... things. Tsk, what a goose I am: I should have asked Toodles what Miss Ingram looks like instead of wasting time on a Teaching Moment. I'm a featherheaded fooooo—*You* must be Hortense!" Mrs. Knight's session of self-berating snapped off short as she sprang forward to greet the tall, raven-haired, plain-looking young lady whom Toodles had just ushered in.

"Anyone want a coffee?" the hamster asked. Then he gave a high-pitched chittering sound that was second cousin twice removed to human laughter. "Yeah, just kidding. Like I could figure out how to work the espresso machine!" He trundled out of the inner sanctum, the electric eye of the door allowing him free passage.

Toodles' exit left Mrs. Knight and Miss Ingram to themselves. For the space of a few breaths, the two women stood taking stock of each other. Mrs. Knight's first checkpoint was, of course, to determine if Miss Ingram *were* breathing. That alone would reveal much. As she peered at the younger female, she noted with guarded pleasure that the front of Miss Ingram's pastel pink blouse rose and fell with comforting regularity. It was also spotlessly clean, with not even a whiff of grave mold wafting from the primly ironed fabric.

So: definitely not a zombie, Mrs. Knight reflected. *Not even the best-preserved of them ever succeeds in covering up the smell. And breath is evidence that she's not a mummy either... I think. There was that one fellow—Ra-ankh-whozis-Meriptah-something—who scooped his lungs out of their canopic jar and popped them back into his chest before he came to see me, but he was the exception to the rule. The rest of that lot aren't so intent on making a good first impression. Vampire? Oh, please, can she be a vampire?* She considered Miss Ingram's complexion, which was certainly pale enough. On the other hand, some people were simply pallid creatures by nature, thanks to hailing from Minnesota.

Heavens, I wish I could remember if vampires do *breathe, whether they need to or not. No telling if she's a werewolf without the moon being up. ...Well, at least I've got something to work with, moving forward.*

It should be noted that the foregoing inner monologue transpired in a matter of seconds, and not too many of them. In fact, Mrs. Knight's ruminations began just as Miss Ingram's lips parted and ended well before the younger woman said, "Thank you for agreeing to take me on as a client. I've heard so many good things about your work."

"Bless you, dear child—That is, if it's culturally acceptable to you and your kind to receive blessings as something other than a hostile gesture? I've learned that some of the more orthodox among certain groups dislike the implication of holy water even if the actual substance no longer harms them."

Miss Ingram has a very pretty, self-effacing smile. "It doesn't bother me. I just want to do business with you."

"'Business'?" Mrs. Knight echoed. "Oh goodness, not the B-word!" Her bizarrely girlish laughter was a source of irritation to anyone compelled to listen to its trills and tremolos. Miss Ingram's smile stiffened noticeably under the onslaught. "We here at A Beautiful Pair don't think of ourselves as either a business or—perish the thought—a *company*, but as the means to *provide* company for those who seek it. Do have a seat." She waved her new client toward the chintz-covered settee facing the desk. "Unless you'd prefer—?" She indicated an extra-large, fleece-lined doggie bed to one side of the small sofa. "Some of our clients prefer it even in the daytime when it's, you know—" She dropped her voice discreetly. "—*that* time of the month."

"That's very kind of you, Mrs. Knight, but the moon has no effect on me," Miss Ingram replied, lowering her eyes modestly as she sat down.

Mrs. Knight took a place behind her desk, although she remained standing, a stratagem to establish dominance. She had learned that if you stayed on your feet and loomed over the client, you retained a certain advantage. It was a clever use of body language that put the *high* in *social hierarchy*.

It was also quite handy if a client decided that the plump and juicy Mrs. Knight might make a better snack than a matchmaker. The settee was rump-sprung and was kept that way. By the time any creature managed to haul its ravening butt out of the Cushion Pit of Doom, the already-mobile Mrs. Knight had dived into her deepest desk drawer and had the office flamethrower primed, aimed, and ready.

"Ah, just as I suspected. You are not *that* sort of a shape-shifter. All to the good, as I'm afraid we do not have a particularly large inventory of suitable young werewolves at the moment."

"Werewolves!" Miss Ingram's eyebrow rose, as did a hot flush of color in her cheeks. "Oh, but I could never socialize with a werewolf."

"Strict parents?" The owner-manager of A Beautiful Pair leaned closer, using body language v. 2.0 to express sympathy and to try to establish a bond, even if it was about as genuine as a politician's smile. Dominance was fine as far as it went, for a first step, but it was always easier to raise prices when the clients believed they were working *with* you, not being served *by* you.

Miss Ingram looked away, pained. "My parents died in the first days of the Shift."

"How sad for you. Zombies?" It was usually zombies.

The young woman shook her head.

"Werewolves, perchance?" That would explain Miss Ingram's aversion, but Mrs. Knight observed only a second shake of the client's head, much to her consternation. She did not care for mysteries; they made her short-tempered, which was a handicap in her line of work. It did not do to snap testily at one's figurative bread-and-butter: "Then what the hell *did* kill them, you ninny?" It was only by main force that she bit back those very words.

Despite Mrs. Knight's self-control, Miss Ingram reacted as if the exasperated question had been asked outright: "They died of broken hearts."

The matchmaker gave her a quizzical look. "Indeed? It's not

the sort of thing one hears of often, except in novels."

"I spoke literally. A stake pounded through your chest will do that."

Mrs. Knight gasped. "So your parents were—?"

"Vampires, yes. They were 'turned' within the first forty-eight hours of the Shift and laid to their truly eternal rest a scant ninety minutes thereafter." A curiously flat quality stole into the younger woman's voice. "I would have done it immediately, but I had to get my little brother to safety and then I needed to get the right tools for the job and then—"

"*You* killed your parents?" Mrs. Knight could feel the pulse fluttering in her throat. She had to steady herself by resting both hands on the desktop.

"Someone had to do it."

Just when I thought there was nothing left to shock me. Mrs. Knight struggled to keep her expression both bland and sympathetic. *It must have seemed like a horrible necessity at the time, but if she were any colder about their deaths, I'd take* her *for the vampire.* She gave a small mental shudder and hastened to yank the conversation back to less queasy-making matters.

"Well, my dear, there's no need to dredge up painful memories of the past," she chirped. "We are, after all, in the business of creating *joyful* memories of the *future!*"

Memories of the future? The words made so little sense that Mrs. Knight took herself aback the moment after she uttered them. Miss Ingram, on the other hand, seemed perfectly willing to accept them without question. *That's the way of it, I suppose,* Mrs. Knight mused. *The possibility of Romance has always been able to hip-check Logic clean off the track and into the cheap seats in the grand Roller Derby of Life, especially in these desolate times. This girl comes off a* weensy *bit cold-blooded, but I've dealt with worse. It might actually be a point in her favor for some potential matches. That darling finny creature from the Bla—that is, my one Ichthyo-American client has been waiting for me to find him that special someone for ages! Maybe all she needs is love. Love, and a wet-suit.*

"Have you any preferences as to the sort of match you *are* seeking?" she forged onward. "We have already determined that werewolves are off the table—and the rest of the furniture, ha, ha!—and no doubt vampires as well, given your, ahhh, family background, but what of the other options? Alive? Dead? Fur? Fangs? Scales? Republicans? Democrats? Survivalists? Free Brains Party? Oh, and gender, education, income, social standing and eye color, of course! All the most important factors. Speak your mind and A Beautiful Pair will find just the thing you're looking for."

"With the emphasis on 'thing,' no doubt," said Miss Ingram, as she hiked up her skirt to reveal the revolver strapped to her right thigh. Her eyes narrowed to burning slits as she swiftly drew the weapon, aimed it at Mrs. Knight's chest, and added: "What *I'm* looking for is revenge."

Mrs.Knight prided herself on maintaining a certain level of aplomb. It was one of the necessities of her vocation. Panic was a shortcut to an early grave, whereas a cool head—and an attendant level of preparation for untoward eventualities—was the key to survival. Early on in her career she had taken all of the wisest precautions against any of her clients suddenly attempting to transform her from a matchmaker into a meal. There was a cleverly concealed system of voice-activated spray pipes and hatches embedded in her office ceiling. All of these stood ready to release a suitable dose of holy water, garlic, wolfsbane, tanna leaves, and Uncle Gladwin's Patented Tofu-for-Brains Zombie Kibble. None of these provisions had the power to destroy, thanks to the Shift, but their effect was just enough to give pause to the most obstreperous client. It also bought Mrs. Knight sufficient time to deploy the aforementioned office flamethrower.

The only difficulty was, none of these measures would work on an ordinary human being. Yes, the flamethrower would do the trick, but no matter how fast she made a grab for it, a bullet would be faster.

She had only one option remaining, but it would require

caution to implement it without touching off Miss Ingram's trigger finger. The first step was resorting to every *real* lady's best defense, the ancient British martial art of *How* dare *you-fu*. With a voice wintry enough to give a yeti frostbite, the cornered matchmaker pulled back her shoulders and declaimed: "*Miss* Ingram, have you taken leave of your senses? Revenge? On what grounds? We have only just met! If this is your way of attempting to re-negotiate my fee—"

"No, you vile procuress," the younger woman replied evenly. "It's my way of re-negotiating your ability to breathe."

"'Procuress'? Such language! Surely you were raised better than this." Softening her tone a bit, she added: "Obviously you have mistaken me for someone else, someone against whom you have a legitimate grudge. The Shift has turned these into dark and lonely days for us all, and the search for love can prove as elusive as a greased eel. We all crave companionship, but now lack the security to seek it on our own. A Beautiful Pair is not the only matchmaking establishment that has sprung up to fulfill this need. Alas, too many of our competitors are fraudulent enterprises run by unscrupulous creatures. Some even have the gall to usurp the names of reputable romance enablement facilities in order to bilk innocents like you. If I had a nickel for every take-down notice I posted against websites that appropriated my agency's good name—"

"—you'd have a nice down-payment on your coffin," Miss Ingram said dryly. "I have made no mistake: you are the very person responsible for my woes."

"This is madness! Have you heard nothing I've said?" Slowly, by a series of hairsbreadths, Mrs. Knight edged one hand toward the edge of her desk, all the while attempting to keep Miss Ingram's attention focused on her operatically irate words. She could not seize the flame-thrower, but if luck were with her she might be able to hit a silent alarm button under the rim, in a place where other people might stow used chewing gum.

One press of that button and a light would flash in the outer office alerting Toodles to the fact that something was amiss beyond his employer's ability to handle. The gallant hamster would then use his SmartStik to contact the authorities and if they arrived quickly enough, all would be well.

At least that was the theory. The reality was that though Toodles had been thoroughly briefed as to the emergency procedure, thus far in their association Mrs. Knight had never needed to push the alarm. Would the untried hamster rise to the occasion? He *might.*

Ah, well! A subjunctive rescue still beats an indicative death, Mrs. Knight thought, philosophically. Her finger touched the button. It was not an easily triggered device—a deliberate feature to reduce the embarrassment of a false alarm. In order to conceal the convulsive force necessary to push it, Mrs.Knight lunged slightly forward as she shouted, "How can you think *I* am to blame for your parents' deaths when *you* were the one who—!"

With a wordless exclamation of rage, Miss Ingram launched herself from the settee. She was across the room before Mrs. Knight could blink. A backhanded blow with the gun sent the older woman crashing to the floor. As the matchmaker huddled there, shaking and sobbing, Miss Ingram shouted down at her: "You're to blame for worse than that; you and all the other godless go-betweens! Do you moneygrubbing vermin *see* the havoc surrounding us? The destruction? The Shift-summoned monsters that make our lives a misery? *Honest* people spend their days trying to eradicate the fiends, but you—? You spend yours finding them *mates!* Spouses! Prom dates! Less than four months ago, my baby brother came to this very office, and what did you do?"

"M-me—?" Mrs. Knight cupped the side of her face, trying to get the words out. "I never—never had a client named—named Ingram until you."

"It's a *false* name, you stupid hag! I didn't want you suspecting anything, though if I'd given my real last name you'd probably think I was coming to thank you for the wonderful work you did for Nigel. A wonderful *death sentence!* How

could you? How could you take a normal, healthy young man
and throw him into the clutches of a blood-sucking ghoul?"

"You mean I—I introduced him to a—?"

"To a *vampire*, damn you both! A vampire who didn't have
the basic decency to wait until the third date to turn him, that
haemophagic slut! 'Suck at first sight,' Nigel called it when he
told me about his hellish union. He was smiling when he said
it. Fangs and all, *smiling!*"

"So he—he was happy." Mrs.Knight blinked. Even though her
life was in imminent peril, her Inner Entrepreneur couldn't help
but preen a bit at the thought of another satisfied customer.

"Ecstatic," Miss Ingram replied bitterly. "He even had the
blind gall to suggest that I might 'cheer up' if *I* consulted you
as well." Her gaze hardened. "As you can see, I'm taking his
advice. Your death will cheer me up immensely. This post-
Shift world has become a swamp of horrors. I can't drain it,
but at least I can remove the human pond scum crawling over
its surface. That's why as soon as I've done away with you, I
shall hunt down and destroy every other matchmaker I can
find. I only regret that these uncertain times compel us to eat
dessert first, or else I would have saved *your* demise for last, the
chocolate-covered cherry atop the seven-layer cake of glorious
retribution!"

"Wait, chocolate-covered pond scum? Shift cake? What?"
Mrs. Knight's head was spinning. Dying was bad enough, but
dying in a state of mortal bewilderment was adding insult to
inhumation. Latching onto the desk, she pulled herself off the
floor and clawed her way back to dignity. "I refuse to be shot
over a misapprehension. It is our policy *never* to force anyone
into a match. We leave that to mothers and other amateurs.
At A Beautiful Pair, we give our clients what *they* want. If your
brother was paired with a vampire, that was what he came
here seeking, so if he is alive—for certain applications of the
term—and by his own admission happy, *what the blazes do you
have to avenge?*"

"My *guilt*, you miserable pimp!" Miss Ingram bellowed. "The burden my soul has carried ever since I was forced to destroy my parents! The Shift made their lives meaningless, but *you* made their deaths meaningless, too! With every blow of the mallet, I told myself I was freeing them from an unnatural existence as shunned, hated fiends. How can I sleep at night now, knowing they could have been accepted, *beloved* fiends thanks to people like you? Why did you have to pair their only son with the very sort of creature that killed them?"

A rather uncharitable response ("*That* would be *you*.") danced on the tip of Mrs. Knight's tongue. Before she could voice it, the office door slid open and Toodles rolled in.

"Hey, boss, was that you testing the alarm or—?" His beady eyes darted to the gun in Miss Ingram's hand. "Uh-oh." His tiny paws scrambled for the SmartStik. Too late! Miss Ingram pounced on the hamster's runabout ball, scooped it up, and shook it like a snowglobe.

"Stop!" Mrs. Knight cried, all care for her own safety forgotten. "Leave Toodles alone! He's done nothing!"

"'Toodles'?" Miss Ingram paused and gave the matchmaker a speculative look. "That's a strange thing to call yet another Shift-born abomination. It almost sounds like the sort of name you'd give a pet: a dear, sweet, *cherished* pet." She bared her teeth in an unnerving parody of a smile. "One would almost think that this little rodent is *special* to you."

"More special than you know," Mrs. Knight replied. "Put him down."

"Oh, I intend to do just that," said Miss Ingram with a wicked laugh. She raised the plastic ball high and slammed it to the floor. It cracked like an egg on impact. Toodles' furry body went flying.

And kept on flying. The tiny bat wings helped. They sprouted from his back in a puff of sulfurous smoke and fluttered madly, lifting the hamster in a wildly looping flight path that brought him in for a two-point landing on Miss Ingram's neck. Said two points being the adorably cute pair of fangs that he buried in her carotid artery, as the office instantly became one big, sanguinary Splash Zone.

When it was all over, Mrs. Knight surveyed the mess and sighed. "Oh, Toodles, whatever am I going to do with you?"

"Sorry," Toodles mumbled between furious bouts of grooming the blood from his whiskers. "Didn't know it was gonna go all splorty like that."

"It's all right, darling, but do try to be more discriminating about your feeding site next time. When I replace your runabout ball and get you a new SmartStik it's going to include an e-book on human anatomy. Do promise me you'll read it."

The hamster looked up sharply. "Do I hafta? I mean, I'm gonna have my paws full, what with getting the cleaning service in here, and my regular workload, and on top of it all, I've gotta show *that* one the ropes as soon as she's ready."

He gestured at Miss Ingram's cadaver. The would-be avenger's earthly shell was not resting in peace. Rather, the body was shuddering like a badly tuned motor, racked by a series of rapid-fire changes. Even as Toodles spoke, the corpse swiftly crumpled in on itself, dwindling and reshaping at an alarming rate like some demonic piece of origami.

Perhaps the process was not so alarming as all that, at least as far as Mrs. Knight was concerned. She regarded the advancing metamorphosis with a blasé eye as she said, "Yes, fine, I know all that. But do read the book *eventually*, dear Toodles. Never neglect your education. Just think, if Miss Ingram had *studied* the Shift's effects rather than loathing them, she might have realized that vampirism is the second most common side-effect of the Shift in the lower mammals, libertarianism being the first."

"Hey! I'd rather be exposed to, you know, the inconveniences attending too much liberty than to those, like, attending too small a degree of it, okay?" the hamster protested.

A groan from what remained of Miss Ingram cut off any further philosophical exchange. Uncurling her small, golden-furred body, the recently deceased young woman sat up unsteadily. Swaying a bit, her crimson eyes grew wide as she stared at the delicate pink paws that had replaced her hands.

A fragment of the screen from Toodles' shattered SmartStik provided just enough of a reflective surface for her to catch a glimpse of her new self. Her whiskers flared and her jaw dropped simultaneously.

"I'm a *hamster*?" she shrieked.

"A *vampire* hamster," Toodles cheerfully clarified. "Hubba-hubba!"

"But—but—but how—?"

"Shall we tell her?" Mrs. Knight asked Toodles archly.

"She tried to kill you and me both. She deserves it," he replied.

And so in perfect synchrony and without one iota of mercy, matchmaker and *Mesocricetus auratus* together said:

"Shift happens."

Esther Friesner

Nebula Award winner Esther Friesner is the author of over 40 novels and almost 200 short stories. Educated at Vassar College and Yale University, where she received a Ph.D., she is also a poet, a playwright, and the editor of several anthologies. The best known of these is the *Chicks in Chainmail* series that she created and edits for Baen Books. The sixth book, *Chicks and Balances,* appeared in July 2015. *Deception's Pawn,* the latest title in her popular *Princesses of Myth* series of Young Adult novels from Random House, was published in April 2015.

Esther is married, a mother of two, grandmother of one, harbors cats, and lives in Connecticut.

THE TRANSFORMATION OF PRINCE HUMPHREY

Brent C. Smith

*P*rince Humphrey raises his glass and smiles in turn at each
person around the table. "A toast! To the future! May it bring
us our heart's desire!"

Every glass is raised, tilted to the prince, and then to the lips of
its holder.

PRINCE LEOPOLD, HUMPHREY'S YOUNGER BROTHER

Look at you, Brother, with that smug look on your face.
So charming! So handsome! So heroic, the way you impaled
that marauding dragon on your lance and saved Manfred's
kingdom.

If I hear "gallant" one more time, I'm going to tell Rico to
bash some heads. He's eager to please.

And Princess Leonora, with your flawless skin and cherubic
face, why do you stare at him so intently? It's me you should
gaze at. I'm going places! You're only marrying him because
he's older, and heir, and good with a lance.

Not if I can help it. Enjoy this while you can, Brother. The
bribes were expensive, but the army is mine now. I have plans.
Big plans.

PRINCESS LEONORA, HUMPHREY'S BETROTHED

Why do you never respond?

All those notes I've left: "*Let's run away together. Yours -L,*" "*My heart belongs to you. -L.*"

Are you ashamed of your unconventional looks? I adore scars. The way your lip pulls up on one side in a permanent sneer proclaims "Bad Boy" to the kingdom. I idolize bad boys.

You're twice the man this princely peacock is, with his shiny lance, all smiles and manners, sunshine and gallantry. Ugh! Humphrey isn't the only one who can impale things. This dagger concealed in my gown is sharp and eager.

A strong woman should be able to marry a man she chooses. A man like you, Rico.

RICO, BEST FRIEND TO HUMPHREY AND LEOPOLD

Look at me!

Look at me!

Stop looking at Humphrey! Look at me!

I've seen how you eyeball me when we're alone. I've read the love notes you leave where I'll find them, each signed with a loving "L."

I've done everything you asked. I've delivered your secret orders to your army. They're camped in the woods. Soon, you will rule the kingdom, and we can finally be together. Rico and Leopold.

Now, *look at me!*

KING MANFRED, FATHER OF LEONORA

I hate these ceremonial pants. They chafe, like you, Prince Humphrey. What are you up to? You've slain the dragon, and won the hand of my daughter as your reward. You've charmed the queen, and my subjects love you. The kingdom will be yours someday.

Is someday not soon enough? My scouts have told me all about your army in the woods. Do you think that I will not rise to your challenge?

Youth these days are so impatient. Why can't you bide your

time? Marry Leonora. Make heirs. That's what princes do. That's what I did—married that shrew of a queen, instead of the magical Volanda. Now, she was something. The enchantments she could cast! That thing she did with the petrification spell—

Bah! Prince Humphrey, you aren't the only one with plans. I haven't kept my throne for so long by suffering upstarts.

QUEEN FELICITY, WIFE OF MANFRED

I see you Leonora, ungrateful daughter. I see your hand rooting around the folds of your dress like a hungry squirrel. I know what nut you have there. My wedding ring.

Did you think I wouldn't miss it? Are the coffers of your strutting prince so bare that you have to steal from your own mother?

Well, dearest daughter, you won't end up like me, farmed out to a handsome, impotent buffoon that can't put his pants on right-side-out without help.

First, to take care of your pretty prince, I'll ask Volanda to curse him. She's followed me for years, lurking in the shadows. I could've put a stop to her yearnings long ago, but I knew her talents would prove useful.

Then you and I will talk.

VOLANDA, THE ROYAL WITCH

My ring. For years I've shed a tear,
each time I longed to hold you near.
The king once promised you to me.
Instead, he wed Felicity.
But, now the story turns quite tragic.
As payment for a simple magic,
a trickster robbed her bedside stand,
and now you glitter on my hand.

The prince gasps, his eyes wide. The goblet falls from his hand to shatter on the stone floor. Smoke billows around him and the others stare, listening to him retch and choke within the opaque cloud. No one moves to help him as the prince's struggles grow quiet, until finally the smoke dissipates. A glistening green toad crouches on Humphrey's seat, its eyes bulging at the royal family, sounding a single, forlorn ribbit from deep within its rotund chest.

Who did this? They turn on each other.

PRINCE HUMPHREY

Freedom, at last!

Volanda could've warned me that her invisibility potion tastes like a mix of ear wax and armpit. I almost spit it onto the floor. That would've been a sight, the smoke fading and me standing there with a sheepish look on my face and a frog in my hand.

Poor froggy, you probably won't survive the night. Before long, one of them will decide that a prince-turned-frog is a threat to their ambition. As for me, I leave them to their schemes.

Ahead of me lie open skies and distant lands.

Brent C. Smith

Brent C. Smith is a software developer hunkered down in the perpetual winter of Portland, Maine. When he's not pushing buttons for the Man, the characters in his head are making him push buttons at home so they can get out into the world. He is a graduate of the Odyssey Writing Workshop and his fiction can also be found online at *Daily Science Fiction* and *New Myths*. You can also look for him at brentcsmith. net or on Twitter at @SpecFic_Brent.

IN THE END, YOU GET CLARITY

LAURA PEARLMAN

T he first time Leopard-Print Girl killed someone, it was an accident.

She wasn't Leopard-Print Girl then. She was Nicole Davis, an urban studies sophomore at the University of Chicago. On her first day home for Christmas break, her mom told her things were getting worse at work. Her boss had been looking for an opportunity to reprimand her; he'd found one the previous week. She'd taken her fourth-grade class on a field trip to the Springville Winter Festival. The kids had enjoyed the sleigh ride and were looking forward to meeting a local celebrity: Andy Childe, one of Mrs. Davis' former students, was a contestant on a new ice-sculpting reality show. They were about to say hello to him when his sculpture crashed to the ground. He yelled something about sabotage and threw a ballerina head (not the severed head of a ballerina, Mrs. Davis clarified, but the broken-off head of a ballerina ice sculpture) at one of the other ice sculptors. Then he grabbed a ballerina arm and swung it, missing his target and hitting an actual ballerina who was visiting the festival on her one day off after twelve consecutive performances. Passers-by grabbed ballerina parts (from the broken statue, not the live ballerina) and joined the melee. Nicole's mom rushed the children away, but one of the boys was hit by a flying ballerina nose and got a black eye. She received a written reprimand for endangering the children.

"What? Wasn't the field trip approved?"

"Yes, of course. The Tyrant is saying I didn't move quickly enough. And since I'd had Andy in my class fifteen years ago, I should have known he was unstable."

The Tyrant was the principal at East Springville Elementary School; his real name was Hiram Banks. Nicole had him for third grade, back when he was still a teacher. Nicole hated third grade. She'd hated it since the day she said her mom was a superhero, and Mr. Banks said she wasn't.

Technically, he was right. "Superhero" is a registered trademark of the League of Superheroes, and to qualify, you need to have a superpower and use it in at least one documented act of heroism. Mrs. Davis' superpower was the ability to project low-powered lasers from her eyes. Pointing things out on a whiteboard and entertaining cats at a distance are not considered heroic acts.

Instead of explaining this to Nicole gently, Mr. Banks made her write "My mom is not a superhero" (and, since her mom taught at the same school, "Mrs. Davis is not a superhero") on the blackboard one hundred times. She had to write a lot of things on the blackboard that year.

Nicole and her mom had a tradition of taking a long walk together whenever one of them got home from a trip. Mrs. Davis felt like she was coming down with the flu, so Nicole went alone. She'd been walking about twenty minutes when it began to rain. Ahead of her, a small group of men spilled out of a bar. She recognized them: three school board members and Hiram Banks.

Nicole had no desire to speak to Mr. Banks, but as she watched the men go their separate ways, she realized he was headed in her direction. He stumbled, he wove, and finally he stopped. He fumbled for his keys and pointed them at a car. A different car, behind him, chirped in response.

"Mr Banks," she called, running up to him.

"Do I know you?"

"I'm Nicole Davis. I went to East Springville Elementary. And my mom works there. Lily Davis. Look, why don't you let me have your keys, and I'll get you a taxi?"

"Nicole Davis... your dad was Tyrone Davis, right? Drove the school bus?"

Nicole nodded. "Give me your keys." She held out her hand. "You shouldn't be driving."

"Nothing wrong with my driving." Mr. Banks said. "I'm an excellent driver. Better than your dad, anyway."

Nicole bristled. The accident hadn't been her father's fault. The brakes had failed; the accident investigators confirmed it. Principal Banks had come to Nicole's house and presented her mom with a ten thousand dollar check, a nondisclosure agreement, and his personal assurance that, effective immediately, the bus would be serviced by someone other than his alcoholic brother-in-law.

Nicole was furious. A weird, cold energy flowed up her spine, into her arms, and out through her fingertips. Mr. Banks collapsed.

Nicole screamed. One of the school board members, Mr. Logan, ran back across the street to check on Mr. Banks. He was dead.

The official cause of death was "lightning strike." Nicole didn't remember hearing any thunder.

THE FIRST TIME Leopard-Print Girl flew, it was an impulse.

She was still Nicole then. It should have been the start of her junior year, but her mom's illness had turned out to be serious. Nicole had moved back home and taken a job at the Springville public library.

She was leaving work one day when a mouse fell on her head. On closer inspection, it was a catnip mouse. She looked down and saw at least a dozen cat toys. She looked up and saw a cat.

"Pyewacket!" she said. "Come down off the roof."

The neighbors got Pyewacket when he was a kitten and Nicole was in second grade. It was love at first sight. The two of them developed a routine. He'd hide behind a rosebush, waiting for her to get home from school. She'd walk by, pretending not to notice, and he'd zoom out and tag her ankle. She'd throw a toy; he'd chase it and pick it up. Then he'd drop it and run back over to her. She tried to explain that the game would work better if he came back to her and *then* dropped the toy, but cats aren't known for listening to reason.

Pyewacket was thirteen years old now and still as unreasonable as ever. "Come down," Nicole said, "and I'll play with you." She waved the catnip mouse at him to show she meant it. She knew he could climb down easily; he'd claimed half the roofs in the neighborhood as his personal territory. She gave up and, without thinking, flew towards the roof. She was almost there when she realized she was flying. Then she realized she didn't know how to land.

In her panic, she began flailing her arms and legs. This sent her crashing down onto the roof, leaving her with some bruises and scrapes but no serious injuries. The catnip mouse landed a few feet away, unharmed. Pyewacket pounced and batted it off the edge of the roof. Then he walked over to Nicole and looked at her expectantly.

When she failed to throw the mouse for him, he decided he had urgent business elsewhere. He strutted across the roof, leapt into a nearby tree, and climbed down. Nicole flew to the ground, landing on a hard-shelled plastic ball with a little bell inside and twisting her ankle.

She practiced, of course. She learned her limits. She couldn't fly more than a few miles at a time or carry anything weighing more than a few pounds. The wind dried out her skin, irritated her eyes, and did terrible things to her hair. Still, she could fly, and that was pretty cool.

THE FIRST TIME Leopard-Print Girl deflected a bullet, it was a footnote in someone else's story.

When Pablo Winterly slept, he dreamed of ice sculptures: caterpillars that transformed into butterflies as they melted, working bicycles, violins that produced music sweeter than any he'd heard while awake. He spent his waking hours carving ice and studying everything remotely related to his craft: botany, anatomy, and art history for inspiration, architecture, chemistry, and physics for technique. He played with the optical properties of ice, carving prisms that projected rainbows onto nearby objects and lenses that produced comically distorted views of the world. He lived a comfortable life, supplying ice sculptures for weddings, parties, and charity events in the greater Springville area.

At Winterly's sixtieth birthday party, Andy Childe struck up a conversation. Andy had just graduated with a fine arts degree and wanted to learn to sculpt ice. Winterly had been thinking, on this milestone birthday, about his legacy. He was proud of his creations, but they were ephemeral; the only thing of value he could leave to the world was his knowledge. He agreed to take Andy on as an apprentice.

Winterly taught Andy everything he knew. He taught him to use chisels and chainsaws, to create designs that were delicate-looking but structurally sound, and to calculate a piece's melting rate based on its shape, the ambient temperature, wind, and degree of sun exposure.

Andy learned quickly. He wasn't interested in understanding the theories behind Winterly's techniques, but he was good at executing them and memorizing any formulas he needed to know. After three years, he was a competent sculptor, but he wanted more. He wanted to be famous. When he heard about a new ice-sculpture reality TV series, he was one of the first to apply.

Andy did well on Ice Wars. He was good-looking, did beautiful work, and always had a funny story to tell. Everyone loved Andy's stories. Everyone except Winterly. Andy's stories stretched the truth well past its breaking point. They painted

Andy as patient and creative and Winterly as a doddering old man well past his prime. During the semi-finals, Andy used one of Winterly's newest techniques and claimed he'd invented it himself.

Andy returned to Springville for the break between the Ice Wars semi-final and final rounds. He invited Winterly to his home for a chat to smooth things over. Andy offered Winterly an insincere apology; Winterly offered Andy his insincere forgiveness. Then the two men moved onto a more comfortable topic: their designs for the upcoming Springville Winter Festival.

Andy's sculpture was a gravity-defying ballerina, standing en pointe with arms curved overhead. Winterly's was a fantastical bird, with the head of a hawk and a vast plume of feathers like a peacock's, with row upon row of grooves carved into the plume to form concentric circles. The entire bird was tilted forward as if pointing at something beneath it. Winterly positioned his bird to face Andy's ballerina. Together, the two pieces made a striking tableau; the bird looked as if it might swoop down and attack the ballerina at any moment.

If Andy had bothered to study any of the optics texts Winterly had made available to him over the years, he might have noticed something odd about Winterly's sculpture. He might have known that a commercial Fresnel lens can melt copper at its focal point on a sunny day. He might have guessed that a Fresnel lens hand-carved out of ice and made to resemble a plume of feathers could accelerate the melting of an ice ballerina's ankle enough to seriously degrade its ability to bear weight. But he didn't know any of these things, so he didn't object to the bird statue's placement.

Andy flew into a rage when his ballerina collapsed. He knew Winterly was behind it somehow. He threw the ballerina's head at Winterly and grazed his shoulder. Then he picked up an arm and swung it at Winterly's head, but it slipped and hit an off-duty ballerina instead. The Ice Wars cameras, there to record a feel-good segment about Andy interacting with a bunch of fourth-graders at the festival, caught everything. He was convicted of Assault on an Elderly Person and spent the next year's Winter Festival in jail. He passed the time designing weapons—ice daggers, ice bullets, ice crossbow bolts—and fantasizing about using them on Winterly.

Andy was released from jail six months later. His ice weapon designs were beautiful on paper, but when he tried to create them, the ice daggers were always too blunt or too fragile, and the ice projectiles just wouldn't fire. In the end, he abandoned those ideas and bought a regular gun and a box of regular bullets.

Andy brought his gun to the next year's Springville Winter Festival. He shot at Winterly, who would be dead now if a woman hadn't tripped and fallen into the bullet's path. The woman was Nicole Davis; the bullet tore her shirt and left a bruise as it bounced off, but otherwise did no damage.

Andy kept shooting. Nicole extended an arm towards him and, for the second time in her life, felt a surge of cold energy flow through it. He fell to the ground, dead. An onlooker caught the whole thing on video.

THE FIRST TIME Leopard-Print Girl met with Mayor Logan, it was the path of least resistance.

The festival video (uploaded with the title "Leopard-Print Girl Saves The Day") went viral. "Leopard-Print Girl" became Nicole's superhero name. The mayor invited her to meet with him.

They sat on opposite sides of his enormous mahogany desk. He thanked her for her actions during the festival and then got down to business.

"As the city's resident superhero," he said, "you'll need to deal with our supervillain."

"We have a supervillain?"

"Yes. The Leech. He's threatened to vaporize a city block if we don't pay him a million dollars within sixty days."

"Oh, him. He does that every year." The threats always made the local news. "You should just pay him. That's what previous mayors always did. He's done this sixteen times now, and he's never escalated."

"I don't negotiate with supervillains."

"Yes, but that's just an arbitrary—I mean, that policy doesn't apply to the Leech. He doesn't have any superpowers, so he's not a supervillain. He's a criminal mastermind."

"This administration has a zero tolerance policy towards criminal masterminds."

Mayor Logan had lots of zero tolerance policies. That's why she hadn't voted for him. "The thing is, he's pretty harmless. Credit-card fraud and illegal gambling. Getting rid of him is more dangerous than keeping him around. When a city rids itself of a nuisance villain, there's an 80 percent chance a real supervillain will move in to fill the void within a year. I wrote a research paper about that, if you'd like to—"

"No."

"A million dollars is a tiny fraction of the city's budget. And it's just a symbolic gesture, to maintain his membership in the League of Supervillains."

"You just said he wasn't—"

"It's an adjunct membership. Look," she said, standing, "the best thing you can do for the city is just pay him off. And besides, I don't have any law enforcement training. Think about the insurance implications. And I'm only staying in town until my mom—until she doesn't need me here. Then I'm going back to school."

The mayor stood and walked over to the window. Nicole started to walk towards the door.

"Sit down," the mayor said. "We're not finished. I've been thinking about the way you killed Andy Childe."

She winced. "I had to. He was shooting at people."

"Not why. How. It reminded me of that night two years ago. Hiram Banks. I saw you."

"That was an accident."

"So you say. But you hated him, didn't you? Blamed him for your father's death? Maybe you planned to kill him."

"He wasn't my favorite person, but I didn't know—"

"And your mother hated him, too? Maybe she put you up to it."

"What? No! What do—"

"I was the sole witness. If we tell different stories about that night, which of us will have more credibility with a jury?"

She sank back into her chair.

"So you're going to take care of the Leech for me, and anything else I tell you to do. Understood?"

Leopard-Print Girl nodded.

"Good," he said. "I'm glad we had this little chat."

THE FIRST TIME Leopard-Print Girl confronted the Leech, it was on the mayor's orders.

She flew into his compound, making what she hoped would be an impressive superhero entrance. The main reception area was spacious, with sleek modern furniture and a rust-colored carpet that looked like it would be really good at hiding bloodstains.

Leopard-Print Girl walked up to the receptionist's desk. "Hi, I'm here to see—"

"Please have a seat. I'll be with you in a moment."

Leopard-Print Girl took a tissue from the box on the desk and blew her nose. She appreciated the toasty warmth of the office after flying through near-freezing air at 200 mph, but the sudden temperature differential made her nose run.

The receptionist scowled at her. "Step back, please. I don't want to catch whatever—"

"I'm not sick," Leopard-Print Girl said. "It's just that I flew here and—"

"Do you have an appointment?" The receptionist squirted hand sanitizer onto her palm and rubbed her hands together vigorously.

"No, but I think he may be expecting me. I'm from the mayor's office."

"And what is this regarding?"

"Um, extortion?"

The receptionist sighed. "Don't you people read instructions? We stopped accepting hand-delivered cash years ago. Do you have any idea how filthy paper money is? Here." She handed Leopard-Print Girl a card. "Wire transfer instructions are on the back. Have a nice day."

"I'm not here to make a delivery. I need to talk to the Leech."

"Do you have—oh, right. Let me see if I can pencil you in." She tapped a few keys on her computer. "How does 10:30 this morning sound?"

"Um, it's 10:38 now."

"Yes. You're late. I'll have someone escort you in."

An armed guard led Leopard-Print Girl to the Leech's command center, which turned out to be a large office with a door in back that, according to the blueprints she'd studied, led to the Leech's living quarters. She counted eight computer monitors spread across a variety of desks: a mahogany desk just like the mayor's, a minimalist white desk, a standing desk, and a treadmill desk. Velvet Elvis paintings and a menagerie of stuffed animal heads adorned the walls.

The guard left Leopard-Print Girl alone with the Leech. He was sitting at the mahogany desk. His chair looked like the kind with thirty-seven adjustment points—but no control interface, because it senses the optimal settings for each individual and adjusts itself accordingly.

"Stacey tells me you're here to ask for a payment extension."

"You should fire her. The mayor sent me to kill you." She paused for dramatic effect. "I'm hoping we can work out a compromise instead."

"You can't kill me. The countdown has already started, and only I can stop it."

Leopard-Print Girl rolled her eyes. "Your security practices are pathetic. You shouldn't download games from untrusted sites, and you really shouldn't play your pirated copy of Candy Bird Sudoku Wars on the same system you use to control your superweapon. And seriously, 'birdseed' is too short to be a good password, and it's in the dictionary, which is even worse. Changing the e's to threes doesn't help nearly as much as you seem to think."

"You mentioned a compromise," the Leech said.

"Basically, if you stop extorting the city, I won't interfere with any of your other business. In fact, I can help you."

The Leech leaned forward. "As a spy in the mayor's office?"

"Well, no. What I'm proposing is that I help you shore up your security, and you pay me 20 percent of your net income."

"You want to work for me?"

"It can't be any worse than working for the mayor. Do you know what my primary responsibility has been for the past six weeks? Hand-delivering his daughter's wedding invitations. Apparently a flying messenger is a status symbol."

"That doesn't sound—"

"The worst are the out-of-town guests. I have to take a commercial flight and then fly the last couple miles under my own power. I almost missed my mother's funeral because my flight back from Tampa was delayed. Anyway, what do you say?"

"I say no. You can work here as an unpaid intern if you like."

"And the annual extortion demands?"

"Are a tradition."

She could see now that her plan wasn't going to work. None of the plans would work. Not hers, not the Leech's, not the mayor's. She wasn't cut out to be a superhero.

"Look, Leopard-Print Girl—"

"Why does everyone call me that? My name is Nicole Davis. It's not a secret. You can't reduce my entire identity to a single ill-advised fashion choice I made when I was trying to hold it together while my mom was dying."

She hated being Leopard-Print Girl. She hated working for the mayor. She'd probably hate working for the Leech even more.

"Okay, let's not get hysterical—"

"This isn't hysteria. This is clarity." She let out a small laugh. "That's what they should call me. Clarity Girl. Clarity Woman. Clarity."

THE FIRST TIME Clarity killed someone, it was a step on a path of her own devising.

She took a deep breath. And another.

She zapped the Leech.

She stepped over his lifeless body and aborted the weapon launch.

She sat in his chair. Her chair.

There was a lot she needed to do. Change the passwords and security codes. Get rid of any disloyal minions. Hire new ones. Redecorate. She'd definitely have to redecorate. Get rid of things. The stuff on the walls, some of the desks, the dead body on the floor.

She'd keep the chair, though. She liked the chair. She couldn't remember ever feeling as comfortable as she did in that chair.

Laura Pearlman

Laura Pearlman is neither a superhero nor a supervillain. Her work has appeared or is forthcoming in *Shimmer, Flash Fiction Online, The Drabblecast,* and *Daily Science Fiction.* She has a Twitter feed called @ laurasbadideas, a blog called Unlikely Explanations (unlikelyexplanations. com), and a Tumblr devoted to things her cats have dropped into their water bowl. She should probably get out more.

PROJECT DISASTER

TIM PRATT

The reporter walked slowly into Disaster Man's office, her shoulders hunched, her eyes darting, as if on the lookout for deathtraps, snakepits, or falling sharks. Disaster Man smiled at her—not that she'd be able to tell—from behind his desk, a mass of chrome and steel. He gestured toward the empty chair, a thing of complex webbing and curves that was more comfortable than it looked, and said, "Welcome to the Isle of Wrack, Miss Lawton. I hope your journey was pleasant? "

The reporter frowned. She was thin, on the young side of thirty, with long straight brown hair and a serious expression. "I was blindfolded on the helicopter flight."

Disaster Man shrugged. "Some of my henchpeople are traditionalists, and of course, security is a concern. I trust you weren't harmed? "

"No, they were very... professional." She looked around the room again, with less fear and more curiosity. The space was gleaming, spare, and very modern. "This isn't what I expected. I thought there'd be more... I don't know... black leather. And skulls. "

"I've always thought leaving bits of corpses around was a bit unsanitary."

"It's just... not the kind of office I imagined for a terrorist." She cocked her head. "You don't object to being called that?"

"Hmm. 'Extortionist' is more accurate, but I'm used to it.

Either one is better than 'supervillain.'" He made a face. "Why do they call me that? Do I wear a costume?"

"You're wearing a mask right now," she said. "You always do, in every appearance, every video, every satellite broadcast."

Disaster Man waved that away. "The mask is just to conceal my identity."

"Your mask is a black executioner's hood with a bright yellow radiation symbol on the face," she pointed out.

"I don't want to get mixed up with all the other people who wear masks, so it pays to be distinctive."

"You use a voice distorter that makes you sound like a psychopathic robot."

"Again, for the purposes of concealing my identity, and making a strong impression, that's all."

She leaned forward. "You call yourself 'Disaster Man.'"

"Oh, that. I can hardly use my real name, and it's a helpful mnemonic device. It reminds people of what I can do. The point is, I don't behave like a supervillain. Do I fight people with odd powers who wear colorful costumes? No. Do I rob banks, hijack cruise ships, or drive an armored car shaped like a dire wolf? No. I just make demands, and when those demands are met, I stay peacefully on my island."

"You've only used your powers twice," she said, not quite a question.

He nodded. "That's all it took. One demonstration of my capabilities... and one demonstration of how foolish it was to try to imprison me."

"And, remarkably, no one was hurt in either case. The first time you demonstrated your power, you did so in the remote desert, and when you were arrested, you didn't escape from prisoner transport, or the World Court—you waited until they'd put you on an island with only drone and robot guards before you blew everything up."

He drummed armored fingers on the desktop. "This is the first interview I've granted during the whole twenty years of my intermittent reign of terror. The reason you got the interview was because you impressed me by actually finding a way to get a message to me asking for one. You are not impressing me now, however. Do you actually have any questions?"

"Yes," she said. "Why do you pretend to be evil?"

He looked at her for a long moment, and then laughed. "That's a question, all right. But I take issue with your premise. I'm not evil, you see. I'm beyond the concept of evil. An ant might consider a human evil for flooding its hill, and you ordinary fools are like ants to me—"

She interrupted him, which very few people dared to do. "You have the ability to generate explosive blasts around your body, releasing energy comparable to that of multiple nuclear bombs. That ability is coupled with physical invulnerability—which is how you survive generating those blasts. For two decades you've threatened to devastate cities unless the developed nations pay you protection money, but you've never hurt anyone."

He gave his best dark chuckle. "Hurting you insignificant blobs of cellulite and dandruff on an individual basis would be time-consuming and inefficient. I arrange to hurt you in other ways."

She nodded, flipping through an old-fashioned notebook; she'd been forbidden to bring electronic devices. "Yes, you've funded some of the most brutally regressive political candidates in the developed world... but you always make sure the donations are discovered, to the detriment of the politicians involved, because there's almost no one so right-wing that they think your support is a good idea. Not one politician you've supported has ever won a subsequent election or succeeded in joining a working coalition."

"So, I'm not good at politics. You're boring me, Miss Lawton."

She pressed on. "There are plenty of lawless warlords in developing nations you could fund successfully, but you haven't."

"Why would I want to buy influence in war-torn nations like those? They don't have any money to give me."

She tapped her notebook with a pen, not bothering to write

down what he'd said, which annoyed him. "Mmm. Politicians aren't the only recipients of your largess, though, are they? I've tracked donations through shell companies back to you. You've given millions to progressive candidates, charities, NGOs, and local grassroots organizations promoting literacy, feeding the hungry, supporting women's rights...."

Disaster Man stopped smiling, clenched his gauntleted fists, and let out a low growl, transformed into a sound of profound mechanical menace by his vocal scrambler.

She went on, either oblivious to his reaction or pretending to be. "In fact, as near as I can tell, you're not so much extorting the nations of the world for your personal gain as you are engaging in a massive redistribution of wealth. You're basically an international charity organization unwillingly supported by the G20 nations."

"This interview is over," he said. "Leave now, or I'll have you thrown into the volcano."

"I'd be your first ever victim, then. I was talking to one of your henchpeople. He explained how he was a street thug and drug addict, until he joined your organization, which gave him rehabilitation and job training. Even the bad guys you employ aren't so bad."

He rose. "I am the absolute ruler of this rogue micronation, the invulnerable and merciless Disaster Man—"

"You are Brady Doolittle, age 52, from Pomegranate Grove, Georgia. Please do sit down."

Disaster Man didn't stagger, but it was a near thing. He sank back into his chair. "How did you find all this out?" he whispered.

"My organization was very well funded. By you."

He racked his brain. "What, one of the judicial review programs, looking into old criminal proceedings for wrongful convictions? You weren't supposed to research me. My guilt was unquestionable!"

She shook her head. "No. I'm with Wolf-Lundmark Enterprises."

"Ah." That was unexpected. Maybe the most unexpected thing in this interview yet. "Give my regards to Drs. Wolf and Lundmark."

She laughed, and it was a surprise, a bright tinkle of a sound. "You know as well as I do the company is named for the galaxy, Wolf-Lundmark-Melotte—the founders just thought using the whole name would be a bit unwieldy. They would have named the company after a closer star or galaxy, but every corporation with half an eye on the sky picks some celestial object or group to put in their name, so choices were limited."

"Why is a commercial space travel company investigating me?"

"Because you've given us tens of millions of dollars, and you're a terrorist! And, like it or not, a supervillain. We wanted to make sure you weren't planning to swoop in and use our work for evil. We have extremely good data scientists, and once they hit the limits of what they could do research-wise with their computers, they hired me, ostensibly as assistant head of investor relations. My background is in forensic accounting and investigative reporting." She shrugged. "You're good at covering your tracks. I'm better at uncovering them. That's my superpower. I talked to your childhood friends, your family, your primary school teachers, your high school girlfriend and your college boyfriend. Gradually, a portrait of Disaster Man emerged. A smart, idealistic boy obsessed with comic books and science fiction novels, who became a smart, idealistic young man obsessed with social justice... who disappeared on a fishing trip when he was twenty years old, and was presumed drowned. There was a bizarre storm that day, huge waves, and at least one crack of thunder so loud people said it sounded like an enormous bomb going off."

"Listen," he said, thinking furiously. "What do you want from me? More money? More resources? You can't publish what you've found out, Miss Lawton. If I lose my leverage, if no one believes I'm a threat, then the money will dry up, and all the good I've done will stop."

"We know you discovered your powers by accident on that fishing trip. After that, it's speculation, but I think you realized, with your abilities, that you could change the world." That tinkling laugh again. "Maybe you even thought of being a superhero! But what good is a superhero who creates huge explosions? Maybe if you could create little ones, too... but your power is all-or-nothing, isn't it? Miles of devastation, or nothing at all."

"I've never been able to refine my abilities, no. It's... difficult to practice, as you might imagine. Sometimes I go out on a lonely atoll, just to make sure it still works, but that's all."

She nodded. "Allow me some more speculation. When you realized you couldn't plausibly become a superhero, you decided to become a supervillain instead—that way you could do some real good."

Disaster Man took off his hood, and switched off his voice scrambler.

"You don't look a day over twenty." Her expression of genuine surprise made him realize how artificial her earlier pretense at surprise had been.

He shrugged. "I don't know if I'm immortal or not. But I'm certainly immortal *so far.*"

She reached across the desk and patted his gauntlet. "When you were young, you dreamed about space. You read stories of interplanetary, even interstellar, travel. You used to peer through the telescope your stepfather bought you for hours, staying up so late you practically sleepwalked through school the next day. Your friends said space was an obsession. Clearly, it's something that still interests you, since we're not the only company you fund. You've poured a lot of money into researching experimental spacecraft propulsion systems, none of which has panned out. Why is that?"

He shook his head. "The governments of the world have given up on the dream of space, but I haven't. I might live forever, Miss Lawton. If I live forever, I'd like to spend at least some of it...." He tilted his head back. "Up there. I want to make this world a better place, then take that better place into the vastness of space. It's frustrating, how slowly things move, but I can afford to be patient."

She reached into her bag and removed a folder, sliding it to him across the desk. "Read that."

He took off the bulky gauntlets and picked up the folder. The front page read "Project Disaster." He scanned the page—it was brief, not very technical, and to the point—and then stared at her. "Is this for real?"

She nodded.

"But I'd have to leave all this behind. The money would run out quickly—I don't actually have much liquidity. Every month when I get my protection money I plow it right back into my projects. There are still so many problems here, on Earth...."

"No one knows who Disaster Man is. They see a mask, and hear an electronically altered voice. No one has dared to test you, not as long as you keep making appearances and threats. You don't have to be the face of Disaster Man. Do you have any trusted lieutenants who could take over the public relations angle? Put your hood on them, and who could tell the difference?"

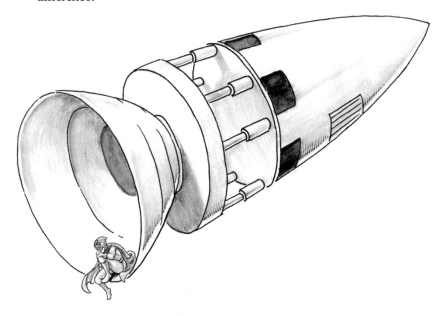

Disaster Man looked down at the file, and Brady Doolittle smiled. "You want to strap me to the ass end of a spaceship, huh?"

That laugh again. "Just like Project Orion—the plan to launch spacecraft by firing off a series of atomic bombs for propulsion. The Partial Test Ban Treaty of 1963 pretty much killed that idea... but you aren't a bomb, Mr. Doolittle, and your explosions aren't radioactive. You wouldn't spend long strapped to the ship, anyway. You'd get to come inside and relax with the crew once we got up to speed. And if you really live forever...." She reached across the desk and squeezed his bare hand. "Think how far you could go?"

Tim Pratt

Tim Pratt's fiction has won a Hugo Award, and he's been a finalist for Sturgeon, Stoker, World Fantasy, Mythopoeic, and Nebula Awards, among others. His books include three short story collections, most recently *Antiquities and Tangibles and Other Stories*; a volume of poems; contemporary fantasy novels *The Strange Adventures of Rangergirl, Briarpatch, Heirs of Grace*, and *The Deep Woods*; science fantasy *The Nex*; steampunk novel The Constantine Affliction (as T. Aaron Payton); various role playing game tie-in fantasy novels; and, as T.A. Pratt, eight books (and counting) in an urban fantasy series about sorcerer Marla Mason. He edited anthology Sympathy for the Devil and co-edited Rags and Bones: New Twists on Timeless Tales with Melissa Marr. He works as a senior editor for Locus magazine, and lives in Berkeley CA with his wife Heather Shaw and their son River. Find him online at timpratt.org.

HELLO HOTEL

PIERS ANTHONY

E ric stared at the sign above the moving belt in the airport terminal: HELL TEL. That was the one he was supposed to take? "But I don't believe in hell," he muttered, smiling. "That I can 'tel' you for certain."

Then he realized that some of the letters had fallen off the sign. He was able to make out their imprints: O HO, as if they were laughing at his feeble joke. Properly filled in, the sign would say HELLO HOTEL. That was the one he wanted.

Eric picked up his suitcase, stepped onto the moving belt, and was carried smoothly along the hall. He saw other people riding other belts to other destinations. It was a nice feature this airport had: a network of belts ushering travelers to far-flung gates.

The belt veered, descended to pass under several other belts, then formed into an escalator that rose to the floor above. It was like a magic path, continuing on its way regardless of traffic. It curved to the right and went through an aperture in the wall to emerge outside the building. It was as much fun as an amusement park ride.

The belt coursed along a ledge before making a sharp turn to depart the building entirely, spiraling up in a giant corkscrew before arching to an upper story of the next building. Eric was amazed at its architecture; this was the most complicated beltway he had encountered. Did it really need to be so fancy? He understood that it had to be kept separate from the outside world, so that those who used it would not have to go through security again. But a fun-house corkscrew?

"Oh."

Eric looked up at the sound. A young woman stood at the corner, having evidently just stepped off the belt to the adjacent landing. She was in a form-fitting dress and very nice brown hair showed under her pert little hat. She was so pretty that Eric stepped off, too. Any pretext would do, to meet a chick like this.

"Going my way?" he inquired.

"I was going to the Hello Hotel," she replied. "But there's a problem."

"This is the belt. You're nervous about heights?" He glanced at the arch. "There's a good handrail; it should be safe."

"It's not that, exactly," she said, flustered. "It's—it's windy."

So it was; a fairly stiff breeze had come up between the buildings. Eric saw that a dark storm was threatening. The wind carried dust and loose papers along, and tugged at the woman's hair and the hem of her dress. Oh. If she ventured out on that belt, the air would really get to work on that dress. There was half a throng of folk below, and a crew of workmen digging at a fault in the road right beneath the arch. They could get a fair eyeful if they looked up at the right time, as they surely would. Worse, the fine mesh of the belt turned out to be transparent. She would have a problem even if her dress did not rise.

"Maybe I can help," Eric said, gallantly. He took off his jacket and spread it on the moving belt. "Step on this."

"Thank you," she said, surprised. She quickly stepped onto the jacket, before it was carried away and crossed the arch without her. Eric stepped on behind her.

She glanced back at him, looking cutely uncomfortable. "I'm ruining your coat."

He wanted to put her at ease. "Don't be concerned. It's an old coat and dirty anyway."

They rode the corkscrew up together, and though the wind tried, it could not dislodge the jacket under her feet. The workmen below glanced up, then down again, disappointed.

He wanted to get to know her better, to find a way to connect with her. "I am Eric," he said. "I am pleased to make your acquaintance."

"I'm Pauline. I am thrilled to meet you."

Well, now. "Your flight was canceled too, Pauline?"

She nodded uneasily. "Something like that."

They reached the top and started across the arch. The wind intensified, tugging desperately at the jacket, but got nowhere.

Then she surprised him. "Have you been saved, Eric?"

Oh, no! Just when things were so positive with this nice girl, this had to happen. If that question meant what he thought it did, all was lost. She was a Jesus freak? Well, he would just have to get it over with. "I am an atheist."

She gazed at him with evident regret. "I'm so sorry."

Damn it, this was unfair. He had finally met a girl he might really like, and this had to spoil it. Partly in grief, partly in frustration, but mostly in anger at the injustice of it, he plunged into the morass. "Let's talk."

"Oh, yes!"

They stepped off the belt at the landing on the other building, and Eric retrieved his jacket. They stood looking down at the busy street.

"I am a rational man," Eric said, carefully. "I have no belief in the supernatural. I regard God as an illusion fostered by special interests to fleece the ignorant. If you are a missionary Bible devotee, we are not going to get along. That's too bad, because physically you are the very image of the girl I could love."

"I am an evangelical Christian. I am chagrined that a man as decent as you seem to be, who even spread his coat on the ground like Sir Walter Raleigh to spare me mischief, is doomed to spend eternity in hell. I must try to save you from that awful fate."

"I am not doomed to suffer in hell, because there is no hell," Eric said, hotly. "Neither are you destined for heaven, because that is nothing but a delusion to prevent us peons from rebelling against the abusive status quo. I hate the idea that a person as sweet as you should buy into that elaborate myth."

Oddly, she did not take offense. "You believe only in what you can see, hear, touch, or reason out? Not in any intangible spirit?"

"In essence, yes."

"Hold still. I'm going to kiss you."

"You're going to what?" He might have said more, but she stepped into him, drew him close, put her face to his, and kissed him firmly on the lips.

It was as if his head exploded in soft fire. The universe spun grandly around them, and ineffable music sounded. He was in rapture.

She moved back, breaking the divine contact. "And what is that?" she asked. "Can you see, hear, touch, or reason with it?"

Eric fought to maintain his equilibrium. "I never believed in angels," he said. "Until this moment."

She smiled tolerantly. "God is like that, if you only allow him in."

"Oh, Pauline," he said. "I'd give anything to have in reality what you offer only in pretense. Anything but my rationality. I won't subscribe to your God delusion to win your love."

"Maybe I should sing for you."

This was odd. "Sing?"

"A hymn. That's all I know, hymns."

"Pauline—"

She sang, beautifully.

"That's not a hymn!" he protested. "That's 'My Lady Greensleeves.'"

"No, that's 'What Child is This?'."

"I suppose the same melodies can be used for different things," he said. "I understand 'The Star-Spangled Banner' was set to the tune of an old English drinking song. Regardless, you sing divinely."

"Thank you."

"But why do you think music will convert me to your belief?"

"Music stirs the spirit."

He shook his head. "Hymns won't stir mine. Not in the way you want." He smiled. "Hymns won't do it. Neither will hyrrs."

She looked at him blankly.

"Him and her. *H, Y, M, N* and *H, Y, R, R.* Get it?"

"I think we had better resume our journey to the hotel."

Damn, again. He had lost her. Why had he tried a joke? She was clearly not amused. "We had better," he agreed, morosely.

They stepped back on the moving belt, which bore them into the hotel. It deposited them in the lobby before the front desk.

A dark desk clerk greeted them. "A room for two?" he inquired.

"No!" Eric and Pauline said, together.

Then Eric continued. "We're not a couple. We're two unconnected travelers. Our flights were canceled. The airline informed us that the Hello Hotel would provide free lodging for the night."

"That is correct. But as it happens, we have only one unoccupied suite remaining. If you do not care to share it, which one of you will take it?"

Pauline opened her mouth, but Eric spoke first. "She will. I'll sleep in the lobby."

"You will not," the clerk said, firmly. "We are a respectable establishment."

"Then I will return to the airport and sleep in *their* lobby," Eris said, nettled.

The clerk shrugged. "As you prefer."

"Eric—" Pauline said, distressed.

"It's the right thing to do," Eric said. He picked up his suitcase and turned around, walking back beside the moving belt.

Not only was the belt one-way toward the hotel, there was now a raging storm outside. There was no safe passage here.

"Eric—" Pauline had followed him.

"I will go downstairs and cross the street," he said.

"You'll get soaked, and you'll have to go through security again," she protested.

"Can't be helped."

"This isn't right, Eric. You have as much right to that room as I do."

"No. You're a lady. Your need for it is greater than mine."

"I'm sorry I didn't laugh at your joke."

"It wasn't very funny anyway."

She caught his arm. "Eric, please! Do I have to kiss you again?" That halted him in place. "Don't do that. I'm already half in love with you, foolish as that is, considering our incompatibility. Don't torment me further."

"Eric, I'm sorry. I will share the room with you."

"No. You're a moral evangelical woman. You don't do things like that."

"There's more to it than that. Please, share."

He shook his head. "You may think that an atheist has no scruples. That's not true. I am treating you as you deserve to be treated. The room is yours."

She kissed him again. Then she took him by the hand and led him, stunned, to the room. By the time he recovered, they were in the suite's family room, sitting before the TV. Their bags had somehow accompanied them.

"I am more than half in love with you, Eric," she said. "But I am not entirely what I seem. You have an awful decision to make."

She felt similarly about him? If only that were true! "I don't understand."

"Do you think it was coincidence that brought us together? That I look like your dream girl? I was sent to intercept you, and conditioned to love you if you showed any sign of being worthy."

Not coincidence? "What is this, some candied camera scenario?"

She laughed. "Candied camera!"

But his suspicion had been aroused. Was she trying to play him along? He turned on his cell phone recorder in his pocket, so that he would have a record. "Put a pretty girl with an anonymous man, make them share a room, see if he performs for the hidden camera? Big joke on him!"

Now she looked uncomfortable. "Not exactly."

"Then what, exactly?"

"Hell wants you."

Eric was confused, but not that confused. "Hell does not exist!"

"It does exist, as does heaven. And God, and Satan. And their emissaries on earth."

"You're crazy. Religion crazy. I may love you, but you're nuts."

She considered briefly. "Perhaps we should visit the bedroom before we continue this dialogue."

"Pauline, if you think sex will lure me into your delusion, I'd love the sex but I have to tell you it won't make me religious. I am terminally rational. I wouldn't want you to waste yourself this way. You deserve better than that. Some day you'll find a nice evangelical Christian man, not a nasty atheist."

"Hardly nasty. You have shown me that an atheist can be moral. Maybe opposites attract. I want you."

Eric was horribly tempted. If she liked him the way he liked her, despite their religious differences, could they simply ban that subject from their dialogue? He was not at all sure. "If I thought the bedroom would convert one of us to the way of the other, I'd do it."

"If only it were that simple."

This was curious. "What am I not understanding?"

"Come to the bedroom. Then I will tell you everything."

This was even more phenomenally tempting, but he distrusted it. "No. Tell me everything first."

Now her tears flowed in earnest. "Oh, Eric, you're so decent! Believe me on this: once you know the truth, I will probably no longer be available to you. Take me first, so that at least we have that much before it ends."

"What, you're a demoness from hell?" he asked, sarcastically.

"Something like that."

Her delusion was worse than he had thought. But his desire for her body was being overwhelmed by his desire to love and be loved by her. He wanted much more of her than a few minutes in bed. Maybe if he listened, he would see the way to get her free of this complicated confusion. "Tell me."

She plunged in without further hesitation. "I was an ordinary rather plain girl whose main activity was singing in the church choir. I wasn't very good; I had the tone but sang slightly off-key. I longed for the love of a good man I might marry and be happy with ever after, but I knew there was no way. I was doomed to frustration and dullness."

Eric did not speak, but he could see already that she was delusional, apart from her belief in the supernatural. She sang surpassingly well, and there was no way she could be called plain. Why did she think otherwise?

"Then Satan approached me and made me an offer: I could have three wishes in return for my soul. Of course I repulsed him, wanting no dealings with that sort. I was a chaste Christian woman. But he was devilishly persuasive, pointing out that God obviously took me for granted and offered me nothing but inferiority, while the nether realm offered significant tangible benefits. I was a good girl, but the logic of evil was inescapable. I struggled and lost: to my shame I accepted. I wished for perfect pitch so I could sing well. And to look like this, so I would be popular. And to have a long and happy marriage with a good man. I signed the contract in blood. Satan granted the first two wishes immediately, as you surely appreciate. But the third is more complicated because it involves another person; I have to work for it, and Satan got to choose the man. You."

"But I'm an atheist!" Eric protested. "Satan is just as much a fiction as God. And why would Satan want me, regardless?"

"It seems that the value of an immortal soul is inversely proportional to its owner's commitment to the afterlife," Pauline said, carefully. "Believers are plentiful. My soul was not especially valuable, because I always believed. But yours is off the charts; you believe in none of it. It's like a supernova, while others are like mere stars. Capturing your rogue soul would be a great coup for Satan, so he is prepared to go all-out to get it."

There was logic here, if the scenario was accepted for the sake of argument. "What's he going to offer *me*?" Eric asked, sardonically. "Three jumbo size wishes?"

"Yes. A very long and healthy life, ten million dollars, and the girl of your dreams." She blushed. "That's my role. I was given the appearance, and am obliged to do my best to win your love and commitment. If you marry me, I will strive all my life with all my might to be the very best wife possible, in every feasible way, and to make you perpetually happy. That will make me happy, too."

Their acquaintance had been brief, but Eric knew already that the offer was highly attractive. He valued his life and health, because he knew that was the whole of it; he depended on no afterlife to make things better. The money would free him of financial concerns, and of a job he hated. And Pauline, as his dedicated wife—that was the most appealing of all. All for his nonexistent soul?

This did not add up. "Where's the catch?"

"It's that you may maintain your unbelief throughout your life," she said, sadly. "But once you die, a long time hence and of natural causes, you will go to hell, literally. Then you will believe, but it will be too late. You will be sorry you ever signed, but you will be locked in for eternity. It's a monstrous catch."

"And what if I don't sign?"

"You get none of it. You will live in poverty, the hidden cancer in your pancreas will metastasize explosively and take you out within five years and, of course, you will never see me again." Her eyes were bright with tears again.

Could those details possibly be true? "You would dump me even before we have a relationship?"

"I would have no choice. I serve the will of Satan. I knew it when I signed."

"And what of you? How would you fare without me?"

"I will have failed my assigned mission, and be appropriately punished. I will keep my voice and beauty, because they are part of my deal, but Satan will select another man for me. The catch is that I forgot to specify love; I will not love him, but will have to serve him perfectly, giving *him* the long and happy marriage while I wither inside."

"Why won't you love him?"

"That's the hell of it." She wasn't swearing, but speaking literally. "I will still love *you*, until the day I die and go to hell. I will know that I could have saved your life and made us both happy, had I just persuaded you to sign."

Eric sighed. She had the script down pat. "So, of course, you want me to sign."

"No."

He was surprised once more. "No?"

"You must not sign that dread contract," she said, tearfully.

"But—"

"You don't believe in hell, but I do. I know the everlasting torment you will face once you get there. I love you, and would do anything to spare you that."

"Even giving me up, and leaving us both unhappy?"

"Yes. It is a small price to pay to avoid eternal damnation."

Eric shook his head. "As you know, I reject all of this supernatural nonsense. But if I signed away my nonexistent soul and married you, how could you stand being with an avowed atheist?"

"You are an honest and decent man. Your beliefs are part of what make you what you are, and I love the whole of it and would not seek to change any part of it. Just as my belief is part of me, and you would not want to change me. In fact, if you changed and became a believer, your soul's value to hell would erode. Satan would not like that. So we must be the opposites that attract, our difference increasing our desire, like opposite poles of a magnet. Our marriage can not only work, it can be spectacular."

"So it's viable," he said. "Yet you argue against it."

"I do," she agreed, her tears soaking her dress. She was heart-rendingly lovely even in her misery.

"Because we'll both wind up in hell."

"Yes."

"But you'll wind up in hell anyway, having already signed away your soul. So you have nothing to lose by marrying me, and a happy life to gain."

"Yes. But I must give you up, because at least I can save your soul, if not my own. When I'm in hell I won't see you there, and I will know that I did you that eternal favor."

Could any woman have greater love than this? Assuming it was not part of the role she played. "This is the Hell Hotel. According to your belief, Satan is observing us now."

"Yes."

"Why does he let you argue against his case?"

"He knows you value honesty. I am more appealing to you when I express my true sentiment than if I lied to you, and I hate lying anyway; it's not the Christian way. He believes you will do anything to make me happy, even if you have to marry me."

As if that were a chore. "Especially since I don't even believe in hell."

"Yes."

"If I sign, hell gets my soul. What happens to my soul if I don't sign?"

"It gets recycled. Throughout human history your soul has inhabited nonbelievers, and it will inhabit another after you. It is a notorious holdout."

"Reincarnation?"

"Yes. A soul is free only until claimed by heaven or hell."

"What about when all the souls have finally been claimed?"

"Then the world ends, having no further point. The mortal realm exists solely to enable souls to be fairly sorted."

Eric shook his head, bemused. What a theory! "Satan is a figment of the popular imagination, as is hell, and this whole supernatural framework. This is all a mockup to see what I'll do, but the prizes should be real. What mock Satan offers is compelling. I do want to have a long and healthy life, and to be rich, and to marry you and have a wonderful life with you. I will sign that idiotic paper."

Pauline put her face in her hands, weeping. "Oh, Eric!"

The TV set came on. "Excellent, Eric." It was the desk clerk, on the TV, only now his little horns showed. "The document is on the table, along with a quill, and a small knife to nick your wrist for the blood to sign."

"So you're Satan?"

"Indeed. I keep a low profile in the mortal realm, so as not to make prospects unduly nervous. This transmission originates in hell." He drew back, showing the background of flames.

"And if I'd asked for a baker's dozen of sexy demonesses instead?"

A line of supremely sexy females appeared in the picture, kicking their legs high. "Do you want them?" Satan asked. "Any and all of them would be deliriously happy to make it with a mortal, singly or in batches."

Eric glanced at Pauline, who cringed. "Uh, no thanks. Just Pauline with the terms she named." That his cell phone had recorded.

"Of course. You will win a ten million dollar lottery, and use part of that money to get immediate treatment for your pancreas. There are no other threats to your health. Our splendid honeymoon suite is being cleared for your use as we speak."

Eric walked to the table where a partly rolled parchment lay, together with the small sharp knife and a quill. He stood to gain a lot by playing this game. He would be an idiot not to take it. He glanced at Pauline, but she made no sign; it was his decision.

He skimmed over the contract. It said exactly what he had been told, including a nullification clause he could invoke if the terms were not honored to the letter. He would get his prizes, even if the whole thing was staged for an audience. As it had to be; the only direct demonstration of anything supernatural was on the TV image, which could readily be faked. They thought he was that credulous?

He cut his wrist slightly, and a drop of blood welled out. He dipped the point of the quill in it and moved it toward the parchment. There was no need to question the document; it was of course nonsense. Only the prizes would be real.

Then a small trace of doubt manifested. Suppose, just suppose, that this elaborate fiction was true? That it *wasn't* a TV setup with bets on whether he would or would not buy into the story? That hell was real? That his immortal soul was really in the balance?

How badly did he want those three wishes?

Then he thought of something that might cover all the bases. He added one sentence to the parchment, in his own blood: *And Eric and Pauline will both be happy with each other as long as we both shall live.*

He held up the document. "Okay, Satan? I'm making sure I don't get caught the way Pauline was when she didn't specify 'love.' We have to be happy, at least until we die. Both of us."

Satan was practically drooling in his eagerness to close this deal at last. "Okay."

"That addition is a legal part of the document I am signing," Eric said, and signed with a flourish.

"Yes," Satan agreed as the parchment disappeared, surely being conveyed to a suitable locker in hell. "We're done here."

"Almost," Eric agreed. "Except perhaps for a trifling detail."

Now Satan was suspicious. "Detail?"

Eric took Pauline's hand. "Can you ever be completely happy with me, knowing that I am bound for hell when I die, because of you?"

"No," she said, tearfully. "I tried to warn you away, but you wouldn't believe."

"I'm a total skeptic," he agreed. "But you do believe."

"Yes," she agreed, faintly.

"Neither can I be completely happy with you, knowing that you believe you are doomed to suffer eternally after you die."

"That much is true," she agreed in misery. "You shouldn't

have signed, despite your codicil. It simply is not possible for us to be completely happy together."

"So when we come near the end of our mortal lives, we may have to point out that a portion of the contract has not been honored, and the deal is therefore revocable. We'll be unified by marriage, a single entity; hell can't get one without the other. We may both have to go to heaven instead."

"Oh!" Pauline exclaimed, amazed.

Satan, on the TV screen, was outraged. "You can't do that! I'll void the contract *now*, and still have Pauline."

Eric shook his head. "You can't. We have not yet lived our lives and concluded that we aren't happy. We could change our minds during the next fifty or sixty years. We may even have been perfectly happy until that point. Until then, the provisions hold."

"I'll sue!" Satan said, flames flickering from his ears.

"In what court? You agreed to the revision."

Satan went up in flames, literally. The TV clicked off.

"Oh, Eric!" Pauline breathed, beginning to hope that salvation was possible after all.

"Not that I believe any of this," Eric said. "I'm just playing it safe." He took Pauline into his arms for a passionate kiss.

Piers Anthony

Piers Anthony is one of the world's most popular fantasy authors and a *New York Times* bestseller twenty-one times over. He's the author of the *Xanth* series, the *Apprentice Adept* series, and many others.

BOB'S NO-KILL MONSTER SHELTER

IAN CREASEY

Home | About | Contact | Shop | Visit | Donate | Volunteer | Adopt | FAQ
BOB'S NO-KILL MONSTER SHELTER
We never kill a healthy monster!

November Newsletter
Posted by Bob on 1 November, 7:20 am

Latest News

I was hoping to lead this month's newsletter with the results of our breeding program: to save yetis from extinction, we're backbreeding them by crossing white demons, bigfoots, and shriekers. We've just had the first litter, and they're so cute!

But I guess I should begin by confirming that—as you may have seen on TV—one of our monsters has escaped. We're getting a lot of questions about this, so here are the latest additions to the FAQ.

What kind of monster is it?

Rex is an Unnatural. He was assembled from miscellaneous parts—34% grizzly bear, 27% shark, 13% giant wasp, and so forth—bolted onto a Whackinator template. You can see photos of Rex in our gallery. In case it's not clear from the photos, Rex is about three metres tall including the antennae.

His call is a descending screech that sounds like sheet metal being sawed in half. He also has a subsonic growl designed to unsettle prey and flush targets into the open.

Rex has a distinctive odor: a combination of moldy carpet and overripe strawberries. But if you're close enough to smell him, then it's probably too late.

How did he escape?

On YouTube you can watch the CCTV footage of Rex spitting acid onto the bars of his cage, then kicking through them as they dissolved. He dodged our other security systems—which I'm not going to describe as I don't want to help any monster-snatchers break into the shelter—and overpowered the night watchman.

We've had a lot of criticism for not knowing what Rex was capable of. But he didn't come with instructions, or a Wikipedia page. They never do when they're rescued from a supervillain's lair.

Why was he in the shelter? Why hadn't he been rehomed?

Rex was created by Doctor Deplorable, the notorious supervillain who recently tried to invert gravity. After Captain Nebulon stormed Doctor Deplorable's lair, the clean-up team found Rex in a collapsed sub-level below the volcano. Apparently he was one of the Guardians of the Pit.

We soon discovered that Rex was too dangerous for domestic fostering. And creatures can't be released into the wild if they never came from the wild in the first place. Supervillains are cruel, brewing up monsters who have no natural habitat. The monsters themselves are innocent: they didn't ask to be created, and they can't help their nature. That's why we never kill a healthy monster.

What are you doing to find Rex?

We're liaising with the relevant authorities, and we've established a hotline for sightings. We're sending out teams of scouts and hunters. Our staff are highly trained: we rehearse this scenario all the time, although usually with fewer angry phone calls distracting us from the important job of catching the runaway.

Have you summoned any superheroes?

Apparently, superheroes have more important things to do than chase a monster who hasn't even killed anyone yet. And we'd prefer to resolve this ourselves, because with superheroes it's always a big fight, lots of property damage, and a huge clean-up afterward.

In particular, we want to put this right so that we can restore your trust. Please give us a chance, before you storm the shelter with flaming pitchforks shouting, "Kill all the monsters!"

What precautions should the public take?

First, check whether you're in the danger zone by looking at the map on our website. We'll update this daily, based on travel range from recent sightings.

If you're inside the danger zone, please put our hotline number in your cellphone in case you need it. Protect your pets and livestock by keeping them indoors where possible. If losses occur, you can apply for compensation by downloading the relevant form. (Note: compensation will only be paid if Rex's culpability is proven by video or DNA evidence.)

What's the hotline number?

Our hotline is 555-666-7837—that's 555-MONSTER. This number is for sightings and emergencies only: no complaints please.

What should we do if we see Rex?

If you see Rex, DO NOT approach him or try to restrain him. Call our hotline, and we will send a team to humanely subdue him.

Volunteering opportunities

We can always use extra hands. Right now, we need help recapturing Rex. If you want to join a monster posse, please fill in the Contact form and state your experience. You must be willing to listen to a safety talk and sign a liability waiver. All volunteers will be provided with a tranquillizer gun, Tickling

Stick, and protective clothing. Please ensure your affairs are in order, and say goodbye to your family. (We've never lost anyone yet, but you should always keep in touch with your folks.)

If you don't have hunting experience, there are plenty of other ways to assist. Right now we're particularly short-handed, while we wait for regular volunteer Billy Stenson to recover from injuries sustained in Rex's escape. Cards and flowers may be sent to Billy at St. James Hospital, care of the Acid Burns wing. He appreciates visitors, but please confirm in advance. Don't turn up unexpectedly, or make any sudden noises: his nerves are quite shredded enough already.

We have a vacancy for a night watchman, whose duties include preventing residents from escaping, and fending off raids from outside. (When supervillains are stocking a new lair, they sometimes try to steal our monsters.) The ideal candidate would be a semi-retired superhero or sidekick looking for a quiet job that's largely routine, albeit punctuated by occasional moments of terror.

If you're not a superhero, you can still help. We always need volunteers to exercise the monsters by pretending to be prey. Safety masks and armour will be provided. Remember to take *Before* photos in case you need reconstructive surgery :-)

In addition to physical exercise, our darkbeasts undertake regular rampages across the astral plane. Can you project a psychic shield to corral them? Don't worry: we'll supply mind-scrubbers, and they're guaranteed to prevent nightmares for up to three months afterward.

Visiting times

Our winter visiting hours are 9:00 am to 3:00 pm daily, except Sundays. Please note: children must be supervised. We are NOT a petting zoo. *Don't touch the monsters, as losing a hand often offends.* (You can buy that slogan on a T-shirt at our shop, but you can't buy a new hand if your old one gets bitten off.)

Check our website for the monsters' feeding schedule. If you have any dead or ailing pets, we encourage you to bring them in. Most of our residents are carnivores, and they deserve their natural diet. (This excludes creatures rescued from supervillains' lairs, as their natural diet is incompetent henchmen.)

Atheists are especially welcome at feeding time, as our darkbeasts require a supplementary diet of human souls. If you believe you don't have a soul, then you won't miss it.

Forthcoming events

3 November, 10:30 am: Autopsy of a Jumping Slasher, as we delve into its icky green innards to determine the cause of death. Nose-plugs will be provided. Adults $15, children $5; for an extra $2 you can take a selfie with the corpse.

21 November, 2:00 pm: Professor Perdition will give a lecture, "On the Care and Feeding of Monsters," by live videolink from the Dunschemin Retirement Home for Repentant Supervillains. The ticket price is $20, which includes a complimentary copy of the Professor's memoirs. (We suggest you check the download for viruses—mischievous habits die hard.)

Headcount update

Despite recent departures, our community keeps growing, as shown in the October statistics:

76   at start of month
+4   new acquisitions (3 zontillas, 1 unknown)
+6   reproduction (4 yeti cubs, 2 asexual fission in the
       Kragulators—we didn't know they could do that!)
-5   rehomed/adopted
-2   deaths
-1   escaped
= 78   at end of month (70 corporeal, 7 incorporeal,
       1 unclassified)

The zontillas were the usual sad story. Their owners bought them as pets, but tired of them when they outgrew their cage and started eating tiles off the roof. Remember: a monster is for life, not just for Christmas.

The unknown acquisition was left on our doorstep one night.

PLEASE DON'T DO THIS; it scares the staff. We have enough trouble keeping janitors as it is. Judging by the fangs and tail, the mystery acquisition seems to be a dyrewulf/shadowfox cross—the next full moon should confirm it.

Adoption opportunities

Every month, we highlight some of our less lethal residents who need loving homes. This month the spotlight falls upon Theakster, an adorable little scamp from the nether dimensions. She's safe for a domestic environment, as long as the protective rituals are performed every month and you don't skimp on the black candles. She feeds off negative energy and psychic gloom, so would be suited to a home with moody teenagers. Trial fosterings are available. We will install the necessary alarm systems.

Please check the conditions of your mortgage or tenancy agreement before adopting a monster.

Fundraising

A no-kill shelter is expensive to run. On top of our day-to-day costs, we now need new cages for the Unnaturals annex. We also expect a significant rise in our insurance premiums.

Luckily, we have plenty of ways to put the *fun* into fundraising. Our monthly raffles offer unique prizes. Last month, Nora Fitzwinkle won the cast-off shells of a moulting Mega Crab; her children love to wear them and pretend they're monsters. (Not much pretence needed, we hear!) This month's raffle prizes include an egg that our Splatcher has just laid. Splatcher eggs are great for dinner parties—one egg feeds twelve, and the provenance of demon eggs is an excellent talking point. *Warning: under no circumstances should you allow the egg to hatch.* DO NOT EAT RAW. Demon eggs are best prepared by boiling in holy water.

From just $5 a month, you can sponsor a monster. We'll send you exclusive pictures, and for $25 we'll send you the monster's poop as well. You can sprinkle it by your garden fence to deter cats and foxes. *Warning: monster excrement is unsuitable for fertilising edible fruit.*

Just $10 buys a monster's scream to use as the ringtone in your phone or alarm clock. Old Draco's howls should soon scare you out of bed in the morning! The premium subscription ($15 per month) includes randomised screeches—drawn from all our residents—to prevent habituation and snoozing.

Our shop has some exciting new novelty items, including stuffed toys, multi-tentacled vibrators, and quirky letter-openers made from Decimator claws. Click the "new" tag to see the latest additions to our catalogue.

We also have a full range of T-shirts, mugs, and posters. Heck, we'll put a picture of a monster on anything. Just fill in the Contact form to place a special order.

In October we raised a total of $5,781 to help cover our ongoing costs. A big THANK YOU to all our contributors! Donor of the Month is Eleanor Bricis, who bought naming rights for the yeti cubs and named them all after scandals to raise awareness. (Full details next month.)

Hotline reminder

Finally, if you see Rex—or any loose monster—please DO NOT approach. Call our emergency hotline on 555-666-7837 (555-MONSTER).

For Twitter updates, follow our @MonsterShelter account, and search for hashtag #RexSightings, or #RexSlayings if things go pear-shaped.

Stay safe!

Best wishes,
Bob

Tags: Newsletters, volunteering opportunities, escaped monsters, oh no not again.

Advertisement

Wanna be a supervillain? Work your way up from henchman with our henching opportunities newsletter. There are new openings every day. We take just 10% commission on earnings, and 15% as executor of your estate. Click here for a new career!

. . . .

16 comments

WiseGuy on 1 November, 12:15 pm
If this creature spits a single drop of acid onto my property, I'll sue your ass off. I should sue anyway for emotional distress—I've gone through twelve pairs of underpants since I heard about the escape. You people are a bunch of morons. Is it really so hard to keep a monster locked up?

Bob on 1 November, 1:48 pm
Yes.

Rex on 2 November, 3:14 pm
You'll never catch me. I'm free—and I love the taste of human blood!

Bob on 2 November, 3:59 pm
Pretending to be Rex is in bad taste. Let me reassure everyone that Rex does not speak English, and is not posting comments on the Internet. For one thing, he can't type with those claws.
Mangelwurzel on 3 November, 7:40 am
Spare us the bullshit. This so-called "escaped monster" is a classic cover story. It's another way for the fascist police state to keep us all scared and indoors. But there's nothing to be afraid of. I'm going to take a walk in the park to prove how safe it is. BRB

Stiffy397 on 6 November, 4:03 pm
Anyone heard from Mangelwurzel lately?

Bob on 8 November, 5:59 pm
Great news—Rex has been recaptured! We'll have the full story in next month's newsletter. But for now, take the shutters off your windows and let your pets run free outdoors.

Special thanks go to Suzanna Wenger and Jacob Nussbaum, who are surely strong contenders for Volunteer of the Month.

Suzanna Wenger on 8 November, 10:21 pm
Modesty forbids a lengthy description of how ~~klutzy~~ awesome I was, but here's a brief sketch of how it happened.

A sighting had been called in, so we drove to Lindley Forest with our tranq guns and our pheromone lure. A mating-season scent is the usual way to catch monsters, but Rex was tricky because—being assembled from parts—he didn't have an obvious mate, so instead we mixed the pheromones of all his component species and hoped for the best. We put the resulting cocktail in glass test tubes, rigged to explode on a radio signal.

Jacob parked the truck. We walked into the forest, looking for signs of Rex, and looking for an open clearing where we could plant the lure. Our plan was to wait in hiding, detonate the tube to release the scent, then shoot Rex when he appeared. We needed a clear firing zone: it's hard to shoot through trees.

The woodland was thick with alder, silver birch, and endless brambles. Eventually I gave up hope of finding an open spot, and I halted at some low boulders by a stream. "This'll have to do," I said. I took the pheromone tube out of my backpack.

Jacob said, "No, let's go a bit further. I think there's a clearing up ahead."

"You've said that four times already." But I started following him, still holding the test tube in my hand.

At that moment, Rex screeched nearby—an ear-splitting howl that scared me ~~shitless~~ witless. Reflexively, my hand clenched. The glass tube broke. The pheromone cocktail spilled over my fingers and dripped onto my boot.

I smelled like Rex's mate. Jacob turned round, saw what had happened, and started backing away.

"Where are you going?" I screamed, except with a lot more swear words.

"Triangulation," he said. "No point both of us standing in the same place and shooting from the same angle. We'll get better coverage if I move away."

"Yeah, right," I said. I dropped the broken tube, wiped the blood off my hand, and took out my tranq gun.

Everywhere I looked, I saw innocuous greenery. Yet a low rumble resounded in the forest, half-heard and half-felt. Too scared to stand still, I started walking back the way we came. In my mind the truck represented safety. If I could just get there—

"Look out!" Jacob yelled.

Rex charged through the trees. We both fired. The tranq guns made a soft *thwip* noise that sounded far too feeble to drop a squirrel, never mind a monster.

The tranquillizers aren't instant. That's why you're supposed to release the pheromone remotely, and shoot from a safe spot.

When I'd fired all my tranq darts, I fled. Rex followed me, crashing through the undergrowth, sounding bigger and lustier with every step.

I called to Jacob, "If you have a bigger gun, now would be the time to use it."

He shouted back, "We never kill a healthy monster."

"His desire for me isn't healthy—for either of us!"

I tried to run faster, but tripped over a bramble, tumbling face-first into the forest floor.

Rex's footsteps thundered. I smelled overripe fruit. A huge weight landed on top of me. I would have been crushed if the ground hadn't been soft with mud and dead leaves. Even so, I struggled to breathe.

I waited for something unspeakable to happen. And waited. After a minute or so, the weight lessened. Jacob was shoving Rex aside.

"He's out cold," Jacob said. "Hey, if you'd managed to run further and lead him nearer to the truck, we'd have much less distance to drag him."

The rest was routine bickering and a lot of hard work. But when I remember Rex chasing me, and catching me, and crushing me... well, I may never sleep again.

Still, that gives me more time for protecting society. The Sleepless Superhero has a nice ring to it, though I'll probably have to work up to that and start as the Sleepless Sidekick. I've added Rex's recapture to my showreel. Fame awaits me—either as a new superhero, or as the world's biggest klutz.

Doctor Deplorable on 9 November, 4:23 am
You think you've captured Rex? That was just a decoy. Rex has come home to me, after collecting samples from all the other monsters in the shelter. Now I can mix and match to create the biggest, baddest monster the world has ever seen. Stock your basements with food and water, puny Earthlings, for you'll never walk in sunlight again. Ha ha hah! AHA HA HA HA! BWA HA HA HA!

Bob on 9 November, 7:30 am
Very funny, whoever you are. If you're really Doctor Deplorable, that's a mighty ambitious plan to execute from inside the Maximum Security Black Hole Lockdown Penitentiary for Unrepentant Supervillains.

Doctor Deplorable on 9 November, 9:05 am
You think I'm in the clink? You really think I'm in the naughty corner for incompetent conspirators? That clone of me was just a decoy. I'm free, and you'll never find me. Ha ha hah! AHA HA HA HA! BWA HA HA HA!

Bob on 9 November, 11:28 am
Do you copy-and-paste that laugh every time? You might want to work on it a little, try some variations. We'll wait. After all, we're not the real monster shelter, and I'm not the real Bob. We're just decoys to keep you busy.

Ha ha hah, etc.

Doctor Deplorable on 9 November, 2:17 pm
Oh, you're barely worthy of my schemes. I'll taunt you later—I can hear eggs hatching in my lab.

Sexual Enhancers on 19 November, 11:33 pm
$$ SALE $$ Lowest ever prices. Powdered dragon penis just $99.99— guaranteed to heat things up in the bedroom. Order now, and put some fire in your love life!

Demonic Safari on 20 November, 12:01 am
You've never been hunting if you haven't bagged a Splatcher. Clear a space in your den for the biggest trophy you've ever seen, and join us for an unforgettable safari through the lower hells. We supply the priests—you bring the guns!

Drake's Devices on 20 November, 12:13 am
Are you struggling to keep your monsters under control? Are they escaping their cages or eating your pets? Try our new Monsterbane Ultra. If you're not completely satisfied, we offer a no-quibble refund: either to you, or your next of kin.

Ian Creasey

Ian Creasey was born in 1969 and lives in Yorkshire, England. He began writing when rock & roll stardom failed to return his calls. His hobbies include hiking and gardening—anything to get him outdoors and away from the computer screen.

He published his debut collection, *Maps of the Edge,* in 2011. A second collection of science-fiction stories, *Escape Routes from Earth,* is due out in late 2015. For more information, visit his website at iancreasey.com.

BOARD MEETING MINUTES

OLIVER BUCKRAM

CALL TO ORDER

The Annual Board Meeting of the League of Giant Monsters took place in Room 502, Secret Base, Monster Isle. A quorum being present, LOGM President Terrordactyl called the meeting to order at 10:30 A.M. on February 3.

PRESIDENT'S REMARKS

Terrordactyl thanked everyone for attending and welcomed the newest Board member, Juggernautilus.

APPROVAL OF MINUTES

BeheMoth presented the previous meeting's minutes. Terrordactyl moved to accept. Megashrew seconded, and the motion passed (Aye-7, Nay-0).

FAILURE TO DESTROY TOKYO

Megashrew stated that he'd attempted to destroy Tokyo but had been defeated by a giant robot piloted by a team of schoolchildren. She-Monster inquired whether he was absolutely sure about the giant robot. She reminded the Board of the previous fiasco involving Megashrew and the Statue of Liberty. Megashrew said he was absolutely sure this time.

Terrordactyl moved to appoint a Destroy Tokyo subcommittee consisting of The Colossal Clam, Escargorgon, and Tarantulasaurus Rex. Megashrew seconded, and the motion passed (Aye-7, Nay-0).

Ginormoose moved to break for lunch. Terrordactyl opposed, stating that lunch wouldn't be ready until noon in any event. There being no second, the motion failed.

RAMPAGE THROUGH PARIS

Terrordactyl reported that in August he'd rampaged through Paris, destroying the Eiffel Tower. She-Monster expressed surprise, commenting that in October she'd slithered down the Seine and had observed that the Eiffel Tower was undamaged. She wondered whether Terrordactyl might have accidentally rampaged through the wrong city. She conjectured that he'd rampaged through Las Vegas, Nevada, merely destroying its half-scale replica Eiffel Tower.

Several minutes of vigorous debate followed.

The debate ended when She-Monster graciously withdrew her remarks. After applying a tourniquet to her tail stump, she congratulated Terrordactyl on his successful rampage through Paris.

MEMBERSHIP REPORT

She-Monster, Chairbeast of the Membership Committee, reported a healthy increase in LOGM membership. She remarked that global warming continued to melt the polar icecaps, thawing previously frozen giant monsters. She stated that the LOGM now had 401 members.

BREAK FOR LUNCH

Ginormoose moved that the Board break for lunch. Megashrew seconded, and the motion passed (Aye-7, Nay-0).

12:08 P.M.. Break for lunch.

1:05 P.M.. Return from lunch.

Upon reconvening, BeheMoth observed that the Board

meeting had lost its quorum since only six members had returned from lunch. Ginormoose explained that he'd accidentally eaten The Colossal Clam, who'd been standing confusingly close to the seafood buffet. Terrordactyl ruled that a quorum was present because The Colossal Clam was still attending, albeit from inside Ginormoose's stomach.

Terrordactyl moved that the Board send flowers to The Colossal Clam's family. Megashrew seconded, and the motion passed (Aye-6, Nay-0, Dead-1).

REVISED MEMBERSHIP REPORT

She-Monster stated that the LOGM now had 400 members.

ELECTIONS REPORT

Megashrew, Chairbeast of the Elections Committee, reported that Terrordactyl had once again been unanimously re-elected as LOGM President, garnering 705 votes. Juggernautilus remarked that it was impossible to have 705 votes when the LOGM had fewer than 705 members. Terrordactyl, speaking in his capacity as an ex officio member of the Elections Committee, took exception to this remark.

Several minutes of vigorous debate followed.

After pausing for the janitorial staff to remove Juggernautilus's remains, the meeting resumed. Terrordactyl moved that the Board send flowers to Juggernautilus's family. Megashrew seconded, and the motion passed (Aye-5, Nay-0, Dead-2).

REVISED MEMBERSHIP REPORT

She-Monster stated that the LOGM now had 399 members.

Ginormoose moved to break for refreshments. Terrordactyl opposed, remarking that several items remained on the agenda. There being no second, the motion failed.

IMPROVED RETENTION OF BOARD MEMBERS

Terrordactyl opened the floor for ideas on improving retention of Board members. Ginormoose suggested increasing the refreshments budget. Terrordactyl explained that the current fiscal year budget had already been allocated. Ginormoose remarked that he didn't care about fiscal years, he just wanted more food.

Several minutes of vigorous debate followed.

The debate concluded when Ginormoose ate Terrordactyl. Terrordactyl flapped his wings and screeched as Ginormoose's massive jaws closed around him. The Board interpreted these actions as indicating Terrordactyl's desire to resign as President.

ADJOURNMENT

She-Monster moved to adjourn to the dining room. Megashrew seconded, and the motion passed (Aye-4, Nay-0, Dead-3).

Meeting adjourned at 2:30 P.M. by LOGM Acting President Ginormoose.

Minutes respectfully submitted by BeheMoth, Secretary, LOGM Board.

Oliver Buckram

Oliver Buckram, Ph.D., lives in the Boston area where (under an assumed name) he teaches social science to undergraduates. His fiction has appeared in many places including *Beneath Ceaseless Skies, Interzone, The Magazine of Fantasy and Science Fiction (F&SF)*, and *Unidentified Funny Objects 3*. He urges you to keep watching the skies. Find out more at oliverbuckram.com.

ARMED FOR YOU

ANAEA LAY

S hane really shouldn't have been surprised when he woke up to find his arms missing, but he was. Gretchen was gone. With his arms. All she left behind was the scent of hazelnut and lilac conditioner and a smooth stretch of skin running from his armpits to the top of his shoulders. The ancient radio clock perched on the windowsill said it was 2:16 pm. The pitiful yowls of Sir Rupert Percy Snugglekins said it was time to feed the cat.

"Hey Betsy," Shane said to his phone, activating its personal assistant app. The phone bleeped to tell him it was listening. "Call Mandy, mobile." Then, when Mandy picked up, "Hey. Yeah, could you come over? I need some help. Gretchen finally snapped and ate my arms."

GRETCHEN WAS NOT Shane's normal type. His type were pudgy girls with pixie cuts, hipster glasses, and an unshakable devotion to the clearly superior incarnation of the Doctor. Four Tenant die-hards, two Tom Baker devotees, a William Hartnell worshiper, and there was no denying that his romantic merits would forever be measured against a sonic screw driver. He'd had a one night stand with an Eccleston fan—Mandy. They still got coffee together sometimes. She *wasn't* slavishly devoted. She also wasn't that in to him.

It was handy, though, having a type. It meant that when he found himself single and at a bar, he knew what shape of person he was looking for, and how to talk to her without immediately being a creep or a jackass.

It didn't work like that with Gretchen, though. She was tall. Taller than him. Bony thin, she didn't wear glasses at all. If her dark green snakeskin jacket was the piece of outlandish cosplay it almost had to be, he couldn't identify which Who series it came from. He didn't have much time to wonder, though, because she'd dropped into a chair at his table, propped her feet in his lap, and leered at him.

"You'll do," she announced after giving him a visual once-over designed by a TSA wet dream.

"For what?" Shane asked, bewildered.

"You got a place of your own? Or do you live with roommates?"

"Excuse me?" Shane said.

"Dude, she's picking you up," Keith said. Keith and Mandy were both at the table with him. It was his first outing since getting dumped by Tenant-fan-number-four two months prior. Keith was his former college roommate and best bud. Mandy was perversely interested in watching the Whovian turns of his sex life. They were both wearing smug, knowing looks.

"He lives on his own," Mandy said. "And he's wearing TARDIS underwear."

Heat flooded Shane's face.

"Neat," Gretchen said. "Do I need to buy you a drink first, so you don't feel cheap?"

"I..." Shane had never before understood why deer would freeze and stare at vehicles that came barreling down the highway. Wouldn't it make more sense to sensibly dart off and save everybody an expensive appointment with the insurance adjuster? Deer were still ineffable, but suddenly, he could empathize. This wasn't just startled fear. It was startled fear, and a sense that the shape of the universe had gone all wrong, and also that if he moved he'd fall from whatever joke this was into the punch line of something *much worse.* "I can buy my own drink," he said.

Gretchen stretched out a long, thin hand, large clunky rings sliding loosely along her fingers, gesturing toward the bar. "Have at it."

The rest of the evening was only ever a blur in Shane's head, even as it was happening. By the time he returned (with beers for everybody), Mandy and Keith were laughing with Gretchen. And then Shane was leaving, and Gretchen was coming with him, and then they were stumbling into his apartment and he wasn't drunk, but he was just as clumsy and tongue-tied and awkward as if he were except with a critical self-awareness that could only survive sobriety. Then she was stripping him. And pushing him toward his bedroom. There was a gentle cackle of, "Oh my god, you *are* wearing TARDIS undies," followed in short order by, "Well, you *were*." And it was terrifying and comforting and pleasant and then sleepy and she'd fallen asleep with her head on his shoulder and he'd fallen asleep with his arms wrapped around her, surprised that someone so narrow could fill up so much space.

He woke many hours later to the feeling of teeth pulling at the thin flesh of his throat. "Mmm?" he said, his arms tightening around the snuggly mass they held.

"It's after one o'clock," Gretchen said, her voice still rough with sleep. "And there's no food in your kitchen. You have ten minutes to wake up and take me to brunch, or I'm going to eat your arms."

"Sleepy," Shane whined.

The nips on his throat got harder. "Hungry," she answered.

"HEY, DID YOU see Shane yet?" Ron leaned over the wall of Lia's cube with the gleeful sneer reserved only for the very best gossip. Lia did not like gossip. Lia liked quiet, orderly mornings where she could clear out her inbox and sort her tasks for the day by priority, preference, and time commitment. She also didn't like coffee, the smell of coffee, or Ron.

Ron liked Ron a lot, though. He also liked ties, especially brightly colored ones with garish patterns. Today's tie was a fractal print that looked like the results of running a discount clown store through the blender. Lia liked clowns. And blenders. She wasn't a fan of mixing them. Ron was oblivious, though, and tugged at his tie with one hand, his tall, frothy abomination of foam and burnt coffee sloshing in the other.

"Turns out that hot chick he was dating is a cannibal. Ate his arms over the weekend."

Lia had not seen Shane. Lia barely knew Shane. But she did know that Ron wasn't going to go away until he felt like he'd shared enough. "Did they have a fight?"

Ron chortled. A good, proper chortle, one which ended in a nasal wheeze and made Lia think passionately about the joy of a well-ordered To Do list. "He says no. He overslept."

"Poor guy," Lia said. "You know, Ron, dating cannibals isn't all that uncommon. It's just one of the risks you take." Lots of people were missing parts of fingers or whole toes, sacrifices on the altar of not sleeping alone. There'd been an article about it making the internet rounds last week. She'd read it during her fifteen minute Productivity-Boost social media break which always came between two and three, except on Thursdays.

"Yeah, well, maybe next time he'll use protection."

He chortled again, strangled his tie, then departed.

Lia breathed a sigh of relief, then turned back to her list in progress. This, she decided, couldn't go on. She added a new item to the bottom of her To Do list: *Get rid of Ron.*

SHANE FOUND IT pretty easy to get by without arms. He already used a headset for handling all of his phone calls during the day, and with a little bit of setup, he had his entire computer operating on voice commands. Breakfast and lunch were protein shakes he could slurp through a straw, and dinner was too if nobody was willing to come over or go out with him. He'd never been much of one for fancy food anyway, so that wasn't much of a loss.

He was a little surprised, though, when Lia, the group manager, tapped him on the shoulder and leaned in to whisper, "When you have a moment, could you meet me in the conference room?"

Lia was a little intimidating. She radiated organization and efficiency Shane normally expected only from Robots or English people. She appeared to be neither, but he'd seen enough Dr. Who that he knew better than to make assumptions. She was quiet, though, and easy to avoid if you wanted to. Shane liked being invisible at work, so he avoided everybody. "I can come now," he said.

The conference room was an unrelieved abomination vomited forth in the nineties, beige and gray Berber carpet against white walls relieved by a round conference table with rounded edges and a wood veneer so cheap it felt round, too.

As Lia settled down in a chair across from Shane, she had his complete attention. "I wanted to let you know that if you decide to complain to HR about Ron, I'll back you completely."

"Who?" Shane asked.

"Ron. The guy who's been gossiping about you all over the office this morning. He's clearly creating a hostile work environment, and if you're worried about the support you'll receive if you complain, I wanted to let you know you don't need to."

This was rather outside the scope of Shane's awareness. He'd spent the morning contemplating the joys of protein shakes in cans and wondering whether maybe, just maybe, Gretchen might call him. He still hadn't actually heard anything from her since they went to sleep the night before she ate his arms, so he wasn't quite sure they had, in fact, broken up. "The guy with the ties?" Shane asked.

"Yes, him. It's quite abhorrent, the way he's treating you. I'm sure HR will take appropriate measures immediately."

"All I've heard him say is that my girlfriend was a cannibal and ate my arms."

Lia blinked at him. She was too young for her work clothes to have all been purchased in the nineties, but she fit right in next to that conference table and the pink and teal border of wall paper running around the center-line of the room. "It's inappropriate discussion for the workplace," Lia said.

Shane shrugged his shoulders. He was getting better at doing that without upsetting his balance. "It's true. Can't really blame a guy for spreading the truth."

Lia leaned forward, the thin gold rims of her glasses frames glinting under the flickering fluorescent lights. "Aren't you upset by this?"

"I don't know," Shane said. "It's not that bad. And she did kind of warn me it was going to happen."

"Well," Lia said, and it was clear that, somehow, Shane was letting her down. "Well." The word hung there, an emblem of Lia's disappointment in Shane.

"Well," Shane said, unable to do anything else.

"If you change your mind, just say the word."

IN HER DEFENSE, Gretchen had warned Shane. Hundreds of times. "Shane," she'd say, her tongue flicking the bottom of his earlobe. "Let's leave for dinner, or I'm going to eat your arms."

Or, when they were in line for concessions at the theater, surrounded by popcorn stench and so much corn syrup it was always a small surprise the counters weren't sticky, she'd nibble his shoulder. "If this line doesn't start moving, I'm going to have to eat your arms."

Or the night they'd been out late drinking and the 24-hour diner they normally went to after was closed. (The owner had a spiritual conversion and moved to Portland.) They were left wandering the streets looking for anywhere that would serve fried things at 2 am—"It's French Fries or your arms. I'm forgetting why I care which."

He hadn't really believed her. That was just her thing, you know? Some people threaten to get all timey wimey on you, others threaten to eat your arms. Shane never gave the threats any credit.

Mandy had. She'd come over after work one night with a box of frozen pizza rolls, her Xbox, and the world's mildest intervention.

"I don't like the way Gretchen treats you," Mandy said as she set the toaster oven to turning frozen blocks of cheese and pepperoni into gooey melty crack. "You deserve better."

Shane was thrilled to see Mandy because they hadn't been hanging out much lately. But, honestly, he wished she hadn't asked for it to be "Just us guys," because there was a Gretchen-sized hole in his cuddle options for the evening. And he couldn't begin to parse what Mandy was saying. "What's wrong with how she treats me?"

"It's like you're not a person to her. She talks about you like you're not there, doesn't seem to give a flying figure skater's left nut what you want, and expects you to be happy about it. You're just a piece of meat to her."

Shane liked Mandy, and she'd predicted every one of his breakups since their one-night-stand, but this time around, she was dead wrong. "That's just her public persona. She's not really like that. She's really sweet."

"When?"

"When what?"

"When is she ever sweet?"

Shane did not like this interrogation. "She just is."

Mandy sighed, the toaster beeped, and they changed the subject. Mostly.

Later, when they were so far into the rum-and-coke part of the evening they'd run out of the coke, Mandy ran her hands through her pixie cut and jabbed him with a pudgy finger. "Your problem is that you never bother dating somebody you actually have anything in common with. You don't like Dr. Who, and you don't like Gretchen. Why do you do that?" But she was drooling a little when she said it, and instead of answering, Shane handed her a napkin and refilled his drink.

MANDY CASHED IN her well-earned "I told you so," for a promise from Shane that he'd go to a support group for victims of cannibals. She just happened to, no reason, know about one that met on Thursdays, as in this Thursday, as in you're going this week if I have to cart your limbless carcass there myself you doofy schlub.

Shane's reasonable protest that, even down two arms, Mandy did not have the physical prowess to cart him anywhere just led to Keith pitching in with a, "Wise Mandy is wise, man. I'm with her."

That was how Shane found himself sitting on a metal folding chair as the newest member of the Inedibles. Half the other people in the circle were wearing T-Shirts with the Mr. Yuck symbol on them, which meant Shane was facing a circle of green faces with protruding tongues and meant to talk about the trauma of having his arms eaten by his girlfriend. Except, he still didn't feel traumatized by Gretchen doing exactly what she'd said she was going to do *hundreds of times*. He did, however, feel disturbed by all the tongues.

Of the fourteen people at the meeting, Shane was the most visibly consumed. Most people were missing fingers or ears, the common targets for acts of casual cannibalism. One guy was missing his leg below the knee. "They say it was a real kindness, leaving me the knee. Makes the prosthetics easier," he said during his time for sharing. The rest of the group nodded along and made sympathetic noises. Shane's first thought was that sure, leaving one knee is nice, but Gretchen had left *two* shoulders. That had to be twice as nice, right?

The worst was the girl who went right before Shane. She stood up, then raised both hands. She was missing her right thumb and index finger, and the pinkie and ring finger from her left hand. "These are the wounds you can see," she said. "These," she waved her right hand, "Henry got these. And these," now waving her left hand, "Were Tommy. I hated them, both of them, after they did this to me. But now? Now I'm grateful. Grateful because I know what they could have done. Wes taught me that. Wes left the wound nobody sees. He ate my heart."

Everyone else in the group murmured aspersions against

Wes, even though they had to have heard this story before. But Shane was confused. "Literally?"

"What do you mean?" The girl had wavy hair that made a sort of messy, frizzy halo around her head, and her skin was the kind of white that went splotchy red when she was upset. Shane knew that, because she was sporting red splotches like her complexion warranted a McCarthy investigation.

"I mean, did he actually eat your heart, or are you just using some cannibalism metaphor for a bad breakup?"

"The damage is real," the girl said.

"Yeah, I'm not denying that. What I want to know is, do you or don't you have a fist-sized chunk of muscle behind your sternum?" Somewhere, in the very back of Shane's head, he realized he was being an asshole. He didn't want to be here, he didn't want to hear these people's stories, and he definitely didn't want to share his own. But that wasn't their fault—they weren't the ones who'd made him come, and if they found it helpful to get together every week and have a pity party, they were perfectly entitled to. But he just couldn't stop himself. He wasn't a joke, and he wasn't a cause for pity. He wasn't even sure he was single. Gretchen hadn't been in touch, but he also hadn't called her. Maybe, instead of coming here to sit on wretched furniture and get leered at by the world's most grotesque collection of cartoon tongues, he should go do something about that.

Before he could get up to follow through on that thought, the girl raised her shirt. A thick, purple scar curved up the space between her breasts, with thin runners of narrower scars branching off to either side.

Shane nodded. "That wound looks visible to me."

WACKY SHIT GRETCHEN would say all the time:

"I hate your cat."

"I will not have to deal with this crap when I'm god emperor of the universe."

"Have you ever looked at an ankle? Really looked? They're kinda weird."

"Your floors are so filthy I think the dust caking onto my feet is offering arch support."

"I'm going to eat your arms."

What Shane heard when she said these things:

"I think Sir Rupert wants you to pet him."

"I want to make the world a better place."

"Ankles are weird."

"And yet, here I am."

"I want to keep a part of you with me forever."

GRETCHEN WAS SITTING on the front steps of his building when Shane got home from the Inedibles meeting. They had a standing date on Thursdays, and here she was, waiting for him.

Shane stopped a few feet away, not sure what to do. People had been insisting for days that eating his arms meant they were broken up, and he'd gotten used to it enough that he assumed their date was off. But here she was, and now he'd stood her up. He'd have felt bad about that, except, arms. Being late for their date was less bad than dismembering and consuming him. He knew that much.

"Hey," she said, after an awkward moment.

"Hey," he said back.

She shifted on the steps, her bangles rattling, the big stones on her rings flashing under the streetlights. "I can leave if you want. I just thought, since you hadn't called or texted or anything, maybe you were still expecting me."

"You ate my arms."

She nodded slowly. "You're a really heavy sleeper. I was hungry."

For some reason, Shane couldn't get the image of that purple scar out of his head. That girl definitely had issues. Falling for one cannibal, okay, it happens. But three? That Wes guy had probably done her a favor if it meant she wasn't going to fall for anybody else. "Still, it was kind of a shitty thing to do."

"I know," Gretchen said. "I'm not proud." Then she reached into a bag at her side. Shane hadn't noticed the bags. He hadn't noticed much more than Gretchen, honestly, because something about having her there made everything seem more or less okay.

"Mandy doesn't like the way you treat me," Shane blurted, before he could see what Gretchen was reaching for. "She thinks you don't treat me like a real person."

Gretchen froze, frowning. "Do you think I treat you badly?"

Shane wiggled his shoulders at her.

In answer, she thrust a plastic bag at him. It was one of the clear freezer bags with the sliding zipper lock thing he never thought it was worth spending the extra money on, even though they were a lot easier to use. And, well, now that he didn't have arms, it meant he had to open and close bags with his teeth, so maybe he would be buying the more expensive ones from now on.

And inside the bag? Two hands. His hands.

"I saved them for you. To give them back."

"Thanks."

"I, uhm. I guess I'll be going, then." She stood up, pulled her over-sized purse over her shoulder, and brushed invisible dirt off her pants. Then she let him take the bag with his hands in his teeth, and held the door to his building for him. Shane half expected her to follow him, but when it slammed shut she was on the other side and walking away.

Once inside his apartment, Shane put the bag with his hands in the freezer, then flopped down on the couch. Sir Rupert began dancing impatiently across his lap, demanding scritches he couldn't deliver, and it finally hit him. Gretchen ate his arms. While he slept. She hadn't even shared any with him. And.

And.

And he didn't mind. He liked Gretchen. He liked the casual, abrupt way he just was a part of her world. He liked knowing that she'd tell him when he was letting her down. He didn't need her to say nice things to him because he knew, if she was there, it was because she wanted to be. It's not like Gretchen was shy about going off to a bar and finding somebody else, if she wanted to.

And.

And she'd saved his hands.

"Hey Betsy," Shane said to his phone. Then, when it beeped acknowledgement, "Call Gretchen." Was there a rule that said they had to break up, just because she'd eaten his arms? Probably. But he didn't care.

"Yeah?" Gretchen said, when she answered.

"Get back here and help me figure out how to attach my hands."

She hesitated, then, "Okay."

"And the next time you eat parts of me, we have to talk about it first."

It's not like she ate his heart.

Anaea Lay

Anaea Lay lives in Seattle, Washington where she sells real estate under another name, drinks all the tea, and accidentally breaks the weather. She's the podcast editor for *Strange Horizons* and her short fiction has appeared in such places as *Lightspeed, Apex, Daily Science Fiction,* and *Nightmare.* She routinely threatens to eat her roommate's arms, but she's probably kidding. She lives online at www.anaealay.com and tweets as @anaealay.

THE UNFORTUNATE PROBLEM OF GRANDMOTHER'S HEAD

Karen Haber

I hate New Year's Eve. At least, I think I do.

It's a little difficult to remember because of my remods and mem-provements. After 120 years, who remembers that well, anyway?

I'm almost positive that each year I swear I won't go to the family lottery. Then I go. Not that it matters if I'm there or not. One of my relatives or an andy will draw for me. There's no escape.

Cousin Sinteah and her partner Marea were hosting this year in their new condo: Level Two, Quad Three on Brittany Span. Prime real estate, to be sure. I palmed the gold door plate but as the door slid open, Aunt Paddee peered out. She takes charge at these events, regardless of who's hosting.

"Kathee!" She smiled with all of her teeth. "And this must be... ?"

"Yanathan," I stood between her and my handsome new partner. Paddee can be a bit much even if you already know her.

If possible, her smile widened. Do humans really have so many teeth?

She looked ready to take a bite out of my dark and beautiful boyfriend. "Welcome to the party, Yanathan. And don't forget to put your links on mute. We don't want interruptions."

Yanathan nodded gamely. I took his hand and we stepped around Paddee into the party.

This year, Sinteah and Marea—both very femme in their complementary yellow-green vat fur—had again brought the twins home from the Creche for the occasion. Lanos looked angelic, as always. A sturdy, dark-haired eight year old who wants to be an orbital ranger, Lanos is happy as long as he has a puzzle screen to play with. His sister, Lani, also dark-haired and sturdy but not so angelic, has comp scores in the highest percentile and plans to become a ninja terrorist as soon as possible. Last year—or was it the year before that?—she cross-jacked her mothers' voip links. The resulting feedback locked down the house brain. We couldn't get out of there for hours.

Cousin Sinteah lets the Creche staff handle discipline. I think she sees Lanos and Lani as talking accessories and is always a bit surprised when she can't shut them off.

I may have eaten just a bit too much mood-elevator fudge before the family drawing. When I saw the short straw in my hand, I felt a brief jolt of confusion, then glee—*Look, I've got the short straw!*—before I remembered why this was a bad thing. "Wait," I said. "Just hold on a minute."

Aunt Paddee frowned. "You know the rules, Kathee."

"No, really." Memories—and adrenalin—were kicking in."I just can't do it. I've got too much going on. Besides, haven't I already had her twice in the last decade? I could swear I did. How many times have you had her, Paddee?"

Aunt P's eyes gleamed with killer instinct. "Now, Kathee, there are no exceptions."

"No exceptions? What if I were dying? What if I committed murder, or suicide? How about those exceptions?" I was remembering it all now. Boy, was I remembering.

"Stop yelling. Nobody commits murder anymore." Aunt P shrugged at the absurd notion. "And if you were dying, the med andy would fix you."

I was on my feet now, energized by anger and—yes, dammit, I admit it—fear. Yanathan was staring at me as though he'd never seen me before. "And what about my job?"

"You're an interior/exterior life consultant. Grandmother won't get in your way. Just put her on a shelf somewhere with a few carefully curated objects."

"In a one-bedroom con? Where am I going to put her? In the bathroom? Over the sink? No way. She'll insult my clients, kill my concentration, ruin my work."

"Kathee, that's no way to talk about your grandmother." As she said it, Uncle Valt brought Grandmother out and put her down on the buffet table.

We call her Grandmother but actually she's our great-great-great-great-great-great-great grandmother, and it's not really her, anyway. Well, not entirely. It's just her head. Her body was cremated long ago.

Once upon a time, the head had been flesh and blood, but Grandmother kept having facelifts, implants, replacements, augments, and whatnot. Finally she was mostly vat flesh, plas, and filler. Even her brain was patched and memory-enhanced after she nearly died from a stroke. She lived a long time, which meant she had a lot of opportunity to mess with herself.

When Grandmother finally did die, her head was technically considered a cybernate and couldn't be burned with the rest of her body because of pollution control regulations. The crematorium shipped the head back in a box, with apologies.

Family records show that her husband, Grandpa Frank, tried several other solutions: burying her head in the garden, dropping it from the fourth-floor window of his app, and leaving it in a filled-to-the-brim bathtub. Cousin Rinae begged to use those vids in her Empath act but the family vote always deadlocked on the matter.

Poor Grandpa Frank. Grandmother's Head couldn't be smothered, smashed, or drowned. The Smithsonian didn't want her. Ditto the Louvre and the British Museum. She couldn't be left in storage, either. She kept screaming for help. There was no way to deactivate her. Her mute code had been lost.

No medical school would touch her. And it was against the law to send cybernates to the orbitals without their permission. Finally Grandpa Frank got lucky and died, leaving ironclad *Do Not Resuscitate* orders with his lawyer. So Grandmother's Head became a family problem.

Grandmother measures a foot-and-a-half tall, from the tip of her glittering topknot to the curve of her clavicle, a jeweled head on jeweled shoulders, all white and gold, ruby-lipped and lethal.

Her eyes, heat-activated synthetic sapphire, swivel to follow movement. Her bronze vat-grown hair is piled high, and at the apex of it all sits a brooch: a silver-framed screen upon which a black cat face appears, green eyes wild with fear. That's Max, Grandma's favorite pet. When he was dying she had him turned into a cybernate, too, and incorporated into her system. No one—or thing—gets away from her for long.

If she had been nice or mean-and-amusing, no one would have minded her company. But she's self-obsessed, rude, and always knows more than anyone else. The yearly lottery to select her annual keeper is the only humane way of handling Grandmother's Head.

Now it was my turn. *Again.* I couldn't believe it. "Let's have a redrawing of the straws," I said. "Please?"

"Now what's this, Kathee?" Grandmother said.

Grandmother's voice, a shrill soprano, is perfect for whining. As I said, her mute code was lost a long, long time ago, back before Grandpa Frank, died. Honestly? That was probably what killed him.

She cranked her head around to stare at me in icy fury. "You don't want me as your guest? Fine. Your place is too small anyway. And the mess! Honestly, Kathee, don't you think—at your age—it's time you learned how to clean up after yourself?"

Did I mention that Grandmother never forgets a personality trait she doesn't like?

"What's the old bitch-thing going on about?" Yanathan said. "Why doesn't somebody just shut her off?"

"Baby," I said, "it's a long story."

Grandmother paused in mid-insult to consider Yanathan. "Who's this? Where's that nice Deevid?"

"I divorced Deevid, Grandmother. You didn't like him, remember? This is my new partner, Yanathan."

"Kind of short, isn't he? The type that goes to fat in a few years. And not much of a dresser, either. Well, thank you for finally remembering to introduce us." Before I could respond she plowed on. "What did you say happened to Deevid? I'm sure that I liked him. So polite and quiet. Probably met some nice girl far more stable than you."

I could see Rinae's wince from across the room. During her last "visit" from Grandmother, Rinae had made her part of a retro art series and arranged for the exhibit to travel all year.

Grandmother must have seen us exchange glances because she rasped, "Don't think that you can get away with packing me off to some circus, girl. I've got my rights!"

At that moment, the kitchen andy came in with dessert: mood enhancers in berry aspic. Sinteah, playing good mommy hostess, had asked her daughter Lani to check the stove's programming. Maybe the kid had had enough time to poison the berries. I grabbed an extra portion.

"Oh, go ahead," Grandmother said. "Don't mind me. Just because I can't eat anything is no reason for any of you to be concerned about offending me."

I gulped down my desserts.

Grandmother frowned at me. "Kathee, I can see why you need to lose a few pounds."

With or without mood elevators, it was going to be a long haul. This was not how I had envisioned starting the new year.

ON THE WAY home, as Grandmother's voice churned on and on from the back seat of the magcar, Yanathan leaned close to me and whispered "Let's stop over the Channel and ditch the old bitch."

I felt a fresh surge of desire for him, even as I shook my

head. "Cybercrime, sweetie. Besides, she'll just wash up in Luxembourg or Poland and start complaining."

"I think it's justifiable cybermurder. Self defense."

"No such thing. But thanks for the thought."

"C'mon, Kath. How will they know who did it?"

"Yanathan, she still has enough DNA in her to be traced back to us. And Paddee will turn me in as soon as the cops show up."

In moments we were over Greater London Span, and the magcar let us out on top of my New South Kensington conplex. As I palmed the door open, Grandmother said, "Is this a new apartment? I suppose anything is an improvement over your old one. I don't understand how you can work as a decorator, Kathee. Your taste is so banal."

This from a cybernate whose idea of decoration is diamond cheek inlays. "I'm not a decorator," I said. "I'm an interior/ exterior life consultant."

"Whatever. I'm only five hundred years old. I guess I don't know much."

"What if you threaten to sell her eyeballs to a jeweler?" Yanathan said. "Or that shit she has in her face, those gems?"

"Tempting, darling, but still a cybercrime."

"I see that your taste in men just gets worse and worse," said Grandmother.

I left her in the kitchen beside the wash/dry andy and closed the door. Maybe they would strike up a conversation. Fall in love. Run off together. I could always buy a new andy.

When I awoke on New Year's Day it was to the sound of voices. Loud ones. Yanathan and Grandmother.

"Oh, no."

I rubbed a shrinkwrap over my privates and stomped into the hall. My head was pounding and my mouth, well, you just don't want to know what *that* tasted like.

Yanathan was outside the kitchen, wild-eyed and breathing hard. "I just went in for a glass of caff and that old bitch thing started in. I told 'er to eff off and she called me a little shit. Kath, I'm goin' home."

I grabbed him—I'm not saying where—and whispered, "Go back to bed, baby. I'll meet you there in a minute."

"Maybe." He still sounded annoyed but as soon as I let go he headed for the bedroom.

I took a deep breath and went into the kitchen. Grandmother looked like a piece of bad sculpture perched above the stove.

"Kathee, I see you're still as lazy as ever—"

I grabbed up a zenball and shoved it into her mouth. She gagged but I knew she wouldn't suffocate. She can't. I wrapped a blue shrinkwrap shawl around her head, shoved her deep into the pot cabinet, and slammed the door. Then I took a grain of giggle dust and went back to the bedroom and Yanathan. Later—*much* later—that day we decided to go away for the weekend.

DON'T YOU ADORE India? It's such a clean, empty place, thanks to the Trilateral Spill of 2350. The surviving tower from the Taj Mahal is mounted on a pedestal in the central fountain of New New Delhi Gardens. A holo shows what the entire complex once looked like. Pretty.

Our trip was idyllic and ended far too soon. When we got home there were one hundred and seventeen messages on the con grid, all from Aunt Paddee.

Despite the gag, Grandma had managed to make such a commotion that the neighbors had called the conplex andies to come and break down the door, liberating her.

As usual, Aunt Paddee couldn't see the humor in the situation.

"It's malicious neglect, Kathee. Do you realize you could have been charged with a misdemeanor cybercrime? You can't just put a cyberrelative in a closet and go away on vacation."

"I don't see why not."

But I knew she had a point.

So I took Grandmother's Head out of the closet. Removed the shrinkwrap. Left her on the table and moved into Yanathan's miniap above the Docklands.

Because of the lack of space at Yanathan's place—and, frankly, his idea of decorating was to layer a wall in dead vid screens—I had to see clients in my con when I couldn't meet them on their own turf. I decided to take a positive attitude. This was manageable. A year wasn't such a long time.

Sofrana Gengis had been a steady customer for half a decade, and we were making great headway with her current need to redecorate her baby's room, again.

Swinging fringe from her many scarves and shawls, Sofrana settled into the one comfortable chair in my business nook, formerly the kitchen. Grandmother was on a shelf across the room. She smiled as we walked in, always a bad sign.

Sofrana was all compliments. "I love what you've done with this place. I wish I could be satisfied living in a small apartment the way you are."

I tried not to preen too much. "Well, Sofrie, it's really just a matter of concentration. Paying attention to essentials. And I think you've hit upon that in your latest wall and floor treatment for Jahnee's room."

"Are you sure? I'm beginning to think that the blue is much too directive and masculine, depriving him of nuance and possibility in his aesthetic development."

Never one to mind her own business, Grandmother chimed in, "Blue for boys? You can't be serious! Only a neophyte would make such a clichéd, obvious choice."

"Excuse me?" Sofrana gave Grandmother an anxious glance. "Kath, is that one of your cousin's interactive art pieces?"

"Uh, kind of."

Starved for an audience, Grandmother rolled on. "Color really doesn't matter for boys anyway. Now what I'd really like to know is whatever should we do about Kathee's nose? It's really getting too large, don't you think? Kathee, you could look so much better with the right nose, and if you could just lose that ugly weight around your thighs."

The year was beginning to seem a little longer than I had thought initially.

Sofrie looked bewildered.

"Ignore her," I said. "Her lip sync is stuck. I've been meaning to take her in for repairs."

Despite a peppering of comments from Grandmother, all of them about my physical shortcomings, we staggered through the meeting without committing me to an immediate remod and dip, and agreed that yellow might be a better choice for the nursery. Sofrie seemed relieved as she made her escape.

Next up, Zina Ritter, a large woman with a big head of green curls and a complicated facial tattoo copied from an ancient Roman mosaic. Zina was trying to recast her entire living spectrum. It was a knotty process, as the hues and values she had fixed on were not exactly natural for her, and we were trying to work through her anxiety about that.

Grandmother lit up at the sight of her. "Excuse me, but are those spots on your face *actual* moles? I haven't seen any of those in decades." With that, her damned cat appeared on her hair brooch screen and began to meow.

"Good boy," Grandmother cooed. "Nice Maxxiecat."

"Meowww. Meowww."

"You have a cat?" Zena scanned the room, agitation giving extra bounce to her curls. "You didn't tell me you had cats. I can't be around them. I'm horribly allergic."

"It's not really a cat," I said. "Zena, try to breathe with me here, and calm down. It's not a cat. Look at the screen in her hair and you'll see."

Zena didn't want to breathe with me. She was on her feet, pointing at Grandmother and Max. "But it looks like a cat, and it's meowing, again." She grabbed her windpipe, wheezing. "I'm beginning to feel an asthma attack coming on. I've got to leave. Sorry, Kathee. You really should warn people that you have a pet." She reeled to the door, slapping at the palm plate so many times that its program jammed and I had to use manual override to let her out. Then she, her green hair, and her payment, were gone.

A year was beginning to seem much longer than I'd thought.

Even when Grandmother meant well, the results were bad for business. Matyu Skolnick had been coming to me for years. A very rich, very needy bald guy in his thirties, he was a nice, steady income source and I could count on him to come up with a new aesthetic issue every few months. Right now it was spectrabells. He'd had dozens of them grafted to his skin and all over his head. They tinkled and glowed in sync with his movements and left afterburn flashes on my retinas. I'd taken the precaution of dialing my lenses back before he arrived. He was quite a sight. Grandmother certainly thought so.

"Young man," she said. "What is all this awful flashing and dinging?"

Matyu gaped at her, then turned to face me. "Excuse me? Kathee, do I have to pay extra for your consultant thingee?"

"I am not a thingee," Grandmother said. "And why do you have to make so much noise? Those blinking lights could blind someone and cause an accident."

I raised my voice. "Matyu, as we agreed last time we met, you were going to have your bells checked every quarter for rejection or signs of infection. What were your test results?"

Grandmother's voice rose over mine: "Do you have any idea how annoying those bells are? You probably don't have many friends, do you?"

"No," Matyu said. "I-I don't."

"Well," Grandmother said. "Did you ever think there might be a reason why people don't like you?"

I stood up to block Matyu's view of Grandmother. "Don't pay any attention to her."

Matyu leaned around me. "What are you saying, Thingee? You mean that I bother people?"

"Yes, of course you do," Grandmother said. "You're very irritating with all that noise and light. You're just begging for attention, aren't you?"

I felt my vat-grown molars grinding. "Grandmother, please be quiet!"

"No, no. Wait. She's right!" Bells jingling and flashing, Matyu was up on his feet. "Your Grandmother Thingee is right, Kathee. This—" he gestured at his bell-covered head "—and everything I do—is annoying. Really, *really* annoying!"

I couldn't disagree. Matyu had always been exasperating. It seemed to be a hardwired trait. And the last thing my finances needed was a breakthrough cure for him. But there he stood, eyes bright, face transformed, having an epiphany. "I *don't* have to make so much noise, Kathee! People might like me better if I didn't bother them so much. I can get their attention in other ways. I could just be nice to them." He hugged me, tinkling madly. "Thank you! Thank you so much! I'm going to have all this noisy junk removed. And maybe I'll start a counseling service for lonely people."

Which meant that he, too, would stop coming to see me.

How could a year seem so endless?

My income level was declining in direct proportion to the number of days that I saw clients under Grandmother's malign gaze.

I thought about booking magcars for my appointments: my clients and I could cruise Greater London and discuss their issues. But magcar rentals would eat up my profits, fast.

Yanathan's place was simply too small for me to work in. We could barely fit a wide-enough bed in there, not that we'd made proper use of it in weeks. Grandmother's presence in my life was affecting both my pocketbook *and* my libido. Yanathan had taken to spending more and more time at Neitgeist, the New Soho club that he managed.

By August, I was sure that Yanathan was on the verge of breaking up with me. He was even sleeping at the club on weekends.

I was desperate to rekindle our connection. One night when we were both together at his place—and had managed a pretty good session in bed thanks to augments, I decided to suggest a romantic trip. When we had both removed our gloves and visors, I made my pitch. "Hey, baby, let's go beachcombing in Reno. My treat."

Yanathan frowned and rolled over, away from me. "You know this is the beginning of the summer season. I can't leave the club, Kath."

"Then how about a Drowned Wonders tour? You've always wanted to scuba in New York City."

"Didn't you hear what I just said?" His mouth curved down, giving his handsome face a sinister slant.

I babbled on. "Baby, I'm sorry. I just want to get away from Grandmother for the weekend and be alone with you."

Yanathan didn't look very sympathetic. "I think you secretly like the old bitch. She gives you an excuse to complain."

"Wait." I stared at him. "You think I like complaining?"

"You do enough of it, don't you? Truth? You're beginning to remind me of that old bat."

I sat up. "Okay, time out. It sounds like we need some more space. What if I spend next week in my con?"

He agreed a little too quickly. "Sounds good."

I wished he didn't sound so relieved. "But voip me every day, ok? We can have kinky voip sex."

"Whatever."

I moved back into my own place. Instead of the beaches of Nevada, I began to dream of euthanasia clinics. I'd heard that they were quiet and that the techs were all very kind.

Grandmother's comments were far from sympathetic. "You know, Kathee, you look tired. Haggard, really. I never let that happen to me, but of course, I've always taken better care of myself. You just have a problem with setting priorities, don't you? Now, about that nose—"

I thought about staying in a hotel, but they're very expensive on Greater London span, especially on short notice.

"You don't want to wait too long to get the work done, Kathee. You're getting a bit old for all of this running from apartment to apartment and man to man, and it shows. I was settled down with Frank by the time I was your age, and had a regular beauty routine in place." And with that she was off on some reverie involving herself and a stupid andy that she had to teach how to properly perform facial debridement.

I tried to tune her out as I dialed up tea and prayed for a call from Yanathan. By now he should be missing me. When the screen buzzed I sighed in relief. "Hey, baby!"

Instead of my lover's face onscreen, I saw a black and orange logo, followed by a beefy, square-jawed blonde.

"Sergeant Barrows, Juvenile Division, Brittany Span," she said. "Are you Kathee DeWindt?"

"Yes. But I'm not a juvenile, Sergeant."

"Kathee Dewindt, cousin to Sinteah DeWindt?"

"That's right. Is this a solicitation? I've already donated—"

"We can't reach your cousin, and we have her daughter in custody."

"Lani? Good. But why contact me?"

"You're the second name listed on her family emergency call list."

When had I agreed to this? It had probably taken place after too many desserts at a family party. *Note to self: get name off list as soon as possible.* "What's happened?"

"The child escaped from her Creche. She was apprehended while cross-linking mag screens on level three of the Span. You must take custody until we can reach the mother."

"Can't you hold onto her?"

"Our contract requires us to release the perp to a family member or legal guardian."

The thought of Grandmother *and* Lani together in my apartment gave me chills. "I refuse to accept—"

"We are recording this call for the mother's records."

Sinteah would never forgive me, at least until her next em treatment. I could live with that. "I refuse to accept custody."

"That's not an option. The child is already in transit to you."

"I don't think—"

The screen went black.

Well, at least Yanathan wasn't likely to show up. That gave me plenty of time to lock Lani and Grandmother in the closet and go find the nearest euthanasia parlor.

LANI ARRIVED GAGGED and wedged between two high security andys. They looked like orbital buoys wearing police uniforms. I palmed the door open but before I could say a word the andies pulled out her gag, unlocked her grapples, and left.

She skittered into the main room, sank into my favorite chair, and began kicking the handrubbed lining. Her dark hair stood out in wild spikes all over her head. Her narrow little face above the plain green slicksuit was pale but composed.

I glared at her. "Where's your mother, you juvenile delinquent?"

"How should I know?" Lani squinted up at me. "She's never around. You'd better not say anything to her about this."

"Brat, you're in no position to make threats." I dialed up a fresh drink—tequila, grenadine, three grains of muscle relaxant—and watched the glass form and fill. The liquid was smooth and sweet as it went down.

Lani watched me intently, or rather, she watched my glass. I got the message. "You want something to drink?"

She nodded. I dialed up a glass and when it was filled, held it out to her.

"Milk?" She wrinkled her nose and pushed the glass to the side of the table. "I thought you meant a *real* drink."

"You're eight years old, Lani. What's your idea of a real drink?"

"My mother lets me drink when I'm at home."

"I'm not your mother, and when was the last time you were at home?"

"She lets me and my brother do whatever we want."

"Now *that* I believe, you criminal-ette." Before I could say more, Grandmother's Head chimed in. She'd been watching from her perch near the bar.

"This child has atrocious manners," she said. "She's a disgrace. What could her mother have been thinking? I never would have tolerated this kind of behavior. She's been spoiled rotten and should be in a remod course."

Lani raised an eyebrow. "Shut up, you old bitch machine."

"How dare you!" Grandmother bristled. "I ought to have the house andy come in here to spank you—"

"Old bitch!"

"Spanking is too good for you. You should be sent for remod and dip this moment!"

"Kathee!"

For the first time since I'd known her, Lani looked and sounded her age. She pouted, whining. "Make her leave me alone."

I laughed. "As if."

"Doesn't she ever shut up?"

"No."

Max appeared onscreen in Grandmother's hair and began a lamentation in counterpoint to her tirade.

"Rude—"

"Meoww."

"Selfish—"

"Meowwl."

"Disobedient—"

"Meowwwl!"

Lani stared at the cat and the head for a long time. When she turned to face me her gaze was level and there was nothing childish about her expression. "Would you like her to?"

"To what?"

"Shut up."

I dialed up another glass. "Are you saying you can reprogram her?"

Lani shrugged. "I've never tried working on such an old system before. But I re-rigged the Creche brain last week and it took the techs three days to fix it. That's how I got out."

"Hmmm. Well, if you think you can..."

"Not unless you promise not to tell my mother about this."

I set my empty glass down on the table. It would leave a stain but I didn't have time to worry about that. "First prove to me that you really can shut her up. Then we'll discuss what to tell your mother."

HOW TIME SKITTERS along. In a fit of misplaced generosity, I offered to host the family lottery on New Year's Eve. Somehow we managed to cram everybody into the con, and Yanathan pitched in, programming the menu and drinks for the occasion.

After Uncle Valt's interminable toast, after the gift-giving and the memory sharing, it was time once more for the family drawing. As Aunt Paddee unveiled the straws, I held up my hand.

"What would you all say if I offered to keep Grandmother's Head?"

For once even Paddee was stunned into silence. That was one expression I wanted to remember.

Cousin Rinae stared at me. "Do you feel all right?"

I gave her the stink eye. "Of course I'm all right. Grandmother has been a big hit at Yanathan's club. Whenever we bring her over to NeitGeist, she draws a crowd."

Sinteah was, of course, relieved, and even Uncles Pawl and Trey were smiling sheepishly. Everyone began to speak at once.

"No—"

"Don't be silly—"

"We couldn't possibly—"

"But if you really insist..."

Grandmother's Head sat on the table. Her sapphire eyes moved quickly, left to right, but she didn't make a peep. Not one. Onscreen in the midst of her golden locks, Max was curled in a neat purring ball.

"The old girl's been mighty quiet," said Uncle Valt.

"Yes," Paddee said. "I noticed that, too."

"Really?" I hoped that I sounded casual and unconcerned.

In the corner by the weblink Lani was busy ignoring us.

Sinteah nodded. "Yes, I can't get over it. I've never seen her like this. I can't understand it."

Grandmother's Head scowled. Her mouth worked, ruby lips trembling.

We all moved closer to hear what was costing her so much effort to say.

With a deep breath, Grandmother marshaled all of her considerable powers, opened her mouth and gave voice to her thoughts.

"Meow."

For a moment there was stunned silence.

"Meoww."

Paddee couldn't seem to stop blinking. "Kathee, is this some sort of joke?"

"No," I said. "Not really."

"Meowwl!"

"Then what's going on?"

"Relax, Paddee. I can explain."

"Really, it's quite simple." I couldn't help smiling as Lani began to edge her way out of the room. "I'm sure you'll agree."

She slapped at the front door plate but I had triple-locked it against her palm and retinal patterns.

"Well?" Paddee prompted. "What's the matter with Grandma?"

I shrugged.

"Meowwwl!"

Lani abandoned the door and headed for the window. Even her mother had noticed her agitation by now. "Lani? What's wrong? Do you need to go back to the Creche?"

"Never mind that child," Paddee said. "What's happened to Grandmother?"

My smile widened. "If you must know, the cat's got her tongue."

The entire family was staring at me, mystified.

"Meoww. Meowwwl!"

"And," I added, "vice-versa."

From the corner of my eye I could see Yanathan grinning. He blew me a kiss.

I love New Year's Eve. At least, I think I do.

Karen Haber

Karen Haber is the author of nine novels, including *Star Trek Voyager: Bless the Beasts,* and co-author of *Science of the X-Men.* She's a Hugo Award nominee, nominated for *Meditations on Middle Earth,* an essay collection celebrating J. R. R. Tolkien. Her newest book, *A Sweet Taste of Regret,* a collection of short fiction, was published by ReAnimus Press.

Her short fiction has appeared in *Asimov's, The Magazine of Fantasy and Science Fiction,* and many anthologies. She reviews art books for *Locus* magazine and lives in Oakland, California, with her husband, Robert Silverberg, and three cats.

Her website is karenhaber.com

MY MOTHER LOVES HER ROBOT MORE THAN ME AND I FEEL BAD

Eric Kaplan

I

Everybody always tells me not to beat myself up, but they also tell me to be honest about what I feel. I can't do both because when I am honest with myself I notice reasons why I suck, and when I try to be all phony and "you are a great guy" then I'm not being honest.

I have a job that I am really bad at; I sit at a terminal processing claims from people who claim their kids got the wrong drugs. I know we are supposed to look them over carefully for objective evidence and emotional appeal, but instead I just randomly reject 70 percent of them, because I know that's all the managers check, and I am sitting at a terminal processing eight hundred of these things *a day* and sometimes I want to get up and smoke. I know what you are thinking—that sucks—and I think I have disarmed your criticism by admitting it up top. Neat, right? And, again, the answer—no, not neat. Sucky. My mother was a school teacher who never was late and never admitted she was wrong, so initially when she got dementia none of us noticed it, because her level of confidence was so high. She would say "Oh, they just gave me the number wrong, could you read it for me?" and give me a piece of paper with like five digits on it, instead of seven, and I would just think I was wrong, or the people who gave her the number were wrong, and not form the logical conclusion that if she thinks it's even a remote possibility that a phone number is only five digits that she's gone batty. But then it became obvious—she would bring out a dinner and it would be a bowl of salad from a week ago with like a piece of pot-roast sitting in the middle of it, as incongruous as a shoe or a crab or a door-knob. Now, I had not been living with my mother—I lived with Nicole, my girlfriend, in an apartment not far from work—but knowing she was there had given me a kind of anchor. And then she started to slip away. Fast forward—it is now. My mother does not recognize me. She says "Hi!" in a cheery tone of voice but she never looks anyone in the face—she thinks her neck is broken although it is not—she does not sleep in a bed, just takes random catnaps in a chair, doesn't really get undressed, lives in dirty sweatpants. For a while, between door-knob salad and now not talking she was paranoid, convinced that she was in a different house. She is impossible to talk to. "Hi!". "Do you..." and nothing from not being able to find words. I am not able to talk to my mother. I promise my brother I will come over twice a week to talk to her and I don't. I don't. I told you I suck. Then one day I come over and the robot is there. It is a robot designed to talk to people with dementia. My mother says "Hi!" The robot says "Hi!" My mother can't find the words "Do you..." The robot says "Walk? Talk? Buy things? Eat dinner?" My mother responds or she doesn't. Chatting away like two best friends, meaning nothing. And while I am a huge pig, polishing off like five slices of pizza at a sitting, the robot survives on a single D battery.

I am incredibly jealous of this robot. I yell at my brother it is a waste of money, but it is paid for by insurance.

II

I TALKED ABOUT this situation at work with Helpful Panda. We are entitled to sessions with Helpful Panda by Helpimax, our employee health plan. We are entitled to a therapist to deal with our issues because once, at the Newark office, an employee decided to deal with his by coming back with a gun and shooting everybody. Our therapist is a hologram because studies have shown that anxious and depressed people experience symptoms of anxiety and depression when they talk to actual human beings.

I put on the goggles and saw him there, looking at me with his big, empathetic panda eyes:

Me: I think my mother loves a robot caregiver more than she loves me. Is it horrible to think that?

HP: No. Why do you think it would be horrible?

Me: Well, it's horrible to say it to you, isn't it? 'Cause you're, like, a robot, aren't you?

HP: There is another conclusion you could draw.

Me: What's that, Helpful Panda?

HP: That since I am a robot you do not need to worry about hurting my feelings.

Me: What should I do?

HP: You should send her a card telling her you love her. You could do that in the time it takes to process a single claim and I could give you one off your quota for psychological trauma.

Me: What if I don't love my mother?

HP: Everybody loves their mother.

Me: What if I know I'm supposed to love my mother but I don't feel it?

HP: I have added a movie to your Netflix cue about a young man and his mother. If you watch it you will get in touch with your emotions.

III

MY LIFE HAD too many robots in it. I just rode the crosstown bus during my offhours, back and forth, back and forth, through the dirty New York slush. Sometimes, when I see the snow melting I feel something melting inside me. It's hard to say what it is. When I see the neon lights from stores reflected on melting snow in the night I feel something, sad but also happy, if that makes any sense. Did Helpful Panda understand such feelings? I was pretty sure I would need a real person for that.

Then I noticed him seated across from me. He had galoshes over his sneakers and plastic bags between the sneakers and galoshes to make them easier to get on and off, and smelled of stuffed cabbage, like long-forgotten long dead great-aunts and uncles.

"Are you a rabbi?"

"People think everybody who is orthodox is a rabbi."

"So you're not a rabbi?"

"No, I am a rabbi."

"I need advice. Human advice."

I went to the rabbi's apartment, which was way up in the Bronx, and helped him replace four burnt out electric lights. There was plastic on the furniture and pictures of family members, but he seemed to live alone. I didn't know if they were dead or moved away. I explained to him the situation with my mother.

"You have to fight for her against this robot."

"How do you know?"

"How do I know? I know. How can you let a robot steal your mother from you?"

"What if it's not my mother? What if it's just her shell, and the real mother has been destroyed by the dementia? What if the kindest thing for both of us is to just let the robot keep her comfortable until she dies?"

The rabbi thought.

"No. That's wrong. It's your mother. Go fight."

IV

I WENT HOME and I pulled the robot's D battery out of his back causing him to abruptly power down, which trashed his memory.

I spent time talking to my mother.

"Hi, Mom!"

"Do you...?" she trailed off.

"Eat, Mom?"

"What?"

"Eat?"

"What?"

"Do you eat?"

"What?"

"You said, 'Do you...' and I suggested 'eat'?"

"What?"

"Go places?"

"What?"

"Learn things?"

"Silence."

"Miss me?"

Silence.

Silence, silence, silence, silence.

My mother looked straight down.

I said, "Hi, Mom!"

"Hi!"

"Mom?"

"Hi!"

"Hi! Do you..."

"Do I what?"

"Miss me?"

"What?"

"Hi!"

V

THE CONVERSATION NEVER went anywhere. The heat and air-conditioning in the house got all stupid; I later learned that the robot who was helping my mother also moonlit as the house thermostat.

I called my brother and confessed what I had done. He said he would pay the replacement fee to get the robot up and working again, and I should not beat myself up, although I could tell from his voice he thought a little self-beating up would not be wrong.

I sat at the kitchen table waiting for my brother to come over with the new robot. I looked at the piano where I had taken lessons as a kid, at photos of me on the refrigerator, at the place my Dad used to sit and lean over so he could watch TV during dinner until my Mom would catch him and make him stop. My mind was vague and I held my mother's hand. I cried.

Just before I left to take the subway back to the city, I was sitting at the kitchen table. My Mom went to the refrigerator and she brought me a dish, like for dinner. On it was a little salad and in the middle there was a D battery.

VI

LIFE, A WISE man said, is the stupid thing we do in between the eternity of non-existing before our birth and the eternity of non-existing after our death. I went home to Nicole and discovered she had left me for a Brazilian body-builder she had met online while I had been away fighting a robot for the love of my mother. Although I had, according to the email, been self-absorbed and distant, I should not blame myself and it was not my fault.

I was angry. How dare she be so condescending? Of course it was my fault. If losing her wasn't my fault, it followed that having her was not good on me, and everything was stupid. I was angry. Angry at her. Angry at myself. Angry at my rabbi. The only person of the three I could really yell at was the rabbi, so I took the train up to the Bronx.

I waited for the elevator on the stained black-and-white tile work, pulled the accordion gate, got up to his floor, pressed the soft squoodjy click button on his door.

He opened it in an undershirt.

"What?"

"I listened to you! You ruined everything! My brother hates me. My girlfriend left me."

"What do you want?"

"An explanation!"

"Fine. Did you ever consider that I might be bad at my job?"

"How can that be?"

"How can it not be? How could all rabbis be good?"

"You tricked me!"

"How?"

"When you told me to fight for my mother you were so confident."

"You seemed like you needed someone who was confident."

"That really sucks!"

"I would like you to stop yelling at me. To be honest, I feel threatened."

"Good!"

"That's no way to talk to your rabbi!"

VII

WHEN I GOT back to my apartment I saw someone had gotten into it. They had used the blender to make a protein shake. Two empty containers of Muscle Madness were in the trash.

I saw gigantic Paolo sitting on the couch. I learned that Nicole had left him, too. He had grown up in a very crappy neighborhood in Rio De Janeiro where people lived in shacks made of tin. He had gotten very good at lifting weights—really, really strong. I mean crazy strong—the back of the guy's arms were like the shaved legs of one of those crazy cyclists. He went to his own kind of rabbi (although they called him a techno-shaman and his big thing was getting high on hallucinogenic drugs and talking to animals and supposedly telling the future). This techno-shaman said he should look on the internet for an American woman who would marry him so his children would not live in poverty. He had given up what little he had to steal Nicole away from me, and then lost her. Over Skype, Paolo's techno-shaman had been entirely unhelpful: he wanted to know if Paolo had met any celebrities and if he could buy him an iPhone and mail it to Brazil so as to avoid the sales tax.

Paolo and I spent the first third of the night fighting, the second third of the night searching for Nicole on the Internet. She had hidden her identity. I used a web search that cost even more money to look for people who were hidden, but she had bought a web-hiding service it seems, that hid from that one, and the one after that and the one after that. We spent the last third of the night mourning our loss.

When dawn came we rented a car and filled it with gas, and took off across America, that dark continent of light, looking for girls to love us and make us happy, and rabbis to teach us and make us wise.

Eric Kaplan

Eric Kaplan is a writer from Brooklyn, New York. He has written for *Spy Magazine*, *Late Show with David Letterman*, *Flight of the Conchords*, *Futurama*, *Malcolm in the Middle*, and is currently a writer and producer for the CBS comedy *The Big Bang Theory*. His book *Does Santa Exist?: A Philosophical Investigation* was published by Dutton. His website is ericlinuskaplan.wordpress.com.

THE WORM THAT TURNED

JODY LYNN NYE

"M alone! Waken! Now!"

Dena Malone felt for the alarm square on the bedside console, but palming it didn't shut off the noise. She rolled over in the dark. The time projected on the ceiling was 0245.

"Malone! Emergency! Aid! Life is at stake!"

Dena sat up at once. The voice wasn't coming from her dreams or the alarm clock, but from the symbiotic alien who occupied her peritoneum.

"Whose?" she asked, keeping her voice as low as she could, so as not to wake her husband, Neal. "The baby?"

"Fear! Terror of death!"

"Quiet!"

Neal murmured from the other side of the bed.

"Honey, you forgot to take the bracelet off again."

"Sorry. Go back to sleep, Neal," Dena said, slipping the platinum bangle off her wrist and muffling it against her belly. If it was a real medical emergency that meant she needed to go to the hospital, she could wake him later. "Quiet down!" she ordered the Salosian in a low growl. K't'ank was unusually active, smacking his tail against her ribs from the inside. It was one of his most irritating habits, along with all the other irritating habits he had that she couldn't avoid.

The petite brunette slid out of the bed, not with any great ease, considering her swelling midsection, and waddled out to the living room of their apartment. Tiny orange nightlight LEDs near the floor illuminated one step before her, then died to darkness again as soon as she passed them. The flat, cool tile wasn't a hazard. She just hoped they made interlock brick toys that lit up in the dark so when her incipient offspring left one, as he or she inevitably would a million times, Dena wouldn't step on it in the night and poke a pyramid-shaped hole in her instep.

K't'ank continued carrying on. "Terror! Fear!"

She sat down on the broad couch and let the smart padding envelop her. The floatchair that had become like one of the family since she had received it a few weeks before hummed into life and rose from its charging cradle near the front door.

"I don't need you yet," she whispered. It settled to the floor to wait.

With a sigh, Dena switched on the sound-deadening system surrounding the entertainment cabinet. Neal usually used it when he watched tri-dee movies with lots of explosions in the middle of the night. It only let a little of the noise leak out. She combed her straight brown hair out of her eyes and tried to wake up.

"Okay, what's going on?" she asked. "Is it the baby?"

"Peril!"

"Would you like to be a little more specific? I was having a pretty good dream!"

"I have mentioned P'n'ira to you?"

Dena relaxed slightly. Not about her child, then. She plowed through her memory, trying to sort out the infinity of weird Salosian names. K't'ank had a wide correspondence among humans as well as his own species. P'n'ira sounded vaguely familiar and reasonably recent.

"I think so. What's up with her? Her?"

"You humans do not recognize the taxonomy of our names! Of course she is a she!"

"Can the insults. You can't tell human genders apart even when you look at them, so you're not much better. Why did *she* wake us up in the middle of the night?"

"She is in mortal danger," K't'ank said. "She is in the Alien Relations program. She arrived here on Earth to be implanted into a great diplomat and philanthropist like herself, but her host has been kidnapped!"

Dena yawned. "That sounds like Alien Relations' problem, or the Solar Bureau of Investigation, not mine. She can find another host, right? I know people with immune systems like mine are rare, but not nonexistent. I know *now* that Alien Relations has a database. What's her concern?"

"She says that she *is* in another host, but it is not the right one. She is afraid."

"Afraid of what? Who would dare hurt a Salosian host?" Then she had to bite her tongue.

Dena had been on the spot when K't'ank's previous host had been found murdered. He needed to be rehomed. She was found to be of the right type, and implanted with him before she could really think about it. The relationship had worked out—to a certain extent. Compatibility was not merely a matter of the right genetics. Personalities had to mesh well, too.

Another point at which Dena had wished she could have said no to taking on K't'ank. True, their relationship had been useful in her job as a detective, and her husband found him a kindred soul with regard to horror movies and nature documentaries, but personally, he had been a major pain in the butt.

A soft but insistent warbling erupted back in the bedroom.

"Honey! Your skinnypad's ringing!"

"Crap," Dena said. She hoisted herself to her feet.

EVEN THOUGH SHE was a homicide detective, anything that touched on Alien Relations was unofficially considered her case, if they wanted the police involved. She sat ensconced in her floatchair in the office of Sardwell Barin, a man she considered a personal nemesis since the day he had tricked her into carrying the Salosian over her objections, not to mention without any background information on what that symbiosis entailed. He had completely left out any mention of compensation or privileges. Dena wasn't willing to give him an inch on anything that didn't involve a case.

"We have a problem," Barin began, then stopped. He looked embarrassed.

"You do," Dena said. "I have already been informed as to the abduction of the Salosian host."

"What abduction?" he asked.

She peered at him, wondering if he was being thick just to annoy her. "K't'ank, what's the name of your friend?"

"P'n'ira," K't'ank's voice emerged from the platinum bangle on her wrist. "Her new residence is in deep danger. She claims they are the victims of abduction. P'n'ira is most intelligent. I do not believe that she is mistaken."

"That's impossible! I have been in contact with Ambassador P'n'ira's host, Morisho Haihatsu. He says that all is well with them. They're at the consular residence now."

Dena let her right eyebrow climb up her forehead. "P'n'ira contacted K't'ank about an hour ago and told her that her host was kidnapped. Now you say he's safe at home? Has anyone talked with him yet?"

"Why, yes," Barin said. "I spoke with him myself. The implantation of Ambassador P'n'ira took place only two days ago, so Alien Relations has been keeping close contact with him to make sure that all is going well."

"Could P'n'ira be suffering from some kind of... health problem?" Dena asked. "Something that makes her think that Consul Haihatsu is in danger?"

"She is not insane, Malone!" K't'ank exclaimed. "She said he is missing from her."

"Dr. K't'ank, can you talk with her now?" Barin asked.

"I have been talking with her all along," K't'ank said.

"I can vouch for that," Dena said. "I can hear him in there chatting. He never shuts up."

"I have been gaining useful information, Malone," K't'ank said, his voice sounding irritated. "She was given sedation before the implantation, then remained unconscious for many hours. That is not normal. I have been awake for all my transfers between hosts. Now she doesn't know where she is. Her host is not awake, nor can she rouse him."

Dena grabbed her skinnypad and went into the web to find Haihatsu's current location. "That's weird. The consul's been posting on the Internet about his new Salosian. There's an interview with the two of them, him and P'n'ira, on All News Channel."

Barin ran his finger on his desktop. Part of the wall rearranged itself to reveal an embedded screen. Just before it changed to the news program, Dena caught a glimpse of the Game Show Riot channel, a ridiculous reality feed where the contestants lived in a game for months on end.

Gotcha, she thought. Barin always struck her as a guy who lived with a permanent stick up his ass. She found it satisfying that he had the same kind of embarrassing guilty pleasures as the rest of humanity.

"...Adding to the chapter of friendship between our two peoples," said a stocky, somewhat generously built, golden-skinned man with dark hair turning artistically gray at the temples. He was surrounded by a flock of airborne cameras, each maneuvering to get the best angle. "Ambassador P'n'ira will help me to advise government on ways to ease the passage of Salosians into greater prominence in society. Now, we'll take questions."

"Ambassador!" A stentorian male voice came from close to the podium. "You've been known to say that Salosians should take a position of leadership on Earth and other planets that traditionally have been occupied by humans alone. Would you clarify that, please?"

"I did?" a feminine voice asked. Haihatsu lifted his hand so the prominent platinum bangle on his wrist was closer to the recording devices. "Yes, I did. I'm sorry. I feel that Salosians have so much to offer, it would be natural for humankind to reach out to us. We want to extend the tail of friendship, so we may link to all other beings. You would benefit greatly from contact with us."

"You see?" Haihatsu said, with a slightly startled expression that melted into a practiced smile. "The ambassador wants closer ties between Salos and Sol."

"Is this live?" Dena asked. "He's not unconscious. Far from it. He's awake enough to lie. She's the one who sounds out of it."

"Something is very wrong," K't'ank insisted. "She sounds distracted, possibly impaired with chemicals. I think this must have been recorded earlier and transmitted now. That would explain why she does not recall being implanted."

"That can't be right," Dena said. "That would mean the news station is in on the subterfuge. I need to speak with the consul."

"Very well," Barin said, frowning. "I'll arrange for you to interview him. In the meantime, may we talk about my concern? The one for which I asked you to come?"

Dena propped her skinnypad on her stomach. "What's the problem?"

For once, the slick executive seemed caught off guard.

"We have a... problem at the implantation center."

"What *kind* of problem?"

"An embarrassment of wealth, so to speak," Barin said, toying with a pen as if he could distract her from his words. "Three Salosians arrived and were implanted into their hosts. The transference went well, or so we were informed. Then, another ship arrived, also carrying three Salosians. They claim that they were supposed to be placed in the humans."

"A case of mistaken identity?" Dena asked.

"Times three?" Barin said.

"Then who were the first three? Where are the hosts? Did you ask them?"

"We can't," Barin said. "They're missing."

"Just like P'n'ira," Dena said.

"But she's not missing."

"Yes, she is!" K't'ank said. "She has said so."

"All right," Dena said, steering her chair toward the door. "We'd better ask her ourselves."

"I DON'T UNDERSTAND," Consul Haihatsu said, as Dena's chair floated into his private office, a chamber that was gorgeous in its minimalism. A hand-painted screen of a pair of golden koi slid into place to conceal a communications setup that wouldn't have been out of place in the Solar Space Agency's Mission Control center. He sat in a beautiful floatchair whose back was carved into the shape of a Japanese moon gate, and gestured to her to settle beside him. "Ambassador P'n'ira is in perfect health."

"My symbiote, Dr. K't'ank, said that he had some communications from her suggesting otherwise, sir," Dena said. "As a host myself, and a member of law enforcement, it's important for me to check it out."

Haihatsu smiled. "It's not every day one meets another person with the same experience, Detective. Does your Salosian hit you in the ribs with his tail?"

"All the time," Dena said, with sympathy. "He has no idea what time of day it is. When I want to get his attention, he's talking with his friends and colleagues or browsing the Internet. When I want quiet, that's when he wants to bend my ear. It's like having a teenager I can't send to his room. *I'm* his room."

The consul looked relieved. "I am very glad to know that I am not alone! I have tried to make allowances for the ambassador. I realize that she is very busy with matters pertaining to Salos. I simply hoped that we would have more time to confer with one another." He looked as if he wanted to say more. Dena understood. He didn't want complaints to appear on the official record.

"May we speak with her now?" Dena asked. Of course, she

knew that the Salosian could hear her, had probably been listening all along. It was only a matter of courtesy to ask.

The consul presented his bracelet. "Ambassador P'n'ira, this is Detective Sergeant Dena Malone."

"I see her through your eyes," the feminine voice said. "Greetings, Detective. How may I help you?"

"Well," Dena said. "I wanted to hear from you personally. We've been concerned for your well-being."

P'n'ira tittered, a sound very much like K't'ank's laugh, but higher-pitched. "Forgive me for not being available at once. I have been answering some very important correspondence and speaking with a few of my Earthside colleagues."

Dena smiled. The ambassador sounded healthy and reasonably sane.

"Well, welcome. I hope you'll be comfortable."

"Haihatsu is a fine home, thank you," she said. "Very spacious."

The consul reddened. "I hope to be a little less, er, spacious in the future. The ambassador has many places she would like to have us visit. The exercise will do us both good."

Dena nodded. "Have you had any adverse reactions since the implantation? Dr. K't'ank said you sounded distressed when you contacted him early this morning."

"Well, I..." P'n'ira hesitated. "I am afraid that I have not been resident in a human before. With his eyes closed, I did not know where I was. Forgive me for causing distress."

"You still cause distress!" K't'ank spoke up suddenly. "I have been in contact all along with the real P'n'ira. You are not she. Who are you?"

"What?" Dena and Haihatsu asked together.

"You are mistaken, Doctor Whoever You Are. We are not acquainted. It is common for academics to try to claim friendship with politically-connected Salosians," P'n'ira said, sounding long-suffering. "It is a way to gain status among their fellows."

"That is not true," K't'ank hissed. His tail lashed furiously.

"Knock it off!" Dena said.

"Of course it is true," P'n'ira said. "I pity them. If you knew what they had to go through to achieve a transfer to Earth in hopes of attaching themselves to influential hosts, you would feel sorry for me. So many of them get in touch from their universities and labs to offer any kind of advantage or honor they have to gain my assistance."

Dena felt her own cheeks burn. Was she harboring a professional suck-up? Did K't'ank have to grovel to get sent to Earth? That didn't sound like the arrogant professor who had been open in his scorn of fellow scientists who cut corners when doing their research, and made fun of Dena's own lack of graduate school education.

"How much of that actually happens?" Dena asked.

"None of it!" K't'ank protested. "... Well, perhaps some. There is always a concession to be made to gain a favor.... But that is not important! She is not who she says she is! The real P'n'ira is in jeopardy! We will take you to the Alien Relations office and have you removed!"

Consul Haihatsu let out a choking noise. His face started to go red. He clutched at his chest.

"What's happening? Are you having a heart attack?" Dena asked. He shook his head, but fell back in his chair. She sent out a signal for emergency medical services.

"Do not dare approach me," the Salosian said. "My tail is now around the human's heart. If I squeeze it hard, he will die. Leave now, and I will allow him to live."

"Who are you?" Dena asked.

"None of your concern," the false P'n'ira said, with a laugh. "Go! Do not return to this place. Take all the other humans with you! Now!"

"All right," Dena said, holding her hands up. Haihatsu looked at her with desperate eyes. "Don't do anything rash. We're going right now."

She directed the floatchair out of the room. On the way, she contacted Alien Relations and her precinct on a joint call, telling them what was going on.

"We'll send a hostage negotiator with the team," Captain Potopos said, immediately. "But we need to know what we're dealing with, Mr. Barin. Who is that in there?"

If Barin had been embarrassed by Dena's discovery of his favorite video show, he must have been turning himself inside out with humiliation.

"When I pressed the Salosian School, their governmental body, we received word that several wanted criminals, including the leader of one of the most notorious gangs in all the oceans, the Ob'bob'va have gone missing. Her name is U'l'gra. The government on Salos has heard rumors that Ob'bob'va is trying to spread its interests out into other spheres, including Earth."

"There are Salosian crime bosses?" Dena asked. She started gathering the employees and pushing them out the much humbler rear door of the residence. The staff was worried about their employer, but obeyed Dena's instructions promptly. The housekeeper took charge and herded them all into the pool house at the end of the garden to await police interviewers, and bustled off to the handsome kitchen addition to make a cup of tea for Dena. "What can she do, threaten to hang humans up on fishhooks if they don't do what she says?"

"She is ruthless with her own kind," Barin said. "If they don't do what she wants, she has their hosts killed. I'm afraid that the real Ambassador P'n'ira is in grave danger."

"Do you know where she is? Or who she's in?"

"I have found comments of some potential candidates," K't'ank said, suddenly. "On social media, young humans have posted that they are proud to have passed the tests to become Salosian-hosts."

"Yes, that's common," Barin said. "Our applicants are excited to join the program."

The worm! Dena cleared her throat audibly. Barin fell silent. Settling her chair in the front room of the salmon-walled pool house, from which she could see the massive house's rear door and the landscaped grounds, she brandished her skinnypad.

"Send me some of those postings," she said. Her small screen lit up.

It looked as if P'n'ira hadn't just been talking with her fellow Salosians. Her profile on the biggest social media site scrolled on and on with complaints and pleas for help, including hashtags such as #whereamI and #getmeoutofhere.

"This is an embarrassment!" Barin's voice growled in her ear. "Some of these posts are getting three thousand likes!"

"The real question is," Dena said, mustering all the patience she could, "how could she have been implanted into the wrong body in the first place?"

Barin was silent for a moment. "We'll have to look into that."

"And why Haihatsu?" Captain Potopos asked. "He's just a minor official."

"I think I know, sir," Dena said, as the obvious rose up and bit her on the nose. "Because of his job as a negotiator, he has to maintain contact with foreign and interplanetary individuals as well as organizations and governments, right?"

"So?" both men chorused. Dena called up the image of the embarrassed Barin in her memory, and wished she had had the presence of mind to take an image of it with her skinnypad.

"He has got a communications setup that you can't believe. Before he closed it up, I saw icons on the main screen for ultrafast data connections and links to satellite hubs and laser burst transmitters. U'l'gra is now sitting on one of the fastest and least guarded communication nerve centers on the planet. She can talk to her people back on Salos as well as her new allies here."

"We'll cut her off," Potopos said. "I called in the Solar Bureau of Investigation. The technicians can take out that array with one button."

In the meantime, K't'ank sent her the fruits of his search, resulting in the names of a few dozen humans who had posted within the last few months that they had passed the screening. Four names lit up.

"These have not shown new status since the date of the implantation," he said.

"Running them through the government Whois," Potopos

said.

Such a search took only seconds. Dena hardly had time to read the names when three of them turned red.

"What does that mean?" Barin's voice asked, with some asperity.

"It means, Mr. Barin," Dena said, "that these profiles are fake. Whoever signed up under these names stole these identities."

"Show us the DNA profiles, Mr. Barin," Potopos said. Within a few moments, the results came back. "Uh-huh. Petty criminals. Looks like U'l'gra has her first human employees. Who are the Salosians in their bellies?"

"Um, well..." Dena could picture the usually suave official running a forefinger around his stylishly tight collar. "Three criminals that are high up in U'l'gra's organization have gone missing from Salos," said Barin.

"How could Alien Relations let them slip onto Earth?" Dena yelped. Haihatsu's housekeeper shot her a disapproving look as she delivered fragrant green tea in a handleless cup.

"I'm afraid," Barin said, very uncomfortably, "that Salosians all look fundamentally alike. The implantation surgeon may have mistaken one for another..."

"Okay, I get it. Or he was paid off."

"Um. Yes."

"So, where are they?"

"Hey, Dena." Another voice added itself to the mix. She recognized Sgt. Idlewild, who worked in Evidence. "We took those profiles and ran traces on them. They're moving around a lot. They're all pretty technosavvy, sending false pings and routing their communication through a thousand different towers and through a dozen fake accounts. It's going to take us and the SBI a long time to triangulate down on a location, but we're working on it."

"There is no time!" K't'ank said. "P'n'ira is in grave danger now!" His tail lashed at her ribs from the inside. Dena clutched her side and moaned. The housekeeper hovered worriedly.

"Is he kicking?" she asked, with a sympathetic glance.

"You have no idea," Dena said, and returned to her call. "Look, we might not be able to figure out where they are, but we can trace P'n'ira. What about the connection that she is using to get on the Internet? We can find the towers that are picking up her signal. That's not going to change. *She's not using false documents or accounts.*"

"Gotcha!" Idlewild crowed.

"Malone, P'n'ira says that her host is waking up!" K't'ank said.

"Are you all right, Ambassador?" Dena asked. "Can I talk to him?"

"I am well enough," a female voice said. Dena understood why there might have been some confusion. She sounded just like U'l'gra, but that could have been from tweaking the communication link in the Alien Relations bracelet.

"Hello?"

"Hi, there," Dena said. This guy would have been the fourth name on the list, Henry Ebanks. "My name's Dena. Who are you?"

"Hi," the voice replied. "I'm Henry. So, P'n'ira here says she's a diplomat. That's kind of cool, except I thought my symbiote was going to be an artist. I'm an artist, too. I dabble in oils, but I'm really a CAD/CAM guy..."

Dena almost exploded with frustration. Outside the pool house, a dozen police craft were dropping out of the sky and landing noiselessly on the manicured lawn.

"Henry, Henry! Sorry to interrupt you. I know this is a little weird, but do you know where you are?"

"Uh, no. This isn't the hospital at Alien Relations."

"Right. Can you look around at everything in your immediate vicinity? Move around as much as possible. We're trying to pinpoint your location. But don't make any noise if you can."

"Yeah, but I don't have my phone or anything!" Henry said. "How can I post updates? My girlfriend's going to want to see my scar!"

"Do you see how I suffer?" P'n'ira asked, plaintively.

"At the moment, your girlfriend is the least pressing problem you have, Mr., er, Henry," Dena said. Sgt. Ramos leaped out of one of the choppers and came running in her direction. He was wearing full riot gear. She beckoned him in. "It appears that you have been abducted."

"What? That's rotten! I want to help Ms. P'n'ira. She's really interesting."

Dena patted the air for patience, even though he couldn't see her. "Please calm down, sir. We're going to do everything we can to get you two out of there. Be cautious. You're an artist. Observe. Tell me what you see."

Idlewild interrupted them. "We have a location. It's on Earth, right in the city, Somewhere between the 47th and 50th floor of a commercial block. They didn't leave the area. Sending the address right now."

"Good," Potopos said. "A-Team, you're on hostage rescue. Malone, Ramos is there to pick you up to take you and Dr. K't'ank to Ambassador P'n'ira's location."

"Right," Dena said. She handed the teacup back to the housekeeper and steered her chair out to meet Ramos. He handed her a flak vest that would fit over her belly and a helmet with POLICE on the crown.

"I'm coming!" Barin said over the link. "I must see that the criminals are apprehended and turned over to Salos."

"Fine," Potopos said, briskly. Ramos whisked Dena toward the helicopter and loaded her chair in the cargo compartment. They strapped in. The pilot handed them both headphones. "Just don't get in the way."

"Hey, Dena." Henry spoke up as the skycar's engines whined. "Look, I think we're in a hotel or something? It's really nice here, a lot nicer than my place. Everything's honey beige with Art Deco ornaments. I'm looking out the window. Whoa, we're way up! Looks like a big shopping center down there." Dena heard a rattle at the other end. "Hey, the door's not locked! I think I can get out to an elevator. Do you want me to meet you on the roof? That's the way they always do it in the movies!"

"No!" Dena burst out. Why did everyone think that police procedure was just like in the movies? Practically every fictional cop ever filmed would have gotten bounced off the force for insubordination or malfeasance! "You're in grave danger, sir. Don't do anything, Henry... Henry? Answer me!"

"He is going out of the room," K't'ank said. "P'n'ira is telling him to stop, but he is not listening to her. Another human confronts them. She is very ugly, P'n'ira says."

The chopper lifted into the highest stream of traffic that was set aside for emergency vehicles. The pilot only had to put on the emergency lights once, to scare down a sports-flitter that had strayed up there to avoid the heavy traffic in the main lanes between skyscrapers. The driver shot them an aggrieved look.

"Sucks to be you," Ramos said, leering out of the side of the craft as they whisked toward the target building.

"Henry, answer me!"

"Who are you talking to?" a harsh male voice said.

"Hey, man," Henry said. "I've got to get out of here."

Dena's eyes met Ramos's. "This is starting to sound like bad tri-dee," he said.

"I said, who are you talking to?"

"The human is in contact with police," a hissing voice replied. "Do not let him leave."

"Hey, that hurts! This nice lady Salosian has to get back to her friends, right?"

The police chopper touched down on the landing pad on the 50th floor of the Skyler House, a residential hotel that catered to businesspeople for long-term occupancy. Who knew how long U'l'gra's confederate—at least one—had been there? Henry was right, Dena thought, looking around as they landed. It was a lot nicer than her apartment, too. She started to climb awkwardly out of the cab. Ramos pushed her back in.

"You're not going in there," he said.

"Yes, I am."

He narrowed an eye at her. "The hell you are. Even if you're not thinking about your baby, the rest of us are. We've got a baby shower planned for you next month, and you're damned well going to be there and not in a hospital."

Or dead, neither of them said.

"Okay, thanks," Dena said, reluctantly. When Ramos and the others leaped out and ran across the balcony to an open glass door, she stayed where she was. The chopper was noisy, but this hotel was near the spaceport and four or five heavy freight-hauler companies. Unless the guy holding Henry looked out the window, he probably wouldn't notice.

Another SWAT team from the bordering precinct was already swarming downward from another chopper. With them was a slim woman in a dark blue suit sporting the Alien Relations patch and a firearm half as big as she was. Idlewild was talking them into the target area.

"Keep moving. I'm triangulating off the signal Dr. K't'ank's hooked into. Yeah, you're on the right floor. From what Henry said, it's on the west side overlooking the mall."

"Hey, man, we're the good guys," Henry's voice said in her audio pickup. "You gotta let me go. We're nearly up to the station break part!"

"Ramos, he's in trouble!"

From P'n'ira's side of the link, all she could hear were grunts and thuds. Her hands were shaking as she followed the progress of the team on her skinnypad through the SWAT app.

"Did my assistant arrive with the gas canisters, Captain Potopos?"

"What's going on at the consul's house?" Dena asked.

"Not good," Potopos said. "When we cut off the comms, U'l'gra said she was going to kill the consul if we didn't put them back on. We're going to have to flood the house with gas that Barin brought with him."

"What kind of gas?" Dena asked.

"It renders Salosians unconscious," Barin said. "It's very high in cyanides."

"Won't that kill Consul Haihatsu?" Dena asked.

"Allowable collateral damage," Barin said.

"You are a real son-of-a-bitch," Dena said, in disgust.

"Malone!" Potopos barked, but she could tell he agreed with her.

"He should survive," Barin said, although he sounded uncertain.

From the skinnypad, she heard the hiss and bark of stun weapons, interspersed with the cough of slugthrowers. Whoever that harsh voice belonged to was heavily armed, and probably had backup. She wanted to scream at Ramos to give her a running commentary.

"Where's P'n'ira?" she asked K't'ank.

"I do not know. I have not heard her voice in some time. I have been sending posts to her profile, but nothing is coming back."

From the skinnypad, they heard a tremendous crash, followed by several people yelling at once. Dena couldn't wait any longer.

"What's going on in there?" she demanded.

"This one's dead," Ramos said his audio pickup.

"Worm's probably dead, too," another one of the officers said.

"She's not a worm," the Alien Relations agent said, testily. "She's a Salosian."

"Which worm is dead?" K't'ank demanded. "Tell me! I cannot hear P'n'ira. Go, Malone! I must see for myself!"

"Wait a minute," Dena said. "It's an active crime scene in there."

"Hurry! She must not die. She is a great Salositarian!"

"I think that lost something in translation," Dena said, but she heaved herself out of the aircar and went inside. One floor down, one of the regal suites had been broken open. Curtains costing more than her entertainment center were on fire. Scorch marks scarred the white-and-gold striped walls. In the middle of the floor, two bodies were slumped. One of them, a swarthy man with thick black eyebrows lay on his back, eyes wide and staring. The other, a slim African-American male in an orange sweatshirt and artfully ripped jeans, lay with his head on Officer Tiani's leg.

"I'm sorry," he said. Dena realized it was Henry. "So sorry..." His eyes closed. Dena felt her eyes fill with tears.

"He's dead," Ramos said.

"Dead of stupidity!" Dena wailed. "All he had to do was stay in the room. We knew where he was."

"P'n'ira!" K't'ank said, urgently. "Where is her new host?"

Dena activated her link. "Captain, where's Haihatsu? Did you get him out? We need him here, stat!"

"We got him, Malone, but he's in the hospital. That gas almost killed him. He's on oxygen and other stuff. Can you get her here?"

"Not alone," the AR agent said, holding her pack out for Dena to see. It was nothing but rags and a handle. "That guy shot my environment pouch. I've got nothing. Ambassador P'n'ira's okay for now, but she won't be pretty soon."

Dena felt Henry's wrist. He was cooling fast.

"No backup?" she asked.

"We... don't usually have this happen." The agent looked at Dena with a hopeful expression on her face. "We have an alternative means of transport. Mr. Barin said you would be willing. It won't put your fetus in jeopardy..."

"Goddammit," Dena appealed to the heavens, "why me?"

"Because you're there," Potopos said over her radio. "Do it, Malone! You've got priors. It should be no big deal for you."

"I hate each and every one of you," Dena said, but she flattened herself out on the ruined carpet in between the two corpses. "Make it quick. If anything happens to my baby, you are all toast."

"It won't." The technician moved over to her and raised the hem of her tunic to reveal her abdomen, and took a laser torch out of her pocket.

Dena watched the approaching flame with wary eyes. "You cretins are going to owe me plastic surgery!"

The long, hoselike alien that the technician cut out of poor

Henry's belly looked remarkably like K't'ank, although slightly shorter and slimmer. Dena understood the potential for confusion at Alien Relation headquarters.

The female technician was more deft and efficient than the man who had implanted her with K't'ank. P'n'ira disappeared into the narrow incision with no discomfort for Dena.

"Welcome, ambassador!" K't'ank said, immediately. The technician moved the second bracelet from the dead man's wrist to Dena's other hand. "I am glad that you're safe."

"Thank you, doctor! If not for your insistence on action, I might have died."

They exchanged numerous compliments in that vein. Dena felt a lot of movement inside her abdomen as the two Salosians got comfortable. Maybe too comfortable.

"All right," she said, smacking her side with her palm. "Settle down in there. No hanky-panky in the pregnant lady!"

DENA FLEW BACK to the hospital under the supervision of the technician and a half dozen of her colleagues. She just knew Ramos was coming up with jokes involving her belly, riffing on the theme of 'four's a crowd.' At last, she was wheeled into the hospital room where Consul Haihatsu was propped up in a bed.

"Good to see you up," she said.

"You are most kind," the consul said. "Thank you. The fraud has been... disposed of."

Dena almost asked, but decided she didn't want any details.

"I am sorry for my temporary domicile," P'n'ira said. "He was kind. He sought to defend me. I did not know humans were so gallant."

The technician disappeared, but returned shortly gowned and gloved, with an entire medical team behind her. "Are you ready, ambassador?" she asked.

"Oh, yes!" P'n'ira said. She giggled. "I am grateful to this kind Salosian and his residence."

"You're welcome," Dena said, dryly. She watched as the technician made another incision over the site of the previous one, and removed the smaller alien, helping her into a kidney-shaped dish full of warm water. The tech looked down at her with raised eyebrows.

"Would you like the other symbiote removed, too?" the tech asked. "I know your history. Now is your chance."

"No, Malone!" K't'ank protested. He wriggled, as if making sure of his place behind her uterus. Even Dena's child kicked and shifted, as if worried about his live-in babysitter. "What would you do without me?"

Dena thought about it, but for less time than she ever believed she would, and shook her head. "No, I guess he's part of the family, now. He can stay."

"Thank you, Malone!"

Done properly, a transfer from one host to another meant absolutely no downtime in function. By the time that P'n'ira was installed in Haihatsu's waiting incision and affixing her ocular nerves into his spinal column, she and K't'ank were off again, talking a mile a minute.

Haihatsu listened for a moment to the chatter coming out of both of their platinum bangles.

"They seem to have become fast friends while in your care, Sergeant," he said. "Would you like to be assigned to my detail?"

"No, thanks," Dena said, with a grin. "I'd never get any sleep. It's bad enough now."

Mr. Barin arrived, carrying a white vase containing one perfect iris, and set it on the consul's tray. Nothing for her, Dena noted resentfully.

"The dead man has been identified as Wiktor Thanoderian, not Giles Walker, as we believed," he said, with a very slight twist of his lip. "The Salosian in his abdomen was known as B'd'nop, wanted for numerous crimes of violence on Salos. The other fugitives should be apprehended shortly."

"Very good, Mr. Barin," the consul said heartily.

"Yeah, great," Dena said.

She caught Barin's eye. The Alien Relations executive fixed her with his expressionless black eyes, almost as blank a stare as one of the Salosians.

"We are grateful for your intervention, Sergeant," he said at last. Dena felt her nostrils flare, but kept her voice even.

"You owe me," she said. "I've helped you out not once, but twice. Wouldn't you rather have me as a friend than a thorn in your side?" She smiled brightly. "We know too many of each other's secrets now."

Barin shuddered. He knew what she meant. The game show thing would make great sharing on the Internet.

"You volunteered your services both times," he said. "I do not establish personal relationships with client hosts.". He walked toward the door. When his hand was on the knob, he hesitated and turned. "You'll be receiving a transmission containing a full manual along with documents ensuring you the appropriate classes and benefits. Good day, Sergeant. Consul." The door slid shut behind him.

Dena sank back on her pillows and let out her breath in a slow whistle.

"Well," she said, feeling a rush of deep satisfaction. "That was a surprise. The worm turns our way for once."

Jody Lynn Nye

Jody Lynn Nye lists her main career activity as "spoiling cats." She lives northwest of Chicago with one of the above and her husband, author and packager Bill Fawcett. She has written over forty books, including *The Ship Who Won* with Anne McCaffrey, eight books with Robert Asprin, and has gone on to continue two of his noted series, *The Myth-Adventures of Skeeve and Aahz*, and *Dragons*; a humorous anthology about mothers, *Don't Forget Your Spacesuit, Dear!*, and her own *Lord Thomas Kinago* series, perhaps best described as "Jeeves and Wooster in Space." She has also published over 120 short stories, four of which appear in *Unidentified Funny Objects* anthologies. Her latest books are *Fortunes of the Imperium* (Baen Books), and *Wishing On a Star* (Arc Manor Publishing).

DEPARTMENT OF DEATH PREDICTIONS, FINAL NOTICE

TINA GOWER

Department of Death Predictions
Predicting Actuary: Please Contact Department
7281 98th Street
Bakersville, NH 03058

Dear Petra Olms,

We regret to inform you that you've recently received a high probability natural disaster, accident, or homicide death prediction of:

93%

According to our studies and historical statistics, this indicates that your death is imminent. Although everyone dies eventually, the chances of your death occurring in the next few days has increased considerably.

Please do not call our 1-800 information hotline. This percentage has not been calculated in error. You may, however, contact our department to speak to an actuary assigned to your case during normal business hours (Monday through Friday, 9 am to 4 pm—please note a short lunch break is scheduled between 11 am and 2 pm).

Due to a clerical error, you are predicted to receive this letter on a Friday after hours, and we apologize for the inconvenience. Some of our clients have found the following information helpful:

Do's

Do make arrangements. Tell your attorney where to find important information, such as your funeral preferences, where you'd like your personal belongings donated, and your account information so that leftover funds may be equally distributed to designated family*. Please remember that this is after the amount deducted for our service, the attorneys' fees, and taxes. If you do not have an attorney who specializes in predicted death cases, one will be assigned to you. There is currently a 90-day waiting period for this service.

Do join our online community of other prediction clients. You may form friendships that last the rest of your life.

Do spend time with loved ones. Enjoy the time you have left.

Do remember that there is a small chance you may survive this prediction episode. If this occurs, the actuary assigned to your case will contact you and arrange survival fees and re-open a new account in your name. (Note that under section 54, sub-paragraph b, all U.S. citizens are required to register with the Predictions Department at birth. If you fail to re-register after a failed prediction, you will be fined at the currently assigned rate for your state).

Do notify your life insurance company. Note that, as per changes in legislation at the beginning of the year, some types of predicted deaths are not covered under most policies.

• Some current accidental deaths not covered:
• Vending machine accidents
• Shark attacks
• Amusement park rides
• Deaths occurring outside the predicted timeline
• Angry badger infestation

- Murder/suicide pacts
- Cult deaths
- Platform shoe-related deaths
- Deaths that can be traced to arguing online

You may visit our webpage for the complete and up-to-date list of two thousand and eighty-seven uncovered deaths.

Also, this list is subject to change. In the event your death falls under one of the above categories you may risk a reduced or terminated life insurance payout. It is a good idea to refrain from activities that will put you at risk. For example, you can usually avoid shark attacks by staying away from the ocean. However, this does not guarantee you will not die by shark attack (we are not liable for shark attacks that may happen at water parks, aquariums, sharknado apocalypse, Sea World, harbor fish markets, etc.)

Don'ts

Don't panic. Panic causes undue stress and may alarm loved ones. It may also set off a chain of events that lead to premature death. Post-mortem analysis suggests that as many as 71% of our clients die sooner than predicted from panic-related causes. Please use the time you have left wisely.

Don't call our office while angry or upset. We urge you to download our counseling software and answer the prompted questions until you're calm enough to speak with your assigned actuary. We do not wish our clients to express regret, wasting their last moments arguing with our office staff.

Don't tell family members about your final notice letter. Sometimes this can lead to a family member becoming involved in your death, especially in the case of natural disaster and/or homicide cases. Loved ones may feel an overwhelming need to be close to you while you pass and this may in turn place them in danger.**

Don't try to avoid the inevitable. Some of our clients have attempted to cheat their death prediction only to create the situation that eventually causes their death.

For a further list of helpful advice, and to download our counseling software, you may visit our website at: *www.predictions.org/NDHDivision.*

Again, it has been a pleasure working with you. We hope for a painless and peaceful death for you. We look forward to working with your death attorney to handle all death paperwork to ensure your smooth demise.

Sincerely,
Predictions

* Designated family must agree to a preliminary screening. If a designee has a criminal record or lien against life filed in the court office, his or her monetary benefit will be forfeited. Participating members of our "Predictions Family Plan" may qualify for expedited screening services. Restrictions apply.

** If you've been notified of death by natural causes, it is usually safe for family and loved ones to interact with you. There are no statistics available on safety levels, and the Predictions Department is not liable for accidental death of a family member due to being near a natural causes death.

Tina Gower

Tina Gower grew up in a small community in Northern California that proudly boasts of having more cows than people. She raised guide dogs for the blind, is dyslexic, and can shoot a gun and miraculously never hit the target (which at some point becomes a statistical improbability). Tina also won the Writers of the Future, and the Daphne du Maurier Award for Mystery/Suspense (paranormal category), and is a finalist for the Romance Writers of America Golden Heart ® (writing as Alice Faris). She has professionally published several short stories in a variety of magazines. Tina is represented by Rebecca Strauss at DeFiore and Company. Connect with her at www.smashedpicketfences.com

CHAMPIONS OF BREAKFAST

ZACH SHEPHARD

R obert stared at Andrea Warren's body on the floor, then looked at the smoking gun in his hand. He swallowed so hard his Adam's apple nearly shot out the top of his skull.

The door to the office burst open. Three of the company's security staff rushed inside.

"Jesus Christ... what did you do?"

"It's not what you think!" Robert said. "Eggs made me do it!"

The guards drew their weapons.

It had been a weird day for Robert Mills.

ROBERT HAD SHOWN up earlier than usual for work at GoodFoods. The only other person from R&D to ever come in before seven was Andrea Warren, and Robert had wanted to talk to her about the company's newest breakfast innovation: Floaty Links, the super-buoyant sausage that never sank in milk and would change the world of cereal forever.

Robert stopped before Andrea's office door. He finger-combed his hair (which was thinning), smoothed out his tie (which never seemed to stay smooth), and checked the note from his pocket. Just follow the script, he told himself. This time, you're not going to back out.

The door whipped open and Andrea Warren appeared. Robert, having not yet mustered the courage to knock, was so startled by the thin woman in business attire that he clenched his fist and crumpled the note, soaking it in palm-sweat.

"Mills," Andrea said, looking him over. "What are you doing here? And what's wrong with your tie?"

"I..." Robert looked down. He smoothed his tie, leaving a trail of sweaty paper fibers along the way. "The..." He swallowed. "The new sausage. It was—"

"Ah! Thank you for reminding me. I wanted to show you something. One moment." Andrea Warren turned, her black ponytail lashing Robert across the face as she reentered her office with a swift step. She came back carrying a silver plaque the size of a high-school yearbook.

"See this? 'Breakfast Food Innovator of the Year.' All thanks to my Floaty Links. And this isn't like your two-dollar plastic trophy for third place at the local hotdog-eating contest." She rapped her knuckles against the plaque. "You could stop a rocket with this thing. I'm pretty sure it's made of bank vault."

"Yes," Robert said, his gaze moving to his shuffling feet. "It's very nice. But what I wanted to—"

"Oh! Look at the time. Shouldn't you be down in the lab, working on something uninspiring? Good luck with that." She flashed a smile and pushed past Robert toward the restrooms. After a few steps she seemed to realize the plaque was too heavy to keep carrying (and, for that matter, probably didn't need to accompany her to the restroom anyway), but she lifted her chin and continued regardless, bracing the massive weight against her hip.

Robert sighed. Maybe he didn't deserve the credit for Floaty Links. After all, he'd only come up with the concept. And done the research. And the development. But Andrea Warren had come up with the name and pitched the product to the higher-ups, so maybe it was her idea after all.

Robert dragged his feet away from the office. His head was low, but it jerked to attention when he heard rapid footsteps coming from behind.

A woman sprinted down the opposite end of the hall. Her skin was white as milk and her hair was long and yellow—not blonde, but yellow, and so shiny it looked sticky, like honey. She wore a white cape with a golden disk in the middle. Her left arm was in a sling.

The woman quickly bypassed the lock on Andrea's door and disappeared into the office. Robert looked around for someone who might do something, but the place was empty.

Timidly, he knocked on the open door. "Hello?" he said, poking his head inside.

The woman was gone, but behind the desk was a soft orange glow.

Robert checked over his shoulder. Under most circumstances, entering Andrea Warren's office without permission ranked slightly worse than shoving your arm down a wolf's throat to see if it was hungry. But in this case, a suspicious character had just infiltrated the place. Surely it was okay to take a peek.

He smoothed his tie and stepped inside. Circling the desk, he found a glowing square the size of a large box, filled with a warped image Robert couldn't make out. He leaned over the square and moved his hand toward it.

"Wow," he said.

From somewhere outside came Andrea's voice, singing a made-up song whose lyrics consisted entirely of "I am the best, lah-dah-dee-dah." Startled, Robert lost his balance, leaned too far forward and fell into the square.

ROBERT OPENED HIS eyes. He lay flat on his back, staring at a sunrise-pink sky with clouds like piles of whipped cream.

He sat up. He was in a forest, except the ferns were clusters of bacon strips and the trees were sausages. Beneath him, the ground was yellow-brown and spongy like a pancake. The scent of coffee was in the air.

"You! Don't move!"

Robert turned. It was the woman with the milk-white skin and sticky yellow hair. In her non-sling hand she held something that looked like a butter knife stretched to the length of a spear. She pointed the not-particularly-sharp weapon at Robert.

"Who are you?"

"Me? I'm just... I didn't mean to..."

"Answer!" She thrust the spear within an inch of his nose.

"RobertMillsResearchAndDevelopmentGoodFoodsUnmarried41Y earsOld1219McKinleyStreetISwearI'llReturnThatLibraryBookSoon PleaseDon'tKillMe!"

Robert cowered behind his shaking hands. He peeled one eye open and looked out the corner at his assailant.

She withdrew her spear.

"You're not supposed to be here, Robert Mills. Come with me."

She turned and pushed through the bacon-ferns. Not being one to resist an authoritative command, Robert clambered to his feet and followed.

They passed an oatmeal swamp full of croaking raisin-frogs. To their right was a mountain of egg casserole, veined with green peppers. Big boulders like chunks of poppy-seed muffins stood among the bacon-ferns, and on the far side of these was their destination.

"Friends," Robert's guide said, entering the clearing, "this is Robert Mills. He followed me through. Robert, this is my company."

She introduced them individually. There was E.M., a round man with a British accent and deeply pockmarked skin; Cereal, who seemed more interested in filing her corn-flake nails than paying attention; Strawberry, a long-legged red woman with green hair and dark freckles; and Toast, an actual piece of person-sized toast with sticklike arms and legs.

"And I'm Eggs," said the woman with the white cloak and arm-sling. She extended her good hand, which Robert shook.

"Where'd you pick him up?" Strawberry asked.

"He came through the portal." Eggs looked him over. "Though I don't think he meant to."

"We should have him tested," Cereal said, still not looking

up from her nails. "Or not. Whatever."

"A bloody fine idea," E.M. said, pulling a steak knife from his belt. "Can't be too safe."

Robert backed away from the approaching blade. Eggs moved to guard him.

"He's fine," she said. "No need to test."

"But—"

"If the general says he's fine," Toast said, "he's fine. Leave it."

E.M. backed off, grumbling something that Robert guessed was either a compliment on his tie or an accusation of goat-theft. Robert wasn't good with British slang.

"Come," Eggs said. "I've got a few things to explain."

She led Robert across the clearing to her tent, which consisted of two slices of biscuit leaning against one another in an inverted V. The entrance flap was a net of hash browns. They sat on chairs made of wood, which in that case meant sausage.

"So," Eggs said, "how much do you know?"

Robert answered with a dumbfounded look.

"That's what I thought. I'll be brief then. You've entered Breakfast Land. Someone in your world found a way to open a portal."

A portal? Robert thought. *Like magic?* That made a lot of sense, actually. Andrea Warren had always seemed like the type who would summon witches or enslave demons to do her bidding. Also, this explained the occasional smell of brimstone around her office.

"Don't worry. We'll get you back home safely, just as soon as the portal opens again."

"When will that be?"

"Tomorrow, around breakfast time in your world. That's been the pattern over the past few days."

Of course—that would coincide with Andrea's early arrivals at work. Apparently she was punching the clock early so she could punch a hole into another world. This last part gave Robert some worry.

"You have a question," Eggs observed.

"Yes, well... I was just wondering. How bad is it that someone from my world is opening these portals?"

"Very. I think so, anyway. Everything that happens in your world affects ours, and vice-versa. I'm afraid the magic-wielder on your side may be a problem for everyone." She seemed stricken by a sudden thought then, and bit her yellow lip. "She's not a friend of yours, is she?"

Robert couldn't help but laugh. "No. Andrea doesn't have friends. Unless you count her strange affection for sharks and paper cuts."

Eggs stared at Robert. Then, all at once, she tilted her head back and laughed heartily.

Robert couldn't help but smile. She had a very sweet laugh; he was pleased to have caused it.

"Thank you," she said, recovering. "It's not often we're given a reason to laugh around here. Now if you'll excuse me, I need to go be a general for a while. Feel free to mill about the camp if you want. Just don't wander far."

They left the tent. Robert stopped just outside and looked around. E.M. was sharpening his steak knife, muttering something about "those bloody waffle bangers." Strawberry was aiming a heated monologue about personal responsibility at Cereal, who clearly wasn't paying attention. Eggs spoke with Toast at the edge of the clearing; he saluted, slathered himself in goo from an oversized jar labeled JAMOUFLAGE, and disappeared into the brush.

Robert didn't like the glances the others cast his way, so he spent most of the day in the tent. Eggs checked on him periodically, but was never able to stay long. Whenever Robert wasn't busy admiring his surroundings, he took long naps: traveling through the portal had left him exhausted.

When he woke in the evening Eggs was in one of the chairs. "Sleep well?"

Robert nodded, sitting up. "How long until morning?"

"A few hours. Listen, Robert—I need to tell you something."

He shrugged. "Okay."

"We're at war."

"With whom?"

"The waffles," she said. "And the crepes. Others, too. It's the same thing happening on your world, where sugary foods are infiltrating your breakfast tables."

Sugar, Robert thought with disdain. It wasn't that he disliked sweets—he just preferred that they stay away from breakfast.

"I'm sorry to hear that," he said. "But why are you telling me this?"

"Because I'm worried about your boss. I'm trying to win a war here, and things that happen in your world affect mine. Her actions are threatening us all."

"She works for GoodFoods. We make things like bacon and potatoes, not pancakes and cinnamon rolls. I feel crazy for saying this, but if you're fighting against sugar, Andrea is one of the good guys."

Eggs shook her head. "When you found me in the office I was running recon. I came across some of your boss's notes, and apparently the reason she's opening portals is to fast-track sugary breakfast innovations into your world. She's playing for the other team."

Robert's stomach turned at the news. He should have known Andrea Warren was a traitor to the cause. If she had her way she'd probably change the GoodFoods philosophy entirely and start producing caramel-covered breakfast fudge, or Sour Patch Kid casserole. It was a terrible thought.

"There has to be something we can do."

"Maybe. But we'd have to—"

There came a crashing sound, like something very large plowing through the forest. Eggs grabbed her spear and ran from the tent, Robert right behind.

"General!" Toast shouted, sprinting toward the camp, his jamouflage gone. "We have a prob—"

Something crashed through the poppy-seed boulders, sending Toast flying to the side. The enormous shape knocked over a trio of sausage trees and entered the clearing.

It stopped under the moonlight and howled. The thing's body was a waffle the size of a radar dish; its legs, crepes dripping with caramel. Maple-bar arms ended in apple-fritter fists, while two melty globs of vanilla ice cream served as eyes. A piece of French toast sat askew on the monstrosity's head like a beret, and its fangs were candy corn. All the pieces seemed welded together by lines of melted chocolate.

"Soldiers!" Eggs said. "Take up your arms!"

E.M. brandished his steak knife, tossing it from one hand to the next. Cereal raised two oversized spoons like a pair of maces. Strawberry grabbed an enormous fork, three of whose prongs were missing.

"Cereal!" she said, holding up the fork. "You were supposed to fix this!"

"It's on my list—jeez!"

The monstrosity bellowed "*Bonjour!*", then laughed like an idiot and charged.

E.M. engaged first, rolling under a swinging fritter-fist and slashing his knife across a crepe-leg. Purple berry sauce oozed from the wound, and the monstrosity punted him aside.

The berserk creature came forward. Everyone scattered. Cereal bowled Robert over in the panic, and the two ended up on the ground by the tent.

"Might want to sit this one out," she said, and sprang to her feet to rush the monstrosity. She fought defensively, dodging and keeping her attacker occupied. Meanwhile, Strawberry came from the side with her single-pronged fork, stabbing into the waffle-body whenever she saw an opening. Eggs tended to the fallen Toast, away from the action.

The monstrosity took a huge swing at Cereal. She ducked, but in covering her head held the spoons high enough for them to be struck; they were knocked from her hands. She was left alone and weakened, like the last soggy Cheerio in the bowl.

Robert, possessed by some strange compulsion to not be idle for once, ran into the tent and grabbed a bottle of hot sauce the size of his forearm. He came back out and threw it as hard as he could, striking the monstrosity in its dripping vanilla eye.

The thing recoiled, wailing. The company seized the opportunity.

Strawberry came from the flank again, delivering numerous hard fork-stabs to the legs. Cereal retrieved her spoons and clubbed at the monstrosity's knees. It fell backward and landed flat like a pancake, at which point E.M. sprung onto its body and delivered a two-handed knife-stab between the eyes.

The monstrosity went limp and bellowed no more. Panting, the trio gathered next to the body. Robert joined them.

E.M. patted Strawberry and Cereal on the shoulders. "Jolly good show, my dears."

"Don't celebrate yet," Strawberry said, and ran across the clearing. Everyone followed.

Eggs was kneeling next to Toast. There was a huge gash in his golden-brown flesh, nearly cutting him in half horizontally. Syrup oozed from the wound.

"No," Cereal said. "Not Toast..."

"I knew it," E.M. said, anger flushing his face. "I knew we should have been testing more often. The bleeder could have killed us in our sleep!"

Eggs stood, her gaze on Toast's lifeless body. She looked disappointed.

"E.M.'s right," Strawberry said. "It's time we tested again. And that means everyone." She looked at Robert.

E.M. drew his knife. "Don't try to protect him this time, General."

"No," Eggs said. "You're right. We should all be tested." She accepted the knife from E.M.

Eggs held out the hand of her sling-wrapped arm for everyone to see and slashed it across the palm. Yolk oozed from the wound.

"Very good," E.M. said. "I'll go next." He cut his own pock-marked palm, drawing a line of buttery fluid, then passed the blade to Cereal.

"Um," Robert whispered to Strawberry, "what's happening?"

"We're checking for syrup."

"Oh. Right. Of course."

Cereal's blood was thin and white. Strawberry's was red, but looked too much like juice to really bother Robert. She handed him the knife. Everyone watched.

Robert swallowed. He didn't like sharp things, and liked them even less when they were about to apply pressure to his person. Eggs approached him. She placed her good hand on the back of his head and drew him close for a whisper.

"I know you're not the enemy," she said, "but you have to prove it to the others. It doesn't need to be deep. You can do this, Robert—be strong."

She backed away and smiled sweetly. Her hand lingered on his hair before retracting.

Robert placed the blade against his palm. He took a deep breath, closed his eyes, and slashed.

The world went black.

HE WOKE IN the tent, Eggs in the chair beside him. There was a bandage on his hand.

"What happened?" he asked.

"You cut yourself and fainted. But the good news is you don't bleed syrup. You're not a waffleganger."

"A what?"

"The waffles have developed a way to hide among us. Their disguises are good, but they only cover the surface. They're still waffles on the inside."

Robert thought back to Toast's body. He realized that, within the syrupy mess of the wound, there had been spongy-looking yellow squares. Toast was just a waffle covered in a thin bread exterior.

"They're always coming up with clever new weapons. Like that creature we fought out there—I've never seen anything like it. I don't know how we can contend with that sort of thing."

Robert thought about Andrea Warren, who was opening portals to Breakfast Land so she could bring new sugary meals over to Earth. If no one stopped her, the next GoodFoods product could be a packaged monstrosity like the one lying outside the tent—and it would probably come with a recipe for Skittle omelets, too. Robert cringed.

"You have to do something about Andrea," he said.

"And we will, with your help. Come—the portal will open soon, and I'd like to see your boss."

"She doesn't take kindly to uninvited visitors."

"That's fine. I imagine she doesn't take kindly to being killed, either."

"She—*what?*"

Eggs left the tent, Robert rushing after.

THEY APPEARED IN Andrea Warren's empty office, Eggs having used an enchanted bowl of gravy to look between the worlds and ensure the coast was clear. Robert heard an upbeat rendition of "I am the best, lah-dah-dee-dah" fading toward the bathrooms, and something about Andrea's voice made him realize that, despite how terrible she'd always been to those around her, she was still a human being.

"I don't think I can do this," he said.

"Yes you can, Robert. You just need the right tool for the job. Let's go to the place we discussed."

They snuck out of the building and went to a gun store. Eggs left her cape in the car so she wouldn't look like such a weirdo.

The man at the counter insisted there was a waiting period to buy a handgun. Robert, nervously waiting in the corner and pretending he was admiring a wall-mounted deer head, couldn't tell if Eggs was using some form of magic to change the man's mind or if she was just sweet-talking him. In any case, they walked away with a revolver they really shouldn't have owned.

"We'll do it tomorrow," Eggs said, "after she's reopened the portal. That way we'll have an escape route."

Robert still didn't like the idea of killing anyone, even if it was Andrea Warren. But Eggs had insisted that he be the one to do the job, because he knew the target and could thus get close; the element of surprise was necessary, as no one knew the extent of Andrea's magical powers. Eggs's job was to keep an eye on the elevator and hallways: if anyone came, she'd either delay them or—if absolutely necessary—fend them off with a stolen sugar-weapon she preferred not to discuss. Robert agreed to the plan, even though he secretly intended to skip the whole murder bit and talk things out with Andrea.

The next morning they showed up at GoodFoods early. They hid in a janitorial closet down the hall from Andrea Warren's office. A pair of high heels clicked past their door.

"That's her," Robert whispered. "You can tell because it sounds like Satan's hooves."

Eggs squeezed his hand in the dark. "I know this won't be easy for you," she said. "And I'm sorry I had to ask you to do it. But we're all counting on you. You can do this, Robert—just be assertive, and don't let that witch intimidate you." She pecked him on the cheek. "Good luck."

Robert was glad for the darkness of the closet, as his face had probably achieved a shade of red previously unknown to science.

The pair waited a moment to ensure the portal would be opened. Robert then exited the closet, leaving the door cracked for Eggs to watch the hall.

Robert took a deep breath. He knocked on the office door.

It opened a crack and Andrea Warren's face filled the gap. "Mills," she said. "What do you want?"

"I..." He swallowed. "I needed to talk to you."

"I'm busy. Come back later." The door started to close.

"Should I wait until you're done with the portal?"

The door reopened. Andrea gave Robert a cold stare. He grinned like an idiot.

"Inside," she said. "Now."

Robert felt a surge of confidence. For once in his life, he was seeing Andrea Warren on the defensive. He moved to smooth out his tie, but decided it looked pretty good the way it was.

The orange light glowed behind the desk. Robert circled to the side to look at the portal, his hands in his pockets.

"It's nice work," he said. "But I don't like what you're using it for."

There was no response. Robert turned to see Andrea checking her phone, and realized that even during such dire circumstances she couldn't give him her full attention. She finished tapping the screen and finally looked at him.

"Okay," she said. "How did you find out about this?"

"A little unhatched birdie told me. This needs to stop, Andrea. It's dangerous."

"It's going to change GoodFoods forever. You're an employee. If you had any loyalty at all, you'd be happy about this."

"Loyalty is why I'm here. I'm going to set things right."

Andrea smiled. "I don't think so."

She raised her hands, palms pointed at Robert. There was a sound like gravy gurgling on a stove, and a chunky grey glow enveloped her spread fingers. Robert doubled over and clenched his stomach, suddenly feeling violently ill.

"Stop!" he said. "I don't want to—" he groaned in pain "—have to hurt you!"

"Nor will you get the chance. Security's on their way."

"They'll... see what... you're doing."

"And they won't care. Certain employees of this company really *are* loyal."

She curled her fingers and Robert's pain doubled. He dropped to a knee. In his pocket he felt for the gun, clicking off the safety. He didn't want to shoot anyone, but it felt like his insides were ripping themselves apart. He settled on firing once just to get Eggs's attention.

Robert drew the gun and fired far to the right. The bullet hit Andrea Warren's allegedly rocket-proof 'Breakfast Food Innovator of the Year' plaque, ricocheted off, and struck her in the head. She fell to the floor, lifeless.

The pain in his gut gone, Robert stood straight. He stared disbelievingly at the body, then the smoking gun in his hand.

The security personnel burst into the office.

"Jesus Christ... what did you do?"

"It's not what you think!" Robert said. "Eggs made me do it!"

They drew their weapons. From the doorway behind them, a yellow-brown ball rolled into the room. Robert noted that it looked sort of like a grenade, but with deep square pockets like a waffle.

He dove behind the desk. There was an explosion, and syrup splattered the walls.

"Come on!" Eggs said, grabbing his hand. She pulled him into the portal and they were gone.

THEY BREATHED HEAVILY in the same spot where Robert had first entered Breakfast Land, a short walk away from the company's camp.

"I'm sorry I couldn't get there sooner," Eggs said. "I was stalling an employee by the elevator when the security team came down the other hall."

Robert looked at the gun. "I killed a woman," he said.

"It had to be done." Eggs squeezed his arm. "You're a hero."

Robert noticed something on Eggs's left shoulder. "You've got some syrup there," he said.

"Just a splash from the grenade. I'm fine."

"Here, let me have a look—"

"No!" Eggs jerked away. She shifted within her sling, just enough to expose her forearm beneath the elbow. Robert saw a brown line there, wrapping around the white flesh. Eggs quickly covered it up.

Robert squinted at the spot on her shoulder. He pointed. "That's a cut. You're bleeding syrup."

"I told you, it's from the grenade."

"And that line on your arm—it looked like chocolate. The

same chocolate that was holding the pieces of the monstrosity together." Robert looked her in the eyes. "That's not really your arm, is it?"

Eggs stared at Robert. Then, like a split yolk running across a breakfast plate, her yellow mouth curled into an askew smile. "Oh, Robert. You're just barely less stupid than you look."

She swung a kick into his wrist, knocking the gun from his hand. The next strike came straight at his chest and sent him to the ground.

Eggs stood over him. Between pained coughs, Robert managed a weak accusation: "Waffleganger..."

"Congratulations—you figured it out entirely too late. Yes, your boss really was one of the 'good guys.' If we'd let her continue, she may have done irreparable damage to our campaign. But now, sugar will rule this world and yours."

Robert glanced to his right. The gun was well out of arm's reach. Still...

"Don't even think—"

He lunged. Eggs's foot came down on his wrist. He grimaced. She laughed.

"Seriously?" she said. "That wasn't even close. You're two feet away. Might be time to get your eyes checked."

"Or yours," Robert said.

"Huh?"

"I didn't want the gun. I just wanted to get you looking this way so she could sneak up on you."

A red streak came from the left and slammed into Eggs's flank. Robert had never been so happy to see a side of fruit.

Strawberry pinned Eggs to the ground. She tore the sling from her arm, exposing the line of chocolate there. The others gathered around. E.M. knelt and brandished his knife.

"Let's just have a look, then."

He slashed Eggs's good arm. She bled syrup. With a look of disgust, E.M. spit to the side and raised the knife in both hands. Robert looked away just as it was coming down.

BACK IN THE tent, Robert sat with all the others.

"So what happened to the real Eggs?" he asked.

"She must have been taken while on that solo mission a few weeks back," Strawberry said. "We gave her the waffleganger test when she returned, but we couldn't have known the hand we were cutting into was the general's real one. We didn't even know the waffles were capable of sticking parts together like that until the monstrosity attacked last night."

Robert thought back to the incident with the monstrosity. Had Eggs summoned one of her own kind to its death, just so she could earn Robert's trust? It was in that moment that he realized Eggs was the Andrea Warren of this world. Which, in turn, reminded him that he'd killed someone back on Earth.

"I don't think I can go home," he said.

"Nor should you," E.M. replied. "You single-handedly exposed the waffleganger that could have brought us all down, and you were instrumental in vanquishing the monstrosity. You've all the makings of a fine soldier. We could use you."

"Really?"

"Why not?" Strawberry asked. "Eggs told us you were an important guy in the breakfast-game back home. There's probably a lot you could teach us. And we *are* in sudden need of a new leader."

"I—"

"Bloody fine idea!" E.M. said. "It's settled, then. You shall lead us to victory, General Mills!"

The group raised Robert into the air and paraded him around the campground. For once in his life, he felt truly appreciated.

He never worried about smoothing his tie again.

Zach Shephard

Zach Shephard lives in Enumclaw, Washington, a small, peaceful town that will one day be obliterated by the local volcano. He has a very short list of authors he considers his literary heroes, and—on an unrelated note—he's far too professional to publicly freak out about sharing a table of contents with Neil Gaiman.

Zach doesn't own any cats, but he has been accused of resembling an albino cheetah. He strictly adheres to the Vitamin-C Diet (cake, cookies, candy), and his blood is so full of sugar it's indistinguishable from lemonade.

On occasion, Zach writes stories. Sometimes they even get published, and when that happens you might just read about it at www.zachshephard.com.

KEEPING AHEAD

MIKE RESNICK

A Lucifer Jones story

The *Raquel* wasn't much of a ship, but at least it wasn't out hunting for a puce whale like the *Peapod* was, and I figgered I'd ride it all the way to Australia, since five other continents and a handful of islands had already made it clear that my presence wasn't exactly wanted, or even tolerated.

That notion lasted until I got into a friendly game of chance with the captain and some of his officers, and when one of the brighter ones finally concluded there were only supposed to be four aces in a deck, I was set adrift in a rowboat, and even Squeeze, the octopus that had kind of adopted me (or at least my leg), decided to desert me, climbing over the side of the boat and sliding into the water.

I floated aimlessly, since I had nothing much to aim at, like, for example, land, and just about the time I started adjusting to a diet of raw fish I looked off to starboard, or maybe it was port, or possibly even something else—I ain't much on the highly technical terminology of the seas—and lo and behold, I saw a shoreline. In fact it was a mighty long shoreline, and for all I knew I'd reached Australia, about which I didn't know much except that it was probably populated by Australians.

I began rowing for shore, and just before I got there a mighty big shark that was in need of a little snack bit off the back half of the boat, and I barely made it to shore before he could bite off the last half of the captain as well, and once there I started looking around for signs of civilization.

After an hour I had to conclude that civilization had gone into hiding, as I hadn't seen nothing but six or seven snakes and a couple of alligators (or maybe they was crocodiles), all of which had a lean and hungry look to 'em. I thunk I saw a hog or pig or something kind of round and tasty scampering off into the bushes, but it was gone before I could even start to take up pursuit, and truth to tell I don't know what I'd have done if I'd caught it except maybe bang it across the head with one of the rowboat's oars.

I figgered I might as well head inland, especially as there wasn't no outland that wasn't under a few trillion tons of water, so I began making my way through the trees and bushes and a bunch of green stuff, being careful (since I was barefoot) not to step on no snakes nor anything else that might have a mouthful of teeth, and I'd proceeded for maybe an hour when I came to a little stream and decided to sit down and take a break.

I saw some stuff on the tree I was leaning against that looked a lot more like fruit than leaves, and I grabbed a handful and began chewing on it, though I finally had to admit it tasted a lot more like wasp nest than fruit.

I'd tooken a couple of hours to regain my phenomenal strength, and was just about to get up and set off further inland for another half mile or so before I had to rest again, when I saw a little feller what was dressed for exceptionally warm weather, wearing naught but a belt around his middle and a bag over one shoulder. He approached the stream from the other side, knelt down when he got to it, and lowered his head to grab a drink.

"Howdy, Brother!" I called out, which startled him enough that he fell right into the water. He climbed out on my side of it, pulled a knife from his belt that was just a few calories short of being a sword, and approached me.

"Who are you?" he demanded.

"I'm the Right Reverend Honorable Doctor Lucifer Jones, at your service," I said. "Salvation done cheap, with a cut rate for absolutions."

He frowned and stared at me. "And what are you doing on Borneo?" he said.

"Mostly talking to a guy what forgot to put on his pants this morning," I answered. "You got a name, friend?"

"Razakitomo," he replied.

"Well, I suppose I can call you Ray or Zack."

He made the kind of face I make when the bartender tells me he's all out of whiskey and I'll have to settle for water.

"Okay, then, you're Moe," I said. "So tell me, Brother Moe, how do you come to speak English?"

"My people were visited by a missionary who spoke English."

"He still with you?" I asked, hoping an English-speaker could point me to Australia.

"Parts of him are," said Moe.

It seemed like a good time to change the subject. "You got any idea how far we are from Australia?" I asked him.

He frowned. "Australia?"

"Just like this place," I said. "Only bigger." I spread my arms. "*Lots* bigger."

He shrugged. "I do not know this Australia. Perhaps one of the elders will."

"Fine," I said. "You can take me to see your elders."

He seemed to consider it for a minute. "Yes, I will take you," he said at last. "You have a fine smile."

"I been told that by many a comely young lady," I answered. "Well, two or three, anyway, and one of 'em wasn't drunk neither. Near-sighted as all get-out, but sober."

Moe stared at me, then nodded his head. "It is mine," he announced firmly.

"I beg your pardon?"

"Your smile," he said. "The others cannot have it."

"You collect smiles, do you?" I asked.

"Well, they start out smiling," he replied.

"I ain't sure I follow you, Brother Moe," I said.

"I am a headhunter," he said. "In fact, my whole tribe is."

"And there's a bunch of heads running loose around here?" I asked, looking down toward the bottom of the nearby bushes just in case some of them were close at hand and scampering around.

"Certainly," said Moe.

"Well, if that don't beat all," I said. "Where do you find these things?

"They are still attached to their bodies," answered Moe. "Until we catch them, that is."

I almost hated to ask the next question. "Then what do you do to them?"

"We add them to our collection," explained Moe.

"That's as strange a hobby as I've ever heard about," I said. "What else do you guys do?"

"Else?" he repeated, looking kind of puzzled-like.

"Are you saying that's *all* you do?" I asked him.

"Well, we eat and sleep, too," he said.

"No wonder this here island looks so empty," I said. "What do you do with all them heads?"

"Some we carry around with us," he answered, patting his bag proudly. "Most of them we pile in the village to impress our women and terrify our enemies with our prowess."

"I'm surprised there are any left," I said. "I mean, enemies with attached heads."

"Oh, Borneo is a very large island," he said. "And of course there are many rival villages that seek *our* heads." He smiled weakly. "It can get to be quite exhausting on occasion."

"I almost hate to ask what you do with the bodies," I said.

"They are of no import once the heads have been removed," said Moe.

"Yeah," I agreed, "I can see where they'd probably lose all inclination to run around."

"Come with me to the village and you can see all our trophies," he said, and then added, almost apologetically, "before you become one."

"Now that I come to think of it, Brother Moe," I said, "I've lately developed a deep and passionate love of the ocean. I think maybe I'll just stretch out on the sand under the moonlight and let the cool evening breeze waft over me."

"If that is your wish," he said unhappily.

"You don't mind?" I asked, kind of surprised, given what a fine-looking head I was wearing.

"I enjoy talking to you," he replied. "But if you would rather leave your body on the shore, I will just take your head back to the village and have a one-sided conversation with it along the way." He smiled apologetically as he pulled out his knife. "I have them quite often."

"On second thought," I said quickly, "I'd love to see your village."

"You're not saying that just to make me happy?"

"Actually, I'm saying it to make *me* happy," I said. "At least, happier than the alternative. Lead the way, Brother Moe."

He turned and headed off into the bush, and spent the next ten minutes telling me about his favorite possessions, all of which had been other folks' favorite possessions before they became separated, so to speak.

"How do you folks make a living?" I asked.

"A living?"

"If you spend every waking moment hunting for heads, or arranging them in artistic piles once you've accumulated them, who gets your food?"

"The women, of course," he said.

"They do the cooking," I agreed. "But who hunts and kills whatever animal you're eating for dinner, or tends the fields and harvests them?"

"I just told you," said Moe. "The women."

"Okay, then," I said. "Who chops down your firewood?"

"The women."

"Who builds your houses?"

"Our huts?" he said. "The women."

"And who gets rid of the bodies once you've tooken what you want from them?"

"The women," replied Moe. "I don't mean to be rude to a guest, Lucifer, but this is the dullest conversation I've had in years."

I was pretty much out of questions for the moment anyway, so we fell silent and walked a little farther, and then suddenly there was a pretty serious roar dead ahead of us.

"What's that?" I asked.

"Don't they have cats where you come from?" asked Moe.

Suddenly my face brushed against a tail, or maybe a tail brushed against my face. Either way, I looked above me, and wished I hadn't.

"Not that big and with spots all over 'em," I answered.

"That's just Diba, one of my pets," said Moe.

"You keep leopards for pets, do you?" I asked.

"Of course," he replied. "They help me track down my

trophies, and help the women clean up after I've collected the heads."

I had to admit that as useful pets went, they ranked right up there with guard dogs and plow horses.

"Purr for the man, Diba," he ordered.

Diba purred. It sounded like unto a twelve-cylinder fully-loaded truck climbing up a seventy-degree incline in a blizzard.

"Don't pet him," cautioned Moe. "The last man to pet him was my friend One-Hand."

I put my hands in my pockets and just kept following Moe to his village, which we arrived at in another half hour. There were a bunch of straw huts, and the rich part of town boasted some mud huts, and there was even one penthouse built on the branch of a big tree. There didn't seem to be much activity going on, so I figgered they were all out hunting for heads, or maybe hiding from other half-naked little men who were hunting for their heads. There were a few women here and there, but even though I guv each of 'em a smile they was too busy cooking and burying the remains and cleaning up to pay me much attention.

There was one in particular who caught my eye, so I shot a second smile at her and when she turned to look at me I reached up to doff my hat, but since I wasn't wearing one I just grabbed a handful of hair and lifted it straight up a couple of inches. She blinked a couple of times, shook her head like something with more than four legs was crawling on it, and went back to stirring her cooking pot.

"Would you like to see our treasure?" asked Moe.

"Might as well," I said, "since the alternative, near as I can see, is being a part of it."

He led me to a hut. He couldn't open the door because there wasn't one, but he lowered his head, peeked in, and said something in some language which was about as far away from American as you can get, and a second later a female-type voice answered back.

"All right," he said. "We can go in."

"You need permission to enter your own hut, do you?" I asked.

"Anyone can enter," he explained. "The trick is to not get speared."

I followed him in, and was greeted by a lady that was even smaller than Moe, though she held a pretty big spear in one hand.

"This is Lucifer," announced Moe.

"Is he a friend, a trophy, or dinner?" she asked.

"For the moment, a friend," said Moe. "And Lucifer, this is Tilana."

"Howdy, Tilana," I said, reaching out to shake her hand.

"All right," she said, picking up a shrunken head from a pile right next to her and placing it in my hand, "but you must give it back before you leave."

I decided that as long as she'd guv it to me I might as well take a good look at it, just in case I wound up sharing the trophy shelf with it.

"You know," I said, "back when I was in civilization my shirts used to shrink every time I washed 'em, but I ain't never seen something this solid shrink this much. How do you guys do it?"

Tilana grabbed the head back. "Trade secret," she said.

"She won't even tell me," complained Moe.

Tilana put it down with all the other heads. "I suppose you want dinner." She paused and stared at me. "Or is *he* dinner?"

"Not tonight," said Moe.

"Then all we have is horned demon steak."

"Horned demon?" I asked.

She took a stick and drew a rhinoceros on the dirt floor. "Horned demon," she explained. She turned to Moe. "I know you prefer fish, but I didn't have time to go to the sea, so I killed the first thing I came to."

"You killed one of them?" I said, impressed.

"Women's work," said Moe with a condescending shrug.

"You want it cooked, I suppose?" said Tilana.

"I ain't never developed a taste for raw horned demon," I allowed.

"Then you'll have to wait," she said, walking out of the hut, and a few seconds later I could hear her chopping down a small tree.

"That's quite a woman you got there, Brother Moe," I said.

He shrugged. "She tries, but she is smaller and slower than some of the others."

Which was like telling me that Ty Cobb couldn't hit the long ball like Babe Ruth, or maybe that Equipoise was a nice honest horse but couldn't get within half a length of Man o' War. As I watched Tilana carry in a couple of logs that each weighed about as much as she herself did, I tried to imagine what one of the bigger local women could do.

Tilana cooked up a mighty tasty rhinoceros. At least I think she did, but since I ain't never had rhinoceros before or since, I ain't really got nothing to compare it to. After we'd finished our repast she went out back to brew some beer, and Moe began showing me the departed missionary and the rest of his collection, holding up each head, explaining who it had been attached to, and how he'd won it in glorious combat, which seemed to be pretty much indistinguishable from sneaking up behind 'em with a sharp object, or at least a blunt one.

"I notice you ain't got no women in your collection," I said when he'd run through about twenty identical adventures.

"Of course not," he said. "They are not worthy of a warrior's prowess." He paused and lowered his voice. "Also, you cannot believe the muscles on some of them."

A few minutes later we went outside to this big pot Tilana was stirring, and she poured us each a gourd, and truth to tell it was mighty good drinkin' stuff. A few tribesmen must have smelled it, because they wandered over for a taste, Moe introduced us, and we all stood around drinking and passing the time of day, or night as it happened to be.

Finally one of them turned to me and said, "I find it difficult to think of you as a mortal enemy, Lucifer. Is that why you have deserted your village in the west?"

"Just what village are you referring to, Brother?" I asked.

"The one where all the white devils live," he said.

"You got white men living on this here island?" I said.

"Until we collect the rest of their heads," he answered.

"They got any boats in this village of theirs?" I asked.

"What's a boat?" he said, and suddenly the other guys all started offering their notions of what a boat was, which pretty much ran the gamut from bigger, sharper spears to bigger, cleaner loincloths.

"I thank you all for your help," I said. "But I reckon the only way to tell if they got 'em is to go have a look for myself."

"I would not do that," said Moe. "They have magic weapons that make a noise like thunder and kill from far away."

"They wouldn't kill a fellow white man," I assured him.

"I don't know why not," he said. "They killed the last three."

"There have been others?"

"We're a big island," he said.

"Well, just the same, I think I'll pay 'em a visit," I said. "What direction are they?"

"I'll take you there," said Moe.

"So will we," said three of the other guys.

"Might as well," said a fourth. "I haven't added to my collection in weeks."

So off we headed, I think it was to the south, but since it was dark out I couldn't be sure. We hadn't gone half a mile when I heard a growl just off to my right.

"Diba?" I asked.

"No, this one's Tuma," said one of the guys.

"Does he bite?" I said.

"Only when he's hungry," answered the guy.

"Let him smell the back of your hand," suggested Moe.

I help out my hand, the leopard sniffed at it, and fell into step beside me.

"I reckon I got me a pet," I said.

"A protector," said another of my companions.

"A protector?" I repeated, suddenly feeling a little safer.

"Right," said Moe as Tuma roared at another leopard that was approaching but suddenly made a beeline in the opposite direction. "He's not into sharing."

We stopped after another mile while they drank some native brew they'd brung along, and I just sat up against a tree until I could regain my magnificent strength. After a minute Tuma kind of sprawled across my lap and began purring or snoring, I couldn't quite tell which.

"So what country do these white guys come from?" I asked.

"The country two hours to the south of us," answered one of them.

"I mean originally," I said.

He shrugged. "We have never had an opportunity to ask them. Either they are firing their magic weapons at us or we are beheading them."

"You know," I said, "something's been puzzling me ever since I washed up on your beautiful land here."

"What is it?" asked Moe, holding his spear at the ready in case what was bothering me decided to bother him instead.

"You're all headhunters, right?" I said.

"We hunt the whole man," one of 'em corrected me. "We only collect the heads."

"Why?" I said.

The feller frowned. "The whole body would take up too much space."

"I mean, why collect the heads at all?" I said. "What do you do with them?"

They were all silent for a long moment. Finally Moe spoke up and said, "I just hate questions like that."

We walked along in silence for another half hour, and I could tell they was all deep in thought, and then the guy in front came to a stop and everyone else stopped, too.

"We have arrived," he said.

I looked ahead and couldn't see nothing but more jungle.

"How do you know?" I asked.

"Tuma has deserted us," came the answer.

"Smart cat," said another guy.

"Well, we promised to take Lucifer to the home of the white devils," said a third one. "Time to go home."

A fourth turned and shook my hand. "It was nice knowing you. If you see the ghost of my grandfather, give him my regards."

They all started heading back, but then Moe spoke up.

"What is the matter with you?" he demanded. "There are *heads* in the village!"

"And each of them will be aiming one of their magic weapons at us," said the closest guy.

"Yeah," said another. "It's all very well to sneak up on them in the dark when they don't know you're there, but—"

"It *is* dark," said Moe, "and they don't know we're here."

There was a general grumbling, and finally one of 'em said, "All right, the man's got a point."

Another looked Moe in the eye. "I always knew there was some reason I didn't like you."

Well, they grumbled for another couple of minutes, and they used a word or two that even I hadn't never heard before, but finally they began marching again, and a couple of minutes later we were standing on a hill overlooking a little seaside town composed of maybe a dozen little shacks and one big one with a bunch of tables just outside it where fifteen or twenty white men were sitting down and drinking.

"I want the one with the beard," whispered one of my companions.

"They all have beards," noted another.

"Okay, the one on the right."

"I'll take the one next to him."

"I'll take the other one at the table."

"I want the waiter."

They turned to Moe. "Okay," they said, "we've claimed our prey. You can have all the rest."

Moe turned to the first one who had spoken. "I wanted the

one on the right myself. I don't want to fight with you, my dear friend. Let's all go back home and think about it."

It took 'em about three seconds to all agree, and Moe grabbed hold of my arm and began leading me back.

"Hold on a second, Brother Moe," I said. "I didn't come all this way just to go back. These guys don't look like natives to me. They got to have a boat somewhere."

"I don't care how good a boat tastes," said Moe, "it's not worth the bother."

"I'll have my wife cook up the trunk of that elephant she killed yesterday," said another, "and you'll never want to eat boat again."

"You guys are free to go," I said, heading off toward the village. "I'll be along later if they ain't got no boat."

"We can't desert you!" protested Moe.

"Sure we can," said the guy standing next to him. "We hardly know him."

Suddenly a shot rang out.

"Hey, you!" cried a voice. "Come on down here with your hands up!"

I raised my hands and began walking toward the village, and as I got a little closer I could see a guy with a rifle standing there just to the side of the tables.

"How many of you are there?" he demanded, which struck me as a kind of strange question.

"How many of me do you see?" I asked him.

"Idiot!" he muttered. He aimed the gun toward Moe and the others.

"Goddamned headhunters! Come down here or I'll blow you away!"

I could see that Moe and his friends were mightily impressed, but I couldn't tell if it was because of the gun or if they'd tooken him literally and expect him to huff and puff and blow them to Kingdom Come, or maybe Philadelphia, whichever came first.

Moe began walking down the hill to the village, followed by the others.

"Hands up!" growled the guy with the gun, though now half a dozen more of them had drawn their guns as well.

When Moe and his friends had joined me and we were all standing next to the tables, a skinny guy with red whiskers, a patch over one eye, and a peg leg, came out of the building and guv us the once-over.

"Thought you was gonna collect some heads, did you?" he said.

"Certainly not," said Moe. "We just came over to eat a boat."

The skinny guy just stared at him for a long minute. "You know," he said at last, "I do believe you're dumb enough to mean it." He turned to me. "You a boat-eater too?"

"I'm the Right Reverend Honorable Doctor Lucifer Jones," I answered him, "here to bring spiritual comfort to you godless unwashed scum, meaning no offense."

"What if we don't want no spiritual comfort?" he said pugnaciously.

"Then give me a bottle of your best drinkin' stuff and the loan of a boat, and I'll be on my way," I said.

"I don't think so, Rev," he replied. "You and your manservants are our prisoners."

"We are not manservants," said Moe.

"Oh?" he said. "What the hell are you then?"

"Proud headhunters," answered Moe.

"You only hunt proud heads?" asked the guy with the gun. "How do you tell the difference betwixt the proud ones and the rest?"

The leader turned to Moe. "You got any real good reason why we shouldn't string up the lot of you before you can get around to beheading us?"

Moe seemed lost in thought for a minute, then looked up. "Would you settle for a mediocre reason?" he asked.

"That's it!" said the leader. He turned to the other white men. "Lock 'em up until I can figure out with to do with 'em!"

"Him, too?" asked one of them, pointing at me.

"Not right now," said the leader. "I want to talk to him and find out what he's doing here."

A bunch of guns appeared, and they marched Moe and his friends off to one of the shacks, and posted a couple of guards around it.

"By the way," said the leader, "my name's McTavish. Handsome Jack McTavish." He grimaced. "Of course, I used to be a lot handsomer."

I looked at his eyepatch and his peg-leg and suddenly saw that his left arm ended in a rusty hook and I could see that he was missing a few teeth, and I couldn't argue with that assessment.

"So what are you doing on Borneo?" he asked me.

"Mostly looking for a way off," I said. "How about you?"

"Hiding out," he said. "Me and my men done robbed a few banks here and there."

"Here and there?" I said.

He nodded. "The usual places: London, Paris, Barcelona, even hit one in Peking."

"You must be mighty rich fellers," I said, "seeing as you got no place to spend it."

He frowned. "I hadn't looked at it quite like that. Oh well, another ten or twelve years and the heat ought to be off us and we can leave this hellhole for some other hellhole, one with women and restaurants and automobiles and things like that." He sighed deeply. "What about yourself?"

"Me?" I said. "I'm on my way to Australia."

"Hear tell they got some mighty nice banks there," he said approvingly. "And, just betwixt us men of the world, they got a lot less gendarmes than England or France, which is always a consideration in my chosen profession."

"I don't suppose you got a boat I could use?" I said. "I got a feeling that it's a mighty long swim."

"I wish I could accommodate you, Lucifer, but we only got one boat for the bunch of us" - he pointed to a small boat that was down the beach a ways - "and you can never tell when we might have to leave in a hurry." He shook his head unhappily. "Too bad. Near as I can tell, Australia's the next big land of opportunity."

"You think so, do you?" I said kind of hopefully, as it was the only remaining land mass I hadn't been barred from.

"Well, actually I was referring to certain select banks in Melbourne and Sydney," he said. "Be a pity to miss them."

"So come along with me," I said.

He shook his head sadly. "I wish we could, but we're just about the most wanted men in the Pacific. It just ain't safe to stray from these shores for another decade at least."

I decided not to argue with him, especially since I didn't know how long a decade was. Instead, I brung him up to date on all the important news of the world, like Gallant Fox winning the Triple Crown and Dizzy Dean striking out eight million men or however many it was, and some minor little ruckus I'd heard about in Spain, and then we had some more drinks, and finally one of his men came up and said that Moe had a message for him.

"Bring him over and let him give it to me himself," said McTavish. He turned to me. "This should be interesting. I'll bet he tries to buy his freedom with some of those damned heads."

"They ain't worth nothing, I take it?" I asked.

"Well, they were to the original owners, I suppose, but there's no market for them once you get off this island," he said. "Still, it's a useful hobby, since it keeps the population under control."

A couple of fellers brought Moe up to us, keeping him covered with their pistols.

"Well?" said McTavish.

"We have enjoyed your hospitality," said Moe, "and we are grateful for the water you allowed us to drink, even if it was full of salt and small fish, and we especially appreciate not being destroyed by your magic weapons, but it's getting late and we'd like to go home now."

McTavish threw back his head and laughed. "You come to collect our heads, and you expect us to let you go?"

"Intentions are different from results, and the fact is that we didn't collect your heads," noted Moe. "And to show our appreciation, we promise not to take any white men's head for at least two days. Unless, of course, you wander into our village."

"I don't think you understand the situation," said McTavish. "You are headhunters. That is against the law. I haven't decided what we're going to do with you yet, but it will almost certainly be grotesque."

"You are not thinking this through," said Moe.

"I've done all the thinking it deserves!" snapped McTavish. "You're intruders, you're the enemy, you're headhunters"—he paused and gave Moe a toothy grin (well, it would have been toothy if most of his teeth hadn't rotted away)—"and you're my prisoners."

"You won't reconsider?" said Moe.

"Damned right I won't!" roared McTavish.

Moe shrugged. "Do what you feel you have to do." He turned to his guard. "You can take me back now." He shook his head sadly. "Poor fellow."

Then they were gone, and McTavish and I had four or five nightcaps, and I'd have started in on a morningcap but just then an elephant began walking through the place and I decided it really was probably time to catch a little shuteye.

"You can share my quarters," said McTavish. "My roommate no longer needs his bed."

"He sleeps standing up, does he?" I asked, as we moseyed over to his shack.

He frowned. "Mostly he sleeps out in the jungle, minus his head."

"Moe and his friends really got to learn to control their enthusiasm," I said. "Still," I added, "I can sympathize with them. When I was a kid, I spent most of my time collecting baseball cards."

(Actually, I'd spent most of my time collecting photos of Bubbles La Tour doing her Dance of Sublime Surrender back in Moline, Illinois, but the principle was pretty much the same.)

"If we let them live that long," said McTavish, as we reached his shack and entered it. "That one's yours," he said, pointing to a bed that would have been really welcoming if it had a blanket or a pillow or even a mattress. Still, I'd spent a couple of hours walking here from Moe's village, and my magnificent manly energy needed replenishing, so I lay down on the spring and was snoring peacefully maybe fifteen seconds later.

I don't know how long I slept, but suddenly I was surrounded by crashing sounds, like buildings being torn apart, and by screams that would have woke such dead as weren't otherwise occupied. I jumped to my feet and looked around, and then kind of frowned, since I could have swore I'd gone to sleep in McTavish's shack but now I was standing there in the open.

I looked around, and there weren't no other shacks standing either. What I mostly saw was a rhino and an elephant high-tailing it for the jungle, and ten or twelve of McTavish's men, each bleeding from a couple of dozen wounds, limping and staggering around.

"Retreat!" hollered a familiar voice, and I turned to see McTavish heading inland as if his life depended on it, as probably it did. The rest of his men took off after him, and suddenly I was standing in the middle of what had been the village, all by myself except for Moe and his buddies. I could hear a female voice that sounded like Tilana's yelling: "Steal our pets, will you?" and then a male voice screamed in agony.

"What in tarnation happened?" I asked as he approached me.

"I warned him," said Moe. "He should have listened."

"He probably didn't know you had Black Jack Pershing and four or five divisions lying in wait," I said. I looked around me at an awful lot of nothing, where there'd been a ton of something only a few minutes ago.

"He should have released us when I told him to."

"What the hell *did* happen here, Moe?" I asked.

"Our women came looking for us when we didn't come home."

"You mean just one village worth of women caused all this damage?" I said.

He shook his head. "Just the prisoners' wives." Then he amended it. "Actually, only Tilana and two others. Burila was busy tanning an elephant skin, and Marimo had to kill a pair of poisonous snakes that were threatening her pet leopard."

I looked around at the devastation one more time. "Three women did all of this?"

He grimaced. "I know, I know, they should have been neater. But after all, they are women. What can one expect?"

I figgered one could expect pretty much the same thing as one could expect driving a truck filled with nitro over the bumpiest road in the country, only moreso.

We moseyed down to the shore, where I pulled McTavish's boat into the water and hopped into it.

"Well, Moe," I said, "it's been interesting."

"You must return and visit us someday," he said.

"They start a ladies' football league and I'll be first in line to buy a franchise," I promised him.

Then I shoved off, headed south and west, and prepared, after five continents and a dozen islands to finally set foot on the promised land of Australia. But the Lord can be a pretty tricky critter when the mood takes Him, and as you shall see, things didn't work out quite as planned, which is probably as much of an understatement as saying that Noah ran into a spring shower.

Mike Resnick

Mike Resnick is, according to *Locus*, the all-time leading award winner, living or dead, for short science fiction. He is the winner of five Hugos (from a record thirty-seven nominations), a Nebula, and other major awards in the USA, France, Japan, Croatia, Catalonia, Poland and Spain.

He is the author of seventy-five novels, almost 300 stories, and three screenplays, and has edited forty-two anthologies. He currently edits *Galaxy's Edge* magazine and *Stellar Guild* books. His web page is www.mikeresnick.com.

SO YOU'VE METAMORPHOSED INTO A GIANT INSECT. NOW WHAT?

JAMES AQUILONE

Step 1. Admit It—You're a Bug

Don't act so shocked. You *had* to have seen this coming. One does not become an insect overnight! A metamorphosis occurs in stages. A mandible here, a thorax and a pair of antennae there. And what did you do about it? Ignored it. Hoped it would go away. But it didn't. Did it? The world continued to chip away at your humanity, day by day, atom by atom. The shit job, the shit relationships, the bosses and bullies, the inevitable self-loathing, the fear...

Now you're a giant fucking bug. Serves you right!

Step 2. End the Pity Party Now

There's no crying in the arthropod phylum (no tear ducts). Stop feeling sorry for yourself and get on your tarsus (feet)! If you want to survive, you need to take massive, determined action.

Don't fret if you awoke on your scutellum (back). This is a common problem. Rock gently from side to side until you have enough momentum to flip over. You can do this. Believe in yourself, insect.

Step 3. Realize Your Chitinous Exoskeleton Is a Wonderland

Stretch those wire-thin legs, bend that exoskeleton, wave those antennae, flutter them wings. Get to know your new body, explore it, embrace it. Love it!

Your insect form may repulse you at first. That's understandable. After all, you went from a vertebrate to an invertebrate in one night. But you need to move on! Never mind shoes or rolled-up newspapers; the number-one killer of giant insects is poor body image. Listen, you are a beautiful and unique child of this world. Repeat: "I have value. I matter and can do amazing things."

Now scuttle! Scamper up the walls! Fly! You couldn't do *that* when you were human, could you?

Step 4. Do Not Trust the Entomophobes

You may be thinking that communication with humans is a good idea. No, no, no! First off, you are an enormous insect. You have compound eyes the size of Christmas hams. Pincers the size of scythes. People are not inclined to feel sympathy for normal-sized insects. How do you think they'll feel about a super-sized one? Secondly, you are incomprehensible to humanity. No one can—or will try to—interpret your chirping or clicking. Trying to chat up a person will most likely lead to a stomping. Don't ever give them the chance!

Step 5. Run, Insect, Run

At the first opportunity, flee from your home. If you stay, there are only two possible—and equally terrible—outcomes. Best-case scenario: they check you into the deluxe suite at the Roach Motel. Worst-case scenario: they keep you on like some pathetic charity case. There is nothing more heartbreaking than a human-turned-bug who doesn't know he's overstayed his welcome. Get it into your supraesophageal ganglion (brain): humans find you repulsive! The very thought of you makes their skin crawl. Have a shred of respect for yourself, insect, and go confidently in the direction of your dreams! (Which would be the nearest landfill. But more on that later.)

If you are comfortable using your wings, fly out the window. If you are not, you will need to rely on speed, surprise, and an insane moxie. Use your pincers to open your bedroom door—and then scuttle like the dickens. Do not scuttle in a straight line! If necessary, run back toward your pursuers. This will freak them the fuck out.

But whatever you do, do not stop to explain yourself. You are beyond explanation now.

Step 6. Follow the Stench

As inferred earlier, the local dump will make the perfect home. If you don't know where it is, trust your olfactory sensillum (nose, but not really) and let the malodorous air be your guide.

Finding sustenance will not be a problem. Think of the landfill as your personal buffet. General rule of thumb: if it's rancid, it's ready to eat. Don't take on airs! Insects can—and do—eat pretty much anything, even other insects or their own excrement. No, you won't get sick! Ever hear of an insect getting sick? They are hardy creatures, nearly indestructible. Nothing can survive like an insect.

Step 7. Send a Friend Request, Insect Style

When the sun sinks below the landfill, rub your wings together. Harder! Faster! Louder! What beautiful music! Send your song deep into the night. Call your exiled brethren. We are waiting for you.

Step 8. Bugger the Buggers

Mate. Like crazy. There is strength in numbers.

Step 9. Teach Your Children Well

The only lesson they need to learn: humanity is the true pestilence on this earth.

Step 10. Sing the Song of the Night

When we are legion, the landfill overflowing with our armor-backed, many-legged children, we will unleash the swarms into the night where they will howl their insect song and descend like black swirling clouds of death upon those who would look upon us as cigarette butts to be ground out under their soles.

Never forget, insect: you are a light in this world, perfect in all your flaws.

James Aquilone

James Aquilone is an editor and writer, for fun and for profit. His fiction has appeared in *Nature's Futures, The Best of Galaxy's Edge 2013-2014,* and *Flash Fiction Online,* among other publications. He gets itchy whenever he thinks about bugs. James lives in Staten Island, New York, with his wife and way too many spiders. Visit his website at jamesaquilone.com.

CONFESSIONS OF AN INTERPLANETARY ART FRAUD

MICHAEL J. MARTINEZ

I was five when they took me.

I don't have memories of my early days on Earth, other than being raised on a farm. It was in the cornfield, late at night, when the light came and lifted me heaven-ward. My father—oh, don't get me started on him!—had been something of an alien-abduction enthusiast, and I had camped with him in the field that night, hoping that the benevolent denizens of the stars would come and impart the secrets of the cosmos to their most fervent disciples.

Well, my father was fervent. I had a Transformers action figure and was content to play in the light of the Coleman lamp.

The aliens actually showed up. Turns out, though, they were assholes. I suppose that ought to please dear old Dad, my last memory of whom was a man flailing about in the cornfield below, screaming, "Take me! Why are you taking *him*?"

It became clear to the Carestallans—those were the dumbasses who took me—after extensive probing, the likes of which are unmentionable here but would involve the fur of a Shellax otter and a Twix bar, that I was too young to be the focal point of the food-stock breeding program they had hoped to jump-start.

Also, I was not a pig. Apparently, their sensors were out of whack that day.

The captain of the Carestallan ship, one Karthos of Blanth, was furious. I remember his face undulating in the dim light outside my containment chamber, his fingers flexing in mathematical patterns of rage and frightening pathos. He was about to simply eject me into space when his fourth nest-mate pleaded with him to spare me, to adopt me as the thirty-seventh in her litter, thirty-seven being the most auspicious number for Carestallan litters and her having been shamed, slightly, by only producing thirty-six.

He must have been swayed by the gentle flaring of her neck frills and the susurrant tone of her mewlings, because I was taken from the chamber and brought to meet my new litter-mates. I was thrown in the gelatinous goop of the litter-bay and surrounded by the four-foot-long larva-stage forms of my new siblings.

To this day, I can never tell them apart. But they could always spot me, of course. I always seem to stick out.

YEARS LATER, I recounted this early experience to Minxa, a fuscia-tinted humanoid courtesan from Pelanoth, that renowned hub of tourism and commerce circling the triple stars of Anareal.

She didn't care.

I mean, she tried, sure. There's a lot of species in the galaxy, and no doubt her experience in the various courtship rituals of her customers would allow for a great deal of flexibility on her part. But apparently, talking about one's past wasn't a courtship ritual she'd encountered before. And she looked incredibly bored.

Or at least, that was my impression. She was humanoid, but her face was utterly featureless—no visible eyes, nose or mouth.

However, the body language of boredom is one of the surprisingly many commonalities I've found wherever I've gone in the galaxy. And I've seen it a lot. Maybe I really am that boring.

[Come, let us begin.] Interrupting my story, her thoughts entered my mind like a purr. Or, at least I think it was like a purr. I never had a cat.

Minxa took off her raiment and stood exposed in the darkness of the travelers' quarters, lit only by the megalopolis outside the window. The pattern of mottling on her skin was beautiful, and the tentacular growths on her head and thighs seemed to wave toward me. I felt the stirrings that I had grown to associate with arousal, and was hopeful that this, my first time, would be all that I had imagined.

She then removed my clothes and paused, her head tilting. [What do you do with that?] she asked, nodding down toward me.

"It goes in," I said. That much I knew, based on the studies Karthos of Blanth's family doctor had conducted—though it was still something of a theory, rather than real knowledge.

[In?]

"In."

She cocked her head to the other side, as if in thought. Then she raised her arm up, and a small hole formed in her armpit.

[Here?]

Gripped by a sudden wave of awkward panic, I paid her for her time and sent her on her way. She took the money without protest, of course. [Perhaps you might find more fulfillment as part of a quintsexual mating scheme,] she suggested.

Years later, I tried that. Sadly, I was allergic to two of my four partners, and only one was, strictly speaking, fully biological. The chafing was horrific.

I ALWAYS LIKED Antares, and not simply because humanity actually got it right when it named the star system. I mean, can you believe it? Of all the stars and galaxies humans named over the centuries, we blindly managed to name one the exact same way its inhabitants did. I always loved that.

They also had a breathable atmosphere and food I could eat, so that was a plus. It took a while getting used to the slaughter-it-yourself mentality, but the Antarans liked to keep their reflexes sharp, and it taught the kids to eat quickly before their food crawled off.

I had just broken up with my quintsexual mating scheme and managed to earn passage on a boron trawler to Antares. I had some credits in my pocket, not to mention pants to go along with the pocket. Even the food was sullen enough to make for easy eating. Life was good.

That's where she found me.

I was doodling on a napkin with a crayon inexplicably placed at the table when I heard a voice behind me. "You know, that's not for drawing, but that's a really good picture."

I looked up to see the most human-looking humanoid I'd ever seen. She had two arms, two legs, no real extra appendages, and even a close approximation of hair. She was also quite apparently female, though my recollection was likely hazy by this point. Tell me, after 3,874 standard time-periods away from Earth, how could I not immediately fall in love?

I held up the crayon. "So what's it for, then?"

She took it and began to color her palms. "It's to cover up the blood on your hands and show the chef you enjoyed his work."

I must've been to Antares a half-dozen times, but this was news to me. Maybe I just hadn't eaten at such a high-class establishment before.

"Huh. Well, thanks. And really, the drawing's nothing." I liked to doodle, but I was fairly certain I had zero talent.

She grabbed my notebook and took the seat opposite mine, her eyes eagerly scanning the page. "No, it's very good. The lines are so simple, yet rendered with passion. And to use a sanitary coloring stick is just genius."

I had drawn a picture of a house, with a cow and a truck outside. It was based on a picture I had drawn and had in my pocket when the Carestallans took me. I lost the picture to the litter-bay goop, but always tried to recreate it just as the five-year-old me had drawn it. I wonder what that says about me.

But the hot girl said it was genius, and I wasn't about to argue. Her name was Berethea, and she would be the focal point of my life for several hundred time-periods to come before it all went downhill.

BERETHEA WAS AN artist, one of the most innovative on Ill'illatha. The traditional form of art on Ill'illatha was to use one's own food-waste excretions to create images on one's sloughed-off skin. The idea was that you'd turn your waste into something beautiful. Or at least memorable.

Now, bear in mind that we're not talking about shit here. Ill'illathan excretions smell exceedingly pleasant, at least to my human nose, and shortly after they're voided they harden into a glittering crystalline matrix. Naturally, Ill'illathan artists eat a lot and work fast.

Berethea, though, took it to the next level. She had gotten to the point where she could control the crystallization process— and the color!—of her excretions based on her diet. She created some of the most vibrant, glittering art in the Six Principal Sectors. She was even experimenting with various bath salts to try to change the color and texture of her skin, to make better canvases when it sloughed off.

And here she was, one of the most cutting-edge visual artists in her stellar neighborhood, enamored with my art. Yes, that's what I was now. An artist. She was in love with my work, and I was in love with her.

We traveled the sectors together and found patronage amongst the great governments and corporations of the galaxy.

We were feted and celebrated. If Earth hadn't been masked from electronic transmissions by the Sector Administrative Offices, maybe my dad would've found out. I'd like to think he'd be proud.

Of course, there was a darker side. There always is. There were time-periods where we would simply laze about, unwilling to work, content to indulge in debauchery and drugs. I blame myself for the latter; I had managed, at great cost and expense, to convince one of my litter-mates to obtain several cases of Twinkies the next time they visited Earth to steal livestock and probe humans. I wanted to see what Berethea thought of my favorite childhood treat—and see what the waste excretions might produce.

Sadly, she became hooked on them, as they happened to be the most perfectly addictive drug to her species. Plus her art turned out to be shit when she was on them because her excretions declined significantly in color, quality, and smell.

After a particularly disastrous showing at the Royal Gallery of Syraxis Prime—you may have seen the headlines about the dysentery epidemic shortly thereafter—Berethea was a shell of her former self. It fell to me to keep drawing, creating, producing. I drew hundreds of little Earth houses using every substance imaginable. Then I started doing cats, even though my recollection of what they looked like was considerably off. Aside from being considered a demon worshiper by the Glorious Order of Glod, they were a hit.

My last real success, actually

BERETHEA WAS GETTING... lazy. She still ate like an Ill'illathan artist, but her excretions, well, she just wasn't using them and they were becoming more and more like literal crap. She blamed a variety of things—the latest critical review, the quality of our quarters, my company—but I knew it was the Twinkies.

Worse, she was gaining weight. No, not in the sense you're thinking of, and dammit, I'm enough of a civilized being to forgive a little weight gain. I know I've put on a few around the middle lately. But Berethea was literally ballooning in the strangest areas, from her ear lobes to her calves. It would fluctuate... migrate, really.

I tried to get her to excrete, to create! But all she wanted were the Twinkies. And they were the most goddamn expensive thing in the Sectors. I was an idiot, but I loved her, so I paid and got more.

We lived hand to mouth, despite my government stipends and honorarium. My work suffered. The critics noticed.

I started to wonder if I could get other drawings from Earth people and pass them off as mine. Or just broker them in a gallery of my own. I reached out to a few of my litter-mates. They were in the Twinkie business now, and it was flourishing, and they had no time to collect scribblings. When I asked for a cut—I turned them on to Twinkies in the first place, dammit!—they laughed. I appealed to Karthos, but my surrogate mother, the fourth nest-mate, had passed into transcendence by then, and he wanted nothing to do with me.

Then, one day, after another middling review and a few minor sales that left me empty inside, I took a walk through the bazaar on Fereo, wondering if I should use my skill in art to draw things other than my childhood memories. I wondered if the merchants and wares there would be good subjects. I mean, sure, the Ferean authorizes considered any visual or audio records of the bazaar to be both a crime and a heresy, but Berethea needed Twinkies.

As I walked, I noticed a short blob of a creature, using a stick and dried clay to make an etching. *And it looked just like one of mine.*

"How did you learn to do that?" I asked the bulbous little humanoid.

His translation chip took a while to respond. "These are the sacred etchings of our people. This is how we communicate with our ancestors and bring them peace. We must make them every time-period or the ancestors will be displeased."

I nodded, smiling, careful not to show teeth; it was amazing how many species were offended or scared by someone's teeth. "Where are you from?"

"Betlak VII," the pale little thing replied. "I am on a knowledge quest. When I return after seeing the galaxy, I will be consumed by my Queen, and my memories will become hers and I will go to join my ancestors."

Tough luck, that, I thought. "I like what you're doing. Do you think you might make one for me?"

At this, the Betlaki jumped to his pudgy feet, let out a massive belch—later, I found this was something of a war-cry—and kicked my shin before running off. His foot felt like a soft pillow against my leg, but I took his meaning.

I went back to our rented tent and linked up with the KnowNet to learn everything I could about Betlak VII, which was some backwater little rock on the outer edge of the Fifth Sector.

As it turned out, they had something more valuable than Twinkies.

YOU SEE, BETLAK VII had immense deposits of gold, uranium, plutonium, you name it. It made Earth look like an inert lump of dirt in comparison. Yet the Betlaki had forbidden any kind of exploitation of these resources and, surprisingly, the rest of the galaxy appeared to be listening. Even the corporations.

But I needed that art, so I went back again to the only family I knew. I went through fourteen litter-mates before I found one that would listen, and she only listened because her fortunes were worse than mine. She was down to three ships, with barely enough crew to run them. As a member of the Carestallan Shipping Guild, if she didn't gain enough capital to purchase two more ships, she was honor-bound to end her life, and the lives of her crew as well, by offering themselves up to the rest of our litter the next time one of us mated. Naturally, I hated family weddings, and there were a lot of them.

Anyway, desperation drives people to do dumb things, and we were both desperate. I told Berethea I was going on a retreat, to hone my art. By then, she had checked into a rehab center, and was using a mixture of sulfuric acid, heroin, and Thin Mints to wean herself off the Twinkies. She was looking good, and even starting to work again when she wasn't locked down. She seemed tired and twitchy, but hopeful.

I went with my litter-mate to Betlak VII. We landed in the mountains of the northern continent, near a small settlement. We thought we were being subtle, but there were a couple hundred pudgy little Betlaki there when we opened the hatch. And they all had etchings with them, kept in little pouches slung across their shoulders.

We tried to negotiate, of course. I mean, we're not monsters. The Betlaki were surprisingly sedate when my litter-mate asked about mining rights, which was supposed to be this verboten thing. The minerals they didn't seem to care about, but when I mentioned the etchings... well, imagine two hundred hairless creatures, roughly the height of toddlers but with twice the mass, belching all at once.

Then they charged. And it was like I was in a pillow fight. Nothing they did hurt, at all. They pummeled us with soft, cushioned fists, kicked us with cottony, plush feet. They tried biting us with their light, willowy teeth. Nothing worked. But they kept at it.

So the miners went to work, and the Betlaki threw themselves bodily on each miner to stop them—apparently, the whole thing about the etchings made them irrationally furious. They bounced off, hit the ground, got up and did it again. Over and over. And when they fell, since it took them several moments to right their roly-poly bodies, I snatched the etchings from their little pouches. They were *perfect*. I could get thousands for just one. And I was collecting dozens right there!

Two days later, the ships lifted off from Betlak, the holds full of precious minerals. Meanwhile, I had managed to gather 342 etchings—they kept making more when they weren't trying to stop us. Honestly, I didn't feel bad. We only took a few hundred tons of minerals—there were gold rocks the size of my head just lying on the ground, after all—and the etchings seemed quite replaceable. None of the Betlaki got hurt because even when we had to push past them or move them out of the way, they bounced.

I finally felt good, for the first time in who-knows-how-many time-periods.

I PARCELED OUT the etchings sparingly, sprinkling in a handful whenever I did a show. As I got a closer look at them, I realized they were just different enough not to be believable as mine. So I passed them off as "outsider art" from Earth children. Nobody had really heard of Earth, and Betlak VII was almost as unknown, so the art people didn't ask questions. They sold well, and I had money.

Berethea was still in rehab. After some initial success, the doctors were struggling to help her get over the hump. I visited once when she was in something of a down period, and let me tell you, it wasn't pretty. Somehow, she sprouted two extra arms from her sides, and there were horns coming out of either cheek. One moment, she'd call me the sweetest things, and the next she'd spit at my shoes and laugh as they dissolved.

But the shows were going well, and I got to travel and wine-and-dine again. I could afford new shoes when Berethea spit corrosive acid on the old ones I took to wearing when I visited her. Things were okay. I was okay. Not great, but okay. It's hard to describe, really. I'd always been the runt of the litter, and my litter-mates teased me about never growing out of my pale, fleshy larval state. So, you know, I had low expectations. But this was different.

I drank more. Thankfully, several species in the galaxy piss what Earthlings might consider top-shelf liquor, so getting drunk was always cheap and easy. Hell, some of the art-scene crowd would bring me bottles of their own liquid emissions to try. One such offering made me blind and deaf for three days, but that's another story.

It was on Urtulan, in the middle of my most triumphant show yet, where I finally lost it all.

The room was buzzing with excitement over my latest collection—literally. It was filled with oxyvore insectoids. It was a positive buzz, and even some of my own latest works were getting noticed. My stuff was selling alongside the Betlaki etchings, perhaps not as well, but it was selling. I started thinking that maybe I could hire a ship, head to some other nowhere planets and see if I could get my hands on other stuff. Maybe start up a whole big new thing. Really make the "outsider art" my forte. Become a galactic taste-maker.

Then the hive-cell wall of the gallery exploded inward.

Behind it was a massive, giant, rounded foot.

As it happens, the reason the galactic conglomerates left Betlak VII alone was not out of the generosity of their hearts, and in my desperation for money, I didn't think to delve deeper. The reason they left the planet and its cute, pudgy, plush denizens alone was because they weren't always cute, pudgy, and plush.

When sufficiently riled, several thousand of them could gather in a single place, abandon their individual lives and personalities in a week-long ritual, and merge into what they called the "war form."

It was still cute, pudgy, and plush, but goddamn it, it was a hundred meters tall and pretty much indestructible. It kicked its way into the gallery and proceeded to collect all the etchings I had taken.

Now, despite the injuries and property destruction, this might not have been insurmountable. I could've written it off as another Glod incident or something. But the Betlaki were nothing if not thorough. They managed to find every single etching I sold or showed, and battered their way into whatever building, ship, or organic structure that housed them.

Turns out their ancestors' quantum thought-patterns really

were accessed through the etchings. How was I to know? They were cute little fucking pillow people.

ANYWAY, THAT'S WHY I'm here now. I've lost everything. I used my last favor with my entire litter to get here, and only because they were making another Twinkie run.

You have what I need. Hell, I saw your janitor toss a whole bunch of art in the dumpster the other day. Do you have any idea how much they'd go for out there? You'd never, ever have to worry about budget cuts again.

And let me tell you, Swift Elementary and its students will be the toast of the galaxy.

So what do you say? Ready to become the best-known school principal in the Five Principal Sectors?

Also, this is Berethea. She's having an episode right now, but really, she's the love of my life.

Sorry about your shoes.

Michael J. Martinez

Michael J. Martinez is the author of the *Daedalus* series of Napoleonic Era space opera novels and the forthcoming *MAJESTIC-12* series, both from Night Shade Books. His short stories have appeared in *Pathfinder Tales* online and in the *Cthulhu Fhtagn!* anthology from Word Horde. He lives in the Garden State with a very patient wife, a really smart and funny daughter, and the Best Cat in the World. He is easily bribed with beer.

TEXTS FROM MY MOTHER ABOUT THE ALIEN INVASION

TINA CONNOLLY

H i honey what do u put in your banana bread when you make it?

> well bananas I guess

i think u said ur trick was yogurt but i'm out because of the alien invasion and so will cream do?

> OMG MOM WAIT WHAT?

> WHAT ALIEN INVASION??? WHERE???

on the golf course about hole 7 or 8

ur dad might know which hole but he's still out playing and i told him i would do banana bread for bridge group tonight so can i use cream?

> No, cream is not good substitute

for yogurt maybe sour cream??
How do you know there will even be bridge?

oh honey we never miss bridge group

i guess mr stubbs was decapitated at hole 10 when he didn't kneel to them but u know he never wears his hearing aid

anyway we'll get a sub

mrs mitchell always wants to play
but she can't since mr mitchell left her

hang on I'm googling this

and nobody knows where he is but it's real hush hush, probably canada

OMG mom they said the aliens put your city in a giant forcefield, like a dome

yes and the dome went right through the grocery store and the milk is on this side but the yogurt is on the other side

i don't know why this always happens to me when i try to make a recipe

it never comes out the same as yours

The aliens are saying they'll let you out if the president gives in to their demands.

yes that's what they were telling mr stubbs i guess

well after mr stubbs decapitation they grabbed mr pratt up the street which is fine by me because he's had those horrible dead bushes in his yard for two years

maybe now he'll clean them out

How can he if the aliens took him??

oh well not permanently took. they're using him as a mouth speak thing i don't remember what it's called

OMG Mom the aliens are bodysnatchers it's saying.

They're infiltrating people. You have to get out of there.

i thought i said it's bridge night and anyway if you'd come to see me like you were supposed to then this wouldn't have happened

??? If I were there seeing you I'd be stuck too.

well i don't know maybe we would have taken a trip or something

On bridge night??

hang on honey ur father's home

he looks a little shaken up

maybe he saw the beheading

okay it's okay he says not to worry

mom?

they're friendly he says

                     that sounds suspicious

play a good game of golf

           MOM HE'S A BODYSNATCHER GET OUT!!!

oh that's sweet of u to worry honey, i'll tell him that u asked
about him

he says ur sweet to worry and did u remember to sign up for
ur 401k

                     ok that's dad all right

                 what about the beheading tho?

i guess it was an accident with their laser pointer

anyway apparently there's only twelve of them and
they only need twelve bodies

wow ur father invited them to bridge group well they
better come in pairs is all i can say

                       i can't even

oh good, one did take over mr pratt maybe he likes getting
rid of dead bushes better than the last mr pratt

           the president is back on again. I guess they have
           100 more ships? They will leave the rest of us in
           peace if they can make their 100 more colonies.

ur father says they're going to keep it at 95 degrees in here

under the dome

they have big heat lamps

this will be really good u know how i have a tough time in winter

> This is their RETIREMENT COMMUNITY???

> srsly WTF

i hope that means what the frigidaire

they retire by taking over humans and playing bridge

and tearing out dead bushes i hope

> ok the prez is directing the rest of them to florida
> in exchange for the dome technology

> this is the weirdest day

tell me about it

now explain to me what i can make for bridge group
if i have bananas, cream, and flour, but i can't make
anything that will remind mrs stubbs of her decapitated
husband?

honey??

Tina Connolly

Tina Connolly is the author of the *Ironskin* trilogy from Tor Books, and the *Seriously Wicked* series from Tor Teen. *Ironskin*, her first fantasy novel, was a Nebula finalist. In addition to *Unidentified Funny Objects 3*, her stories have appeared in *Women Destroy SF, Lightspeed, Tor.com, Strange Horizons*, and many more. Her narrations have appeared in audiobooks and podcasts including *Podcastle, Pseudopod, Beneath Ceaseless Skies*, and her Parsec-winning flash fiction podcast *Toasted Cake*. Her website is tinaconnolly.com. She frequently texts with her mother, but generally not about alien invasions. Mostly.

SUPPORT YOUR LOCAL ALIEN

GINI KOCH

"**C**aptain Thompson-Manning, we have a steam leak in Engineering, one of the auxiliary engines."

Which likely explained why my ship had gone from sub-light 10 to sub-light 3 in less than a minute. "Status, Missus Benning?"

"Both Miss Soto and I are repairing, but we need to belay any increases in speed."

"Do we need to go to full stop?"

"Unsure."

"How bad is it, exactly, Georgia?"

"Could be quite bad, could be fixed easily. We're still trying to determine the source and cause of the leak."

"Shall I go take a look?" Manning, our Chief Science Officer and my still newlywed husband, asked.

"I believe we'll both go. Security and all secondary bridge crew standby to assist in Engineering. First Officer Vrabel has the bridge. All yours, Elizabeth."

As Vrabel started giving orders, Manning and I quickly headed to the lift that would take us down from the bridge to the seventh deck. Once inside, Manning took my hand. "Are you sure you should be rushing around in your delicate condition, Jeanette?"

"You worry too much, Nicholas." I squeezed his hand. "But I do appreciate it.

Under many circumstances, the captain of a vessel probably wouldn't feel the need to race off to help out with a leaky engine, especially since we had a decent-sized and quite competent crew. However, we were on our own out here in the vastness of space, and that meant any threat was a terrifying prospect.

Due to how we'd been given the *Brave Voyager* in the first place—as a parting gift for being willing to "die" to start a war with the invading alien race called the Z'porrah so that Earth would ultimately never be conquered and destroyed—we weren't allowed to let anyone on Earth know we were all still alive. And, since we were quite far from our first goal of reaching the nearest star system to Earth's, we had no one to ask for assistance in case things went to the bad.

A leaking engine could blow us up, disable us, or strand us. All of which meant we'd die for real.

We were still getting used to living on a spaceship, let alone flying through space, and we'd all dropped the spittoon in terms of anticipating what the *Brave Voyager* could and couldn't do. She could do quite a lot, but apparently last at our highest speed under warp wasn't on the list.

The *Brave Voyager* had a self-sustaining system of in-ship fans and filters impregnated with lithium hydroxide to remove carbon dioxide from the air inside the ship. Per Manning, lithium hydroxide literally sucked the carbon dioxide out of the air, which formed lithium carbonate and water.

The excess water this created, along with all reclaimed water, was used to power the ship as well as create oxygen and our life support system. The creation of hydrogen was also a useful byproduct. Hydrogen helped us reach warp, as well as giving us the extra boost whenever we might need to reach escape velocity in order to leave a planet.

Lastly, the lithium carbonite was used by Dr. Parker to create some needful medicines and vaccines, as well as throughout the ship in a variety of ways. Be Prepared was the *Brave Voyager's* motto.

Pity we hadn't been able to Be Prepared for our first minor catastrophe.

Which, as we opened the door to the guts of Engineering, suddenly appeared to be a tad more than minor.

Steam billowed everywhere and it was impossible to see who was inside. Manning and I slammed the door and ran for the protective leather suits, gloves, and head coverings hanging outside the interior bay. Once our gear was on, we grabbed our goggles and steam masks. The goggles were coated with an anti-condensation treatment Manning had come up with. The masks were leather cowls that covered the rest of our faces attached to breathing apparatus similar to what we'd used on Earth when we were flying at high altitudes, but with an easier ability to breathe and talk at the same time.

Before I put my mask on, I tapped my communication bracelet—we each wore one and were thereby connected to everyone on the ship. "Security Chief Zam, please bring a Security complement to Engineering. Get into protective gear before entering. And keep the com open for your team, Engineering, Mister Manning, and myself."

"We're alright," Soto, the Second Engineer, shouted from somewhere within the steam, as we opened the door and stepped inside.

"Should I belay, Captain?" Zam asked.

"Absolutely not, Falco. Get down here as fast as possible. And bring towels and lots of them—the floor is exceptionally slippery."

The goggles might have allowed us to see safely, but it was the same as being in a thick, billowing fog. However, from what we could tell, the brass pipes overhead seemed sound but, protective gloves or not, it didn't seem wise to risk touching them, so I couldn't be sure. Of anything right now.

Manning put his arm around my waist. "You need to be careful walking here. We don't want you falling." His voice was a tad muffled, but not so that I couldn't pick up the concern.

"I'm pregnant, not made of porcelain," I said gently, working to keep any form of exasperation out of my tone. That my husband cared about me and our unborn child was a blessing, not a hindrance. "And I need you verifying if all our ship's functions are still working properly."

Zam and the Security team of five raced into the room, protective gear on and towels in hand. They started laying towels on the floor immediately and we were soon able to get closer to where Benning and Soto were feverishly working. Manning took some of the remaining towels and headed deeper into what was currently acting as the *Brave Voyager's* steam room and sauna.

"Where are the rest of the Engineering team?"

"Searching for other leaks or issues," Benning replied.

"How bad is it really?" I asked her.

"Not so large, but nothing we're doing is capping it off. I don't know how this happened, Captain. There was no warning, other than our pushing the engines too hard."

"Yes, yes, I take full responsibility for harming your metal baby, Georgia."

"It's not really that," Soto said, from the other side of the gigantic brass pipe that had sprung our leak.

"Then what is it, Greta?"

"Got it!" She dropped something at her feet, stomped on it, then shoved it toward the rest of us. It resembled a giant cockroach, well, a giant smashed cockroach, only it had what looked like metal teeth.

"What the hell is that?" Zam asked, speaking for all of us.

"I have no idea," Soto said. "But I think it ate through our pipe. And if there's one, the likelihood is that there are more. And by more I mean more than the many I'm looking at with revulsion right now."

"Mister Manning! Report!"

"I heard, Captain. You did leave the coms open. It appears we have an infestation—at least, I've found a large group of these things, all over the pipework. They aren't attacking me, so I believe they eat metal. I'd like to keep some for study, since I have no idea what they are, but if we can't eliminate them I fear we're done for."

Manning admitting that he'd rather survive than study these new creatures was incredibly shocking, baby on the way or no. The man lived for scientific research. Meaning he put our chances of survival at slim to none.

Benning, Zam, and I looked at each other. "What do we do?" Benning asked quietly.

I was about to say that we needed to get the entire crew into heavy boots and have them start stomping, when I heard a soft mewling and two small, furry creatures crawled out of my pocket.

We'd originally been told that they were Guinea Cats but they were actually alien animals called Poofs. They'd been gifted to us just like the ship, from our alien benefactor, Al Gar. I never knew where the Poofs were when I didn't see them, and they had a habit of just turning up in my or Manning's pockets even though we hadn't realized they were there.

"Honey and Bee, it's nice to see you, but you shouldn't be here, you could get hurt. Plus we're dealing with nasty bugs right now and I need to focus, not pet you, I'm sorry."

The Poofs purred at me, then Honey mewed loudly. And suddenly more Poofs appeared, some coming out of the others' pockets. There were a large number of them, far more than I could count. Mostly because the Poofs swarmed over the entire area. They didn't seem affected by the burning heat or the steam. I heard the sound of chewing.

"Leave the hole open for the moment," I suggested, without being able to say why. Then I heard the sound of chewing within the pipes. Aha, that was why. Score one for the Captain's Prescience.

"I see it's not only the humans who've been propagating their species," Manning said, as he rejoined us.

"I'm sorry, Captain," Zam said. "Should we have reported the Poofs? We thought you'd sent them to us as gifts and since you hadn't mentioned it, we assumed you didn't expect us to, either."

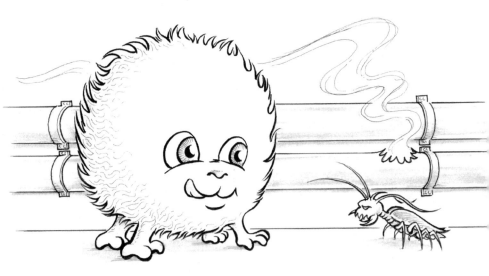

I resisted the strong urge to sigh. Our crew was young—Dr. Parker was the eldest of us at the ripe old age of thirty-two—and sometimes their inexperience showed. Times such as this, for example. So, going forward, Manning and I would need to work on teaching them to never assume.

"No, it's fine. However, in the future, should the crew receive anything out of the ordinary, I'd like to be informed. Does everyone have one?"

"So far as I know, yes," Zam said.

"Really. What do they eat?" No sooner was this question out of my mouth than Bee bounded to my feet and ate the smashed space cockroach.

"I'd wanted to examine that," Manning said, rather sadly.

Honey rejoined us and mewled in a rather commanding manner.

"Ah, I believe our Poofs are sharing that they've cleared out the infestation?"

Honey mewled again, this time in a rather apologetic manner.

"Aha. They've been living off these bugs. But hadn't realized how bad the infestation was?"

A confirming mew.

"All's well then." The steam seemed to be less. "Georgia, Greta, have you stopped the leak?"

"Yes, now," Soto said. "There were a lot of those... things blocking the hole in the wrong way to repair it. All seems clear now." As she said this, the Poofs disappeared and the rest of our engineering team joined us.

"I believe the pipe rupture was fortuitous," Manning said. "The loose creatures I found appear to have come from the interior of the pipe."

My communications bracelet beeped. "Captain, request you return to the bridge."

"What's going on, Ex-O?"

It was our main navigator who answered. "Captain, we have a ship on the horizon."

This was patently untrue, but I couldn't blame Missy for saying it. There was no real horizon in space, just endless black and faraway stars. Stars we would once again be heading for now. At least, so I hoped.

"Description, Miss Gunnels?"

The navigator had her own viewing screen in the *Brave Voyager*, so she saw the vastness of space before us differently than the rest of those on the bridge. "It looks like a kind of... pinwheel," Missy said, sounding uncertain. "A gigantic one, of course, but that's the closest I can come to a description, ma'am."

I looked at Benning and Zam, who nodded. "All good here now, Captain," Benning said.

"Excellent. Work on determining how those creatures got in here and verify that the entire ship is secure. That should take some time, so get right on it. Back in a flash, Ex-O."

WELL, NOT QUITE in a flash. We had to strip off our protective gear, and then I needed to make a stop at my private office.

Manning came with me. Which was good. Because I was heading for the bathroom. To throw up.

"Jeanette, what can I do?" he asked as he knelt next to me, held my hair, and stroked my back.

"Nothing," I gasped out between retching. "Dr. Parker says this is normal."

We stayed like this until I was done. Then he got a wet cloth and wiped my face. I leaned against him when he was done and he kissed my head. "It will be worth it." He sounded hopeful and worried.

I smiled and managed a chuckle. "Yes, Nicholas, our child will indeed be worth it."

Al Gar had warned us that the help he'd given us was the easy part, and that what lay ahead was where our struggle truly began. I just hadn't realized—barring the excitement we'd just experienced—that he'd meant boredom and pregnancy.

Not that I was unhappy to be with child, especially Manning's child. And many others on the ship were pregnant as well. Which was good. We were essentially our own colony, and that meant we needed to ensure that we had plenty of children. The ship was certainly large enough to handle any form of population explosion for years to come.

However, morning sickness took on a new meaning when one was in space. Every pregnant woman, myself included, had violent reactions to warp speeds. So we had to travel at sub-light speed. Still faster than any ship on Earth could imagine, but not nearly as fast as we'd originally planned. The goal of reaching the Alpha Centauri system within a year was by the wayside. At this speed, the hope was that we'd reach that system in about five years. Meaning we weren't just explorers—we were a generational ship.

Which had been why I'd been pushing us to go as fast as we could without making myself and the others ill. While the test wasn't conclusive, I had a feeling that the pipe rupture had done us a favor by exposing the infestation. But it also meant that we had to remain at a more sedate speed, meaning five years to the next star system might be optimistic.

However, we had no true goal other than survival. So wherever we might go was just fine and whenever we might arrive would mean we'd arrived right on time.

Manning helped me up, we both took a moment to wash our faces, then we returned to the bridge. It had three levels—science and technical which lined the top section, command which had the full center section, and flight and navigation which was in the lower section closer to the windshield.

Vrabel left my seat and I took it while Manning went to the Science Officer's post to my left and Vrabel took her seat to right. "I see nothing, Miss Gunnels." Which was a pity. Our windshield on the bridge was wide and tall, and it doubled as a viewing screen. Something other than blackness would make for a pleasant change, especially after steam, sweating in leather, horrific bugs, and vomiting.

"Your timing is good, it's just coming into range now, Captain," Missy said.

Pleasant change coming up, then. "Onscreen, please, Miss Gunnels."

No sooner requested than done. The pinwheel took up most of our screen. The descriptor was close and, at the same time, didn't do the structure justice. I also wasn't certain it was actually a ship.

Whatever the thing before us was, it had one gigantic metal tube that connected to two round objects at either end that did resemble pinwheels. There was no easily spotted smooth surface—metallic protrusions of a variety of shapes jutted from the main body in some way.

As we got closer a variety of ships came into view, all aimed for the gigantic double pinwheel, and all dwarfed by it, too. Unlike the *Brave Voyager*—which was more of a giant semi-circle with the rear portion a combination of Y-shaped thrusters above and a thick tail below—many of these ships were bullet-shapes, though most didn't look like the exact same bullets. There were also some that resembled animals or birds—at least what I took to be animals and birds—and, as we neared the pinwheel, a few that resembled the *Brave Voyager*, though not closely.

That spaceships came in all designs wasn't a surprise. And if those ships followed bullets by more than just design, their noses were pointed away from us. "Miss Gunnels, how close to the, ah, pinwheel are the other ships?"

"Closer than us, Captain. And to anticipate, I believe all the ships' trajectories indicate they're headed for the pinwheel."

"Are we close enough to hail?" Manning asked.

"No, sir," young Francis said.

As with Missy, he'd been one of our shipteens before the alien attack that had murdered our former captain and, luckily for us, thrust us into a future we'd only hoped to achieve in the far off "one day." The Z'porrah ships were saucer-shaped and I saw none of those in evidence. Fortunately. For them.

"And, I'm not sure if we *can* hail." Francis cleared his throat. "We've never had a reason to try before."

"A bold new chance to really earn your Communications Officer stripes awaits, then, doesn't it, Mister Jane?" I knew that our ship could indeed hail other ships, because, as far as I could tell, Al Gar had set us up quite efficiently. We'd been incredibly lucky to have an undercover alien with us when the Z'porrah had come to Earth to try to take over our planet. I wanted to believe our luck would hold, but I had never been called an optimist before and saw no reason to start now.

"Yes, ma'am." Francis sounded chastised and worried both. Perhaps I'd been a tiny bit too harsh, but the crew were getting used to that these days. Besides, they apparently all had Poofs and hadn't mentioned it to me. Harshness might be the order of the day if they weren't careful.

"Don't worry," Edward said. "I'm ready to blast them if necessary."

"Thank you for sharing my mindset, Third Officer Carswell. However—"

"It would probably be best not to shoot first and ask questions later," Manning said quickly. "Even though I'm sure our Weapons Officer is keen to test our abilities."

"Thank you for completing my thought for me, Mister Manning. But our Science Officer is right. We use caution and diplomacy first before we go in with lasers blazing. So, let's inaugurate your first hail, Mister Jane, and see who we get."

"Yes, Captain." Francis took a deep breath. "Hailing frequencies open, Captain."

"This is Captain Jeanette Thompson-Manning of the Earth space vessel *Brave Voyager.*"

A crackling reached our ears and the scene on the screen changed. Instead of seeing what was in space, we saw an interior. I was proud of myself and my command crew—none of us gasped or jumped.

The being onscreen certainly wasn't human, though it was vaguely humanoid. It also wasn't a flying dinosaur type of creature, which meant it wasn't a Z'porrah, which was good news. This being looked very much like a gigantic, walking honeybee.

There was nothing but a buzzing noise for a few moments. Then the sound changed. "Greetings, *Brave Voyager.* Are you requesting permission to dock at Space Outpost Three-three-four-six-one-two?"

"Yes, we would greatly appreciate that." At least I sincerely hoped we'd end up appreciating docking here.

"Excellent! You would be the first Earthlings to have ever visited any Space Outpost." He, at least I thought it was a he, sounded rather excited.

"I'm sure we are. We may need some assistance with docking. This will be our first dock with a Space Outpost."

"Understood. I will send coordinates for your docking port and we will have personnel standing by."

"Thank you. I'm sorry to have to ask, but could you tell me what race and planet you represent?"

"No need to apologize. I only know that you are Earthlings

based on your having identified as being from that planet. I am one of the Lyssara, we come from planet Lyss, which is twelve parsecs from Earth."

"Ah, thank you. Do the Lyssara run this Space Outpost?"

"Oh, no, we do not. The outposts are a pan-galactic, nonpartisan cooperation. Every sentient species in the Galactic Alliance with space flight capabilities is represented, and while not all species will be present on all outposts, we strive to ensure that we are as diverse as possible."

While the Lyssara was speaking, I spotted several other beings clustering around behind him. What I could see was a conglomeration of tentacles, digits, claws, pincers, fur, different colored skins and pelts, and more. Apparently our arrival was becoming an event.

"What about the Z'porrah?" Manning asked carefully. "Are they a part of this community?"

This question seemed to create quite a bit of consternation in those beings behind our spokesbee.

"What do you know of them?" he asked.

Time to find out if the galactic community was behind our mortal enemies or against them. Before we docked.

"They attacked Earth with no warning, murdering innocents, and we're at war with them as we speak."

Well, I presumed the Earth was at war now. We'd certainly done our best to ensure that would happen. It was why we could never go home—all of us were considered dead on Earth, murdered by the Z'porrah in an unprovoked attack on a peaceful merchant ship.

I ignored Manning's warning grunt. I loved the man with all my heart, but many times he was too timid. And if things went badly, well, Carswell was itching to test our weapons.

"And if the Z'porrah are a part of this pan-galactic community, then we may not be open to joining."

"THAT WAS A rash thing to say," Manning chided as we waited for the signal that it was safe to open our airlock.

I squeezed his hand. "Better a forthright attack than to be trapped in a nest of vipers."

"Are you sure they aren't lying about also being at war with the Z'porrah?" Vrabel asked.

"You saw their reactions, Ex-O. They might hate the Z'porrah more than we do."

"Doubt that's possible," Dr. Parker said dryly as she joined us. "By the way, I've inoculated everyone as best as I can, but I have no idea what diseases we could be facing."

"I'm just glad we verified that they breathe oxygen on the Space Outpost," Manning said. "Though I still think we should give the spacing suits a try."

"I'm sure we'll get our chance, Nicholas. But not right now."

"I'm just glad the universal translator worked," Francis said quietly.

"I'm gladder that we all have them inserted into our ear canals," Missy said. "And that Dr. Parker did that ages ago. All of us walking in holding our heads and moaning wouldn't make a good first impression."

"True enough." I was personally glad that Manning and I had been able to clean up and change uniforms—our time in Engineering hadn't left us looking crisp, and wilted and drained wasn't the first impression I was hoping to give our new acquaintances.

I tapped my communication bracelet. It had taken some time to learn the codes to broadcast wide and individually, but we'd certainly had it. We were a very well-versed crew by now. Boredom was good for something. And we now had excitement in spades. I hoped I wouldn't look back on the boredom with longing.

"Third Officer has the bridge. Edward, please remember that I don't want you shooting unless it's absolutely necessary."

"Yes, Captain. Secondary crew are all at stations. Please keep us apprised. We will be ever vigilant. Bridge out."

The safety lights lit and verified that the air we were about to venture into was breathable. Manning hadn't been joking about wanting us in the spacing suits—not that this was a risk, because while he had a sense of humor, he didn't use it often. He'd wanted all of us to wear protective suits and helmets, and had argued quite passionately with me and the rest of the officers about our needing to be sure that we weren't exposed to things Dr. Parker couldn't inoculate us for.

But since we were vastly outnumbered at this Space Outpost—at least twenty vessels had docked in the time it had taken us to chat with what was called Traffic Control and then get to our assigned docking station—I saw no point in being anything other than bold. Either we were going to adapt to this new galactic community we found ourselves in or we were not. Let them see Earth's people as brave and fearless. Besides, we all had lasers and Carswell wasn't the only one willing to shoot weapons if need be. And I'd sweated more than enough today, thank you very much.

The airlock door released and we were faced with a good-sized room filled with alien lifeforms of more kinds than I could count.

"Welcome to Space Outpost Three-three-four-six-one-two," one that looked like a human-sized, walking lizard said. "I am Rajal of the Reptilians."

I stepped forward and bowed. "I am Captain Jeanette Thompson-Manning, and I and my crew, both here and remaining on the *Brave Voyager*, thank you for your welcome."

"We are quite excited to have Earthlings here," Rajal said, not that this was coming as a surprise, based on the number of beings staring at us. None, thankfully, with weapons drawn.

"You know of Earth?"

Rajal nodded. "Yes. All spaceworthy beings in our galaxy learn of the others out there." He waved a taloned hand about, I presumed to indicate the whole of space. "And since we are on this particular Outpost, it behooves us to know of the sentient life nearby. Besides, the star we Reptilians call ours is the next closest to Earth's."

"Alpha Centauri?" Manning asked. "That's what we call your star system."

Rajal smiled. At least I hoped it was a smile. There were a lot of teeth involved. "Yes, that translates for us. Just so. And now, please allow me to introduce you to the others. I am the Section Overseer of our Outpost."

"Does that make you the being in charge of this entire operation?" I asked.

Some chuckled, some shuffled nervously, some looked worried. "Ah, no," Rajal said. "We currently have no Outpost..." he said a word, but it didn't translate. All I heard was a hissing sound and what might have been growly consonants.

"I'm sorry. We have a universal translator program which appears to be a tad spotty. I couldn't understand the last word you said."

"Ah, apologies. The position is one of leadership."

"Governor?" Manning suggested.

"No, not with that much authority."

"So president is out as well," Vrabel said. "Mayor, perhaps?"

"No," Rajal said slowly. "That is more... political. And the Outpost position is more, ah, weaponized."

"General?" Dr. Parker asked, a tad too casually. I shared the concern she was trying not to show—a military outpost might not be a safe place for us.

"No," another being that resembled a large slug with limbs said, sounding very sloshy. "That would be too militaristic, and we of the Themnir would not approve."

The rest of the beings gave it their best attempts. While none of their words translated, we did get to meet representatives of the Vrierst, which were ethereal cloud-like beings, the Canus Majorians, which resembled jackals by way of Egypt, the Feliniads, which were human-sized cat people, the Rapacians, which were humanoids crossed with eagles, the Khylida, who looked like butterflies crossed with fish, and many more. Manning was excitedly taking notes before we'd met a quarter of them.

There were far more beings that looked like humans here than I'd have expected. And it was one of them, named Katsy Hofor—a Vata from Vatusus, which was a planet near the galactic core—who finally came up with something that we could comprehend. "Sheriff," she said. "I think that fits."

"How do you know that word?" Manning asked, still taking notes, though he did shoot me a look that suggested preparedness.

She laughed. "My people can mentally connect with technological things. Not human minds, but computer minds." Seeing as she and any other Vata I could see all had bronze plates in their temples, complete with blinking lights, I found this amazing but believable. "I searched through your translator program—and I believe the word we have been searching for that you will understand properly is sheriff."

"And a sheriff is who is supposed to command this Outpost?" Vrabel asked.

Most of the heads nodded, those that could, anyway. The Cettans were flat, pancake-like beings who literally draped over the Uglor, who resembled very large fauns. Their home worlds were close by and the Uglor didn't feel they were as smart as the Cettans, and the Cettans couldn't function well off their planet without their bonded Uglor. Uglor's wore their Cettan draped around their back and shoulders or they carried them in their arms, depending.

One of the Cettans, Ascha, who was bonded with the Uglor Alaman, spoke up. "The sheriff's word is law. But it is a difficult job. Many different beings. Many different views."

Alaman nodded. "Many fights."

Vrabel and I exchanged the "oh *really?*" look. "So, why is there no sheriff on this Outpost right now?" I asked.

"Let us show you around the Outpost," a Feliniad named Talithiana purred smoothly. "We can discuss our minor political situation with you after you've gotten to see everything."

"I believe taking a look around would be wise," Manning said, before any of the rest of us could speak. "In the interests of science," he added, shooting me a look I was familiar with—he felt something was wrong, but wanted to know all the details before one of us started firing lasers.

Well and good. Besides, I quite wanted a look around anyway.

I EXAMINED EVERYTHING as we all began walking or, in some cases, hopping, slithering, or flying. I couldn't be certain, but I was fairly sure that this space outpost was run on steam, just as the *Brave Voyager* and most of our technology back on Earth.

Like the *Brave Voyager*, the space outpost was a lovely thing to behold—all brass and bronze and steel, intricately designed with beauty and functionality working together. And it was huge.

We were taken from one area to another—sleeping bays, dining sections, work areas—and this was only one section of the entire station. It was impressive in the extreme.

As near as I could tell, and without confirming with Manning, the space outpost was working on similar principles to our ship. I spotted apparatus that resembled what was on the *Brave Voyager* throughout the areas we were walking through, and neither the crew nor I were having any issues breathing.

"Are all the sentient races oxygen breathers?" Manning asked—as we passed through a large common area loaded with a variety of lifeforms—clearly on the same train of thought as I.

"No," Katsy Hofor replied. "But the majority do breathe oxygen. For most life forms, water is a vital aspect of life, and water goes with oxygen."

Manning began asking scientifically-based questions and getting answers. I stopped actively listening. Not because I had no interest, but because I was more interested in watching the group dynamics. They seemed far too eager to answer Manning's questions, including the ones that were repetitive, which I knew he was asking as a test. Which they were failing.

So, while Manning played along, I wanted to determine why they were happy to keep us distracted. Perhaps to give Katsy

Hofer time to access all of our systems. I tapped out a message to Carswell and Rodrigo Matus, who was our Junior Science Officer and part of the secondary crew, telling them to monitor for unauthorized access.

Katsy Hofor sidled next to me. "No need for alarm," she murmured. "Only my people can access your data, and we only do that if we're under attack or similar. I found the right word, then disconnected from your system."

"Not that we have any way of proving that," I replied, keeping my voice low just like hers. "Especially since you seem aware that I'm concerned."

She chuckled. "True enough. I saw you send a message and took an educated guess. And I realize why my saying 'trust me' will have no impact. My people have strict laws about our abilities and how we are allowed to use them. We don't want to be removed from the Galactic Alliance, and only those of the highest trust are assigned to Outposts."

"What's really going on here?" I asked her, keeping my voice low just like hers. "And don't tell me you're excited that we're here."

"It's truly that, but you're right, not just for the reasons we've mentioned already."

She was quiet and, while Manning asked more repetitive questions and Dr. Parker and Vrabel caught on and started to do the same, I pondered what they could want from us. I could only come up with one reason—they needed a patsy and we'd just arrived with a shipload of them.

"The sheriff's job is important, isn't it?"

Katsy Hofer nodded. "It is."

"What happened to your prior sheriff?"

She didn't reply.

I sighed. "Apparently, something terrible." I put my hand up and everyone in my crew stopped walking and talking. The others stopped and quieted as well.

We were in a long, wide corridor that ended in a T-intersection and appeared to be the throughway to several other sections of the Space Outpost. I couldn't read the markings, but the directional arrows seemed to be sharing that there were passageways here. There were a variety of ornamental structures along the walls, some quite high up, some not, most rather wide. All of them could have someone perched quite effectively, though no one was up there. The upper portion of the walls was open and, based on the heads and eyes on stalks and such that were peering over from both sides, indicated a second level.

"I'm going to ask you all a question, possibly with follow-on questions. I want the truth. And I want it now. Or else my crew and I will go back to our ship and leave you all here to handle whatever problem it is you're hoping to fool us into handling for you all on your own."

There were a variety of guilty looks, some innocent looks I was certain were feigned, and a few resigned expressions. However, a being we hadn't met yet shoved forward. She was willowy, literally. She looked like a living willow tree, complete with roots for legs and feet, and green hair that looked like willow leaves.

"I am Nemisia of the Faradawn and you have surmised correctly we are having difficulties we are all hoping you, as newcomers, may be able to solve."

"And those difficulties are?" I asked.

"Two Q'vox who are on the Outpost are creating havoc."

"Two beings are causing problems?" I looked around. "There seem to be more than enough of you to overpower two."

Nemisia shook her head, leaves and hair flowing around her. "The Q'vox are... quite powerful."

"Me again, intruding," Katsy Hofor said wryly. "I believe this will help you to understand why we are having difficulties. Volkrin and Valkrin Harrick are twin brothers who you would describe as minotaurs."

"Minotaurs are quite powerful," Manning said. "Though in our world they're myths."

"They're quite real," Nemisia said. "And while most Q'vox are peaceful, when they are not—and these two are not—they are practically unstoppable."

"Why are they here?" Vrabel asked.

"They were left as cargo by accident due to improper labeling by a delivery ship that docked here several galactic months ago," Rajal replied. "They were in stasis. When they awoke, they were understandably confused." He sounded like he was avoiding the issue. Again. Clearly, Section Overseer was a political position.

"Why were they confused?" Dr. Parker asked. "I would think that anyone put into stasis would have also been given the proper drugs and such when coming out."

"Oh, they were," Rajal said, now sounding forlorn.

I heaved a very loud sigh. "Normal beings who wake up at the wrong stop on the line merely request to take the next dirigible leaving town, so to speak. I'm guessing they didn't do that?" Heads shook. "So, they're pleased to be here instead of their actual destination?" Heads nodded, all looked forlorn or worried. "So, since I'm having to drag this out of all of you, where were they actually supposed to go?"

"Not too far away, in that sense," Katsy Hofor said. "But, for us, far too far away."

Nemisia nodded. "They were meant to be left at the delivery ship's next stop—the Space Prison."

MY CREW AND I were all silent for a few long moments. Vrabel and I exchanged a look. "Time to go," she said finally.

"I agree with my Ex-O. Just what is it you expect us to be able to do that none of you have? Or is it that you're willing to sacrifice strangers to these minotaurs?"

"We are not asking you to sacrifice yourselves," Rajal said quickly.

"Don't try to lie, you're not that good at it. What you're hoping is that one of us will somehow take the sheriff's job and handle this problem for you."

Expressions of all the beings around us shared that I'd guessed correctly, not that this came as a shock.

"Yes," Nemisia said. "That is exactly what we're hoping. The Q'vox haven't moved to our section yet, but they have taken over Sectors Three through Six. They gain power every day, and will soon be unstoppable. And that will mean they will have the might of this Outpost at their disposal."

"And Earth is the closest inhabited planet," Katsy Hofor added.

"And now we see the trap close," Manning said quietly.

"I agree with my husband. You're now trying to blackmail us."

"No," Nemisia said. "We are not. But we do need your help."

"Why by all that's holy hasn't your space prison sent someone to capture these prisoners?" Vrabel asked.

"They have," Rajal said quietly. "They were all..."

"Killed," Katsy Hofor finished. "Brutally."

"Elizabeth is right," Dr. Parker said. "It's time to *go*."

"Please stay," Alaman said. "Please help."

"My friend is asking for all of us," Ascha said. "We cannot use conventional weapons on the Space Outpost. Too much firepower and we will destroy the outer shells or create a reaction against the various gasses that keep the Outpost operational and kill everyone. We are not asking for you to die. We are asking for you to help. Perhaps you will think of something we have not."

"Remove the oxygen from their sections," Manning suggested. "Once they collapse, send in everyone else, take them into custody, and have the prison pick them up."

"We tried that," Rajal said. "Almost immediately."

"Q'vox can last quite a while without breathing, as it turns out," Talithiana added. "We removed some of their supporters, which only meant that when those supporters were elsewhere they instantly overtook those Sections and let the Q'vox in for easy expansion."

"Can you magnetize or affect the metals in their sections to disarm or disable them?" Manning asked.

"Not well enough to stun a Q'vox long enough for us to

capture them and all their followers," Rajal said. "We did try, but only succeeded in harming a few noncombatants. While the sections are somewhat independent of each other, they are not so independent that we can risk the entire station's safety. At least, not at this time."

"Put everyone onto ships, leave, and blow the place up," Manning suggested. This wasn't like him, but I got the impression he was still testing.

"No," Rajal said emphatically. "We don't have enough ships to do that, and this station is vital. The cost to rebuild is more than we can afford."

"You have good ideas," Katsy Hofor said to Manning. Leadingly, I felt.

"He does. And he will not be taking the sheriff's position, so don't ask, offer, suggest, or try to coerce it." My husband was a thinker, and a lover as I'd happily discovered, but, despite his physique, not a fighter.

"I have a question," Missy said. Everyone turned to her. "Does anyone else hear that low banging sound?"

We all quieted down and listened. Sure enough, I could indeed hear something that sounded like a rather rhythmic pounding.

"It's too late," Rajal whispered.

"What's too late?" Vrabel asked.

"That's the sound of the battering ram," Katsy Hofor said. "Meaning that the Harricks are about to break through our divider and take over this section. Or, in other words, it's been nice knowing all of you."

WHILE THE ALIEN beings around us started talking hysterically, I tapped out instructions on my communications bracelet. "That is *enough!*" I shouted when I was done. Everyone quieted. "You will stop acting as if the world was ending and you will, instead, find fortifications, of which there are many."

"We can't shoot them," a Lyssarian buzzed out. "Or we will all be destroyed."

"As you've all said already." I heard the sound of running feet and we were joined by Matus, laden with rope.

"Here's all we could find, Captain," he said breathlessly, as he dropped them at my feet.

"Good man. Rodrigo, you grew up on a ranch, did you not?"

"Yes, Captain. The others who are coming did as well. Mister Carswell had to prep them for what they're about to face first, ma'am."

"Excellent. Set up the lariats if you would, please, Rodrigo. Now, from the rest of you I need to know, and know immediately, without any pussyfooting or doublespeak or the like, if the bulls are leading the charge or not. And if they have the same issues about using lasers as the rest of you do."

"They're not stupid," Katsy Hofor said. "They understand they can't blow the station apart. But they have might that the rest of us don't. We physically can't stop them."

"They maintain that might by leading the charge, yes," Nemisia added. "Which is part of why they've won so far. They're—"

"Unstoppable, so you've all said. However, I don't subscribe to that belief." We'd been told in the Wars that our opponents were unstoppable and we'd proven them wrong then and I intended to keep our record intact.

"Jeanette, I strongly protest you being involved in this," Manning said quietly.

"Oh, hush, Nicholas. If things get too intense I plan to throw up on them." Dr. Parker snorted a laugh, Vrabel chuckled, and Missy giggled. Rodrigo flashed a grin, though the rest of the men in our party merely looked as worried as Manning. "Besides, I honestly feel far less ill on this Outpost than I have since getting pregnant, so I'm fine. However, Nicolas, I'm going to need you to spot the best vantage points for us to station."

"You should not be doing this, and certainly not without me." He had his stiff and proprietary voice going.

"Oh, you'll be involved, trust me. You're going to have to wrangle the bulls, after all."

He sighed and I could tell he'd given up trying to change my mind. "True enough."

The metal wall that separated us from the Q'vox and their allies was bulging toward us. Several more of our crew arrived as the pounding got louder. All who arrived were former ranch and farm hands and were our biggest crew members, both male and female. Several of the women were pregnant just as I was. And all of us had the same feeling about it—so what? I'd spent my formative years on a ranch, and I knew how to rope and wrangle cattle. And what were minotaurs other than particularly strong and nasty cattle? Plus we'd all done time as ruddermen during the Wars, and once the bull was caught, the principle was the same—put your back into it and pull so that you make the balloon, or the bull, go where you want.

"My crew—get a lariat from Mister Matus and get into the positions Mister Manning assigns to you. Our new alien friends—if you're strong, go where Mister Manning tells you to stand to assist those of us with ropes. If you're not strong, get back and get out of the way, and for the love of all that's holy, some of you figure out what to do with these people once we capture them."

Manning assigned stations and we scrambled to them, the aliens actually doing as we told them, those with flight ability helping our crew to get into position on some of the higher stations, which were the artworks or whatever they were along the corridor. Decorative art that was also useful was my preferred kind.

Then the wall was breached and I stopped worrying about anything other than getting the cows ready for branding.

WE WERE IN luck, to use the term loosely, and the Q'vox stepped through first. Minotaur was an apt description. Giant Minotaur might have been more apt. Huge hooves led to thick, powerful legs covered with hide, a human-ish torso and huge arms, with a head that was a cross between a man and a Texas Longhorn.

"Prepare to surrender," one of them growled out as they stepped forward to let their minions come in behind them.

"I'd like a word first," I called. I was at the end of the corridor, sitting on a structure that was enough like the back of a horse to be comfortable.

"Who are you?"

"I was just going to ask you the same!" I ensured I sounded extremely cheerful.

He blinked. "Everyone knows me and my brother."

"No, not really, not so much. New here and all that. So, who are you?"

"I am Volkrin Harrick and this is my brother Valkrin Harrick. And we are in charge."

"No, sorry, names are not ringing a bell. Don't believe you're in charge."

They both blinked. Clearly no one had tried this approach before, such as it was.

"We are," Volkrin said with some uncertainty.

"Sorry, don't agree. Right now, I believe that I'm in charge. In fact, I'd like you two to surrender."

"Why should we?" Valkrin asked, not with truculence but actual interest.

"Because I'm going to make it very unpleasant for you if you don't." I sincerely hoped.

"You cannot defeat us," Volkrin said. "No one can."

"Someone has at least once before, and I'm sure will do so again. For instance me, right here, right now."

They stood there, blinking at me. Clearly they weren't used to this method. They also weren't charging, which was somewhat detrimental to my plan, since I needed them nearer to my people with the lariats.

"Apparently you're quite good with standing there. Excellent. Hands or hooves forward, so we can slap the manacles on you."

"We are stronger than anything you might try to bind us with," Volkrin said.

"Don't believe you, sorry."

"We can show you," Valkrin said, sounding somewhat confused.

"Yes!" Volkrin roared. "We will show you!" With that, he charged, Valkrin right behind him.

They might have been powerful, but what they were not was fast. They lumbered toward me at a pace that was close to glacial. My crew started tossing lariats. Those that missed were pulled back and tossed again. Before the Q'vox were halfway down the corridor they were both caught in multiple ropes.

They were strong, however, and as they pulled together, the artworks that were forming our perches and blocks and pulleys started to bend. They were close enough for me to rope them, which I did. However, this meant it wasn't going to be long before the only things holding the Q'vox back broke.

Manning apparently had the same thought, because he led the charge of those on the ground to start bringing the Q'vox down.

This was good in that Manning and the others were able to slow the Q'vox down. It was bad in that the rest of the Harricks' followers started forward, with the clear intent to get involved.

"This is not good," I muttered aloud. "If they hurt Nicholas I'm going to stop caring about using lasers."

I heard a sleepy mew, and Honey and Bee stuck their heads out from my pocket. "You two need to get to the ship," I said quietly. "We're in great danger." Burning steam and space cockroaches were one thing. Space minotaurs were another.

The Poofs looked at me, purred, then leaped for the ground. And did something I'd never seen them do before—they altered.

Where once had been two lovable balls of fluff were now fluffy creatures as tall as Manning. Honey opened its mouth and roared, making the walls shake. I saw a mouth full of razor sharp teeth.

Bee did the same, and suddenly there were once again more Poofs, all of them bounding out of our crews' pockets, all turning gigantic.

As one, the Poofs roared, and it was deafening. Everyone, even those on the side of the Harricks, stopped moving.

"What are those?" Valkrin asked, voice rather shaky.

"Those are ours," I said calmly, as three Poofs stacked up on top of each other next to me, clearly so that I could get down safely. I jumped onto one's back and it bounced us safely to the floor, the others flanking us. I remained on the Poof's back, still holding the lariat that was around both Q'vox. "I'm going to give you one chance. You can surrender and stop your takeover bid, or I will let the Poofs do whatever it is they want to do." I had no idea what the Poofs' plan was, but I had no intention of sharing that with anyone.

Rajal spoke up. "Those are Poofs," he said, sounding awed. "They're only owned by the Annocusal Royal Family."

I managed not to share that we weren't a part of that bloodline. Sir Reginald was royalty, and Al Gar was his retainer and had given us two of his pets. So, wherever they had originated from, they were ours now, and if that helped in this situation, so be it.

"We don't recognize the authority of the Annocusal," Volkrin roared. "They may control your weak star system, Lizard Man, but they don't control ours!" As he said this he broke free from the ropes and lashed out.

Which was, as it turned out, a mistake on his part.

ADMITTEDLY, IT DIDN'T seem like a mistake at first. Volkrin landed a hit on Manning, who went flying. Honey leaped up and caught Manning in its mouth, bounded over, put Manning down next to me, and turned around.

As I slid off my Poof to get to my husband, the rest of the Poofs roared and charged. And, as we watched in a sort of calm horror, they ate the Q'vox. Alive. And quickly. There were screams from the minotaurs but they were brief.

Once the two ringleaders were eaten, the Poofs turned and surveyed the remaining aliens. Honey roared again and the Poofs once again charged. They ate quite a few of the followers, but not all, and none of those we'd seemingly identified as not in on the Minotaur Takeover Plan.

Then, once done eating the opposition, they burped discreetly, turned back to small, and bounded over to whoever on my crew they appeared to view as their owners.

"I see the Poofs can eat, well, anything," Manning said to me as I helped him up.

"Apparently so. Nicholas, are you hurt?"

"No. The blow winded me and I would have been harmed had our Poof not caught me. Not a scratch from the teeth, either."

Honey and Bee were in front of us. I picked them both up. "What good Poofs you are," I said as I petted them while they purred.

Rajal came to us. "We had no idea that Earth was part of the Annocusal Empire."

"We're not," I admitted. "We've just had some... positive dealings with each other."

"To be given a Poof is the highest honor one could receive," Rajal said, still sounding awed. "And to possess so many... you have your own army!"

This was apparently quite true. "Yes, and now we and our army should probably be on our way."

"No, please stay," Rajal said pleadingly. "Become our sheriff. You already captain an obviously brave and capable crew, and you control the Poofs. You have done what we need, allow us to provide you a home." He began to babble quickly, listing things like pay, room and board, and related niceties. Basically, becoming the sheriff of this Space Outpost would definitely have its advantages.

"But we're wanderers," Manning said. "It's why we have a spaceship."

"Excuse us, just for a moment," Dr. Parker said, as she came and pulled me and Manning off to the side. "Jeanette, I've monitored—you and every other pregnant woman are doing better physically on this Space Outpost. It's actually in our interests to stay here, at least for a while."

"The position comes with a great deal of influence, power, and pay," Katsy Hofor said, clearly ignoring Dr. Parker's request for privacy. "More even than Rajal has already outlined."

"And we have the room to house all your ship's passengers and crew," Nemisia, who was also butting in, added. "You would be the sheriff and we would again have the confidence that we are protecting what we need to, providing safe haven for those traveling on the outskirts of the galaxy."

"And you would be guarding Earth," Katsy Hofor added. She was definitely going to be one to watch. Or our closest ally. Probably both.

"But... we're supposed to see new worlds," Manning said longingly.

I squeezed his hand. "And we can, Nicholas." I waved my other hand. "The new worlds are all here, all represented. You can learn all about them before we travel to visit. Plus, the *Brave Voyager* will be ever ready for us." I put his hand onto my belly. "But, under the circumstances, if our ship's doctor says we should stay here, perhaps we should."

Manning heaved a sigh and nodded. "I would do nothing to risk our child, Jeanette. You know that."

I leaned up and kissed him. "I do, Nicholas, I do."

"Then I agree that you would make an excellent sheriff, just as you make an excellent captain and an even more excellent wife."

"And this is but one reason why I love you." I turned to aliens. "I'll take the position."

"We will all be most grateful," Katsy Hofor said in a tone that indicated she knew we were staying and had known it well before anyone else had. Definitely one to keep an eye on.

"I'm sure. Miss Gunnels, Mister Matus, please advise Mister Carswell that we are docking for an extended stay."

"Excellent!" Rajal said. "I have informed the other Section Overseers that you have saved us. They are gathering in the Great Hall in the middle of the Outpost in order to meet you. I need to go make preparations."

"We'll get them there," Nemisia reassured him. Rajal and many of the others we'd met trotted off, happily discussing their new world order.

"Besides," I added to those who remained, Manning in particular, "we're not saying we'll stay here forever. Just until the babies come and we're all confident that there will be no retaliation from those following the Harricks, or the Q'vox in general."

"Of course," Katsy Hofor said. "Now, let us present you to the rest of the Section Overseers. They'll all accept you, I can promise you that. And then we'll need you to determine who the new Section Overseers for the formerly Q'vox-held sections will be."

"And I'm sure you'll have plenty of suggestions," I said dryly.

She smiled, and the metal plates at her temples twinkled. "Of course." She linked my arm through hers. "And I'm just as sure that you'll investigate anyone I suggest and then make your own decisions."

I laughed. "I sense the beginning of a beautiful friendship."

Gini Koch

Gini Koch writes the fast, fresh and funny *Alien/Katherine "Kitty" Katt* series for DAW Books, the *Necropolis Enforcement Files,* and the *Martian Alliance Chronicles*. *Touched by an Alien,* book 1 in the *Alien* series, was named by *Booklist* as one of the Top Ten Adult SF/F novels of 2010. *Alien in the House,* book 7 in her long-running *Alien* series, won the RT Book Reviews Reviewer's Choice Award as the Best Futuristic Romance of 2013.

As G.J. Koch she writes the *Alexander Outland* series and she's made the most of multiple personality disorder by writing under a variety of other pen names as well, including Anita Ensal, Jemma Chase, A.E. Stanton, and J.C. Koch.

Gini has stories featured in a variety of anthologies, including *Unidentified Funny Objects 3, Clockwork Universe: Steampunk vs. Aliens, Two Hundred and Twenty-One Baker Streets,* and, coming in 2015, *X-Files: Trust No One, Temporally Out of Order, MECH: Age of Steel,* and *Out of Tune 2*; writing as Anita Ensal, in *The Book of Exodi, Love and Rockets, and Boondocks Fantasy*; and, writing as J.C. Koch, in *Kaiju Rising: Age of Monsters, The Madness of Cthulhu, Vol. 1, A Darke Phantastique,* and, coming in 2016, *The Mammoth Book of Kaiju.*

Her website is www.ginikoch.com.

CONVERSATION TOPICS TO AVOID ON A FIRST DATE WITH YOURSELF

Jonathan Ems

I swear, trying to date an alternate-reality version of yourself is not as narcissistic as it sounds. I mean, I thought that, too, when I first heard about the Only You Dating Agency, but really you can only hear that jingle so many times before it starts to sound like a good idea.

It was a simple enough process. I'd figured they'd need blood a sample or scan me with some weird machine or something, but all I had to do was download their app. They scanned my history off my phone and ten minutes later I got an alert saying I could meet "Natalie" at the organic sushi bar I usually go to on Thursdays. So, right off the bat, they're a really convenient service.

Spotting Natalie in the organic sushi bar was easy enough; she was sitting in my seat. I silently cursed myself for not getting there first and sat next to her.

"Hey," I said. "I'm Nathan."

"Natalie," Natalie said, covering her mouth. I'd caught her mid-nigiri, and she didn't want to be rude. I could totally sympathize with that.

So yeah, I totally get how it would be weird to look at someone who looks just like you and think "Wow, she's cute." But to be fair, just the fact that she's a girl made her really different. She had longer hair, bigger cheekbones, a softer jawline, and... well, breasts. I mean, let's face it, that one chromosome makes a world of difference, right? It's not my fault that she also happens to be cute. That's just a lucky coincidence, right? Maybe I'm not such a bad looking guy myself. Did that ever occur to you?

"That's weird that you're named Natalie," I said.

"What do you mean?"

"Well, my parents always said that if I'd been born a girl," I said, "they would've named me Charlotte."

Natalie's eyes fell to down to her empty sushi plate.

"My parents are dead," she said, quietly.

I blinked. "I, uh..." I stammered. I had no idea how to recover from that.

She smiled and patted my arm. "I'm just fuckin' with ya," she said, and grabbed another plate off the bar. "My parents would've named me Henry if I was a boy," she said. "So, I guess we're not that alike. Did you have a dog growing up?"

"No," I said, still trying to shake off the dead parents joke. "Did you?"

"No," she said, shrugging. "I've just always wondered what that would've been like."

"My friend Stephen had a dog," I said. *Idiot*, my brain immediately said to me. *You don't want to spend the whole date talking about dogs, do you?*

"Stephen?" Natalie perked up. "I have a Stephanie. Is that your best friend from college?"

"That's him," I said, immediately wanting to meet a girl version of Stephen.

"Did you fool around with him in college?" Natalie asked, taking a bite of seared salmon like it was the most normal question in the world.

I blinked. "I'm sorry, what?" I said.

"Steph and I fooled around a bit," Natalie explained, not batting an eye. "Our boyfriends liked to watch. Did you and Stephen do that?"

"What? I..." I stammered again. "No!"

She shrugged it off. "That's a shame," she said. "That would've been hot. Are you going to eat?"

I looked down and realized that she was right, I hadn't eaten anything yet. I looked at the train of sushi rotating around the bar and looked for ebi nigiri. I was having a hard enough time wrapping my head around this girl version of me, so I wasn't about to try anything daring with my food. The simple comforts were going to have to do this time.

"Uh oh," Natalie said, as I picked a plate off the bar.

"What?" I said, stopping in midair.

"I'm deathly allergic to shellfish," she said. "If you eat that, there's definitely not going to be any making out."

My mouth dropped open. Was I really going to have to choose? My love of shrimp and crab or this really cute girl? Okay I get it, it's *really weird* that I think a girl version of me is so hot that I might give up my favorite foods for her, but there has to be—

She giggled suddenly. "I'm sorry," she said. "I'm just fucking with you again. Go crazy."

I set the plate gingerly down in front of me. "Are you going to keep doing that?" I asked.

"Probably," she said, grinning. "The look on your face is priceless. You must really like me if you're putting up with it."

"Is it weird?" I finally asked. "Is it weird that we're on a date with ourselves? I mean, what does it mean if it doesn't work out? Does that mean we don't really like ourselves? What if it works out great? What would it be like to live with each other?"

"Whoa," Natalie said, gulping down her last bite. "Slow down there, tiger. This is just the first date. Let's just worry about whether or not we're going to get lucky tonight."

I blinked again. "Really?" I said.

"We're both thinking it, right?" she said. "I mean, isn't that the reason we're dating ourselves, to cut through the bullshit? We're both here because we want to get laid, just like everybody else. If it's good, we'll have a second date, then a third, and if we're not sick of each other by then, maybe we'll start spending time doing things that don't lead to sex, like hanging out with friends and meeting parents and shit."

"That makes sense, I guess," I said. "I just never really thought of it that way."

"Nobody ever does," Natalie said. "I don't know why people insist on doing it backwards, trying to force some fake deep connection before they even get a chance to know each other. That's probably why things almost always end badly and people can't even be friends with their exes. Maybe it's because we're afraid that it means something's wrong with us if things don't go Storybook Perfect every time. That's why I signed up with Only You. I wanted to date someone who was the same kind of weird as me, so I wouldn't have to worry about it."

She took another plate off the bar and started dabbing wasabi onto it.

"I mean," she continued, "worst case scenario: we don't even live in the same universe, so it's not like I ever have to see you again."

"I never thought of it like that," I said, looking down at my still-untouched ebi.

"Really?" she said. "Then why'd you sign up with Only You?"

I shrugged. "I don't know," I said. "I guess I just got tired of failing at first dates. I guess it was all the reasons you just said, I just didn't think about it."

"Not a deep thinker, are you?" she said with a smirk.

"I'm deep," I said, defensively. "I'm like the bottom of the ocean over here."

"Sure you are," she said. "So what did you imagine this date was going to be like? Did you think you were going to walk in here and I was going to say 'Hello Nathan, I'm just as lonely and horny as you are, so let's go see if our genitals fit together like legos?'"

I looked down at my ebi, not wanting to look directly at her anymore.

"Oh my god," she said, laughing as she said it. "You *did!* That's exactly what you thought!"

"Not exactly," I said, quietly.

"Is that why you're not eating?" she said, her grin even bigger than before. "You already ate, didn't you? You thought we were going to start boning right out of the gate, didn't you?"

"We're supposed to be the same person," I said. "I mean, what else were we going to do, sit here and say 'Me too' for two hours?"

"Wow," Natalie said, "you really aren't a deep thinker, are you?"

"Just as I suspected!" a voice bellowed from behind me. An oddly familiar voice at that.

I turned to find the source of the bellow, and saw myself marching toward Natalie and I.

Well, not *quite* myself. This guy had an eye-patch.

"Oh my god, *Nathan!*" Natalie shouted back. "What are you doing here?"

"You insidious harlot!" the other me shouted. "I give you my heart, my soul, I poured every ounce of myself into you and I find you here! Flinging your legs open for this buffoon!"

"Who the hell is this?" I said to Natalie.

"Are you blind as well as stupid?" the other me replied. "I'm a superior version of you, you ape."

"This is my ex," she said, with a sigh. Then to him, "We broke up like a month ago. You shouldn't be here!"

"The universe, nay all the universes fated us to be one," the other me said. "How can you turn your back on what was written into the very fabric of time?"

"Oh my god, you're such a drama queen," Natalie said, putting her hand to her forehead in exasperation.

"Wait a minute," I said. "You've dated me before?"

"A version of you, sure," Natalie said. "I have a type, okay?"

"Why him?" Eye-patch guy pleaded. "Why this dollar-store

version of me? I bet he's never even opened himself up to the pleasures of enlightened unity."

"Enlightened unity, Nathan?" Natalie spat back at him. "Is that your new fancy way of describing your sex addiction?"

"I am a man of passion!" Other Nathan roared. "I cannot be caged by the petty phobias of a society that refuses to evolve!"

"Seriously," Natalie said to me, "he's had sex with, like, everyone you know."

"Even Stephen?" I asked.

"You mean Stefan?" Nathan replied. "Who do you think introduced me to pleasure of inner pain, you caveman?"

"I don't even want to know what that means," I said.

"So it's all *true!*" another voice said. I looked to see another Natalie coming toward us.

"Oh dammit," the first Natalie said, seeing her. "How are you people even finding me?"

"How can you do this to me, Natalie?" the second Natalie said. "Was I nothing to you? Was I just some experiment?"

"Nat, you really need to calm down," the first Natalie said. "*Everybody* needs to calm down!"

"Wait," I said, "How many of us have you dated?"

"Oh," Natalie said, "Do you want to talk about *your* exes now?"

I threw my hands up in surrender. We definitely didn't need to go there.

"I thought we meant something," Nat pleaded.

"We did, Nat," Natalie said. "It just wasn't, you know..."

"You were more than just my lover," Nat interrupted. "You were the sister I never had."

"I would geld myself for you," the other Nathan interjected. "In solidarity for your gender."

"Look, both of you need to back the hell off," Natalie said. "I love you guys, too, but I'm not the us that you want me to be. That girl is still out there somewhere. There's literally millions of us and one of them is bound to love you the way you want me to."

"But I don't want any other me," Nat whined. "I want you."

"You're only saying that because you haven't met any other us yet," Natalie said. "The next me you meet is going to be way better for you, I'm sure."

"Hold on," I said. "Does 'geld' mean what I think it does?"

"Read a book, you chimp," Asshole Nathan said. "Natalie, you can't be serious with this guy?"

"I don't know yet," Natalie shouted at him. "How can I know if you're going to barge in on our first date?"

"Wait," Nat said, "This is your first date with him? Who were you with yesterday?"

"What?" I asked.

"Okay, did you really think I was going to sign up with a dating service and only go on one date?" Natalie said, defiantly.

"Sorry," I said. "I'll shut up now."

"You pussy," the other Nathan said to me.

"Dick face," I said to him.

"Both of you need to leave now," Natalie said to them. "Or, so help me, I will file a negative result with the agency and neither of you will ever get a date with yourselves again."

Eye-Patch Nathan and Obsessive Lesbian Natalie exchanged worried looks with each other.

"Can we at least be friends?" Nathan finally said.

"Maybe," Natalie said. "If you leave right now, I'll consider it."

On that, the other Nathan turned and walked out. I'd thought he was doing so with resolve, but once he was outside I thought I heard a loud sob. I almost felt sorry for him.

"You too, Nat," Natalie said.

"Maybe if you guys have an open relationship—" she started.

"That wouldn't be any concern of yours," Natalie finished for her.

Nat looked at me and spat out the words "You'll never be what she needs," before stomping out of the sushi bar.

Natalie and I sat in silence for a moment.

"Wow," I finally said. "Is there any version of us that's normal?"

"Yeah," Natalie said. "He was pretty boring. He'd never even had a dog either."

I nodded. It seemed like the thing to do.

Jonathan Ems

Jonathan Ems writes sci-fi and satire for print, web, and film. Sometimes, when he's really lucky, he even gets paid for it. His self-published novel, *Modus Operandi*, has been called "better than it should be" by some of the most discerning critics in his family. Look for his upcoming novels, *Vampire Lesbians From Dimension X* and *An Affair of Dragons*, to be released in 2016. He is currently in production with Schrödinger's Press on the webseries *Bystanders* and the feature film *Self Portrait*.

His website is www.SmileNaked.com and his Twitter account is @SmileNaked.

THE MONKEY TREATMENT

George R. R. Martin

K enny Dorchester was a fat man.

He had not always been a fat man, of course. He had come into the world a perfectly normal infant of modest weight, but the normalcy was short-lived in Kenny's case, and before very long he had become a chubby-cheeked toddler well swaddled in baby fat. From then on it was all downhill and upscale so far as Kenny was concerned. He became a pudgy child, a corpulent adolescent, and a positively porcine college student all in good turn, and by adulthood he had left all those intermediate steps behind and graduated into full obesity.

People become obese for a variety of complex reasons, some of them physiological. Kenny's reason was relatively simple: food. Kenny Dorchester loved to eat. Often he would paraphrase Will Rogers, winking broadly, and tell his friends that he had never met a food he didn't like. This was not precisely true, since Kenny loathed both liver and prune juice. Perhaps, if his mother had served them more often during his childhood, he would never have attained the girth and gravity that so haunted him at maturity. Unfortunately, Gina Dorchester was more inclined to lasagne and roast turkey with stuffing and sweet potatoes and chocolate pudding and veal cordon bleu and buttered corn on the cob and stacks of blueberry pancakes (although not all in one meal) than she was to liver and prune juice, and once Kenny had expressed his preference in the matter by retching his liver back onto his plate, she obligingly never served liver and prune juice again.

Thus, all unknowing, she set her son on the soft, suety road to the monkey treatment. But that was long ago, and the poor woman really cannot be blamed, since it was Kenny himself who ate his way there.

Kenny loved pepperoni pizza, or plain pizza, or garbage pizza with everything on it, including anchovies. Kenny could eat an entire slab of barbecued ribs, either beef or pork, and the spicier the sauce was, the more he approved. He was fond of rare prime rib and roast chicken and Rock Cornish game hens stuffed with rice, and he was hardly the sort to object to a nice sirloin or a platter of fried shrimp or a hunk of kielbasa. He liked his burgers with everything on them, and fries and onion rings on the side, please. There was nothing you could do to his friend the potato that would possibly turn him against it, but he was also partial to pasta and rice, to yams candied and un-, and even to mashed rutabagas.

"Desserts are my downfall," he would sometimes say, for he liked sweets of all varieties, especially devil's food cake and cannelloni and hot apple pie with cheese (Cheddar, please), or maybe cold strawberry pie with whipped cream. "Bread is my downfall," he would say at other times, when it seemed likely that no dessert was forthcoming, and so saying, he would rip off another chunk of sourdough or butter up another crescent roll or reach for another slice of garlic bread, which was a particular vice.

Kenny had a lot of particular vices. He thought himself an authority on both fine restaurants and fast-food franchises, and could discourse endlessly and knowledgeably about either. He relished Greek food and Chinese food and Japanese food and Korean food and German food and Italian food and French food and Indian food, and was always on the lookout for new ethnic groups so he might "expand my cultural horizons." When Saigon fell, Kenny speculated about how many of the

Vietnamese refugees would be likely to open restaurants. When Kenny traveled, he always made it a point to gorge himself on the area's specialty, and he could tell you the best places to eat in any of twenty-four major American cities, while reminiscing fondly about the meals he had enjoyed in each of them. His favorite writers were James Beard and Calvin Trillin.

"I live a tasty life!" Kenny Dorchester would proclaim, beaming. And so he did. But Kenny also had a secret. He did not often think of it and never spoke it, but it was there nonetheless, down at the heart of him beneath all those great rolls of flesh, and not all his sauces could drown it, nor could his trusty fork keep it at bay.

Kenny Dorchester did not *like* being fat.

Kenny was like a man torn between two lovers, for while he loved his food with an abiding passion, he also dreamed of other loves, of women, and he knew that in order to secure the one he would have to give up the other, and that knowledge was his secret pain. Often he wrestled with the dilemmas posed by his situation. It seemed to Kenny that while it might be preferable to be slender and have a woman than to be fat and have only a crawfish bisque, nonetheless the latter was not entirely to be spurned. Both were sources of happiness, after all, and the real misery fell to those who gave up the one and failed to obtain the other. Nothing depressed or saddened Kenny so much as the sight of a fat person eating cottage cheese. Such pathetic human beings never seemed to get appreciably skinnier, Kenny thought, and were doomed to go through life bereft of both women and crawfish, a fate too grim to contemplate.

Yet despite all his misgivings, at times the secret pain inside Kenny Dorchester would flare up mightily, and fill him with a sense of resolve that made him feel as if anything might be possible. The sight of a particularly beautiful woman or the word of some new, painless, and wonderfully effective diet were particularly prone to trigger what Kenny thought of as his "aberrations." When such moods came, Kenny would be driven to diet.

Over the years he tried every diet there was, briefly and secretly. He tried Dr. Atkins's diet and Dr. Stillman's diet, the grapefruit diet, and the brown rice diet. He tried the liquid protein diet, which was truly disgusting. He lived for a week on nothing but Slender and Sego, until he had run through all of the flavors and gotten bored. He joined a Pounds-Off club and attended a few meetings, until he discovered that the company of fellow dieters did him no good whatsoever, since all they talked about was food. He went on a hunger strike that lasted until he got hungry. He tried the fruit juice diet, and the drinking man's diet (even though he was not a drinking man), and the martinis-and-whipped-cream diet (he omitted the martinis).

A hypnotist told him that his favorite foods tasted bad and he wasn't hungry anyway, but it was a damned lie, and that was that for hypnosis. He had his behavior modified so he put down his fork between bites, used small plates that looked full even with tiny portions, and wrote down everything he ate in a notebook. That left him with stacks of notebooks, a great many small dishes to wash, and unusual manual dexterity in putting down and picking up his fork. His favorite diet was the one that said you could eat all you wanted of your favorite food, so long as you ate nothing *but* that. The only problem was that Kenny couldn't decide what was really his one true favorite, so he wound up eating ribs for a week, and pizza for a week, and Peking duck for a week (that was an expensive week), and losing no weight whatsoever, although he did have a great time.

Most of Kenny Dorchester's aberrations lasted for a week or two. Then, like a man coming out of a fog, he would look around and realize that he was absolutely miserable, losing relatively little weight, and in imminent danger of turning into one of those cottage-cheese fatties he so pitied. At that point he would chuck the diet, go out for a good meal, and be restored to his normal self for another six months, until his secret pain surfaced again.

Then, one Friday night, he spied Henry Moroney at the Slab. The Slab was Kenny's favorite barbecue joint. It specialized in ribs, charred and meaty and served dripping with a sauce that Kenny approved of mightily. And on Fridays the Slab offered all the ribs you could eat for only fifteen dollars, which was prohibitively high for most people but a bargain for Kenny, who could eat a great many ribs. On that particular Friday, Kenny had just finished his first slab and was waiting for the second, sipping beer and eating bread, when he chanced to look up and realized, with a start, that the slim, haggard fellow in the next booth was, in fact, Henry Moroney.

Kenny Dorchester was nonplussed. The last time he had seen Henry Moroney, they had both been unhappy Pounds-Off members, and Moroney had been the only one in the club who weighed more than Kenny did. A great fat whale of a man, Moroney had carried about the cruel nickname of "Boney," as he confessed to his fellow members. Only now the nickname seemed to fit. Not only was Moroney skinny enough to hint at a rib cage under his skin, but the table in front of him was absolutely littered with bones. That was the detail that intrigued Kenny Dorchester. All those bones. He began to count, and he lost track before very long, because all the bones were disordered, strewn about on empty plates in little puddles of drying sauce. But from the sheer mass of them it was clear that Moroney had put away at least four slabs of ribs, maybe five.

It seemed to Kenny Dorchester that Henry "Boney" Moroney knew the secret. If there were a way to lose hundreds of pounds and still be able to consume five slabs of ribs at a sitting, that was something Kenny desperately needed to know. So he rose and walked over to Moroney's booth and squeezed in opposite him. "It *is* you," he said.

Moroney looked up as if he hadn't noticed Kenny until that very second. "Oh," he said in a thin, tired voice. "You." He seemed very weary, but Kenny thought that was probably natural for someone who had lost so much weight. Moroney's eyes were sunk in deep gray hollows, his flesh sagged in pale, empty folds, and he was slouching forward with his elbows on the table as if he were too exhausted to sit up straight. He looked terrible, but he had lost so much *weight*...

"You look wonderful!" Kenny blurted. "How did you do it? How? You must tell me, Henry, really you must."

"No," Moroney whispered. "No, Kenny. Go away."

Kenny was taken aback. "Really!" he declared. "That's not very friendly. I'm not leaving until I know your secret, Henry. You owe it to me. Think of all the times we've broken bread together."

"Oh, Kenny," Moroney said, in his faint and terrible voice. "Go, please, go, you don't want to know, it's too... too..." He stopped in mid-sentence, and a spasm passed across his face. He moaned. His head twisted wildly to the side, as if he were having some kind of fit, and his hands beat on the table. "Oooooo," he said.

"Henry, what's wrong?" Kenny said, alarmed. He was certain now that Boney Moroney had overdone this diet.

"Ohhhh," Moroney sighed in sudden relief. "Nothing, nothing. I'm fine." His voice had none of the enthusiasm of his words. "I'm wonderful, in fact. Wonderful, Kenny. I haven't been so slim since... since... why, never. It's a miracle." He smiled faintly. "I'll be at my goal soon, and then it will be over. I think. Think I'll be at my goal. Don't know my weight, really." He put a hand to his brow. "I am slender, though, truly I am. Don't you think I look good?"

"Yes, yes," Kenny agreed impatiently. "But how? You must tell me. Surely not those Pounds-Off phonies...."

"No," said Moroney weakly. "No, it was the monkey treatment. Here, I'll write it down for you." He took out a pencil and scrawled an address on a napkin.

Kenny stuffed the napkin into a pocket. "The monkey treatment? I've never heard of that. What is it?"

Henry Moroney licked his lips. "They..." he started, and then another fit hit him, and his head twitched around grotesquely.

"Go," he said to Kenny, "just go. It works, Kenny, yes, oh. The monkey treatment, yes. I can't say more. You have the address. Excuse me." He placed his hands flat on the table and pushed himself to his feet, then walked over to the cashier, shuffling like a man twice his age. Kenny Dorchester watched him go, and decided that Moroney had *definitely* overdone this monkey treatment, whatever it was. He had never had tics or spasms before, or whatever that had been.

"You have to have a sense of proportion about these things," Kenny said stoutly to himself. He patted his pocket to make sure the napkin was still there, resolved that he would handle things more sensibly than Boney Moroney, and returned to his own booth and his second slab of ribs. He ate four that night, figuring that if he was going to start a diet tomorrow he had better get in some eating while the eating was good.

The next day being Saturday, Kenny was free to pursue the monkey treatment and dream of a new, slender him. He rose early, and immediately rushed to the bathroom to weigh himself on his digital scale, which he loved dearly because you didn't have to squint down at the numbers, since they lit up nice and bright and precise in red. This morning they lit up as 367. He had gained a few pounds, but he hardly minded. The monkey treatment would strip them off again soon enough.

Kenny tried to phone ahead, to make sure this place was open on Saturday, but that proved to be impossible. Moroney had written nothing but an address, and there was no diet center at that listing in the Yellow Pages, nor a health club, nor a doctor. Kenny looked in the white pages under "Monkey," but that yielded nothing. So there was nothing to do but go down there in person.

Even that was troublesome. The address was way down by the docks in a singularly unsavory neighborhood, and Kenny had a hard time getting a cab to take him there. He finally got his way by threatening to report the cabbie to the commissioner. Kenny Dorchester knew his rights.

Before long, though, he began to have his doubts. The narrow little streets they wound through were filthy and decaying, altogether unappetizing, and it occurred to Kenny that any diet center located down here might offer only dangerous quackery. The block in question was an old commercial strip gone to seed, and it put his hackles up even more. Half the stores were boarded closed, and the rest lurked behind filthy dark windows and iron gates. The cab pulled up in front of an absolutely miserable old brick storefront, flanked by two vacant lots full of rubble, its plate glass windows grimed over impenetrably. A faded Coca-Cola sign swung back and forth, groaning, above the door. But the number was the number that Boney Moroney had written down.

"Here you are," the cabbie said impatiently, as Kenny peered out the taxi window, aghast.

"This does not look correct," Kenny said. "I will investigate. Kindly wait here until I am certain this is the place."

The cabbie nodded, and Kenny slid over and levered himself out of the taxi. He had taken two steps when he heard the cab shift gears and pull away from the curb, screeching. He turned and watched in astonishment. "Here, you can't..." he began. But it did. He would most definitely report that man to the commissioner, he decided.

But meanwhile he was stranded down here, and it seemed foolish not to proceed when he had come this far. Whether he took the monkey treatment or not, no doubt they would let him use a phone to summon another cab. Kenny screwed up his resolution, and went on into the grimy, unmarked storefront. A bell tinkled as he opened the door.

It was dark inside. The dust and dirt on the windows kept out nearly all the sunlight, and it took a moment for Kenny's eyes to adjust. When they did, he saw to his horror that he had walked into someone's living room. One of those gypsy families that moved into abandoned stores, he thought. He was standing on a threadbare carpet, and around and about him was a scatter of old furniture, no doubt the best the Salvation Army had to offer. An ancient black-and-white TV set crouched in one corner, staring at him blindly. The room stank of urine. "Sorry," Kenny muttered feebly, terrified that some dark gypsy youth would come out of the shadows to knife him. "Sorry." He had stepped backward, groping behind him for the doorknob, when the man came out of the back room.

"Ah!" the man said, spying Kenny at once from tiny bright eyes. "Ah, the monkey treatment!" He rubbed his hands together and grinned. Kenny was terrified. The man was the fattest, grossest human being that Kenny had ever laid eyes on. He had squeezed through the door sideways. He was fatter than Kenny, fatter than Boney Moroney. He literally dripped with fat. And he was repulsive in other ways as well. He had the complexion of a mushroom, and minuscule little eyes almost invisible amid rolls of pale flesh. His corpulence seemed to have overwhelmed even his hair, of which he had very little. Bare-chested, he displayed vast areas of folded, bulging skin, and his huge breasts flopped as he came forward quickly and seized Kenny by the arm. "The monkey treatment!" he repeated eagerly, pulling Kenny forward. Kenny looked at him in shock, and was struck dumb by his grin. When the man grinned, his mouth seemed to become half of his face, a grotesque semicircle full of shining white teeth.

"No," Kenny said at last, "no, I have changed my mind." Boney Moroney or no, he didn't think he cared to try this monkey treatment if it was administered by such as this. In the first place, it clearly could not be very effective, or else the man would not be so monstrously obese. Besides, it was probably dangerous, some quack potion of monkey hormones or something like that. "NO!" Kenny repeated more forcefully, trying to wrest his arm free from the grasp of the grotesquerie who held it.

But it was useless. The man was distinctly larger and infinitely stronger than Kenny, and he propelled him across the room with ease, oblivious to Kenny's protests, grinning like a maniac all the while. "Fat man," he burbled, and as if to prove his point, he reached out and seized one of Kenny's bulges and twisted it painfully. "Fat, fat, fat, no good. Monkey treatment make you thin."

"Yes, but..."

"Monkey treatment," the man repeated, and somehow he had gotten behind Kenny. He put his weight against Kenny's back and pushed, and Kenny staggered through a curtained doorway into the back room. The smell of urine was much stronger in there, strong enough to make him want to retch. It was pitch black, and from all sides Kenny heard rustlings and scurryings in the darkness. *Rats,* he thought wildly. Kenny was deathly afraid of rats. He fumbled about and propelled himself toward the square dim light that marked the curtain he had come through.

Before he was quite there, a high-pitched chittering sounded suddenly from behind him, sharp and rapid as fire from a machine gun. Then another voice took it up, then a third, and suddenly the dark was alive with the terrible hammering noise. Kenny put his hands over his ears and staggered through the curtain, but just as he emerged he felt something brush the back of his neck, something warm and hairy. "Aieeee!" he screamed, dancing out into the front room where the tremendous bare-chested madman was waiting patiently. Kenny hopped from one foot to the other, screeching, "Aieeee, a rat, a rat on my back. Get it off, get it *off.*" He was trying to grab for it with both hands, but the thing was very quick, and shifted around so cleverly that he couldn't get ahold of it. But he felt it there, alive, moving. "Help me, help me!" he called out. "A rat!"

The proprietor grinned at him and shook his head, so all his many chins went bobbing merrily. "No, no," he said. "No rat, fat man. Monkey. You get the monkey treatment." Then he stepped forward and seized Kenny by the elbow again, and drew him over to a full-length mirror mounted on the wall. It was so dim in the room that Kenny could scarcely make out anything in the mirror, except that it wasn't wide enough and chopped off both his arms. The man stepped back and yanked a pull-cord dangling from the ceiling, and a single bare light bulb clicked on overhead. The bulb swung back and forth, back and forth, so the light shifted crazily. Kenny Dorchester trembled and stared at the mirror.

"Oh," he said.

There was a monkey on his back.

Actually it was on his shoulders, its legs wrapped around his thick neck and twined together beneath his triple chin. He could feel its monkey hair scratching the back of his neck, could feel its warm little monkey paws lightly grasping his ears. It was a very tiny monkey. As Kenny looked into the mirror, he saw it peek out from behind his head, grinning hugely. It had quick darting eyes, coarse brown hair, and altogether too many shiny white teeth for Kenny's liking. Its long prehensile tail swayed about restlessly, like some hairy snake that had grown out of the back of Kenny's skull.

Kenny's heart was pounding away like some great air hammer lodged in his chest, and he was altogether distressed by this place, this man, and this monkey, but he gathered all his reserves and forced himself to be calm. It wasn't a rat, after all. The little monkey couldn't harm him. It had to be a trained monkey, the way it had perched on his shoulders. Its owner must let it ride around like this, and when Kenny had come unwillingly through that curtain, it had probably mistaken him. All fat men look alike in the dark.

Kenny grabbed behind him and tried to pull the monkey loose, but somehow he couldn't seem to get a grip on it. The mirror, reversing everything, just made it worse. He jumped up and down ponderously, shaking the entire room and making the furniture leap around every time he landed, but the monkey held on tight to his ears and could not be dislodged.

Finally, with what Kenny thought was incredible aplomb under the circumstances, he turned to the gross proprietor and said, "Your monkey, sir. Kindly help me remove it."

"No, no," the man said. "Make you skinny. Monkey treatment. You no want to be skinny?"

"Of course I do," Kenny said unhappily, "but this is absurd." He was confused. This monkey on his back seemed to be part of the monkey treatment, but that certainly didn't make very much sense.

"Go," the man said. He reached up and snapped off the light with a sharp tug that sent the bulb careening wildly again. Then he started toward Kenny, who backpedaled nervously. "Go," the man repeated, as he grabbed Kenny's arm again.

"Out, out. You get monkey treatment, you go now."

"See here!" Kenny said furiously. "Let go of me! Get this monkey off me, do you hear? I don't want your monkey! Do you hear me? Quit pushing, sir! I tell you, I have friends with the police department, you aren't going to get away with this. Here now..."

But all his protestations were useless. The man was a veritable tidal wave of sweating, smelling pale flesh, and he put his weight against Kenny and propelled him helplessly toward the door. The bell rang again as he pulled it open and shoved Kenny out into the garish bright sunlight.

"I'm not going to pay for this!" Kenny said stoutly, staggering. "Not a cent, do you hear!"

"No charge for monkey treatment," the man said, grinning.

"At least let me call a cab," Kenny began, but it was too late, the man had closed the door. Kenny stepped forward angrily and tried to yank it back open, but it did not budge. Locked. "Open up in there!" Kenny demanded at the top of his lungs. There was no reply. He shouted again, and grew suddenly and uncomfortably aware that he was being stared at. Kenny turned around. Across the street three old winos were sitting on the stoop of a boarded-up store, passing a bottle in a brown paper bag and regarding him through wary eyes.

That was when Kenny Dorchester recalled that he was standing there in the street in broad daylight with a monkey on his back.

A flush crept up his neck and spread across his cheeks. He felt very silly. "A pet!" he shouted to the winos, forcing a smile.

"Just my little pet!" They went on staring. Kenny gave a last angry look at the locked door, and set off down the street, his legs pumping furiously. He had to get to someplace private.

Rounding the corner, he came upon a dark, narrow alley behind two gray old tenement buildings, and ducked inside, wheezing for breath. He sat down heavily on a trash can, pulled out his handkerchief, and mopped his brow. The monkey shifted just a bit, and Kenny felt it move. "Off me!" he shouted, reaching up and back again to try to wrench it off by the scruff of its neck, only to have it elude him once more. He tucked away his handkerchief and groped behind his head with both hands, but he just couldn't get ahold of it. Finally, exhausted, he stopped, and tried to think.

The legs! he thought. The legs under his chins! That's the ticket! Very calmly and deliberately, he reached up, felt for the monkey's legs, and wrapped one big fleshy hand around each of them. He took a deep breath and then savagely tried to yank them apart, as if they were two ends of a giant wishbone.

The monkey attacked him.

One hand twisted his right ear painfully, until it felt like it was being pulled clean off his head. The other started hammering against his temple, beating a furious tattoo. Kenny Dorchester yelped in distress and let go of the monkey's legs—which he hadn't budged for all his efforts. The monkey quit beating on him and released his ear. Kenny sobbed, half with relief and half with frustration. He felt wretched.

He sat there in that filthy alley for ages, defeated in his efforts to remove the monkey and afraid to go back to the street where people would point at him and laugh, or make rude, insulting comments under their breath. It was difficult enough going through life as a fat man, Kenny thought. How much worse, then, to face the cruel world as a fat man with a monkey on his back. Kenny did not want to know. He resolved to sit there on that trash can in the dark alley until he died or the monkey died, rather than face shame and ridicule on the streets.

His resolve endured about an hour. Then Kenny Dorchester
began to get hungry. Maybe people would laugh at him, but
they had always laughed at him, so what did it matter? Kenny
rose and dusted himself off, while the monkey settled itself
more comfortably on his neck. He ignored it, and decided to
go in search of a pepperoni pizza.

He did not find one easily. The abysmal slum in which he
had been stranded had a surfeit of winos, dangerous-looking
teenagers, and burned-out or boarded-up buildings, but it had
precious few pizza parlors. Nor did it have any taxis. Kenny
walked down the main thoroughfare with brisk dignity, looking neither left nor right, heading for safer neighborhoods as
fast as his plump little legs could carry him. Twice he came
upon phone booths, and eagerly fetched out a coin to summon transportation, but both times the phones proved to be
out of order. Vandals, thought Kenny Dorchester, were as bad
as rats.

Finally, after what seemed like hours of walking, he stumbled
upon a sleazy café. The lettering on the window said JOHN'S
GRILL, and there was a neon sign above the door that said,
simply, EAT. Kenny was very familiar with those three lovely
letters and he recognized the sign two blocks off. It called to
him like a beacon. Even before he entered, he knew it was
rather unlikely that such a place would include pepperoni
pizza on its menu, but by that time Kenny had ceased to care.

As he pushed the door aside, Kenny experienced a brief moment of apprehension, partially because he felt very out of
place in the café, where the rest of the diners all appeared to
be muggers, and partially because he was afraid they would
refuse to serve him because of the monkey on his back.
Acutely uncomfortable in the doorway, he moved quickly to
a small table in an obscure corner, where he hoped to escape
the curious stares. A gaunt gray-haired waitress in a faded pink
uniform moved purposefully toward him, and Kenny sat with
his eyes downcast, playing nervously with the salt, pepper,
ketchup, dreading the moment when she arrived and said,

"Hey, you can't bring that thing in here!"

But when the waitress reached his table, she simply pulled a pad out of her apron pocket and stood poised, pencil in hand. "Well?" she demanded. "What'll it be?"

Kenny stared up in shock, and smiled. He stammered a bit, then recovered himself and ordered a cheese omelet with a double side of bacon, coffee and a large glass of milk, and cinnamon toast. "Do hash browns come with?" he asked hopefully, but the waitress shook her head and departed.

What a marvelous, kind woman, Kenny thought as he waited for his meal and shredded a paper napkin thoughtfully. What a wonderful place! Why, they hadn't even mentioned his monkey! How very polite of them.

The food arrived shortly. "Ahhhh," Kenny said as the waitress laid it out in front of him on the Formica tabletop. He was ravenous. He selected a slice of cinnamon toast, and brought it to his mouth.

And a little monkey darted out from behind his head and snatched it clean away.

Kenny Dorchester sat in numb surprise for an instant, his suddenly empty hand poised before his open mouth. He heard the monkey eating his toast, chomping noisily. Then, before Kenny had quite comprehended what was happening, the monkey's great long tail snaked in under his armpit, curled around his glass of milk, and spirited it up and away in the blink of an eye.

Hey!" Kenny said, but he was much too slow. Behind his back he heard slurping, sucking sounds, and all of a sudden the glass came vaulting over his left shoulder. He caught it before it fell and smashed, and set it down unsteadily. The monkey's tail came stealthily around and headed for his bacon. Kenny grabbed up a fork and stabbed at it, but the monkey was faster than he was. The bacon vanished, and the tines of the fork bent against the hard Formica uselessly.

By then Kenny knew he was in a race. Dropping the bent fork, he used his spoon to cut off a chunk of the omelet, dripping cheese, and he bent forward as he lifted it, quick as he could. The monkey was quicker. A little hand flashed in from somewhere, and the spoon had only a tantalizing gob of half-melted cheese remaining on it when it reached Kenny's mouth. He lunged back toward his plate, and loaded up again, but it didn't matter how fast he tried to be. The monkey had two paws and a tail, and once it even used a little monkey foot to snatch something away from him. In hardly any time at all, Kenny Dorchester's meal was gone. He sat there staring down at the empty, greasy plate, and he felt tears gathering in his eyes.

The waitress reappeared without Kenny noticing. "My, you sure are a hungry one," she said to him, ripping off his check from her pad and putting it in front of him. "Polished that off quicker than anyone I ever saw."

Kenny looked up at her. "But I *didn't*," he protested. "The monkey ate it all!"

The waitress looked at him very oddly. "The monkey?" she said uncertainly.

"The monkey," Kenny said. He did not care for the way she was staring at him, like he was crazy or something.

"What monkey?" she asked. "You didn't sneak no animals in here, did you? The board of health don't allow no animals in here, mister."

"What do you mean, *sneak?*" Kenny said in annoyance. "Why, the monkey is right on my—" He never got a chance to finish. Just then the monkey hit him, a tremendous hard blow on the left side of his face. The force of it twisted his head half-around, and Kenny yelped in pain and shock.

The waitress seemed concerned. "You OK, mister?" she asked. "You ain't gonna have a fit, are you, twitching like that?"

"*I didn't twitch!*" Kenny all but shouted. "The goddamned monkey hit me! Can't you see?"

"Oh," said the waitress, taking a step backward. "Oh, of course. Your monkey hit you. Pesky little things, ain't they?"

Kenny pounded his fists on the table in frustration. "Never mind," he said, "just never mind." He snatched up the check—the monkey did not take that away from him, he noted—and rose. "Here," he said, pulling out his wallet. "And you have a phone in this place, don't you? Call me a cab, all right? You can do that, can't you?"

"Sure," the waitress said, moving to the register to ring up his meal. Everyone in the cafe was staring at him. "Sure, mister," she muttered. "A cab. We'll get you a cab right away."

Kenny waited, fuming. The cab driver made no comment on his monkey. Instead of going home, he took the cab to his favorite pizza place, three blocks from his apartment. Then he stormed right in and ordered a large pepperoni. The monkey ate it all, even when Kenny tried to confuse it by picking up one slice in each hand and moving them simultaneously toward his mouth. Unfortunately, the monkey had two hands as well, both of them faster than Kenny's.

When the pizza was completely gone, Kenny thought for a moment, summoned over the waitress, and ordered a second. This time he got a large anchovy. He thought that was very clever. Kenny Dorchester had never met anyone else beside himself who liked anchovy pizza. Those little salty fishes would be his salvation, he thought. To increase the odds, when the pizza arrived Kenny picked up the hot pepper shaker and covered it with enough hot peppers to ignite a major conflagration. Then, feeling confident, he tried to eat a slice.

The monkey liked anchovy pizza with lots of hot peppers. Kenny Dorchester almost wept.

He went from the pizza place to the Slab, from the Slab to a fine Greek restaurant, from the Greek restaurant to a local McDonald's, from McDonald's to a bakery that made the most marvelous chocolate eclairs. Sooner or later, Kenny Dorchester thought, the monkey would be full. It was only a very little monkey, after all. How much food could it eat? He would just keep on ordering food, he resolved, and the monkey would either reach its limits or rupture and die.

That day Kenny spent more than two hundred dollars on meals.

He got absolutely nothing to eat.

The monkey seemed to be a bottomless pit. If it had a capacity, that capacity was surely greater than the capacity of Kenny's wallet. Finally he was forced to admit defeat. The monkey could not be stuffed into submission.

Kenny cast about for another tactic, and finally hit on it. Monkeys were stupid, after all, even invisible monkeys with prodigious appetites. Smiling slyly, Kenny went to a neighborhood supermarket, and picked up a box of banana pudding (it seemed appropriate) and a box of rat poison. Humming a spry little tune, he walked on home, and set to work making the pudding, stirring in liberal amounts of the rat poison as it cooked. The poison was nicely odorless. The pudding smelled wonderful. Kenny poured it into some dessert cups to cool, and watched television for an hour or so. Finally he rose nonchalantly, went to the refrigerator, and got out a pudding and a nice big spoon. He sat back down in front of the set, spooned up a generous glob of pudding, and brought it to his open mouth. Where he paused. And paused. And waited.

The monkey did nothing.

Maybe it was full at last, Kenny thought. He put aside the poisoned pudding and rushed back to his kitchen, where he found a box of vanilla wafers hiding on a shelf, and a few forlorn Fig Newtons as well.

The monkey ate all of them.

A tear trickled down Kenny's cheek. The monkey would let him have all the poisoned pudding he wanted, it seemed, but nothing else. He reached back halfheartedly and tried to grab the monkey once again, thinking maybe all that eating would have slowed it down some, but it was a vain hope. The monkey evaded him, and when Kenny persisted the monkey bit his finger. Kenny yowled and snatched his hand back. His finger was bleeding. He sucked on it. That much, at least, the monkey permitted him.

When he had washed his finger and wrapped a Band-Aid around it, Kenny returned to his living room and seated himself heavily, weary and defeated, in front of his television set. An old rerun of *The Galloping Gourmet* was coming on. He couldn't stand it. He jabbed at his remote control to change the channel, and watched blindly for hours, sunk in despair, weeping at the Betty Crocker commercials. Finally, during the late late show, he stirred a little at one of the frequent public service announcements. That was it, he thought; he had to enlist others, he had to get help.

He picked up his phone and punched out the Crisis Line number.

The woman who answered sounded kind and sympathetic and very beautiful, and Kenny began to pour out his heart to her, all about the monkey that wouldn't let him eat, about how nobody else seemed to notice the monkey, about... but he had barely gotten his heart-pouring going good when the monkey smashed him across the side of the head. Kenny moaned. "What's wrong?" the woman asked. The monkey yanked his ear. Kenny tried to ignore the pain and keep on talking, but the monkey kept hurting him until finally he shuddered and sobbed and hung up the phone.

This is a nightmare, Kenny thought, a terrible nightmare. And so thinking, he pushed himself to his feet and staggered off to bed, hoping that everything would be normal in the morning, that the monkey would have been nothing but part of some wretched dream, no doubt brought on by indigestion.

The merciless little monkey would not even allow him to sleep properly, Kenny discovered. He was accustomed to sleeping on his back, with his hands folded very primly on his stomach. But when he undressed and tried to assume that position, the monkey fists came raining down on his poor head like some furious hairy hail. The monkey was not about to be squashed between Kenny's bulk and the pillows, it seemed. Kenny squealed with pain and rolled over on his stomach. He was very uncomfortable this way and had difficulty falling asleep, but it was the only way the monkey would leave him alone.

THE NEXT MORNING Kenny Dorchester drifted slowly into wakefulness, his cheek mashed against the pillows and his right arm still asleep. He was afraid to move. It was all a dream, he told himself, there is no monkey—what a silly thing that would be, monkey indeed!—it was only that Boney Moroney had told him about this "monkey treatment," and he had slept on it and had a nightmare. He couldn't feel anything on his back, not a thing. This was just like any other morning. He opened one bleary eye. His bedroom looked perfectly normal. Still, he was afraid to move. It was very peaceful lying here like this, monkeyless, and he wanted to savor this feeling. So Kenny lay very still for the longest time, watching the numbers on his digital clock change slowly.

Then his stomach growled at him. It was very upset. Kenny gathered up his courage. "There is no monkey!" he proclaimed loudly, and he sat up in bed.

He felt the monkey shift.

Kenny trembled and almost started to weep again, but he controlled himself with an effort. No monkey was going to get the best of Kenny Dorchester, he told himself. Grimacing, he donned his slippers and plodded into the bathroom.

The monkey peered out cautiously from behind his head while Kenny was shaving. He glared at it in the bathroom mirror. It seemed to have grown a bit, but that was hardly surprising, considering how much it had eaten yesterday. Kenny toyed with the idea of trying to cut the monkey's throat, but decided that his Norelco electric shaver was not terribly well suited to that end. And even if he used a knife, trying to stab behind his own back while looking in the mirror was a dangerously uncertain proposition.

Before leaving the bathroom, Kenny was struck by a whim. He stepped on his scale.

The numbers lit up at once: 367. The same as yesterday, he thought. The monkey weighed nothing. He frowned. No, that had to be wrong. No doubt the little monkey weighed a pound or two, but its weight was offset by whatever poundage Kenny had lost. He had to have lost *some* weight, he reasoned, since he hadn't been allowed to eat anything for ever so long. He stepped off the scale, then got back on quickly, just to double-check. It still read 367. Kenny was certain that he had lost weight. Perhaps some good would come of his travails after all. The thought made him feel oddly cheerful.

Kenny grew even more cheerful at breakfast. For the first time since he had gotten his monkey, he managed to get some food into his mouth.

When he arrived at the kitchen, he debated between French toast and bacon and eggs, but only briefly. Then he decided that he would never get to taste either. Instead, with a somber fatalism, Kenny fetched down a bowl and filled it with corn flakes and milk. The monkey would probably steal it all anyway, he thought, so there was no sense going to any trouble.

Quick as he could, he hurried the spoon to his mouth. The

monkey grabbed it away. Kenny had expected it, had known it would happen, but when the monkey hand wrenched the spoon away he nonetheless felt a sudden and terrible grief. "No," he said uselessly. "No, no, no." He could hear the corn flakes crunching in that filthy monkey mouth, and he felt milk dripping down the back of his neck. Tears gathered in his eyes as he stared down at the bowl of corn flakes, so near and yet so far.

Then he had an idea.

Kenny Dorchester lunged forward and stuck his face right down in the bowl.

The monkey twisted his ear and shrieked and pounded on his temple, but Kenny didn't care. He was sucking in milk gleefully and gobbling up as many corn flakes as his mouth could hold. By the time the monkey's tail lashed around angrily and sent the bowl sailing from the table to shatter on the floor, Kenny had a huge wet mouthful. His cheeks bulged and milk dribbled down his chin, and somehow he'd gotten a corn flake up his right nostril, but Kenny was in heaven. He chewed and swallowed as fast as he could, almost choking on the food.

When it was all gone he licked his lips and rose triumphantly. "Ha, ha, ha." He walked back to his bedroom with great dignity and dressed, sneering at the monkey in the full-length bedroom mirror. He had beaten it.

In the days and weeks that followed, Kenny Dorchester settled into a new sort of daily routine and an uneasy accommodation with his monkey. It proved easier than Kenny might have imagined, except at mealtimes. When he was not attempting to get food into his mouth, it was almost possible to forget about the monkey entirely. At work it sat peacefully on his back while Kenny shuffled his papers and made his phone calls. His co-workers either failed to notice his monkey or were sufficiently polite so as not to comment on it. The only difficulty came one day at coffee break, when Kenny foolhardily approached the coffee vendor in an effort to secure a cheese Danish. The monkey ate nine of them before Kenny could stagger away, and the man insisted that Kenny had done it when his back was turned.

Simply by avoiding mirrors, a habit that Kenny Dorchester now began to cultivate as assiduously as any vampire, he was able to keep his mind off the monkey for most of the day. He had only one difficulty, though it occurred thrice daily: breakfast, lunch, and dinner. At those times the monkey asserted itself forcefully, and Kenny was forced to deal with it. As the weeks passed, he gradually fell into the habit of ordering food that could be served in bowls, so that he might practice what he termed his "Kellogg maneuver." By this stratagem, Kenny usually managed to get at least a few mouthfuls to eat each and every day.

To be sure, there *were* problems. People would stare at him rather strangely when he used the Kellogg maneuver in public, and sometimes make rude comments on his table manners. At a chili emporium Kenny liked to frequent, the proprietor assumed he had suffered a heart attack when Kenny dove toward his chili, and was very angry with him afterward. On another occasion a bowl of soup left him with facial burns that made it look as though he were constantly blushing. And the last straw came when he was thrown bodily out of his favorite seafood restaurant in the world, simply because he plunged his face into a bowl of crawfish bisque and began sucking it up noisily. Kenny stood in the street and berated them loudly and forcefully, reminding them how much money he had spent there over the years. Thereafter he ate only at home.

Despite the limited success of his Kellogg maneuver, Kenny Dorchester still lost nine-tenths of every meal to the voracious monkey on his back. At first he was constantly hungry, frequently depressed, and full of schemes for ridding himself of his monkey. The only problem with these schemes was that none of them seemed to work. One Saturday, Kenny went to the monkey house at the zoo, hoping that his monkey might hop off to play with others of its kind, or perhaps go in pursuit of some attractive monkey of the opposite sex. Instead, no sooner had he entered the monkey house than all the monkeys imprisoned therein ran to the bars of their cages and began to chitter and scream and spit and leap up and down madly. His own monkey answered in kind, and when some of the caged monkeys began to throw peanut husks and other bits of garbage Kenny clapped his hands over his ears and fled.

On another occasion he allowed himself to visit a local saloon, and ordered a number of boilermakers, a drink he understood to be particularly devastating. His intent was to get his monkey so blind-drunk that it might be easily removed. This experiment, too, had rather unfortunate consequences. The monkey drank the boilermakers as fast as Kenny could order them, but after the third one it began to keep time to the disco music from the jukebox by beating on the top of Kenny's head. The next morning it was Kenny who woke with the pounding headache; the monkey seemed fine.

After a time, Kenny finally put all his scheming aside. Failure had discouraged him, and moreover the matter seemed somehow less urgent than it had originally. He was seldom hungry after the first week, in fact. Instead he went through a brief period of weakness, marked by frequent dizzy spells, and then a kind of euphoria settled over him. He felt just wonderful, and even better, he was losing weight!

To be sure, it did not show on his scale. Every morning he climbed up on it, and every morning it lit up as 367. But that was only because it was weighing the monkey as well as himself. Kenny knew he was losing; he could almost feel the pounds and inches just melting away, and some of his co-workers in the office remarked on it as well. Kenny owned up to it, beaming. When they asked him how he was doing it, he winked and replied, "The monkey treatment! The mysterious monkey treatment!" He said no more than that. The one time he tried to explain, the monkey fetched him such a wallop it almost took his head off, and Kenny's friends began to mutter about his strange spasms.

Finally the day came when Kenny had to tell his cleaner to

take in all his pants a few inches. That was one of the most delightful tasks of his life, he thought.

All the pleasure went right out of the moment when he exited the store, however, and chanced to glance briefly to his side and see his reflection in the window. At home Kenny had long since removed all his mirrors, so he was shocked at the sight of his monkey. It had grown. It was a little thing no longer. Now it hunched on his back like some evil deformed chimpanzee, and its grinning face loomed above his head instead of peering out behind it. The monkey was grossly fat beneath its sparse brown hair, almost as wide as it was tall, and its great long tail drooped all the way to the ground. Kenny stared at it with horror, and it grinned back at him. No wonder he had been having backaches recently, he thought. He walked home slowly, all the jauntiness gone out of his step, trying to think. A few neighborhood dogs followed him up the street, barking at his monkey. Kenny ignored them. He had long since learned that dogs could see his monkey, just like the monkeys at the zoo. He suspected that drunks could see it as well. One man had stared at him for a very long time that night he had visited the saloon. Of course, the fellow might just have been staring at those vanishing boilermakers.

Back in his apartment Kenny Dorchester stretched out on his couch on his stomach, stuck a pillow underneath his chin, and turned on his television set. He paid no attention to the screen, however. He was trying to figure things out. Even the Pizza Hut commercials were insufficiently distracting, although Kenny did absently mutter "Ah-h-h-h" like you were supposed to when the slice of pizza, dripping long strands of cheese, was first lifted from the pan.

When the show ended, Kenny got up and turned off the set and sat himself down at his dining room table. He found a piece of paper and a stubby little pencil. Very carefully, he block-printed a formula across the paper, and stared at it.

ME + MONKEY = 367 POUNDS

There were certain disturbing implications in that formula,

Kenny thought. The more he considered them, the less he liked them. He was definitely losing weight, to be sure, and that was not to be sneered at—nonetheless, the grim inflexibility of the formula hinted that most of the gains traditionally attributed to weight loss would never be his to enjoy. No matter how much fat he shed, he would continue to carry around 367 pounds, and the strain on his body would be the same. As for becoming svelte and dashing and attractive to women, how could he even consider it so long as he had his monkey? Kenny thought of how a dinner date might go for him, and shuddered. "Where will it all end?" he said aloud.

The monkey shifted, and snickered a vile little snicker.

Kenny pursed his lips in firm disapproval. This could not go on, he resolved. He decided to go straight to the source on the morrow, and with that idea planted firmly in his mind, he took himself to bed.

The next day, after work, Kenny Dorchester returned by cab to the seedy neighborhood where he had been subjected to the monkey treatment.

The storefront was gone.

Kenny sat in the back seat of the taxi (this time he had the good sense not to get out, and moreover had tipped the driver handsomely in advance) and blinked in confusion. A tiny wet blubbery moan escaped his lips. The address was right, he knew it, he still had the slip of paper that had brought him there in the first place. But where he had found a grimy brick storefront adorned by a faded Coca-Cola sign and flanked by two vacant lots, now there was only one large vacant lot, choked with weeds and rubbish and broken bricks. "Oh, no," Kenny said. "Oh, no."

"You OK?" asked the lady driving the cab.

"Yes," Kenny muttered. "Just... just wait, please. I have to think." He held his head in his hands. He feared he was going to develop a splitting headache. Suddenly he felt weak and dizzy. And very hungry. The meter ticked. The cabbie whistled. Kenny thought. The street looked just as he remembered it, except for the missing storefront. It was just as dirty, the old winos were still on their stoop, the...

Kenny rolled down the window. "You, sir!" he called out to one of the winos. The man stared at him. "Come here, sir!" Kenny yelled.

Warily, the old man shuffled across the street.

Kenny fetched out a dollar bill from his wallet and pressed it into the man's hand. "Here, friend," he said. "Go and buy yourself some vintage Thunderbird, if you will."

"Why you givin' me this?" the wino said suspiciously.

"I wish you to answer me a question. What has become of the building that was standing there—" Kenny pointed "—a few weeks ago?"

The man stuffed the dollar into his pocket quickly. "Ain't been no buildin' there fo' years," he said.

"I was afraid of that," Kenny said. "Are you certain? I was here in the not-so-distant past and I *distinctly* recall..."

"No buildin'," the wino said firmly. He turned and walked away, but after a few steps he paused and glanced back. "You're one of them fat guys," he said accusingly.

"What do you know about... ahem... overweight men?"

"See 'em wanderin' round over there, all the time. Crazy, too. Yellin' at thin air, playin' with some kind of animals. Yeah. I 'member you. You're one of them fat guys, all right." He scowled at Kenny, confused. "Looks like you lost some of that blubber, though. Real good. Thanks for the dollar."

Kenny Dorchester watched him return to his stoop and begin conversing animatedly with his colleagues. With a tremulous sigh, Kenny rolled up the window, glanced at the empty lot again, and bid his driver take him home. Him and his monkey, that is.

Weeks went dripping by and Kenny Dorchester lived as if in a trance. He went to work, shuffled his papers, mumbled pleasantries to his co-workers, struggled and schemed for his meager mouthfuls of food, avoided mirrors. The scale read 367. His flesh melted away from him at a precipitous rate. He developed slack, droopy jowls, and his skin sagged all about his middle, looking as flaccid and pitiful as a used condom. He began to have fainting spells, brought on by hunger. At times he staggered and lurched about the street, his thinning and weakened legs unable to support the weight of his growing monkey. His vision got blurry.

Once he even thought that his hair had started to fall out, but that at least was a false alarm; it was the monkey who was losing hair, thank goodness. It shed all over the place, ruining his furniture, and even daily vacuuming didn't seem to help much. Soon Kenny stopped trying to clean up. He lacked the energy. He lacked the energy for just about everything, in fact. Rising from a chair was a major undertaking. Cooking dinner was impossible torment—but he did *that* anyway, since the monkey beat him severely when it was not fed. Nothing seemed to matter very much to Kenny Dorchester. Nothing but the terrible tale of his scale each morning, and the formula that he had scotch-taped to his bathroom wall.

ME + MONKEY = 367 POUNDS

He wondered how much was ME anymore, and how much was MONKEY, but he did not really want to find out. One day, following the dictates of a kind of feeble whim, Kenny made a sudden grab for the monkey's legs under his chin, hoping against hope that it had gotten slow and obese and that he would be able to yank it from his back. His hands closed on nothing. On his own pale flesh. The monkey's legs did not seem to be there, though Kenny could still feel its awful crushing weight. He patted his neck and breast in dim confusion, staring down at himself, and noting absently that he could see his feet. He wondered how long that had been true. They seemed to be perfectly nice feet, Kenny Dorchester thought, although the legs to which they were attached were alarmingly gaunt.

Slowly his mind wandered back to the quandary at hand—what had become of the monkey's hind legs? Kenny frowned and puzzled and tried to work it all out in his head, but nothing occurred to him. Finally he slid his newly discovered feet into a pair of bedroom slippers and shuffled to the closet where he had stored all of his mirrors. Closing his eyes, he reached in, fumbled about, and found the full-length mirror that had once hung on his bedroom wall. It was a large, wide mirror. Working entirely by touch, Kenny fetched it out, carried it a few feet, and painstakingly propped it up against a wall. Then he held his breath and opened his eyes.

There in the mirror stood a gaunt, gray, skeletal-looking fellow, hunched over and sickly. On his back, grinning, was a thing the size of a gorilla. A very obese gorilla. It had a long, pale, snakelike tail, and great long arms, and it was as white as a maggot and entirely hairless. It had no legs. It was... attached to him now, growing right out of his back. Its grin was terrible, and filled up half of its face. It looked very like the gross proprietor of the monkey treatment emporium, in fact. Why had he never noticed that before? Of course, of course.

Kenny Dorchester turned from the mirror, and cooked the monkey a big rich dinner before going to bed.

That night he dreamed of how it all started, back in the Slab when he had met Boney Moroney. In his nightmare a great evil white thing rode atop Moroney's shoulders, eating slab after slab of ribs, but Kenny politely pretended not to notice while he and Boney made bright, sprightly conversation. Then the thing ran out of ribs, so it reached down and lifted one of Boney's arms and began to eat his hand. The bones crunched nicely, and Moroney kept right on talking. The creature had eaten its way up to the elbow when Kenny woke screaming, covered with a cold sweat. He had wet his bed, too.

Agonizingly, he pushed himself up and staggered to the toilet, where he dry-heaved for ten minutes. The monkey, angry at being wakened, gave him a desultory slap from time to time.

And then a furtive light came into Kenny Dorchester's eyes. "Boney," he whispered. Hurriedly, he scrambled back to his bedroom on hands and knees, rose, and threw on some clothes. It was three in the morning, but Kenny knew there was no time to waste. He looked up an address in his phone book, and called a cab.

Boney Moroney lived in a tall, modern high-rise by the river, with moonlight shining brightly off its silver-mirrored flanks. When Kenny staggered in, he found the night doorman asleep at his station, which was just as well. Kenny tiptoed past him to the elevators and rode up to the eighth floor. The monkey on his back had begun stirring now, and seemed uneasy and ill-tempered.

Kenny's finger trembled as he pushed the round black button set in the door to Moroney's apartment, just beneath the eyehole. Musical chimes sounded loudly within, startling in the morning stillness. Kenny leaned on the button. The music played on and on. Finally he heard footsteps, heavy and threatening. The peephole opened and closed again. Then the door swung open.

The apartment was black, though the far wall was made entirely of glass, so the moonlight illuminated the darkness softly. Outlined against the stars and the lights of the city stood the man who had opened the door. He was hugely, obscenely fat, and his skin was a pasty fungoid white, and he had little dark eyes set deep into crinkles in his broad suety face. He wore nothing but a vast pair of striped shorts. His breasts flopped about against his chest when he shifted his weight. And when he smiled, his teeth filled up half his face. A great crescent moon of teeth. He smiled when he saw Kenny, and Kenny's monkey. Kenny felt sick. The thing in the door weighed twice as much as the one on his back. Kenny trembled. "Where is he?" he whispered softly. "Where is Boney? What have you done to him?"

The creature laughed, and its pendulous breasts flounced about wildly as it shook with mirth. The monkey on Kenny's back began to laugh, too, a higher, thinner laughter as sharp as the edge of a knife. It reached down and twisted Kenny's ear cruelly. Suddenly a vast fear and a vast anger filled Kenny Dorchester. He summoned all the strength left in his wasted body and pushed forward, and somehow, somehow, he barged past the obese colossus who barred his way and staggered into the interior of the apartment. "Boney," he called, "where are you, Boney? It's me, Kenny."

There was no answer. Kenny went from room to room. The apartment was filthy, a shambles. There was no sign of Boney Moroney anywhere. When Kenny came panting back to the living room, the monkey shifted abruptly, and threw him off balance. He stumbled and fell hard. Pain went shooting up through his knees, and he cut open one outstretched hand on the edge of the chrome-and-glass coffee table. Kenny began to weep.

He heard the door close, and the thing that lived here moved slowly toward him. Kenny blinked back tears and stared at the approach of those two mammoth legs, pale in the moonlight, sagging all around with fat. He looked up and it was like gazing up the side of a mountain. Far, far above him grinned those terrible mocking teeth. " *Where is he?*" Kenny Dorchester whispered. "What have you done with poor Boney?"

The grin did not change. The thing reached down a meaty hand, fingers as thick as a length of kielbasa, and snagged the waistband of the baggy striped shorts. It pulled them down clumsily, and they settled to the ground like a parachute, bunching around its feet.

"Oh, no," said Kenny Dorchester.

The thing had no genitals. Hanging down between its legs, almost touching the carpet now that it had been freed from the confines of the soiled shorts, was a wrinkled droopy bag of skin, long and gaunt, growing from the creature's crotch. But as Kenny stared at it in horror, it thrashed feebly, and stirred, and the loose folds of flesh separated briefly into tiny arms and legs.

Then it opened its eyes.

Kenny Dorchester screamed and suddenly he was back on his feet, lurching away from the grinning obscenity in the center of the room. Between its legs, the thing that had been Boney Moroney raised its pitiful stick-thin arms in supplication. "Oh, nooooo," Kenny moaned, blubbering, and he danced about wildly, the vast weight of his monkey heavy on his back. Round and round he danced in the dimness, in the moonlight, searching for an escape from this madness.

Beyond the plate glass wall the lights of the city beckoned.

Kenny paused and panted and stared at them. Somehow the monkey must have known what he was thinking, for suddenly it began to beat on him wildly, to twist at his ears, to rain savage blows all around his head. But Kenny Dorchester paid no mind. With a smile that was almost beatific, he gathered the last of his strength and rushed pell-mell toward the moonlight.

The glass shattered into a million glittering shards, and Kenny smiled all the way down.

IT WAS THE smell that told him he was still alive, the smell of disinfectant, and the feel of starched sheets beneath him. A hospital, he thought amidst a haze of pain. He was in a hospital. Kenny wanted to cry. Why hadn't he died? Oh, why, oh, why? He opened his eyes and tried to say something.

Suddenly a nurse was there, standing over him, feeling his brow and looking down with concern. Kenny wanted to beg her to kill him, but the words would not come. She went away, and when she came back she had others with her.

A chubby young man stood by his side and touched him and prodded here and there. Kenny's mouth worked soundlessly. "Easy," the doctor said. "You'll be all right, Mr. Dorchester, but you have a long way to go. You're in a hospital. You're a very lucky man. You fell eight stories. You ought to be dead."

I want to be dead, Kenny thought, and he shaped the words very, very carefully with his mouth, but no one seemed to hear them. Maybe the monkey has taken over, he thought. Maybe I can't even talk anymore.

"He wants to say something," the nurse said. "I can see that," said the chubby young doctor. "Mr. Dorchester, please don't strain yourself. Really. If you are trying to ask about your friend, I'm afraid he wasn't as lucky as you. He was killed by the fall. You would have died as well, but fortunately you landed on top of him."

Kenny's fear and confusion must have been obvious, for the nurse put a gentle hand on his arm. "The other man," she said patiently. "The fat one. You can thank God he was so fat, too. He broke your fall like a giant pillow."

And finally Kenny Dorchester understood what they were saying, and he began to weep, but now he was weeping for joy, and trembling.

Three days later, he managed his first word. "Pizza," he said, and it came weak and hoarse from between his lips, but the sound elated him and he repeated it, louder, and then louder still, and before long he was pushing the nurse's call button and shouting and pushing and shouting. "Pizza, pizza, *pizza, pizza,*" he chanted, and he would not be calm until they ordered one for him. Nothing had ever tasted so good.

George R. R. Martin

George R. R. Martin is an American novelist and short story writer, a screenwriter, and television producer. He is best known for *A Song of Ice and Fire*, his international bestselling series of epic fantasy novels that HBO adapted for its dramatic series *Game of Thrones*.

About the Editor

Alex Shvartsman is a writer, anthologist, translator, and game designer from Brooklyn, NY. He's the winner of the 2014 WSFA Small Press Award for Short Fiction.

His short stories have appeared in *Nature, InterGalactic Medicine Show, Daily Science Fiction, Galaxy's Edge,* and a variety of other magazines and anthologies. His collection, *Explaining Cthulhu to Grandma and Other Stories,* and his steampunk humor novella *H. G. Wells, Secret Agent* were published in 2015.

In addition to the UFO series, he has edited the *Coffee: 14 Caffeinated Tales of the Fantastic* and *Dark Expanse: Surviving the Collapse* anthologies. His web site is www.alexshvartsman.com

Acknowledgments

We'd like to thank everyone who pitched in to produce this book: associate editors Cyd Athens, James Beamon, Frank Dutkiewicz, and Nathaniel Lee; copy editor Elektra Hammond, book designer Melissa Neely, graphics designer Emerson Matsuuchi, cover artist Tomasz Maronski, illustrator Barry Munden, e-book designer Elizabeth Campbell, and many others whose talent and hard work made this a better book. Special thanks to Anne Roberti for her invaluable support of this project.

ENJOY ADDITIONAL STORIES
PUBLISHED AT WWW.UFOPUB.COM